Exhibited
A Gentle Love Story
Nellie Wilson

Contents

This one's for all the little kids who spent more of their childhood outside than inside.

Author's Note & Content Warnings

Hello there —

Thank you for picking up this book. I hope you enjoy it. While a gentle love story between two men from very different backgrounds, there is heavier content in this book. I provide these content warnings so you, the reader, can ensure that you are in a good place to read Jeremy and Davis's story.

Content Warnings:

- on page sexual content (but with discussions of consent, testing, and protection)

- adult language

- alcohol and marijuana use

- a sober character with a history of alcoholism (does not relapse)

- death of parents of one main character (previous), ongoing experiences with grief

- mentions of previous experiences with homophobia (does not occur on-page in book)

- depiction of forest fires.

There's a dog, and I promise that nothing happens to the dog. She remains perfect the entire time.

Take care of your heart and mind as you read this and all books.

Much love,

Nellie

Davis

New jobs were always stressful, even in an industry one knew well, an industry that seemed to fit like a second skin. And Nathaniel (never Nate) Davis — who, actually, always went by Davis and never Nathaniel Davis — knew forestry. He reminded himself of that as he took a deep breath, letting the pine-infused air soak deep into his lungs. He focused on the ache in his left knee left over from a particularly nasty fall during his last ride in West Virginia. He could also take in the trees, because this part of Colorado had a particularly excellent old-growth forest.

He also knew that a year in, it wasn't considered a *new* job, per se. It still felt new, because the mountains he got to see every morning were so different from the mountains of his youth and early adulthood. The Rockies were large and imposing, cutting through the clouds with defined peaks and arguing with the sky at the tree line. The Appalachians in West Virginia were more subtle, older, more like rolling hills with a golden sunset above them.

There was probably a metaphor in there if Davis looked hard enough, but he hadn't had enough coffee yet, and his back hurt. He needed a new mattress. He ignored the stiffness in his back, just like he ignored the brown tips that poked up and meant that Pine Bark Beetles had taken residence in this part of the forest. He ignored the whistling that meant there was a crack in the window behind him that he needed to fix.

Heading in from the rear porch, groaning as he stretched his back, Davis prepared a pot of coffee. It was quiet outside, one of the reasons he headed to the porch every morning to collect his thoughts, but it was too quiet in his cabin. He thought about getting a speaker for the cabin. While Davis loved the crisp silence of the morning, after a year, he had begun to feel like the place was missing something, a bit empty. He hadn't really begun to set up until recently, convinced that he would be told to leave. But he was beginning to feel settled. Music could help.

Or someone in his bed.

Shaking *that* thought off, Davis threw on a hoodie and beanie and walked over to the main office for the morning ranger meeting.

"Morning," he grunted at Alex and Yesenia, who were always early. Davis was, too, but not as early as those two. Somehow, they usually managed to go for a trail run or a mountain bike ride before work most days, too. Not for the first time, Davis thought about asking to go along or scheduling a weekend bike ride. He wasn't going to be fired. His coworkers liked him. He was doing well at his job, had consistently booked programming throughout the past year, and had organized a series of educational hikes that had even gotten a write-up in the Denver Post, even if the reporter had paraphrased most of the answers that Davis had stammered through.

It's been a year, Nathaniel, he berated himself, using his full name like it was his gram chastising him for not doing chores on the weekend. There was a list a mile long of reasons that this move to Colorado had been right for Davis, and one of them was that it was his chance to work for the federal government, which felt a bit like getting called up to the MLB after struggling through AAA.

Plus, he got to learn new species of trees.

Chokecherry. *Prunus virginiana.*

Quaking aspen. *Populus tremuloides.*

Rocky Mountain Juniper. *Juniperus scopulorum.*

And yellow-bellied marmots. *Marmota flaviventris.*

And those little critters were cute.

Just like Alex when he yawned in the morning and scrunched his nose. Just like his boss, Eric, was. Silver hair and crinkles around his eyes from a career spent in various nature-focused jobs. A prominent nose that Davis found intimidating and sexy. But Davis had a rule about never mixing work and pleasure, and that definitely extended to his boss. Especially the boss who had gotten him out of West Virginia once and for all over a year ago.

Back then, while working for WV State Parks, Davis, who struggled even on the best days with text-heavy websites, had spent the better part of three months battling with the US-AJobs site, uploading his resume and experience and jumping through every other hoop imaginable to prove to some computer somewhere that he was actually qualified to be doing the job he had already done for the past decade. And once he had successfully put everything into the computer, he had to wait. Wait so long that he had honestly forgotten all the places he had applied to, until he received a phone call from Head Ranger Eubank, inviting him to interview at the national forest in Klarluft, Colorado.

Fast forward another agonizing seven months, and here he was, the newest outreach and education forest ranger at the Klarluft National Forest and the newest employee of the Department of Agriculture. Though he'd had the same position at the state park in West Virginia, it had felt like a new start.

And god knows, Davis had needed a new start.

That had been over a year ago, and Davis still felt like it was his first day. He couldn't nail down *why*, only that thirty-odd years in West Virginia had taught him that if something was too good to be true, it probably was.

"Good morning, good morning," Eric said to the assembled crew of forest rangers and support staff. It was early spring, still too early for any seasonal staff to be around. So it was Eric, who led the group, then Davis, who oversaw educational programming and outreach, Yesenia, who managed the endangered species conservation plan in conjunction with a host of other governmental organizations and nonprofits, and Alex, who worked in water conservation and testing. It was an odd crew, but in Davis's experience, most people who were drawn to jobs in conservation were. When he had moved from West Virginia to Colorado a year ago, it felt like the culmination of everything that he had been struggling through for years. The jobs he worked to afford community college and undergrad, then weird seasonal jobs with state parks that had led to a full-time job. It felt odd to finally be figuring out that he might be in the right job at the age of thirty-eight, but Davis wasn't used to following any sort of normal path or fitting in where he was supposed to.

Davis knew that he was going to help save the forest. Or, as the mission would be for the Forest Service, make sure that it was properly managed and conserved. People like Davis had to be practical.

He was really good at pretending to be listening as the meeting kicked off, which wasn't unusual. It was how he had gotten through high school and stuttered through seven years of college. That, plus a very corny Appalachian ability to connect with the trees in a very deep manner. Davis didn't need to look at a dichotomous key to know if something was a pine or a spruce. Flora and fauna were able to be ordered in his brain the way that the shapes of words never could have been.

Davis wanted more than anything to prove that he belonged here, that he was someone who deserved to work for the national forest system and speak for the trees.

"What's going on?" Yesenia asked. "I have a group coming in to do a bird count this afternoon, and I need to get started on looking at last year's data so we can understand —"

"You're good. Yes," Alex said, kicking one booted foot over his thigh and leaning back in the chair. "You know that group is going to be late anyway."

"Heh, true. Remember that one year —" And so it went. Alex and Yesenia were the only two staff members who'd stayed on site during lockdown, so they had an incredibly close relationship that Davis was jealous of. Eric, he had managed to surmise, had been transferred to Colorado from a national forest in Arizona, a goal of his for a long time, as his grandmother lived in the area. Davis felt like an outsider, an interloper, and had been waiting every day for them to let him know that the newest budget had come out and his position had been cut. Or that they'd discovered why he occasionally visited Denver and had decided to fire him.

Davis knew you couldn't fire people for being queer anymore, but it still didn't stop him from imagining the worst possible outcome.

"Anyway, as I was saying," Eric said, raising his voice just enough to take over the room. "I was informed today that we have been the beneficiaries of a grant that needs to be used quickly."

"Why so quickly?" Yesenia asked the question that Davis would have asked if he had a bit more courage and a bit more coffee this early in the morning.

"Shitty communication," Eric said. "You know how government work is. Hurry up and wait, and then wait, and then it's a damned emergency." He rubbed his hands together as he went over the details and the three rangers tossed ideas around. Alex wanted to invest in new monitoring equipment. Yesenia wanted to try to use it to advocate for wildlife crossings over one of the major roads near the forest.

But Davis had an idea. Not only something to bring people into the forest, but to educate. It would help his job, yes, but it would also benefit them all, because it would bring people to the national forest, and it could help with education and outreach.

Davis cleared his throat. "I think we should update the visitor center."

"But no one *goes* to the visitor center," Alex said.

"That's the point, dumbass," Yesenia said, and Davis hazarded a smile, which she met.

Davis felt as if he'd gained a power-up in one of the animated driving games he loved and continued, detailing how an updated visitor center would not only bring more recreational hikers and families but could help the overall mission by spreading education back to the cities.

"Should we vote?" Eric asked.

"Nah, Davis's idea is a good one," Alex said. Yesenia agreed, and all of a sudden, Davis was on his way to live his dream of being the Lorax.

Okay, well, he wasn't the Lorax, but he would try. Plus, the Lorax hadn't actually saved the forest. Maybe Davis could. And the first thing he was going to tackle was this god-awful, horrible, no good visitor center. Davis couldn't draw, but he could communicate his ideas to a professional. He pulled out his computer and googled *Colorado Exhibit Consultants*, pulled out his phone, and began to speech-to-text a message detailing what he imagined.

Jeremy

At what point did a job stop being new and interesting and start being old hat? Was it after you'd maintained the same career for over a decade? Or lived through a global pandemic and taken your very much in-person job online and then back in person? Or was it when you had to learn an entire new aspect of your job when budget cuts forced your workplace to merge with another?

Jeremy Rinci wasn't sure when it had happened, but his work had become stale. Boring.

Old.

Not that old things were necessarily bad. Jeremy looked forward to every day he got older, considered each one a gift that he certainly knew he wasn't guaranteed. He had studied art history in school, knew that some of the oldest paintings were handprints and smudges on rock walls that meant *I am here*.

But in this case, Jeremy's job as the lead exhibit designer for the Vanberg Museum of Science and Technology (the university still hadn't come up with a more interesting name, which meant that no wealthy family had tried to clean up their name by donating a lot of money) had become old and stale and boring. He couldn't move, not with his entire financial life tied up in a house he had purchased at twenty-four and his emotional life tangled deeply with an eclectic cast of characters that were his best friends. But something had to change, and god knew he wasn't going to take up running ultramarathons or skiing or whatever people did in Colorado when they were going a bit out of their mind.

One night, however, sitting on his couch with a glass of pinot noir and an especially melancholy selection of 1940s love ballads playing through his speakers, Jeremy tried to remember the last time he had really felt creatively inspired. Not just the figure drawing classes he took once a month, but the kind of work that gave him a reason to breathe. To create something that could be a lasting legacy and teach and inspire all at once.

Which had led him to booting up his computer and trying his hand at being an independent businessman again. Because what said "a little bit desperate" more than a creative trying to have a second business on the side in this present set of unprecedented times?

He had gotten into this world as an excuse to combine both of his family's interests. His dad had been an engineer, and his mom had been an artist who illustrated children's books. He had, while in graduate school, dreamed of taking his parents to his first exhibit opening, but that dream had been taken from him suddenly over the series of two months. And while he hadn't ever been able to show them what he did, he still did it professionally, and occasionally, that spilled over into his personal life. For a while, it had become a go-to date, to take a man to a museum exhibit and explain the ways that a color complemented the artifacts or was chosen to evoke a certain era or emotion. The delicate manner that fossils were mounted so they looked like they were floating in midair. The choice to feature a solitary artifact versus an array of a collection. He knew a date was going well if the man's eyes didn't entirely glaze over when he began talking about font choice for labels. Or, at the very least, if he pretended to be interested.

So, dusting off his old consulting website and checking the email that had been unchecked since 2018 had been a step to reclaiming that interest. And if it had been because he hadn't had a date in a while and was bored, well, no one needed to question that either. The website was quickly updated, and the inbox remained empty, but only for a few days. After an especially exhausting week at work, Jeremy had clicked open the website to see a message from an NDavis at the United States Forest Service.

Hello, Mr. Rinci —

I'm attaching an RFP that I've developed to utilize grant money to renovate and reinterpret the visitor center here in Klarkuft National Forest. From what I gather, the exhibit was last updated during the Kennedy administration and could use some love. I would be happy to set up a meeting with you at your convenience to discuss our plans for the center and our budget constraints.

Sincerely,

N. Davis

Educational Ranger

USFS

There was a picture of Smokey Bear at the bottom of the email. Maybe that was why Jeremy immediately opened the RFP — *request for proposal*, the fancy title of *here's what we want* — or maybe it was because of the humor he swore emanated from this email. Whatever it was, Jeremy lightly danced his fingers across the keyboard and, within hours, had set up a meeting with this NDavis for the weekend.

Luckily, he had been able to squeeze in an eight-a.m. spin class with his best friend, Foster, before driving up to ease off some of the nerves. Though it was less relaxing than expected, considering that Foster was both sweating out rum next to him and pouting over the end of a relationship with another woman he'd claimed he was going to marry when he saw her at a bar.

So here Jeremy was, driving out to his least favorite place in the entire world — the outside — to revive his old pipe dream. He loved his work at the university, thought the exhibits were interesting and a good addition to his portfolio, and loved his coworkers. They understood that Jeremy was an indoor cat. There was one time, just over a year ago, when his museum had merged with another on campus and he had been forced to do a stupid high ropes course out at a camp here.

He had liked the zip line, but the mosquitoes really ruined the entire experience.

Driving his trusty Prius out to the mountains taxed its engine, but at least he had a car and could operate it today. He dutifully followed his GPS directions and daydreamed about public transit in major cities.

The BART.

The NY Subway.

Hell, even Philadelphia's SEPTA system, which he had always joked should have been called the SEPTIC system. That joke had gotten him, if he remembered correctly, three excellent orgasms from two decent men and one boyfriend that he'd had to break up with when he made the middle-of-the night decision to move to Colorado.

Which had *so* much nature. An absurd amount of it. It also, apparently, had very little cell phone reception, as the map on his center panel went blank except for a crude outline of a road and the blue dot that Jeremy was now blindly following.

He took a sip of his Tension Tamer tea, set the thermos back in the center console, then steeled himself to head outside. He could do this. He could pretend to be outdoorsy for just a little bit if it meant getting a chance to actually put some decent color schemes in an exhibit and a nice sans serif font.

Jeremy turned down his music to help him navigate the final twists of the forest service roads, looking for what NDavis had described as "something you'll know when you see."

He followed that dot, praying that the technology gods were going to be on his side today (they had argued against his ability to save a mockup yesterday in SketchUp after he told his computer that it was being a "fucking asshole," so he wasn't taking chances). He followed the blue dot until it led him to a very sad cabin with a peeling sign that said *Visitor Center*. The paint was so peeled it actually looked more like *Visitor Cunter*, but he figured that wasn't the best idea to open with.

Cringing as the undercarriage of his car scraped on a mound of gravel, Jeremy parked and gathered his sketchbook and iPad, a bit horrified that this crumbling building was going to be his return to exhibit design.

He sighed. Everyone had to start somewhere.

"Hello?" Jeremy called, eyeing a welcome sign that reminded him of the one time he visited a friend outside of some city in Ohio that started with a C. It was hand lettered, which was impressive, but half had been erased and there was a white splatter of something on one side. Bird shit, he assumed.

He hoped.

"Mr. Rinci?" came a voice from the other side of the door. A cough, then a suppressed sneeze.

"It's just Jeremy," Jeremy said, stepping gingerly onto the porch of the cabin and being reminded of Boo Radley's house.

"Welcome to the visitor center, Just Jeremy," replied the voice, accompanied by a warm, gravelly laugh. Jeremy's shoulders dropped just an inch. The door opened, and Jeremy was greeted by NDavis, who was, by an objective measure, uncomfortably attractive.

Jeremy was no stranger to attractive men, had spent a lot of his twenties dancing at clubs and flipping through apps and then quietly dating in his thirties. Emphasis on quietly, because his three best friends in Colorado were all nuisances. Emmy was suspicious of everyone and loudly investigated all of their backgrounds and scraped the internet for any detail that meant it wasn't up to her standards. Phoebe was subtler in her investigations but gave advice that was too honest and too accurate, and often, Jeremy wanted willful ignorance about the toxic men he dated.

The worst, however, was Foster, a straight man who believed in true love and happily ever after and probably fairies, which were the same level of fantasy.

Jeremy knew from experience that even if you did find true love, happily ever after wasn't guaranteed.

Regardless, Jeremy liked dating and adored flirting but never expected it to go anywhere. And of course he knew the two standard rules — don't fuck anyone you work with and don't hit on straight men.

Which was definitely NDavis, because the man in front of him was devastatingly, ruggedly handsome and also painfully straight.

"Hi, Just Jeremy," he said, reaching out a hand that Jeremy imagined was roughly the size of a bear's paw. Were there Grizzlies in Colorado? He'd have to ask a biologist he knew.

"Hello, uh, Mr. Davis?" Jeremy said, swallowing a groan at the awkward introduction. Way to be professional, Rinci.

"Just Davis," he said. Jeremy slipped his slender hand into Davis's rough palm and had an unwelcome image of Davis swinging an axe and splitting a log in half. He was a head shorter than Jeremy, who was often the tallest in the room at six-five, but Davis was probably twice as wide. No, wide wasn't the right word. *Thick.*

Like a fucking tree trunk or something else in nature.

Another image, this one of a children's book that his mom had illustrated about Paul Bunyan.

Did Paul Bunyan have cropped dark blond hair that was the perfect level of disheveled? If Jeremy had clocked Davis at a bar in Denver, he'd assume that it was intentional, full of products and styling gel, but out here in the trees, where Davis had just pulled a beanie off his head and scrubbed a hand through his hair, it was natural. As was the beard that was just this side of too long, a bit unkempt, not a drop of beard oil in sight. Davis wore a dark green flannel with the forest service logo on the chest, buttoned up over a thermal shirt, and work pants that looked like they were actually worked in, the thick cotton worn thin and soft over time.

"Welcome to the visitor center," Davis said, releasing Jeremy's hand quickly and shrugging his shoulders. "It's not much, but it's what we've got here."

"Government funding is no joke," Jeremy laughed drily. "I work for the university's museum down in the city, and it's been an interesting couple of years." Which was the understatement of the century, but Davis didn't need to know that.

"Do you want to see the visitor center? I can give you a tour of what we have now and, uh, maybe even what I have planned?" Davis was saying, kicking at a rock in the dirt.

"Yes, of course," Jeremy said, compartmentalizing the part of his brain that recognized Davis as an attractive man and activating the part of his brain that was an exhibit designer. He rifled through a portfolio in his head, remembering the career he had built. A beautiful reinterpretation of an inaccurate diorama. A retrospective of a queer photographer whose negatives had been found in a basement. A stunning spotlight on the university's last remaining passenger pigeon specimen to make a statement about the Anthropocene era, whatever that was.

He definitely kept his eyes on the trees and the ornate gables of the visitor center instead of letting them drop below Davis's worn leather belt. At least the design of the cabin seemed architecturally sound. The door creaked, and Jeremy was hit with the musty odor of damp wood, old glue, and another funk that he didn't want to consider. He'd been in some sad museums and some weird archival rooms, but this one? Well, it was probably one of the saddest things he'd ever seen.

There was, as far as Jeremy could see, one large room full of multiple smaller exhibits (if you could call them that) and what looked like two doors that led to an *assroom* and a *water los t*, if the signs were to be believed. The exhibits were standard nature center — a collection of slightly off-looking stuffed animals with signs set in a typeface that had gone out of style with Members Only jackets, a few sun-faded posters that Jeremy would bet didn't represent the most up-to-date science, and a crumbling model on a table of what Jeremy guessed was the traditional house of the local native peoples. Attempting to control his face, he took a tentative step forward to look at the taxidermy collection. The floor creaked.

"I know it's not great," Davis said, "but the building is structurally sound, and we've got a new grant to rehab this place, but I'd like to focus more on the content."

"That's a good sign," Jeremy said, bending closer to look at a fox missing its front left foot. "The cabin is beautiful. I'd guess, what, 1905-1910?"

"1907," Davis replied, sounding impressed.

"We could probably interpret the architecture, too, if you wanted, not just the, well —" Jeremy paused and realized that he hadn't even asked what the overall goals of the visitor center were. Who were the visitors? Who did they want them to be?

He'd never tell Emmy. She'd kill him for only thinking about design instead of the people who used it. "I'm sorry. I started thinking. What did you have in mind?"

"I could show you some ideas I had."

Jeremy looked up from where he was trying to decide whether one specimen was a squirrel or a small, furry alien creature to see Davis, whose cheeks had turned a slightly ruddy pink, standing by an open laptop with photos on it.

"I'd love that," Jeremy said, bringing himself to his full height. "Is there a place we could sit down? I'm not exactly trusting whatever is on the floor," he said, gesturing at a faint trail of his footprints in the dust on the floor.

"Yeah, this place gives off a real Hanta Hut vibe," Davis said, opening the door to the outside.

"What?" Jeremy asked, assuming it was a nature-related joke he didn't get.

"Hantavirus," Davis explained, guiding him toward a portable trailer which, he assumed, held the ranger offices. A sign — with all of its letters! — confirmed that he was correct.

"Yeah, I was an art kid," Jeremy said, defaulting to his usual jokes. "I can learn science for an exhibit, but I'm not, like, a scientist."

"Hantavirus is a potentially deadly condition you can get by inhaling rodent droppings," Davis said, far too calmly for Jeremy's liking.

Davis

Davis wasn't the best with new people. He tended to be a bit shy and awkward at first, which was why he struggled with dating in high school and during his long path to his college degree, especially after he got sober. But Davis also knew that his tendency to ramble on about topics he was passionate about — which, strangely, included zoonotic diseases, because keeping people safe was what a ranger *did* — did not exactly make people comfortable. And Jeremy, even though he tried to hide it, was not comfortable. As they stepped outside, Jeremy swatted at an invisible mosquito on his arm and stepped delicately, like a critter might be underfoot at all times.

It was cute.

Davis engaged in a lovely cycle of self-delusion as he led Jeremy away from the visitor center (which did not have any evidence of hantavirus but did have a family of raccoons living in the crawl space who did not appear to be rabid, though they were cute in a feral sort of way). It was a cycle that Davis had begun entertaining in middle school, workshopped in high school, tossed out in college, but then embraced wholeheartedly when he got hired at West Virginia State Parks.

The cycle went like this: 1) See attractive man; 2) tell himself that anyone would objectively notice an attractive man; 3) wonder if he looked as good as the other man; 4) panic that someone would notice him thinking about male attractiveness; 5) remind himself that he also thought women were attractive; 6) think a bit more about a woman; 7) repeat ad nauseam.

It didn't work.

It never did.

Davis wasn't ashamed of being bisexual. He had accepted it as a part of himself since he realized that the other guys he was friends with in high school didn't think about other men like *that*. But just like he didn't advertise his sobriety when he met someone, he didn't think it was anyone's business to know that about him. It was a safety mechanism, a protection. Not shame.

In the back of his brain, Davis knew that the ranger uniforms were hideous. But he had never thought about it, because he had always tried to keep the part of himself that cared about what he looked like around other men suppressed at work. Because when he had imagined Jeremy Rinci, who emailed back quickly and attached a YouTube video about the history of Smokey Bear that made Davis laugh, he imagined an old Italian designer. Someone who was wrapped in the pashminas that had been popular among his mom and his aunts when he was in high school (and boys like Davis from Anthracite Springs were definitely *not* supposed to know what a pashmina was). He wasn't off, per se, because Jeremy emerged from his Prius in a small cloud of expensive smelling cologne. How did he smell more like nature than the actual nature that Davis lived in? Pine and leather?

Davis probably smelled like sweat and dirt and whatever deodorant was cheapest when he went into the closest city.

Davis opened the door and suppressed the impulse to tidy things up. Jeremy was a colleague, a coworker. He was probably used to offices. But for the first time, Davis was seeing his office through the eyes of someone else — someone he wanted to impress — and it was mediocre, to say the least. He had two offices; one in his cabin and this one, which was in the main staff building. He clearly had spent more time in his cabin office, because this one was, well, kind of gross. The walls were a sickly sort of beige, and his desk was cluttered. He did have a nice hand-crocheted afghan over the back of his desk chair, so that made it look almost personalized.

Davis had been preparing for this meeting because updating the visitor center and getting more people of all types out here *was* a goal of his. Which meant that he had been scrolling through dozens and dozens of photographs of beautifully designed exhibits and had seen every single paint swatch that could possibly be nature related. Drawings and photographs, like trees, had always been easier for Davis to wrap his brain around than the written word. Davis settled into his chair, the afghan knitted by his cousin a comfortable lumpy reminder of home and support behind him.

"Where should I...?" Jeremy asked, looking around the office.

Cursing himself, Davis got up and pulled the plastic chair with the fewest number of cracks over next to his desk chair so Jeremy could see the screen. Davis sat back down and Jeremy folded his long body around the chair. Davis did everything he could to focus on inputting his password correctly the first time instead of obsessing over how close Jeremy's knee was to his.

"Do you mind if I take notes?" Jeremy asked.

"Of course not," Davis said, clicking at his computer. "You're the expert here." He clicked around on his computer and wished that the federal government didn't always have to go with the lowest bidder when it came to IT.

"I prefer to view exhibit design as a true union of experts who have something to teach each other," Jeremy was saying. Davis peeked at him out of the corner of his eye, surprised to find that he had kept his iPad away and had pulled out a sketch pad. He assumed everyone down in cities had moved to entirely digital work these days. Davis focused on the way he crafted the letters of *visitor center* and not the way that Jeremy's long, delicate fingers gripped his pencil. Davis, once again, compared Jeremy's grace to his own. If Davis was holding a pencil right now, he felt like it would look like a caveman gripping a stone tool or the grubby fist of a toddler.

A beep from his computer turned his attention back. "Well, thank you," Davis replied. "I want the visitor center to be a welcoming space to meet anyone who is venturing out to the forest where they are." He swallowed and wished he had a seltzer in the room to ease the tickle in his throat.

"Tell me what that means to you," Jeremy encouraged, and Davis focused on his computer screen, the images he had collected, while Jeremy's pencil scratched at his sketch pad.

"Well, for me, nature is comforting. So I want the visitor center to be a place that feels welcoming and familiar for people like me —" Davis paused at Jeremy's slightly confused look. "You know, White dudes," Davis added, hoping that Jeremy would assume what most people did and make it *White straight dudes*. "Anyway, I want to encourage them to look a bit deeper at the forest they think they know. Look past the tree to think about all the species that rely on this one pine, or encourage them to roll a rotting log back and see that there's a tiny ecosystem below. But I also want it to be a call to action for those people, that we can't take the forest for granted with the pressures of climate change and, well, everything."

Jeremy made a thoughtful noise that encouraged Davis to continue talking.

"And there are other people, of course, who feel like nature is a reminder of what's been taken from them. My boss is a member of the tribe whose land was a part of this forest, and he struggles with working for the government office that helped take it away from his people. So I'd like there to be a portion that is Native-designed — I can connect you with Eric, because that's not for me to say."

"I have some professional relationships with Tribal Archaeologists at the University," Jeremy added. "I'll reach out and see if they're willing to consult. You have a budget to pay them, right?"

"Of course," Davis said quickly.

"What else?"

"I think it's important that people realize that a tree or an elk doesn't give a shit about who you are," Davis said, immediately feeling bad for swearing. His gram would have pinched him. Jeremy gave a questioning look, and Davis continued talking. "But the people who manage the land do. Like the color of your skin or the clothes you wear or who you love means more than your connection with the land." Davis didn't know why he was still talking, feeling his cheeks warm under his beard and stumbling his way through a sentence that probably made Jeremy Rinci think he was even dumber than he was. "I mean, a lot of people feel like the forest isn't for them. I want to change that." That was as close as Davis ever got to acknowledging his sexuality at work, couching the need to make natural spaces more welcoming to queer people in the general discourse of diversity and inclusion. Which was a half-assed attempt, really, considering the fact that just last week, he had seen a drag queen climb Half Dome on his social media.

Everyone has their own journey, he reminded himself. Something he had learned from one of his counselors.

"I love that," Jeremy commented, his pencil stroking across the paper. Davis felt a warm pulse below his sternum, the way he would before he stepped up to the plate and knew he would smash a home run in high school. Emboldened and maybe a little cocky, which was a feeling that Davis didn't often get in school. A feeling he never really got until he took his first ecology course at the local community college and realized that he was *good* at this, that it didn't involve reading books, because it was about listening to the natural world around him.

"And there are people who are afraid of the forest. Who think that it's scary out here or dangerous, when really, the only dangerous thing is being unaware of your surroundings." Davis let out the remainder of his breath, realizing he had been talking more to Jeremy than he had to most people over the past few months. And perhaps had just slightly insulted him.

Jeremy's pencil stopped moving. "Are you alluding to the fact that I am not a nature person?" A shock of fear bolted through Davis. He worried that he had offended Jeremy and would have to find a new exhibit designer. That fear was assuaged when Jeremy let out a surprisingly loud and goose-like laugh. "I'm just saying, maybe don't lead with a virus carried by mouse poop in the exhibit."

Davis let out a nervous laugh. "Oh, well. Yeah. Sorry about that." The two men shared a small laugh, looking at each other for just a moment. Davis noticed that Jeremy had light blue eyes, the color of a glacial creek at the height of the snowmelt. He looked down at the sketch pad, where Jeremy had taken notes and drawn a few trees. Aspens, from the look of it.

"Have you been out here before?" Davis asked, breaking the silence.

"Eh, no," Jeremy replied. "I'm much more of an indoor cat. As you may have noticed." Well, if Jeremy was an indoor cat, then Davis was a feral tomcat who was probably missing half of one ear.

And he didn't know what inspired the next words, but Davis opened his mouth and said, "Would you like me to take you on a hike?" When he saw a look of slight terror flash across Jeremy's face, Davis quickly added, "Just the little visitor center loop. It doesn't even have any elevation."

Jeremy looked indecisive for a second, like he was having a conversation with himself, then replied, "I guess it's good for me to understand what this whole forest is all about." Davis clicked out of his computer, then dusted his hands on his pant legs, partially out of nerves, but partially because there was always a light layer of dust and dirt on everything out here. He took another peek at Jeremy's linen pants and hoped that there weren't any mud puddles on the trail.

"We can talk more about your process as we walk," Davis added.

"I'm better at that." Jeremy sniffed.

Davis led Jeremy outside and around the back to the small, one-mile loop that wound through a patch of aspen trees to a clearing where Davis would sometimes teach lessons to school groups but more often went to clear his head when he was stuck underneath a mountain of emails and the letters started to look more like squiggles on a page and less like words he could hear in his head. Walking helped. Movement helped.

"This is gorgeous," Jeremy said, and Davis turned around, assuming that Jeremy was talking about the small wildflower garden that was used to show the native plants of the area. But when he turned, he saw Jeremy looking at a trail sign, tracing the script with one delicate finger. The trail sign that Davis had made himself, wood burning a quote by Gifford Pinchot to add a bit of a personal touch to the trail:

Conservation is the application of common sense to the common problems for the common good.

Something that Davis had learned about in his first ecological history course, in a discussion about the theoretical differences between John Muir and Gifford Pinchot, who had founded the government office he worked for. While Davis had loved Muir's writing, something about Pinchot's practicality spoke to Davis. People like Davis couldn't wait for fancy policies and grand plans, but it was the day to day, a series of small, good deeds to better his community, that Davis was drawn to.

"Thanks," Davis said, bringing himself back to the present. "My pressure was a bit inconsistent on the first few words, but I'm happy with the way it turned out."

"You made this?" Jeremy asked, surprised.

"Don't sound too shocked. I'm not just a dumb redneck." Perhaps a bit too defensive; perhaps Davis showed his own anxiety a bit too freely.

"Never crossed my mind," Jeremy replied breezily, and Davis wished he could believe him.

Jeremy

It had been a long time since Jeremy had willingly gone on a hike, though he didn't think most of his friends would agree that's what he had done. It was a gentle stroll through some trees at best, but it had been...not terrible.

It was the end of summer. The first breaths of fall were a bit more apparent in the mountains, it seemed. One yellow leaf, solitary among a field of green and the whites of the bark, created a lovely contrast that was already giving Jeremy ideas about the color scheme he could use for the opening exhibition. A way to bring the outside into the visitor center, to allow the visitor to extend the experience beyond the boundaries of the house. In Davis's plans, he had said he wanted the first exhibit to be about the concept of noticing, of emphasizing the ability that anyone had to experience the forest, then to go deeper with each subsequent panel — animals (though he had said "charismatic megafauna"), then smaller, plants and microorganisms that created small worlds underneath even a log. As they walked, Davis had pointed out things that Jeremy wouldn't have looked twice at. The way that one brown tree indicated the presence of an invasive beetle. A pressed down area of grass that indicated it was where a family of deer would sleep at night. A pile of rocks, which Davis angrily kicked over, mumbling that it wasn't appropriate to make trail markers that were unauthorized.

"People can get lost," he had said. "It's our job to manage this forest, but it's also our job to keep the forest and the people who use it safe."

Jeremy couldn't have imagined someone better to embody *safe*. Davis had a quiet presence that filled a room, though it was clear the man was more comfortable outside. The minute they had stepped foot on the trail, he had become infinitely more verbose, the words flowing as they picked up their pace. Davis had shared a bit about the history of the area and this specific forest, then his plans for the exhibit, using his hands to talk. His hands that, Jeremy had imagined, looked perfectly comfortable wrapped around an axe or using a chainsaw.

Sitting on his couch later that evening, a cup of tea freshly brewed, Jeremy examined his own hands. He kept his fingernails trimmed short for *purposes*, but, even in graduate school, where he was writing papers and making art constantly, he had been good about washing his hands of ink, paint, or charcoal. An image of what his delicate hands would look like next to — or tangled with — Davis's rough hands flashed in his mind. He took an annoyed sip of tea. The last thing he needed was to develop a crush on a straight man.

He looked around his house, the Craftsman with gorgeous curved doorways and original doors and windows, which he had impulsively purchased when he moved from Philadelphia to Colorado. It had needed work — still needed work — but even though he had never been to Vanberg before, something about the house called to him. He knew that his parents had met at the university in town, had raised him with stories of their parties and friends and, of course, the moment they saw each other across a lecture hall and *knew*. An engineering student and a fine arts major who somehow spoke the same language of their souls.

It wasn't like Jeremy didn't believe in true love. He had seen it with his parents, had seen it with his friends and their families. But it was harder and harder to see that path opening up for him when hookup culture was still in his blood. Though his propensity for nine to ten hours of sleep kept that from happening as often anymore. Dating was annoying, and the pool in Vanberg was small. It was one of those places full of straight people who loved to post Pride flags on their windows and go to drag brunches. Which was wonderful, and Jeremy knew he was lucky to live in a place like that, but it would be nice if there were more men to date. So he enjoyed himself with occasional swipes and glasses of red wine, nights laughing at bars and sweating out the booze the next morning with his best friends. He went to exhibits, went to art openings, begged the woman who ran the Tea House in town to special order flavors from around the world. He worked on his house, designed exhibits. It was more than enough.

But still, Jeremy thought, turning on soft lo-fi music, sometimes the house felt empty. He didn't want a roommate — living with Foster during lockdown had proved that — but building a life with someone seemed special.

For now, he sighed, opening up his iPad and, subsequently, the mood board Davis had emailed. Designing this visitor center exhibition was something to keep his mind occupied. A consolation, perhaps.

—

Morning brought a six o'clock spin class, one of his favorites, taught by a twink with a British accent who never failed to make Jeremy laugh or make Foster complain about the number of sprints. Following class and a shower, the two men headed to the Jumping Goat, the local coffee shop, for their Monday morning catch-up. Usually, Jeremy would pass along gossip from the museum he worked at, while Foster would bemoan his love life or, alternatively, gush to Jeremy about the most recent woman who had stolen his heart.

Foster ordered a triple white mocha with a caramel drizzle, while Jeremy contented himself with a London Fog. Their tea selection was crap, but Foster liked this place, and Jeremy loved his friend.

"Weekend report?" Foster asked as they sat down, licking a dollop of whipped cream off the side of his mug.

"I, uh, went hiking? For a job?" Jeremy said, blowing a stream of cool air across his drink.

"Have you been body swapped? What has Emmy been up to since she's been getting dicked down? Concocting some sort of magic potion?"

"Don't say *dicked down*. That's disgusting, and I have to work with both of them," Jeremy said, pulling a face.

"I mean, a witch's spell is the only reason that you'd willingly set foot in the mountains. We've tried to get you to go skiing a million times!" Foster whined slightly.

"It's different. It was for a job."

"I didn't know that the museum had a site out there." Foster dipped a finger in his whipped cream, and Jeremy watched the barista eye him hungrily. What most annoyed him about his best friend, other than his cockeyed optimism about the world and need for mundane gossip, was that he knew exactly how attractive he was and utilized it all the time. Foster was never *not* dating someone, though they never met the impossible standard that he had set.

"Nah, a private consulting thing. Something I tried once when I first moved here. Recently I wanted to, I dunno, stretch my wings or something." Jeremy made a flapping hand gesture that he hoped encompassed *my life is great, but I'm still feeling like there's something missing, which feels greedy but also necessary. And also, I feel like I need to live up to a legacy my parents never expressed.*

"Dope." A real poet, his best friend.

"What about you? Brewery news? Dating news?" Foster ran the business side of Mountain Friend, Vanberg's most popular craft brewery, while his older sister, Flo, was the brewer. Foster was surprisingly savvy, though he hid behind good looks and a goofy demeanor.

"Business is good. Flo is still talking about bringing on an assistant brewer. She needs one if she wants to open another location, honestly. But she's hesitant to trust people with recipes after her ex. Trivia is consistent. I'm considering a few movie nights in the spring. Hoping to replicate the hype around the Hallmark series we run in December." He took another sip of his drink and tossed a grin to the barista. Jeremy rolled his eyes. "Had a few dates this weekend. Nothing panned out." He drained his coffee and stood up, clearly intent on getting a number.

Jeremy wanted to ask Foster if he ever felt stuck, if he ever felt like he had wedged himself into one corner of a career that he loved and a personality that had fit perfectly at twenty-four but had grown a bit threadbare at thirty-four. But instead, he gave a false huff of frustration. "Go get 'em, tiger."

Davis

It was just an ordinary Saturday, really. Nothing to suggest it would shift Davis's thinking. Though on Friday, after work, he had asked Alex and Yesenia if he could join them on their Saturday ride. He had managed to hold his own, which shouldn't have surprised him. He was a good cyclist in West Virginia. Not good enough to enter races or anything, but confident and capable enough to not injure himself on some of the more difficult trails around the New River Gorge. Colorado was terrifying. The rankings were much higher than anything he had experienced, but over the last year, Davis had become a more technical rider, looking at the details of a trail before he got to the beginning. There was a metaphor there for the way his life had shifted since sobriety, but he would need more coffee before he could make the words connect in his brain.

After the ride and a shower, Davis settled in for his morning routine — a cup of coffee on the back porch, something that he had done even in the depth of winter. It tended to ground him and help him remember where he was, how far he had come. Then he would repeat a poem that a counselor had given him years ago that had somehow lodged in his brain.

I am the master of my fate.
I am the captain of my soul.

After his fingers or the tip of his nose were too cold or his coffee was empty, Davis headed back inside and spent a solid thirty minutes mindlessly scrolling on social media.

You had to have *some* vice, he supposed.

Between baseball highlights, depressing international news, witty captions from the National Park Service, and GoPro videos of mountain biking, Davis's thumb stopped his scroll.

Clear the Shelters! National Shelter Pet Day

A rescue, just a few exits down the highway.

And maybe it was the budget that had gotten approved for the visitor center exhibit, or maybe it was the way that Jeremy had sent a GIF of Pattie Gonia saying "Forest, Serve!" in celebration, or maybe it was the fact that Yesenia had complimented Davis's riding, but something shifted into place. Colorado, this forest, this odd little cabin he lived in, was his home. And this odd little cabin would be a lot better with a furry friend. Fifteen minutes later, Davis was parking at the shelter and filling out a form with his name, address, and history with pets.

The volunteer, an older woman who was wearing cat ears, smiled at him and asked, "Dog person or cat person?"

"Dog," Davis answered immediately, then explained that he worked at the national forest, which was good, because dogs were able to go on the trails through national forests. He didn't mind cats, per se — there were always some prowling around his uncle's farm and in his backyard when he was a child. But something about a dog and the physical affection pulled at Davis's heartstrings in a different way. The woman put up a small sign at the desk and led him down a concrete-block hallway, where he was met by another volunteer, who unlocked the kennel. He stepped into the damp kennel. It smelled a bit antiseptic and a lot like his uncle's living room, like *dog*, and was overcome with the immediate desire to somehow find a way to take home every single dog here.

"Most people like to walk up and down the aisles a few times and see the whole pack," the volunteer was saying. "I'll be in the hallway. Let me know if there are any dogs that you'd like to take out in the yard."

Davis began to slowly walk up and down the room, a little unsure of what he was doing. How did you pick just *one* dog when there were thirty here that needed a home?

He felt something cold brush against his left hand and looked down to where a stubby dog nose was pushing against his palm. There had been very few moments in Davis's life where he instinctively *knew* something. He knew the first time he learned that there were people whose job it was to protect nature that he would be one of them. He knew the first time he went hunting that he would never go again. He knew one arbitrary afternoon during a summer home from finishing his undergrad degree that he should probably not have another drink, maybe ever. He knew the first time he set foot in Colorado that the ground here called to him. And when he looked into this tan pit bull's soft and gentle blue eyes, he knew that this dog had stolen his heart.

He crouched down to get eye level with the dog, ignoring the ache in his low back. "You're an angel, huh?" he whispered, putting out his hand for the dog to continue to smell. Two little sniffs, then a tentative lick of his hand. "What's your name, sweetheart?" He looked at the tag — *Mary Anne* — along with a printed photo. A flashback to sitting on Gram's couch, wrapped up in a scratchy blanket that somehow felt good, sipping warm ginger ale and eating broth and dumplings while reruns of *Gilligan's Island* played on her television. "Mary Anne, huh? I always liked her more than Ginger." Davis scratched behind her ears, earning himself a pleased groan from the dog. "Well, I also liked the Professor, too."

The paperwork took a bit to fill out, and Davis ended up purchasing a probably overpriced bag of dog food and a harness from the shelter, telling himself that Mary Anne deserved everything as she made her way to her new home and that even if he was overcharged, the shelters deserved it. When he had first moved to Colorado, he had done what, to him, was a standard nature dork orientation — looked up the state flower (Columbine), state bird (lark bunting), mammal (big horn sheep), and tree (blue spruce). He had ended up discovering that Colorado also had a state amphibian (tiger salamander), fossil (stegosaurus), rock (yule marble) and a state pet. Davis had expected the state pet to be something painfully all-American and unaffordable, like a purebred golden retriever or one of those doodle dogs that weren't as cute as everyone had him believe. But no, the Colorado state pet was a shelter dog and shelter cat. As he took the leash from the volunteer, officially confirming that Mary Anne was *his* dog, he began to feel his roots here grow just a bit deeper.

"Are you afraid of cars, big girl?" Davis asked as Mary Anne gave his truck a tentative sniff. "Or are you more afraid of the fact that I don't think this truck has ever been washed?" Davis opened up the passenger door, and the dog leaped into the cab, immediately heading across the center console and sitting in the driver's seat. "Not afraid, apparently," Davis said. "But I don't think you'll meet the federal requirements for driving a government vehicle." Davis laughed, and Mary Anne answered with a sniff before plopping down on the passenger seat, facing backward. He maintained a steady conversation with the dog as he drove back to the national forest and was rewarded with Mary Anne's delightful selection of groans, sniffs, yips, and one large sneeze. By the time he pulled into his driveway and headed to the passenger door to make sure he had a firm grip on Mary Anne's leash before she ran away into the mountains, he was fully, 100 percent, deeply in love with this dog.

He brought her inside, double checking to make sure that every door and window was locked, and he supervised as she tentatively walked through every room in the small cabin. "You like it here?" he asked, watching as Mary Anne hopped up on his bed, turned around three times, and collapsed into an impossibly small ball of dog and immediately began snoring. "Yeah, darling, you like it here." Davis closed his bedroom door, then unloaded everything he had purchased, sliding a towel under the mixing bowl full of water and a soup bowl for kibbles that would do for now. He grabbed his phone and headed back into the bedroom, where Mary Anne hadn't moved an inch. Settling into bed, and already contorting his body around the dog, who, of course, decided that the center of the bed was the perfect place for her, he scrolled through a shopping app. A set of food bowls, dog bed, toys, a running leash, poop bags, a few more toys, and then a set of winter booties in case her feet got cold — all added to the cart.

Jeremy

"Never again," Emmy said, wringing sweat from the thick, black bangs that were stuck to her forehead. "Never a-fucking-gain will you drag me to this discotheque masquerading as a gym."

"The towel at the end was nice," Phoebe said. "And the music wasn't terrible."

"False," Declan added, stealing a sip of Phoebe's water. "The music was terrible and my ass is sore."

"That's because you have no ass," Phoebe replied, planting a kiss on his cheek.

"Watch it, Feathers," he replied in a low voice, eliciting a giggle from Phoebe.

"I had fun," Ryan said, taking an obnoxiously loud gulp of water.

"It's not fair. You're built for cardio," Emmy grumbled.

"I've *trained* for cardio, sweetheart, and so have you, if you know what I mean." Ryan waggled his eyebrows at her. Emmy tried to frown, but a slightly embarrassed smile snuck through.

"Blech," Dec said. "Straights."

"Coffee?" Foster asked.

"Yes, but I can't stay long," Flo said, blowing a chestnut curl out of her face. "I have résumés to look through for the brewery."

"You're hiring?" Dec asked. "If you need a bartender, Lina would pick up a shift or two."

"Nah, we're good on bartenders, but I finally need an assistant brewer."

These were his best friends, he thought as he laughed to himself. They were a chaotic mess that, when his mind wandered to other things, often continued chattering away like a very loud, very academic white noise machine. The chatter continued as they meandered down the street, the couples pairing off on the walk to the coffee shop. Foster, single again, dropped back next to Jeremy's side.

"Good music this morning," Foster said.

"Yeah."

"Nice weather."

"Yep."

"Crazy to hear about that alien landing yesterday."

"Sure." Jeremy's lack of engagement was rewarded with a punch to his upper bicep from Foster. "What the hell was that for?"

"Just bringing you back to the present moment. Your mind is all over the place." Foster, as he said this, slipped his phone out of his pocket and subtly checked for messages.

"Really? I'm the one who isn't *in the present moment*?" Jeremy asked, rolling his eyes.

"It's business."

"Funny business."

"You're not a comedian. Don't quit your day job, Jer," Foster said, laughing. The group approached the coffee shop, placed their orders, and settled around a low table. Emmy and Ryan took the couch in the middle. Phoebe pulled her feet up underneath her as she folded into a chair. Dec found the armchair next to hers, and Foster pulled up a stool. Jeremy perched on a footstool, something coursing through his veins today in a way that made it impossible for him to sit still.

Even though the tea selection was horrible, he had a decent affection for the Jumping Goat. It was close to campus and his friends loved it. If he needed to actually work, he would head to the Tea House and focus. Today, he craved community. Needed a reminder of the life he had built here. It was worth suffering through their Earl Grey.

"Jeremy Philip Rinci," Emmy said, turning her body to face Jeremy, away from where Ryan was discussing baseball with Declan. "Distract me from these boys and their sports talk. What's new with you? I feel like you've been a ghost recently."

"Are you sure you're not distracted by the flames of new love?" Jeremy replied sarcastically.

"Bah!" Emmy said. "He's fine. I'm only with him for the house." Though she played it off casually, Jeremy had been privy to Emmy's nerves about moving in with Ryan. How she loved him but was used to her independence and solitude. Jeremy had shared the way his parents kept separate spaces that the other never went into — his mother had her studio where she painted her professional work, and his father had a small corner where he tinkered with radios and other small electronics. Emmy and Jeremy were the singular only children in their group of friends and had often bonded over their love of quiet and their need to recharge away from their friends who had grown up with siblings. Emmy also knew enough about Jeremy's background that she didn't ask prying questions. She was content to trust Jeremy to share when things were necessary. Jeremy was grateful for friends who minded their own business.

"Whatever you say, Em," he replied. "Things are good."

"House things? Work things? Love things? Life things?"

"I need fewer friends who have gone to therapy," Jeremy said as a response. When Emmy raised her eyebrows into her blunt bangs and simply stared, Jeremy relented. "House things are a mess. My garbage disposal is broken, so my trash smells horrible. Work things are fine, but boring —"

"God knows we needed some silence in the office," Emmy interjected.

"You and your man are the cause of the majority of my work stress," Jeremy replied, but there was no heat behind the accusation. Emmy and Ryan had brought national attention to their tiny museum with their collaborative exhibition, and they were both anxious for the next exhibit to top their first.

"You love me," Emmy replied, wrinkling her nose.

"I guess. I've been consulting again, and I started a new exhibit design —" And before he could get to *life things* and talk about how he was feeling stuck at their shared workplace, Emmy pounced.

"What kind of exhibit are you working on? Can you chat about it? Have you signed an NDA? Who's the client?" she asked in rapid fire succession, setting her dirty chai down on the table to lean forward, closer to Jeremy.

He rolled his eyes. "It's nothing fancy. Just a visitor center out in the forest."

"What forest?" Phoebe asked, jumping into the conversation.

"Klarluft, right by where Colin and June live."

"I think he leads some summer overnights through their wilderness space," she said, pulling out her phone to either google or text her brother. "What's the exhibit on?" she asked, typing and swiping as she talked.

Jeremy didn't quite know yet. Davis had a lot of ideas, and the forest was beautiful, but he wanted to pick his friends' brains. "The forest?" he replied. "It's about bringing people in and teaching them. But I don't want them to be lectured to or to be bored."

And all of a sudden, here were seven people adding ideas, and Jeremy's hand couldn't work fast enough to write them all down.

"Make sure there's a good photo shoot location for social media, because that's free advertising for the forest," Phoebe mused.

"Have you reached out to tribal consultants?" Emmy asked. "Oh! And you should probably talk about the history of American preservation and its ties to white supremacy."

"You're such a ray of sunshine, darling," Ryan said, wryly, to which Emmy rolled her eyes. "Even though it's accurate." Ryan sipped a vanilla latte. "Did you know the Rockies are some of the youngest mountains in the world, and they're still growing every year?"

"Why would any normal person know that?" Dec added, resulting in Phoebe pinching him in the side.

"Do they want to open an attached tasting room for the brewery?" Foster asked. "I can also help with budgeting and production connections. We had a great fabricator who made all of our signs for the Great American Beer Festival last year, and I know good suppliers for the brewery's furniture." Foster was already pulling out his phone to text Jeremy but made a surprised noise when he found a series of alerts on the screen.

"You know, we could use spruce tips from the forest to add to an IPA and have some of the proceeds benefit the national forest," Flo said, fixing the bandanna that tamed her curly hair.

"Slow down, slow down," Jeremy said, holding his hands up and mimicking pumping the brakes in his car. "My brain doesn't work this quickly, and neither does my hand." He made a dramatic show of rolling his wrist. "Plus, I don't want to get ahead of myself. I'm not the content expert. I'm just the facilitator." It wasn't that Jeremy didn't like learning — you couldn't work in this field without being a bit of a nerd about everything — but the *what* of an exhibit wasn't as important to him as the *how*. The challenge and craft of taking complex ideas formulated by experts and translating them in a beautiful way to the general public? That was what made Jeremy's brain zing. It was the same way that historic research affected Emmy, or event planning got Foster firing on all cylinders. For the content of the exhibit, he'd defer to Davis. And something about that man, his new colleague, his *client*, made Jeremy want to take things easy and slow. To make him feel comfortable and not push too hard, but to communicate excitement. To be a partner in this design process.

The conversation transitioned away from ideas for Jeremy's exhibit (*the exhibit for the national forest*, he internally corrected himself) to plans for the upcoming long weekend, which allowed Jeremy to slip back into his comfortable role of observer of his friends.

Dec mentioned a showing of *City Lights* he wanted to attend, which led to Emmy and Phoebe chatting about the development of talkies and how it limited the opportunities for actors with accents. Ryan had turned to Foster and attempted to make idle small talk about the upcoming college football season, to which Foster reminded him that he hated organized sports. Ryan, rolling his eyes, grumbled, "I'll just text Julian, he gets me," while Foster contented himself, smiling at his own phone. Flo and Phoebe batted ideas back and forth for beer names. Phoebe's love of wordplay came in handy as she suggested more and more double entendre–laced rhymes with pale ale.

Jeremy smiled, content with the band of buffoons he had chosen to surround himself with. This was what he had hoped for when he moved to Colorado. The type of community his parents had cultivated in Greenwich Village. There was always someone joining their family of three for dinner. Sometimes it was an author that his mother was illustrating for or a visiting professor that Jeremy's father had charmed into giving a talk at his engineering firm. Often, though, it was one of the friends his parents had accumulated since their move to New York City — playwrights, activists, dancers, poets, ham radio broadcasters, chefs, and journalists for the *Village Voice*. It's why Jeremy had purchased his house, hoping to open it up to his friends. He also imagined that someone would be there with him as he opened it up, but Jeremy, for all his talk of embracing change, was fearful. Because love meant loss and risk. Friendship love was a beautiful thing, and Jeremy was lucky to experience that.

Unprovoked, Davis's face floated into Jeremy's mind as Ryan and Foster engaged in an arm-wrestling contest.

How was he spending his long weekend?

More importantly, why did Jeremy care?

Davis

One of Davis's favorite moments was the second after he finished a mountain bike ride and took off his helmet. There was a clarity in that space, with your heart still racing and your hair damp. The lactic acid in his muscles still burned pleasantly, a reminder that Davis had *done something* with his body today. In those moments, he was giddy, almost high. It was the closest thing he had found to the buzz he used to get from a steady intake of alcohol. Mountain biking, however, resulted in a clarity of mind, as opposed to the conscious numbness he chased from drinking.

Lots of addicts swapped their substances for something else. His counselor had suggested running marathons at first, but then took one look at Davis's *dense* form and had suggested that he find something else or attend some meetings. He tried a few twelve step meetings, but, after talking it over with his counselor, decided it wasn't the framework for him. He knew that some of the people kept attending meetings, knew that it worked for them, how they loved to fidget with a chip in their pocket or on a key ring. For Davis, he couldn't admit his failings to a God that had abandoned his family and their homesteads, no matter how close to heaven it had claimed to be. For a young boy who had felt that so much was out of his control — his brain, his attractions, his family's finances, the coal industry his town was built on — he couldn't be a young man who admitted he didn't have control over his own choices. So, with the help of his counselor and his college adviser, he'd signed up for a beginner mountain biking course at the community college and had given it a shot. It was rough at first. Growing up in rural West Virginia meant that he didn't have sidewalks to bike on, unless he wanted to take a bike down a rural highway that was full of trucks carrying coal and, as he worked as a college student, drilling for the new jobs that were promised by fracking. But something about being in nature, combined with the exertion and confidence he gained with each completed ride, worked for him. He hadn't looked back since.

Today, he took his helmet off and felt the cool breeze along his sweaty hairline, causing a shiver to run down his spine. He had finished first, which was unusual, but he had felt fully in the moment today. In *flow*, as Yesenia called it. This morning's trail had been a new one for Davis, but it was one that Yesenia said had an especially great portion of curves that made the climbing worth it.

She was right, of course, as Davis had learned, she usually was about mountain biking. She was the best of the three of them. Alex, unsurprisingly, preferred bombing down hills and, more often than not, ended up in a bush or a ditch at least once during every ride. Davis thought he had heard Alex take a tumble behind him, but he was already too deep in the momentum of his descent to be able to stop. He only felt a touch guilty about it, and only until Alex flew down the hill, a few small leaves and branches sticking out of his helmet, a goofy smile on his face.

"Amazing!" he said, skidding to a stop in front of Davis, taking off his own helmet to join Davis in watching Yesenia expertly navigate the single track, choosing to go over the jump that Davis had avoided.

"That was a great one," Yesenia said. "I wish that we could ride all day instead of working."

"Agreed," Alex said. "How does work always get in the way of fun?" He turned to Davis. "Speaking of which, I think it's time we met the new love of your life."

The good mood from the ride vanished in an instant. Did Alex know he was queer? Was he going to tell Eric? Yesenia? Was Davis safe?

"What did you name your dog?" Yesenia asked.

"C'mon, man, we want to meet her! My dog would love her," Alex whined.

Oh.

Of course.

A friend's aunt, a former nurse from upstate New York, had once given Davis a piece of advice she used to keep her head straight when they didn't know what was wrong with a patient. "If you hear hoofbeats, they're probably horses, not zebras," she had said. Davis, growing up in Anthracite Springs, felt like he had been hearing zebras for decades. He wasn't bullied in high school, because no one knew he was queer, but he was on the baseball team and had heard gay slurs tossed around between teammates more than handfuls of sunflower seeds in the dugout. Community college was a time for quiet experimentation with an openly gay classmate in his intro to biology class. Something that Davis told himself he could have written off as taking the class incredibly literally. When he dated men, or whatever you called a regular hookup, it was in a different city. Hell, it was in a different state, and Pittsburgh and Wheeling could sometimes seem like two different universes.

What he did was his business and his business alone.

Moving out here, it was easy to keep it quiet, even though his onboarding from the Department of Agriculture and the

Forest Service emphasized their new commitment to diversity and inclusion. He had scribbled the phone number for the Forest Service harassment reporting center on a Post-it, folded it up, and tucked it into a corner of a drawer in his desk. He'd read the press releases about how the forests were celebrating Pride throughout June, the feel-good stories about queer rangers and organizations that helped LGBTQ+ people experience the outdoors. Davis wanted to be the type of ranger that would be featured in the article, but he felt like he had used up all his good luck in even getting this job, what with his mediocre GPA from a decent forestry school. A few nights in Denver shortly after he'd moved here were enough so far, but Klarluft was far. National forests, as a rule, tended to be a long way from larger cities with their Pride parades and gay bars. A child of a small town, Davis wasn't ready to chance it out here.

"Hello?" Yesenia asked. "Dog time?"

"Of course," Davis said, walking his bike over to his cabin. "Her name is Mary Anne, like on *Gilligan's Island*, and she's a sweetheart." He tilted the bike against the outside wall, then unlocked his door. Mary Anne, who had been snoring in her crate when Davis left, perked up when she heard the door and knocked a paw against the lock. She was a strong girl, and Davis couldn't help the smile that spread across his face when she began wagging her tail so much that the crate began to skitter across the floor. "She's affectionate!" he called as Mary Anne zoomed out to the front porch and immediately put both paws on Alex's chest and a sloppy kiss on his face.

"We just met, Mary Anne!" Alex laughed. "Let me buy you dinner first!" Suitably pleased with her greeting to Alex, the dog gave an aggressive sniff of Yesenia's shoes, then rolled over, showing her belly.

"See? She knows I'm the alpha," Yesenia preened, kneeling down to scratch the dog's belly. Mary Anne let out a pleased groan, even more when Alex joined in on the pets.

"She'll have to play with my dog," Alex said. "Caveman gets along with everyone, too."

"Well, I'm pretty free," Davis said. "It's mostly just me and this girl these days."

"How's the exhibit coming? The one with the grant money?" Yesenia looked up at Davis from where she had sprawled out on the floor, allowing Mary Anne to engage her in a full-body snuggle.

"Uh, it's good. We've hired an exhibit consultant who is also a designer, and we had an initial meeting—kickoff; whatever you want to call it—to get started."

"Sweet," Alex said. "She's a good designer, then?"

"He," Davis corrected, and felt his face heat. "And yeah, his portfolio is really impressive. Works down at some museum in Vanberg, I think." Davis didn't think; he knew. Because he had spent an embarrassing amount of time on both Jeremy's website and then his staff bio on the university's website. He had read just enough to become even more intimidated by the man, who already carried himself with a confidence that was foreign to Davis. According to his biography, Jeremy had an undergraduate degree from NYU, which Davis thought of as one of the schools that only existed for rich kids, famous people, or fictional characters, like Harvard or Cornell. Real people, people Davis had known, didn't go to schools like that. And then Jeremy had an MFA. Davis had to google that term to find out what it stood for. He had laughed out loud in his cabin, startling Mary Anne, imagining if he had come back home to Anthracite Springs and told his Dad and his brother that he was going to get a Master in Fine Arts.

"Well," Yesenia said, giving Mary Anne a scratch behind the ears and pressing herself up to standing. "Keep us updated. When are you meeting next?"

"I think in two or three weeks," Davis said. Again, he knew. The date was highlighted in bright yellow on his desk calendar. It was in two and a half weeks.

"Let's go for a ride afterward, and you can tell us all about it," Alex said.

"Okay, yeah," Davis said. "Thanks."

He watched his coworkers head to their respective cabins, then turned to Mary Anne, who cocked her head in return. "I have to work today," he said to her. She groaned, and Davis nodded in agreement. "I know, sweetheart, but I have to go to work and get paid so I can feed you." At the mention of food, Mary Anne began to trot in circles, edging closer and closer to the door that led inside to the kitchen where her bowl was, and Davis laughed again.

Jeremy

Jeremy spent the long weekend bouncing between activities with his friends, avoiding the running list of things that he needed to fix around his house. Did people really *need* a garbage disposal, anyway? People probably didn't use them in Europe. He attended his monthly figure drawing class and had gotten a glass of Lambrusco with his friend Yuna. Both of the artists embraced the best parts of a Colorado spring and reminisced about Jeremy's first year in Vanberg. That year, he had awoken in early May to find two feet of snow on the ground, so you could never be too sure when the next beautiful Sunday would occur. Sunday morning was a spin class with Foster, followed by lunch with Emmy and Ryan that had, of course, devolved into an exhibit planning session before Jeremy made an excuse about grocery shopping so he could extricate himself. He overslept his alarm on Monday and was able to sneak into his studio without Emmy or Phoebe accosting him and making him social.

An only child, Jeremy preferred the days where he was given tasks via email and could allow his brain to wander down whatever path would end up being the most efficient for creativity to flourish in order to get his work done. At the moment, his biggest task was figuring out a design that integrated history and science, which was enjoyable, but for some reason wasn't holding his attention. Jeremy had even tried a new, more caffeinated tea blend from his office stash, which had only succeeded in making him feel like he was vibrating slightly. Trying to jog his creativity, Jeremy tried a new playlist, taking his desk from sitting to standing, then finally, he opened his YouTube account. Perhaps visual stimulation would help.

His eyes caught on the Smokey Bear documentary that he had sent Davis in their first email. A strange overture, he realized, but something that he remembered one of his first advisers in graduate school talking about. Making a personal connection was important for so many of the people you would work with in exhibit design. These were people who were experts in their field, who were used to talking at such a nuanced level of detail about their work that trust between a designer and a client was essential. People had to trust that you would represent their research, their community, their *forest* with the same kind of care and affection they had for it. And while Jeremy knew he would never be an expert in these fields, he liked being able to brush shoulders with the brilliant minds for these moments.

Hoping to spark something that would allow him to work on any exhibit he was supposed to be working on, Jeremy clicked on the channel that hosted the Smokey documentary and found one on something called *Mission 66*. Vaguely worried about the title, Jeremy found himself enraptured by the history of how modernist architects were used in national park visitor center design.

Yes.

This was interesting.

There was so much to pull from here, so many stories.

And damn gorgeous design.

The interplay between the sleek modernism and the rustic surroundings would make for an eye-catching contrast, in addition to connecting the Klarluft National Forest with a larger national conversation in design. And it would be unexpected, too.

Jeremy felt a spark in his fingertips akin to the first time he had participated in a charette, when the entire curatorial and design team was holed up together in an office, bouncing ideas off each other. It was invigorating. He opened his sketchbook, and a mockup of an exhibit took place that took the visitor through the establishment of the forest. Jeremy could connect it to all the grandiose spots of the west: Mesa Verde, Yosemite, Yellowstone.

Grateful, not for the first time, for his studio in the attic of The House, a Queen Anne Victorian that held the offices for a combined history and science museum, Jeremy opened his personal computer and his business email and tapped out an email.

Davis,

I have a few design ideas that I think would be best to discuss with you in person...

Davis

Focusing on work, especially when it involved a lot of emails, was something that Davis had to strive to accomplish. Which was difficult, because he needed another coffee. Because when his brain got tired and frustrated, it made reading even harder.

Davis left the administrative building and its harsh fluorescent lights, laptop in hand, and decided to work from his cabin office. Mary Anne would be happy, at least. Hopping down from the couch, the dog gave a dutiful lick and followed Davis to his office, where she flopped dramatically down on her newest bed and was snoring in seconds. Laughing, Davis sat down at this desk, placing one booted foot on a drawer he'd left open last time as a makeshift footrest. It was nice being able to choose where he worked, and nicer when there was a snoring dog next to him. After the computer booted up, Davis's eyes flicked down to his screen, to an alert in the corner that announced even more emails had arrived in the last four minutes. Davis got a million emails a day, mostly from the white noise of the federal government. Bureaucratic red tape meant that everyone had to be informed of everything, which, of course, meant that no one was informed of anything.

Responding to emails at the cabin's office was easier. He could use his speech-to-text program and make sure that no one heard the awkward way he had to announce punctuation.

He could do this. Davis sighed and reminded himself that it was the dumbest thing to be afraid of. It wasn't a mountain lion or an alligator tortoise; just an email. From her bed, Mary Anne sighed in agreement.

Opening his email, he saw that the newest message was from the tall exhibit designer who had, frustratingly, not left his daydreams since they had gone on the walk together.

Davis,

I have a few design ideas that I think would be best to discuss with you in person...

He quickly typed a response back, skimming it over twice to see if there were any typos.

J -

Any afternoon this week works for me. One perk of life out here is that my schedule is always open because we don't have that many visitors.

D.

The minute that he pressed *send*, Davis felt a cold chill rush through his body. Why had he added that line about his schedule? He could have been professional and just provided times. No one — especially not Jeremy Rinci — needed a justification for his schedule. He wished the government would have let him install the program that held the email in the outbox for ten minutes, which had been a lifesaver in West Virginia. It had been hard enough to convince the onboarding HR staff that he needed the text reading program, having to give the staff member a stern reminder that even senators were using programs like this in chambers.

A quick reply.

D-

Thursday? Should I bring hiking boots for another excursion?

J.

Davis chuckled. He had taken Jeremy on a 1.5-mile flat loop that he routinely took second graders on in flip-flops. Excursion would be a generous term for what they had done.

J -

No excursions this time, I promise. I will bring out some specimens and old photographs if you're interested.

D.

Another moment of internal screaming. Specimens, yes, but the idea that Jeremy would be interested in dusty photographs of boring old forest rangers —

D-

I'd love that.

See you Thursday at 1.

J.

Davis looked around this office and was hit with an overwhelming desire to make it look, well, better. He had a box of ephemera from home, from the tiny corner cubicle he had been able to claim at the office in Charleston. A Smokey Bear sticker, a WVU pennant. A framed advertisement for the CCC that featured strong, striking men that was incredibly homoerotic in the way that most Great Depression marketing was. A poster from his high school best friend's bluegrass band. All in a box in the corner, collecting dust, and Davis wanted to hang them up. Make it feel lived in.

Davis put everything on the wall, then decided it didn't feel right and moved all the posters again, grateful for the blue tacky stuff the government provided. Looking at the collection of art, something was off, but he couldn't figure out *what*. This was why he hired an exhibit designer. He turned to his desk and attempted to organize it into something that wasn't just piles. He started with the books that had shaped him — *A Sand Country Almanac, The Wilderness Warrior,*

Losing Eden, Braiding Sweetgrass — stacked in a neat pile on the corner of his desk.

A knock on Davis's cabin door interrupted his consideration of whether it was weird to have a snow globe on his desk, even if it was from Yosemite. "You stay here," Davis said to Mary Anne, closing his office door behind him. When Davis opened the front door, Alex was there, accompanied by a large black dog with long hair and one spotted hind leg.

"Hey," he said. "I, uh, brought my dog over so he could meet Mary Anne. Is that okay?"

"Of course. Come on in." Alex ambled in, the dog by his side.

"This is Caveman, and he's the best dog in the world," Alex said with the same kind of pride a parent had about their newborn.

"Hey, boy," Davis said, putting his hand down for Caveman to sniff.

"Looks nice in here!" Alex said. "It seems like you've decided to stay with us?"

"Yes?" Davis said. Had he been making his coworkers feel like he was leaving? He wanted to make sure that he did everything normally, made them feel comfortable. He didn't want to give them any reason to look at him twice or question his behavior. His goal was to fade into the background. Not to be invisible, but to be unnoticed.

To be *normal*, whatever that entailed.

Because if someone noticed you, they could be interested in you.

And interested people asked questions.

So if he was just *there*, he could blend in.

Normal.

"A few of us are headed to the local bar later for a drink if you want to join," Alex offered. "Yesenia and I realized that we've never invited you."

Normal. He could grab a Diet Coke or a seltzer, stealthy. It might even be advantageous to pull the bartender aside and ask that he be served tonic and lime when he asks for a drink. It's what he had done in Charleston, which had worked well. His coworkers never knew, and the bartender checked in on him. It was a nice arrangement and something he should replicate here. But Klarluft was smaller than Charleston, and if Davis knew anything about small towns, it's that everyone knew everyone else's business. And if he was going to be staying here for a while, he wanted firm control over what aspects of his personal business were able to be shared.

"I can't," Davis said, waving at his computer screen. "I'm working on sorting through the pile of emails I've let build up this week. Next time?" He could start talking about his sobriety at some point with them, and then that way it wouldn't be a shock when he didn't drink. He had just gotten his first invite to a happy hour. He couldn't be the wet blanket that reminded everybody he was sober. Davis knew that wasn't a good way to make friends.

So he distracted Alex with a dog. "Want to meet Mary Anne?"

Alex grinned like a second grader who just came back from a doctor's appointment with McDonald's. He let Caveman out to the backyard, and Davis let Mary Anne out. After the ritual exchange of butt sniffs, the dogs engaged in a classic game of *whose mouth is bigger*, then settled for chasing each other around the small, fenced-in meadow.

It was nice to chat with Alex as something more than a coworker, as someone he could imagine being friends with. Alex, it turned out, shared a love of sports and went on a long rant about how the college football playoffs needed to stop changing all the time. Davis, still a huge WVU fan, wanted them to keep changing so he could see the Mountaineers anywhere near the playoffs. For a moment, it felt like Davis was back in West Virginia, shooting the shit and talking trash on Pitt with his cousin Bruce.

Alex whistled for Caveman and offered another invite out to the bar, to which Davis used emails as an excuse. After he had left, Davis sat back down at his computer, and Mary Anne let out a long sigh. "I know, girl," he said to the dog. "But we'll have a lovely night at home, working our way through that new game." Over the last year, Davis had started playing more video games, as he didn't have many friends, and was surprised at the way the narratives had increased in complexity. Working away at a story, bit by bit, slowly uncovering how the puzzle piece slotted together. It seemed to Davis how his friend who loved reading talked about getting lost in a book. Tonight, Davis would be an assassin sneaking around Ancient Greece.

Once he got through these damn emails. And found some photographs for Jeremy.

"On second thought," Davis said to Mary Anne. "I'll probably spend some time looking through the digital archives instead. That okay with you?"

Mary Anne answered with a snore, and Davis opened up the National Archives website, finding the records for his forest. Maybe he could find other people who felt connected to this same piece of land throughout history...

Jeremy

Jeremy knew that most of his friends saw him as confident, aloof, even. He worked hard to cultivate that image, a bit of a playboy, a bit of a metropolitan man-about-town. The truth was, he had tried on a few versions of himself in undergrad — the slutty twink who was covered in glitter, the academic man who was serious about art history and scholarship, the friend who was down to try anything once — and had settled on the current version of himself after his life was thrown off-kilter. What his friends didn't see was that he worked hard to stay calm and spent every Sunday evening organizing his outfits for the week and planning out his schedule that somehow still fell apart at the last minute. Regardless, it was about preparation so he couldn't be caught entirely off guard.

There were certain things he liked to keep to himself. Like the figure drawing class he took, or how he spent a lot of time working on Davis's exhibit designs and researching the cheapest fabricators so the grant money could go as far as possible.

And so, after a few days of documentaries and archival research, Jeremy had pulled together a new mood board for Davis's planning. One that echoed the great architects that had been commissioned for national park visitor centers and drew a common thread of the development of the visitor experience. Bringing the past into the present through the experience. There, he had some help from Emmy, who had been overjoyed to come over one night and split a bottle of wine and chat about accessibility of natural spaces for various audiences.

Equipped with a new playlist he had downloaded from a favorite music blog he had started following in college (during his pretentious vinyl-purchasing phase, where he attempted to drink coffee), Jeremy drove back out to the national forest. He had remembered, this time, to download music instead of streaming it, because cell reception was spotty once he turned off the highway. He had also remembered to download everything he needed to his iPad, as the wi-fi needed a government username to connect with. That was something that Emmy had brought up in her recommendations after two glasses of wine: that people needed to be able to post about their visit to the forest.

"Wi-fi, or whatever fucking stupid technology they'll come up with next," she had said, laughing at her own joke into the glass of wine. "These things are important to experience, but they're important to share. And—" She took a breath, and Jeremy knew that he was in for one of her patented rambles (or lectures, depending on your perspective). "And while everyone can shit on social media — as well they should — it's been a way to open up the world to a lot of people who wouldn't be able to experience that exhibit or even know that it exists."

Davis would like Emmy, Jeremy thought, laughing to himself. It was rare that he thought that about his prickly friend. Emmy had softened since moving in with Ryan and achieving a bit of success with her recent research and exhibit contents, but she was still an acquired taste. But Emmy and Jeremy had always seen each other in a way that was special to their friendship, an understanding of what growing up talking mostly to adults did to a child. And she had seemed to really enjoy helping out on Davis's exhibit.

The exhibit for *the forest*, Jeremy corrected. Davis wasn't his client. He was just a representative. Jeremy, once again, dutifully followed the blue dot and pulled into the visitor center, laughing to himself as it still read *Visitor Cunter*. When all this was over, he wanted that sign in his house. At least a photograph of it. Expecting to walk into the office, he was surprised to see Davis standing outside the building. He was bent over, pulling up a weed, but straightened quickly when he took notice of Jeremy's car.

Davis looked much as Jeremy remembered him. Which, he reminded himself, just meant he was being an especially thorough consultant. Even if he didn't usually remember the exact blending of green and gold that comprised a client's eyes. Even if he did take note of the fact that Davis wore a hoodie this time, instead of a flannel. Jeremy studied the logo on the chest — the incredibly broad, barrel chest — and could make out a few music notes around a name that had faded with time. Jeremy didn't think he owned anything in his closet that dated to pre-COVID, let alone anything old enough to have a peeling logo. Other than his house and a few close friends, nothing in Jeremy's life was that permanent.

"Hey," Jeremy said, getting out of his car and pushing his sunglasses into his hair. He had thought about what to wear today, opting for a practical pair of jeans and a light shirt, just in case he went hiking again. And because he liked the way the jeans hugged his ass and the shirt showed off his arms.

"Hi, Jeremy," Davis said, brushing dirt off his hands onto his thighs. He took off his baseball cap, ran a hand through his hair, and put the hat back on. He wasn't wearing sunglasses, and he smiled as Jeremy approached, slight lines crinkling at the corners of his eyes. "You have some new ideas for me?"

"I did some research over the past few days and talked to a few friends at the museum down in Vanberg so they could explain some ecology things to me." Jeremy held out his iPad. "I put together some additions to your mood board. Hope that's okay."

Davis shrugged, a neutral reaction. "Sure. I mean, you're the expert." And Jeremy had a knee-jerk reaction to comfort this man, to tell him that no, actually, *Davis* was the expert, and Jeremy's job was to translate his ideas into a setting that was more accessible for people.

What Jeremy said instead was "nah." And then he followed Davis into the administrative building.

Davis

Davis said the absolute stupidest things around Jeremy, he decided. Things that, in his head, sounded smooth and flirtatious, but felt awkward and clumsy when he said them. Jeremy had followed Davis into his office and had sat down in the chair he had settled into last time, the one that had a tiny table next to it. Jeremy flipped open his tablet case and performed a series of what seemed like complicated maneuvers to set it up so it displayed a well-designed presentation.

Davis, once again not enjoying the comparisons that seemed to spring up between himself and Jeremy, fumbled with his clunky government-provided computer. Jeremy had a sleek iPad that could probably easily send a spaceship to Mars. Davis's computer seemed to have been designed to operate a bomb shelter during the height of the Cold War.

"Uh, Jeremy?" He always felt weird saying someone's name, especially when it was someone he was attracted to. What if they could *tell* by the way he said it? Like maybe there was an advanced version of gaydar that Davis wasn't equipped with as a bisexual man.

"Hmm?"

"What are you presenting on?"

"New exhibit idea," Jeremy said, and then launched into a deep discussion of how he planned to connect the architecture and history of the grand national parks of the west to the national forest.

And while Davis wanted to hear this handsome man — who talked with his hands and had one piece of hair that was curling around his ear in a devastating manner — continue to talk about the fact that the National Park Service had demolished the Gettysburg Cyclorama ("which was designed by *Neutra*!" he had huffed), he had to stop him.

Because it wasn't about linking this patch of trees to something else.

Because the National Forest Service wasn't the National Park Service.

Because Jeremy was wrong.

Because this wasn't the type of exhibit that *this* forest needed.

Davis cleared his throat. "Uh, Jeremy?"

"Yes?"

"I work for the Forest Service."

"Of course, yes," Jeremy said, nodding in agreement. He wasn't getting it, so Davis continued.

"I work for the Department of Agriculture, with the national forests. National parks are under the Department of the Interior," Davis explained carefully. "They're different offices of the federal government." Davis remembered when *he* learned that, the complicated diagram in his text book listing *interior, state, treasury, defense, labor, justice, agriculture* and about a dozen others.

A light pink flush spread across the top of Jeremy's cheeks. "Oh," he said simply.

"Yeah, and..." Davis swallowed, tried to remember that *he* was the expert here and that he did actually know what he was talking about. A reminder, this time from a therapist he still talked to occasionally through video chats, that he was enough. Confident. In charge of his own choices. "I actually disagree with this approach."

Jeremy looked at him. Actually, it was more accurate to say he *studied* him, and Davis felt like he was under the microscope, like the lichen in his ecology class.

Lichen were critical to the ecosystem.

So Davis continued. "It's not about tying our forest to other, more famous natural spaces. It's about allowing people to see that what they have right here, right now, is special and important. There's enough here that's amazing, you know, like —" Davis's brain pulled for something that he could talk about in depth, something that would convince Jeremy that what looked to be an average forest was full of nuance and wonder. "Lichen."

"What is a lichen?" Jeremy asked. It took a moment for Davis's brain to catch up with the reality of the situation. Part of Davis's upbringing was *loud*. Even when people agreed with you in West Virginia, they yelled at you about it. Jeremy, however, was calm and measured, which, sometimes, Davis mistook for the type of sullen anger that took over his dad after another round of layoffs at the mine. But Jeremy wasn't angry, not by his body language or his tone of voice. He had simply cocked his head, hair moving in a distractingly attractive way, and given Davis a small smile. A small smile that Davis hoped meant *keep talking, I'm curious*.

So Davis took a deep breath and did. "Well, lichen aren't well known to a lot of people, but they're the cornerstone of ecosystems all over the globe, including right here. They don't fit into the classification systems that we have, because they're both fungi and plants. It's an example of a healthy symbiotic relationship. They're potentially the oldest living organisms on the planet, and I think there's something to learn from the fact that two species working together like this have lasted the longest." Davis took another breath and continued, somehow recalling things that he had learned from his favorite professor, Dr. Bibee. "They're beautiful and add this fascinating spark and life to a forest, even on boulders and old logs. They're so old and so unchanging that we can date some by seeing them on tombstones from the 1800s in historic photos. They can tell us when glaciers melted from the last ice age. Plus, they're able to be used as an indicator of air quality. Back home, there are some places that are using them to see how superfund sites are faring and other places that are using them to monitor emissions."

"Where's home?" Jeremy asked.

"West Virginia," Davis replied.

"I have a friend from eastern Ohio. You could bond about running away from steel mills," Jeremy said. Again, Davis was worried that he had given too much of himself away, that he had somehow become the bitter person he worked hard to *not* be, but again, he realized Jeremy was joking.

"I didn't run away," Davis said, trying to inflect some lightness into his voice. "I simply moved to find a better opportunity. Plus, the mountain biking out here is way better."

Jeremy gave a small sniff, and Davis couldn't tell whether it was to indicate a positive or negative emotion. "I ran away here. It's not so bad."

Davis recalled that Jeremy had lived in cities that seemed, to him, full of life and opportunity and community — New York City, Philadelphia. He had seen the Liberty Bell on a school trip in 6th grade and was more shocked by the number of people around him than by the fundamental part of American history. Davis didn't know how to respond to someone who admitted running away from that, so he defaulted to what was comfortable — silence. "Anyway," Jeremy said, "that's good to know. Keep it local. Keep it intimate." Hearing that word from this man's mouth was a bit too much for Davis right now, so he excused himself, offering Jeremy a seltzer from the mini fridge he kept in the corner of his office.

Jeremy

Jeremy took the offered seltzer, appreciating the cutesy design of the mulberry and a small ginger root that made Jeremy want to put it on a T-shirt. Or a sticker. Or a water bottle.

"This is cute," Jeremy said, holding up the can. "Imagine if the forest had little characters like this we could use as marketing."

Davis, who had a seltzer of his own in the same flavor, gave a wry grin. "Is Smokey not good enough for you?"

"Considering that I apparently don't know what organization I'm even consulting with, I shouldn't be suggesting anything right now." Jeremy laughed a bit, hoping to put Davis at ease. Taking a page out of his bartender friend Declan's playbook, Jeremy asked an inviting question and left a bit of silence afterward as an invitation for Davis to respond when he felt comfortable. "Can you tell me the difference?"

"So, uh," Davis began, then took a sip. "National parks are under the Department of the Interior, and they're about preservation — keeping things as they are. Untouched. Right? Forests are under the Department of Agriculture, because lumber was considered a commodity. Something to be maintained and managed. National forests started as forest reserves so that lumber companies wouldn't take everything all at once. It all stems back to Gifford Pinchot and the establishment of forestry as a profession in the United States as a true craft, rather than just lumbermen taking anything they could get. There were arguments with people like John Muir about preservation — which is what parks do — and conservation — which is what forests do. People like to paint them as opposite forces, but I like to think that they're two approaches to the same goal. Especially in recent years. Like we now have a duty to preserve old growth forests within the national forest system, and that's important because —" Davis took a breath and then closed his mouth. "Sorry, I'm probably boring you. You don't care about this." Davis looked away, like he was embarrassed or he'd said something out of turn. Jeremy took a sip of his seltzer and thought about how to respond, because yeah, he probably didn't care about the technical definition of *old-growth forest*, but Jeremy liked learning. And he especially liked learning from good teachers, like Davis.

A silence settled, the only noise Davis playing with the tab on his seltzer can.

"No," Jeremy said. "It's fascinating. You explain things in a way that makes sense. It's not simple, but it's easy to follow. Comforting." He tapped the quilt behind him. "Like this quilt. Handmade, right?"

"My aunt made it," Davis answered. "Well, if you get bored, let me know. At least you have Aunt Ellen's blanket to keep you warm if you fall asleep."

Jeremy had friends who loved to go on tangents, a natural consequence of working in a museum. He had heard lectures on how dinosaurs swallowed rocks to help their digestion. He had heard about the importance of looking for gap in the museum archives, the necessity of providing multiple means of access for children to experience a museum, the development of hand-drawn animation in post-war Japan, even details about why Jimmy Carter was the reason craft beer exploded in the 2000s. His friends were brilliant and knew it. They didn't underestimate their own expertise, and they loved to bandy about their ideas and things they'd learned with each other. Jeremy saw himself more as a sponge, soaking it all up for when he would eventually need it later.

Davis, however, seemed bashful about the fact that he knew this, was an expert on it. Every few sentences, he would stop and ask Jeremy if he was really, truly interested in what he was talking about. And while maybe Jeremy didn't care as much about the ways in which the Vanderbilts' house gardens connected to the national forest or how *carbon sequestration* worked, he was interested in the ways that Davis talked with his hands to explain a concept. The way the man's hazel eyes shone a bit gold when he was excited, and Jeremy was reminded, oddly, of Yukon Cornelius, on the hunt to find silver and gold. Davis's voice grew a bit husky at times as he spun a yarn about how people didn't understand what forests meant to this country, the ways that even rangers had shifted their understanding to be one of appreciation and care, rather than utilization and practicality.

When Davis attempted to describe the size of some of the redwoods that had existed in California and struggled for words, he finally pulled up a photograph on his computer that had stunned Jeremy into silence. A dozen or so men, all standing within a slice made into a tree. Davis excused himself and grabbed a tissue from the desk, wiped his eyes, and continued on by discussing changing policies toward forest fires in the last thirty years. The entire time, Jeremy soaked it in like an Epsom bath while his hand skimmed across his sketchpad.

Davis reached a natural stopping point, and Jeremy couldn't tell whether it was because he was done speaking or he had finished the can of seltzer that had been a prop through his entire narrative. "Sorry, that was a lot," he said, crushing the can slightly with his hand.

"No," Jeremy said honestly, shaking his head like he couldn't believe it. "Shit, I wish we could just put a hologram of you telling that story in the visitor center."

"Something tells me that we don't have the budget for that," Davis replied, deadpan.

"Yeah, that might be a bit ambitious for federal funding," Jeremy said, grinning. "While you were talking, I wrote some ideas down." Jeremy passed his sketch pad over and watched Davis take in the information. "I think we could make it about breaking down these former divisions. The goal could be for people to realize the interconnectedness of all things. Different groups of people, humans and animals, the way the forests intertwine with the city." Now it was Jeremy's turn to feel embarrassed. Maybe he had misspoken.

"That's perfect," Davis said softly. "I don't know how you distilled all my rambling down to that."

"You're a great storyteller," Jeremy replied. "My mo—uh, a mentor I had was a storyteller, too. It's an amazing skill. I bet you're great around kids."

Davis flushed again. "I do love leading the elementary tours. There's this pure awe and appreciation in children, you know?" Jeremy didn't know. He had been raised around adults more than younger children, and, growing up, most of his friends were only children. His version of New York City didn't seem like a place that ever catered to little kids unless they were working in a factory in 1900.

Jeremy studied Davis, who was taking his finger and tracing over the ideas that Jeremy had written down, along with a few sketches of titles and phrases that had particularly struck Jeremy while Davis was speaking. He was still staring, Jeremy realized, when Davis looked up and made eye contact with him, those green-gold eyes widening ever so slightly, then relaxing. Jeremy felt *seen*, but only for a moment.

Davis stood up abruptly, handing the sketchbook back to Jeremy. "This all is great," he said quickly.

Jeremy felt like he was being dismissed. "Okay, um. I'll take these ideas and get back to you during our next meeting," he said.

"Next week?" Davis asked, sounding hopeful.

"Next week," Jeremy responded, nodding, and was rewarded with a small smile from Davis.

Jeremy

Even though Jeremy did the vast majority of his professional work on a computer or tablet these days, there was something about the tactile nature of charcoal that nothing could replace. Since lockdown had ended, Jeremy had been working harder and harder to remember the original reasons he had pursued art. He tried pottery, painting, metalwork, watercolor, and photography — all mediums he had worked in during college and his MFA — and he had enjoyed them all, but it was the figure drawing class that met at the community arts center he kept coming back to.

Unsurprisingly late and carrying a large newspaper pad under his arm and a small case for his charcoals, he quietly settled into his usual spot as the instructor was introducing their models and focus for the session. Next to him, an Asian woman with a blackwork sleeve of cherry blossoms, chrysanthemums, and tigers grinned at him in greeting. Jeremy had a routine habit of leaving for events around the time that they were due to begin, so Yuna had begun putting her bag on a stool next to her so Jeremy would be able to sit there. Yuna, a friend that none of his other friends knew, was a bit of a life raft at times. Plus, it was better than being stuck in the back of the class with the boomers who had moved to Vanberg in the '60s and still thought that everything could be bought and sold for the approximate cost of a small joint.

When he had first met Yuna, they had been seated next to each other in one of the first sessions Jeremy attended and had struck up polite conversation. During the first break, Yuna had commented on what Jeremy had drawn — the life model in a contrapposto pose to echo a classic statue — then showed her own work. Yuna had drawn their life model in with fine lines and pastel colors.

"It's *ukiyo-e*," Yuna had said. "It translates to *pictures of the floating world* in Japanese." Following class, Jeremy had asked Yuna out to tea, where she explained her desire to take back the style of Japanese woodblock printing from the way it had been used by western artists in the 1800s. Jeremy, feeling like he could use his art history degree for the first time ever, had immediately felt a friendship connection. Since then, the two had attended an unlikely series of exhibition openings in stuffy, stark white halls and cramped, sweaty dive bars, making fun of each of them in their own ways. Yuna was working as a tattoo apprentice and understood the struggles and successes of freelance art.

They gave each other friendly nods, then Jeremy took a deep breath and closed his eyes, thinking about what his mother used to look like when she sat down at her watercolor easel. She would take a deep breath and stretch her arms out and wiggle her fingers. She told Jeremy when he was younger that she took a moment to see the finished piece in her mind's eye and she tried to send that image to her fingers to be easier to transfer to the paper.

Maybe it was sitting at an easel. Maybe it was the white noise of pencils and charcoal scratching across papers or the quiet jazz put on by the master teacher, with just the occasional murmur of their voice as they mingled through the easels, offering critique and commentary on the art. What-ever it was, something about figure drawing was calming and centering to Jeremy. He found he could lose himself in the snippets of the body he focused on. Some days, it was a detailed study of the way the elbow bent. Others, the way to highlight the definition of muscle along the calf. Today, he was particularly focused on how to capture the detail of the model's hair as she moved, the beads at the end of her long, thin braids providing a comforting noise when she switched poses that reminded Jeremy of a rainstick used by his preschool teacher.

It was moments like this that Jeremy was at his most reflective. He loved the push of his body in spin classes, but when his charcoal was in hand and that limb was perfectly in communication with his mind, he felt most centered. Emmy, surprisingly, when he had told her about his love of sketching, had suggested it was because he was reminded that life is a process that you can always adjust and tweak, just like a sketch. He liked the reminder that things could be messy and fragmented but still contain beauty. He had just figured out the particular flick of the charcoal he needed to represent the baby hairs around the woman's forehead when the master artist rang a tiny bell, which meant a stretch break.

A younger Jeremy would have sketched straight through. Thirty-four-year-old Jeremy knew that his carpal tunnels were only good for so long if he didn't engage in regular stretches. As he was stretching, he caught a glimpse of Yuna's work and saw that she had chosen to use a piece of black newsprint and white chalk.

"What's that?"

"Flash for white tattoos. I want to explore ways of tattooing on different hues of skin, and white tattoos look stunning on skin that's her tone," Yuna indicated to the model.

"Yuna," Jeremy scolded, "you cannot keep sleeping with our figure models."

She snorted. "It was, like, three times." Jeremy kept looking at her, eyebrows raised. "Okay three times last *year*, but you have to kiss a lot of frogs to find your princess." She playfully pushed his arm. "What about you? How's the Jeremy Rinci frog-and-prince situation?"

"Not my priority," he said, perhaps a bit too defensively. "My consulting business is actually consulting." She gave a small round of applause. "Well, I have my first client right now, so most of my off time is working on that exhibit. I'm out in the national forest at least once a week, which means I'm playing catch-up all weekend."

"Well, at least you don't have to worry about getting into trouble with mixing business and pleasure," Yuna said, laughing to hide her bitterness. Shortly after she had met Jeremy, she had lost her first tattoo apprenticeship with her uncle after she slept with one of her clients. She'd been working to earn back the trust of her family's tattoo business ever since and mostly worked as a guest artist in shops around Colorado and the mountain West. "I can't imagine there are many rangers and mountain men who bat for your team." Davis's face while he was explaining the nuance of lichen versus mosses flashed into Jeremy's mind.

"Yeah, I think it's a pretty straight place," Jeremy replied. Oddly, he realized he hadn't even opened an app since he started working on the project for the national forest. He supposed it was because he spent his free evenings with his friends or trying to fit in a bit of extra time on that project. Yes, that had to be it.

"Tea?" Yuna asked when class was over.

"Of course." Yuna biked and Jeremy drove to Dragon Tea Salon, a hidden treasure that Jeremy had discovered in Vanberg during his first month living here, desperate to find some place that wasn't his home office or mess of a house to exist.

A traditional Japanese Chashitsu, dating back to 1700, it had been dismantled piece by piece from a village in Japan and carefully reassembled on a flat piece of land next to Vatten Creek in the early 1990s when the two small towns had become sister cities. When Jeremy had asked Emmy about it, he had been treated to a small lesson on Vanberg's attempts to become a mountainous Silicon Valley and how the city council's overtures to Japan had less to do with international goodwill and more to do with luring Japanese companies to locate their headquarters in the university town. Regardless of how the building had come to be, it was another reason Jeremy couldn't imagine leaving Vanberg. Nothing like this existed in any other city in the United States. As Yuna biked up on her customized fixed gear, pulling off her helmet, Jeremy thought about how any other city wouldn't have a Yuna either.

Wouldn't have an Emmy or a Phoebe. Wouldn't have a bar run by Declan. Wouldn't have a Foster. Wouldn't have a Ryan either.

The two ordered their tea and grabbed two floor cushions and settled into a table near a large window with a traditional wooden screen cutting some of the harshness of the early afternoon sun. They made small talk until their tea arrived, poured with the utmost care and confidence. Jeremy watched the small sachet in his cup open, leaves and flowers blossoming. "How did you know you loved tattooing?" he asked Yuna.

A dry laugh was her response. "Because even when I hate it, I can't imagine doing anything else. It's a way for me to do art that feels relevant. An honor that things I draw, from my culture, end up on people's skin. It's that trust." She took a sip of her own tea, the ginger wafting over to Jeremy as she did so. "Why? Are you considering leaving exhibit design?"

"No. God, not at all. I have no transferable skills. No one wants a salesman who's more concerned with font selection than the product he's selling." He looked down at his cup again, where two of the leaves had become tangled together, dancing in circles in the currents created by the tea. "I have just been feeling a bit stuck, but I can't imagine doing anything else." He finally committed and took a sip of his tea. "I guess that's why I started consulting. Like maybe this will shake me up. I'm already learning new things."

"Oh?" Yuna raised an eyebrow, and then Jeremy was telling her about the project out in the forest, about the ideas and how he had been so wrong, and then how he and Davis had stumbled upon an idea that energized them both. Jeremy had left the forest after their previous visit feeling like he was on the right track, but he had worried that he'd somehow offended Davis. There was no reason in particular. Just a sense that a current in the air had shifted slightly, and Jeremy wasn't sure what it meant.

That fear had been assuaged early the next morning when he received a voice memo from Davis, his voice still a bit scratchy with sleep. Which Jeremy didn't notice or have any reaction to at all. The voice memo had thanked Jeremy for listening to Davis's "rambles" and for adding some new ideas. Jeremy wondered why Davis always felt that he had to thank Jeremy for listening, when anyone who had half a brain would have liked to listen to Davis talk about how national forests often surrounded national parks and were hidden treasures that most tourists didn't spend time in. After that meeting and Davis's message, it was like the floodgates had been opened. Davis had been sending him articles and photographs, the shared Pinterest board growing by dozens of photographs by the day. Podcast episodes, too, enough that Jeremy could listen to all of them for a week straight and probably not repeat one.

"Sounds like you're well on your way to finding spark again," she said after Jeremy finished. "How is the client?" It took Jeremy a few moments to realize that the client was Davis. He didn't feel like other clients he had worked with years ago, pretentious artists in Boulder or stuffy old men who ran historical societies in small towns in eastern Colorado. Davis was *real* and genuine and just a pure soul.

"He, uh, I mean the national forest is a great client."

"He?" Yuna said, catching Jeremy's verbal misstep.

"Yeah, a guy named Davis. The primary contact at the forest. He's an educational ranger, which makes sense, because he's taught me a lot about —"

"So much for the forest being a straight place, eh?" Yuna interrupted. Jeremy sipped his tea. "Is this Davis cute?"

"I plead the fifth," Jeremy replied delicately.

"Oh, you're in danger," she said, chuckling. "Trust me, I know better than anyone how that goes."

"Yuna, I say this with all the love in my heart, but you're wrong. First off, it's work —"

"Didn't two of your coworkers just move in together?" she interjected.

"Well, yes, but that's not the point. Davis is, well, *Davis*. He's a forest ranger. Out there. And he's not like me. We established that," Jeremy said, hoping Yuna got the point. Jeremy had long passed the point where he tried to hit on men of an undetermined sexuality. He was himself, which was openly gay and proud of it, and that made it apparent to anyone where his preferences lay. If Davis had been *looking*, Jeremy would have known it.

He conveniently ignored the moment their eyes had met across a sketchpad, or the way Davis had blushed when Jeremy complimented his wood-burned sign.

"Your phone is buzzing," Yuna said, shaking Jeremy out of his thoughts.

He looked down at his phone and saw a short email from Davis, asking if they could do the next work session down in Vanberg. Without thinking, he smiled.

"A hot date? New match?"

"It's the exhibit," Jeremy said. "Give me a few seconds to send a response." The pointed exhale Yuna answered with communicated her thoughts on the matter.

And because the universe had an absolutely pathological sense of irony, when Jeremy swiped to unlock his phone, the photo widget on his home screen showed him a photograph of his family on NYU's graduation day, the violet commencement gown a contrast with his pale skin. He was skinnier then, a lanky undergrad who spent late nights in the studio finishing his final portfolio for his minor in studio art and early mornings in the library working on his thesis in art history. But his smile was bigger than anything he'd seen in photographs in a long time, because he was sandwiched between his parents. His mom wore a long, felted tunic, probably made by one of the fiber artists she was friends with. Her gray hair was pulled back in her usual low ponytail, the unruly curls that Jeremy inherited doing their best to escape from the clip in the New York spring breeze. His father had insisted on wearing the *NYU Dad* T-shirt that Jeremy had bought him freshman year, tucked into a pair of khakis held up with a braided leather belt. It wasn't in the photograph, but Jeremy was sure he was wearing bright red Chuck Taylors. They were something that, according to his mother, he had found in graduate school decided he never needed another type of shoe.

Jeremy's smile faltered, his heart aching in a way that made the grief feel fresh. He took his photo album out at specific times — their birthdays, their anniversary, the dates of their passings — and he was able to contain his grief on those days. To see it here, after his heart had skipped a beat talking about Davis, was a cruel reminder of how dangerous love could be.

"You good, Jer?" Yuna asked softly.

"Just fine," he said. "Too many emails." And if Yuna noticed his eyes watering or the way he wasn't typing on his phone, she was a good enough friend to not mention it.

Davis

Davis had no idea why he had sent that email, but, once again, what was sent through the internet was done and out in the world.

Jeremy —

You've been out to the forest the last two meetings. I'm happy to head down to Vanberg for our next meeting. I need to pick up some things down the mountain anyway.

Davis

Again, he felt himself over-explaining his reasons for wanting to be down in the city, as if he needed something custom ordered. When Davis went shopping in the city, he usually ended up buying a piece of gear he didn't actually need at an outdoor store or another blanket for his couch. This time, he had marked a few pet stores that specialized in outdoor gear for dogs. He thought Mary Anne needed a backpack for their adventures. He wasn't exactly sure what a dog would carry in a backpack, but the photos on the website were too adorable for reason.

The reality, other than making his dog look like an L.L. Bean model, was that Davis was interested in seeing Jeremy in his element, which was very clearly not the national forest. While he had been polite about it, it was obvious in the way that Jeremy twitched at every small insect landing on him and aggressively ducked at every branch that poked out across the short loop around the visitor center they had walked on last week.

So he wanted Jeremy to feel more at ease. Which was a very normal, perfectly standard thing to do with a new work friend. Work person. Colleague? Just two bros hanging out, talking about exhibit design.

When Jeremy had finally responded to Davis's email after a day — a time frame that seemed absurdly long, like the first weeks of quarantine — he had emailed an address for Davis to drive to. Davis, who wasn't super familiar with Vanberg other than grocery stores, a mechanic, and the outdoor store, figured they'd meet at a coffee shop. Probably some place that handwrote their signs in ornate cursive, which made it harder for Davis to read, so he would just order whatever Jeremy did and hope it would taste okay. However, he pulled up in front of a gorgeous house painted in a dark red with deep green and white accents and ornate stonework on the porch. He first assumed he had typed the address wrong. It wouldn't have been the first time when transferring numbers from one message to another. But even as he double-checked, this *was* correct. And it was confirmed when Jeremy opened the front door, a mug in his hand, waving.

He was wearing a short-sleeved knit button-up shirt paired with loose linen pants. Davis imagined that he would be more at home sipping from his mug on a balcony in Paris or a patio in Mykonos than in Colorado, where there were still gray piles of slush in every parking lot. Davis glanced down at himself and groaned. He had worn his standard Carhartt pants, broken into the perfect level of comfort, paired with a West Virginia State Parks T-shirt that most likely had a hole in it somewhere. Probably in the armpit. Why didn't work shirts have reinforced armpits? Seemed like something the government should address, right after the seven thousand other issues that were probably more pressing.

With another groan, Davis grabbed for his backpack, which contained his behemoth of a computer, and got out of his truck. "Mornin'," he said, waving at Jeremy.

"Welcome to *Casa di Rinci*," Jeremy said, waving the mug at the ornate lamps that framed each side of the large door. Oak, Davis guessed, based on the pattern of the wood grain. He focused on the wood instead of the way Jeremy rolled his last name around in his mouth.

"Italian?" Davis guessed. He knew basic Spanish and a touch of American Sign Language, but he struggled enough with English as it was.

"*Si*," Jeremy replied, grinning. "My dad's family was from Milan."

"Ah," Davis replied. Most of the Italians he knew back in Western Virginia had been descended from immigrants that came from southern Italy or Sicily, darker complexions and thick dark hair. "I wish my background was a little more interesting, but it's just 'hillbilly.'"

"There's a lot of beautiful outsider art from Appalachia" — Davis was impressed by Jeremy's correct pronunciation — "and a strong legacy of pottery in West Virginia especially."

Now this, Davis knew. "Fiesta Ware," he said, following Jeremy through the front door. The natural light in the living room was warm, though the couches and chairs looked less like they should be sat on and more like they belonged in a museum. "The older stuff is radioactive." Could he sound any more like a dumb hick?

"Can I get you anything?" Jeremy said. "I don't drink coffee, but I have some for, um, guests." A faint blush appeared on his fair skin. "I've got mountains of tea, and water, and wine, if you're into that this early."

"Tea sounds lovely," Davis said, following Jeremy to the kitchen. He pulled open two drawers, and Davis was astounded. This was a mother lode of tea, with every flavor he could dream of. His eye caught on a familiar flavor, and Davis felt a tingle in his chest. "You have sassafras tea? Here?"

Jeremy's eyes twinkled. "Don't narc on me to the government."

"Why? Because you have tea that's illegal in some countries because of some chemical compound? Tea that was cultivated by Indigenous communities until White growers took over most of its native range?" Davis could taste the distinctive flavor from the sassafras tea his aunt made when he had a cold or too many mosquito bites.

"I buy from ethical suppliers," Jeremy added quickly. "The tea shop in town gets these for me, and my friends have researched their sourcing practices."

Davis smiled. "I'm kidding, Jeremy," Davis replied, still feeling uncomfortable using his first name. He talked to people with names all the time. Why did this feel odd? "I'm descended from folks who made and still make moonshine. This is nothing."

"And now you." Jeremy waved at Davis's bag after turning on his kettle. He looked down and saw his USDA backpack. Ah yes, now he worked for the federal government.

"Yeah, yeah, but the Department of Agriculture isn't exactly the ATF." Not that certain family members of his hadn't been furious when he joined the state government and began to remind them of hunting regulations, especially during archery season.

"How do forest rangers feel about hunting?" Jeremy wondered as if he could read Davis's mind. Davis opened his mouth to begin to explain the long and tangled history of how sport hunters were intertwined with early preservation and conservation movements and his complicated feelings on Teddy Roosevelt, but he was interrupted by Jeremy again. "Never mind. You can tell me over a drink after we finish working. You've been sending me a lot of amazing information. What's your latest idea about the exhibit?"

Davis rolled his shoulders back and opened his computer. As the kettle whistled, Davis entered his password, then entered it again when he clumsily mistyped it. It was annoying how the government made him change his password so often. He ended up writing it down on a Post-it, defeating all the extra firewalls and magic that the IT department put on his brick of a computer so that no one stole whatever information was contained there.

"Uh, wi-fi password?" Davis asked as Jeremy walked back over, holding two mugs of steaming tea. Jeremy set the red mug near Davis, and Davis tried to ignore the fact that it was his favorite color. The exact red of a maple leaf during autumn in the Appalachian mountains.

"Courier New, twelve point," Jeremy replied, typing away at his own sleek laptop. It was fancy and high tech and out of Davis's price range and tech ability, he was sure.

"Could you write it down?" Davis asked, a bit embarrassed. He knew that he would need to refer to it again, plus there was always the annoyance of capitalization and numbers in these things.

"Sure," Jeremy said. He grabbed a mechanical pencil from a cup on the table and scratched away on a notepad. Davis studied the wood, running the tip of one finger over the grain. Pine, he guessed. He thought about how bourbon barrels needed only virgin white oak and what a waste it was. He thought about how his attraction to a man like Jeremy would have made him reach for a glass or three of bourbon a decade ago. He thought about how he wanted to share both of these facts with Jeremy.

People usually reacted in one of two ways when Davis told them about his sobriety. One was overcorrection. They asked if he could be around alcohol, acted like they had to pretend that the entire liquid category of booze didn't exist for them. That wasn't great, but what was worse was pity. The way they looked at Davis like he was broken, or like he had crawled out of some gutter. He didn't have the heart to tell them that there was no grandiose story, no dramatic stint in rehab. Just a cold West Virginia night and an uncomfortable realization about himself, then a regular series of meetings with a counselor, a southern woman who called him *sweetie* and shared her own sobriety story as he unraveled his reasons for drinking. He needed to call Mabel, who took checks in the mail as payment and still acted as his counselor when he needed a session.

As for coming out? The one time he had done that hadn't gone well, and he kept his business to himself. After that, the men he had been with had been able to pick it up from context clues. Namely, Davis's tongue down their throat.

"Here," Jeremy said, passing Davis the note. *Couriernew12point*, it read. Davis typed it into his computer, activated the firewall or VPN or whatever Eric had explained to him during his tech orientation, and then he was on.

"Sorry that took forever," Davis said.

"Drink your tea." Jeremy smiled back. Davis took a sip, the familiar burn of the sassafras singeing his throat. He remembered his aunt and mom making this type of tea every winter to prevent colds. That and Vicks VapoRub were the majority of his medical care growing up.

"Tastes nice," Davis said instead of unspooling his history with Appalachian folk medicine. His document finally up, he pointed to the screen. Things were easier when he spoke about ecology. "So the phrase that I think should guide the exhibit design is *think like a mountain*, from my hero, Aldo Leopold. We can't talk about the trees of the forest without thinking about the water that allows them to grow, and we can't think about the water without thinking about the animals that drink from streams and rivers, and their food chains. We humans like to separate. A mountain doesn't, but embraces the whole complex web." Davis took a sip of tea, looked up to see if Jeremy was still listening. His right hand was moving, alternating between sketching and drawing on a pad of paper. It seemed like he was engaged, so Davis continued. He spoke about the ways that Leopold had listened and changed his field but also didn't shy away from some of the criticism he had learned. How the idea of wilderness being a place without cars was what one podcast had called "pathetic nostalgia" which "ignored how White settlers had already reshaped Native life." How horses were seen as a fine introduced species but dogs weren't. Davis almost mentioned Mary Anne, how when he got to see her run on trails, he felt more in touch with some primal part of himself, feeling more human than he ever did in the city.

"Seriously, we could feature you in a video," Jeremy said, and Davis felt embarrassed and a bit frustrated.

"No, I said before. I don't think we need a White man telling visitors what to think," Davis said curtly.

And immediately, Davis was worried again that he had overstepped. God *damn*, he had hired Jeremy to be the expert in exhibit design, and here Davis was, interrupting him and telling him he was wrong again. But, dammit, Davis knew he was right. He didn't know much, wasn't worldly in any way that would matter to people like Jeremy and his friends down in the city, but this he knew. "I mean, *another* White guy telling people what they should learn?" Davis let out a laugh that he hoped didn't let Jeremy know how nervous he was. "I had enough of that growing up, and I'm pretty sure everyone else did, too."

"One of my best friends, any time she encounters something that doesn't work, likes to blame whatever straight, White man invented it, which, statistically, is probably correct," Jeremy said, and Davis didn't bother to correct him. This wasn't the time. Probably, there would never be a time where he would ever need to tell Jeremy about himself, which was perfectly fine. "I think I've been going about this all wrong," Jeremy continued, and Davis had a moment of fear that he was going to quit the project. Say that Davis was too difficult of a client to work with, or too stupid or something. Something that voice in the back of Davis's mind liked to whisper when he couldn't sleep, the one that often had him sending a text to Mabel, asking for a small reminder.

Under the bludgeonings of chance | My head is bloody but unbowed, Davis reminded himself. Even if Jeremy quit, Davis could bounce back and find a new consultant.

"How so?" Davis asked.

"I don't know if this has been truly collaborative," Jeremy explained, closing his sketchbook and setting it to the side. Davis braced himself to hear the words *this isn't working out*, but instead, Jeremy asked, "Let me grab some Post-its."

"Huh?" Davis asked. Jeremy returned with a giant pile of brightly colored Post-its. Super sticky ones, he imagined, not the shitty pale-yellow ones the government could afford that barely stayed on a flat table, let alone on his computer monitor.

"This is how one of my best friends likes to plan exhibits," Jeremy explained, tossing him the bright blue stack. He took the green for himself, leaving the pink and purple on the table. "We'll chat about ideas, put them down on the table, and start to group them together as themes and patterns reveal themselves."

This Davis could understand. "This is awesome. I would do this when planning papers in college." He had a class in high school called "Research Paper," where students had an entire semester to write one paper, and the first half had been dedicated to *just* an outline. Davis remembered being in his bedroom, hot and angry tears falling down his face because his brain did not understand why he had to use this format. Roman numerals here, then capital letters — that's not how Davis understood information. It was bad enough that everything in that class was based on written sources. That had been before he knew about speech to text, back when books on tape meant packages of cassettes for grandfathers who read thrillers or books about old boats.

Surprisingly, community college had been what opened Davis's mind up. He was in a remedial English course, something that had embarrassed him at first, until his professor — a noted poet in the area — had told the class on the first day that he had spent his entire elementary, middle, and high school experience in special education. "I'm not stupid," the professor had said. "I just didn't learn how they taught." That professor had proceeded to toss out dozens of strategies for reading and writing to the class, telling them to take what fit and leave the rest, which was kind of how Davis had grown up attending church. Once he figured out that there was no requirement to use any one format, that it was just one approach, that the arbitrary rules he was taught in high school were just that — made up and made to be broken — he had succeeded more than he had ever dreamed.

"I like this," Davis said, scratching the Aldo Leopold quote on a Post-it and setting it down in the center of the coffee table that Jeremy had cleared off.

"Okay, well, here is everything I've written down from your last two lectures," Jeremy said, flipping open his notebook. The way Jeremy said *lectures* made it sound more like a compliment, rather than a sneered joke at how Davis could talk too much when he was nervous. He decided to accept it as such, because Jeremy had *listened* and written down more things than Davis remembered saying. "If we transfer all these to Post-it notes, you can sort them in the ways that make sense to you."

Davis nodded and picked up a pencil and wrote the question *Who does the forest belong to?* on a bright green pad. "Sounds excellent. If you can read my writing, that is."

"Davis, I can read your writing." And a part of Davis wished he had said *Davis, I can read you*.

Jeremy

After about three dozen Post-it notes were scattered on the table, Davis began sorting them, chewing on his lip as he moved the slips of paper around.

"Can you tell me what you're thinking as you sort?" Jeremy asked. Davis went pink but began to explain the web of connections he was creating, why certain things were grouped together. And Jeremy realized he was doing it *again*. He had asked Davis to explain something and had settled for half listening. He was still a professional, of course, though he thought that there was a small chance that his right hand was operating independently of his mind. Because while he still sketched ideas and wrote down key phrases that Davis was saying, Jeremy's brain remained entirely focused on his eyes when Davis looked up at him. Those golden glimmers that sparked when he made a wry ecology joke that Jeremy didn't quite get. The way he effortlessly tied concepts together made Jeremy nearly weep. He wanted to introduce him to Phoebe and have them go down rabbit holes about educational interpretation. He wanted to watch Davis explain why it was so important to "leave no trace" to a group of first graders and have them all go on a trash expedition. He wanted to know if those golden eyes flickered when someone touched him.

He *wanted*, and that was a dangerous emotion. Jeremy drew an especially harsh line and grunted as he struggled to erase it.

"What?" Davis said, interrupting Jeremy's thoughts.

"Nothing," Jeremy said with a forced laugh. "I believe you were telling me about a forest fire in 1910?"

After about an hour more, a map of ideas was organized and laid out on the table, and they had assigned tasks for both of them. Jeremy would do a bit of online testing of a few exhibit concepts to see which ones people were drawn to. Davis would talk to the rangers in the field to see who would like to share their expertise and stories in the exhibit and in a series of online videos that Jeremy suggested.

"I produced a few videos for the museum during lockdown," he said.

"A few?" Davis said, raising his eyebrows. He had caught on to the way Jeremy liked to play down his accomplishments.

"I mean, it was a series," Jeremy admitted.

"Hmm," Davis said, leaning back in his chair. "You don't like to talk about yourself much, huh?"

Jeremy shifted uncomfortably in his chair. "I mean, it's not polite to brag."

Davis snorted. "City boy," he laughed, leaning back in his chair and spreading his legs wide. A straight man's position, but one that was obscenely attractive, showing off the expanse of his thighs.

"What makes you say that?" Jeremy asked, straightening again in his chair.

"Nothin'," Davis said, and Jeremy noticed that the more relaxed he became, the more his speech changed. Became a bit rounder, softer, the vowels drawing out and seeming to sway in the space between the men. When Jeremy didn't respond, Davis leaned forward, his forearms on his thighs. "It's not a bad thing. Just different. You dress nice and hold yourself in the way that tells me you went to good schools. What city?"

"New York," Jeremy admitted. "Greenwich Village."

"Even I've heard of that," Davis laughed. "What brought you out here?"

An icy chill ran through Jeremy's body, the same way it always did when someone asked him how he ended up in Vanberg. Usually, he laughed and talked about choosing a job or, if he was in a flirtatious mood, he would tell the man that he needed to up the percentage of queer men near the mountains.

But something about Davis made Jeremy feel honest, feel open. Davis had this uncanny ability to look at Jeremy and suss out whether he was being true. He had seen it with other people as well, in the visitors he encountered on the trail or the stories he told about former coworkers as they worked. But Jeremy didn't think he was ready to fully tell the story of what brought him to Colorado without some liquid courage. "I'm happy to tell you my life path," Jeremy said, getting up and happy to move, "but I'm going to need a glass of wine." He crossed the living room and found a bottle of pinot noir, something he had been gifted as a thank-you from the museum's board of directors for some reason or another. "Do you want one?" He looked over his shoulder, expecting to see Davis's wide smile.

Instead, he found Davis looking up at the ceiling and, for a moment, wondered if he had a crack in the ceiling, had a desire to grab plaster and fix it so Davis wouldn't find his place wanting. "I, uh," Davis began, crossing his legs. "I don't drink."

"Oh," Jeremy said, unsure of what to say next. He knew it wouldn't be proper to ask *why* or to inquire for more details. Sometimes people didn't drink. Phoebe, one of his best friends, often preferred to smoke weed instead of consuming alcohol. Before Jeremy could change the subject to something less awkward, he heard Davis take a deep breath. He interjected first. "Sorry. I can make a cup of tea for myself." There. That was a good solution. And then, the next time Davis came out, Jeremy could make sure to hide all the alcohol in his house, empty the fridge of the few beers Foster had brought over.

"No, no," Davis chuckled. "I'm not at that stage anymore. I can be around alcohol. I just don't drink it. I'm not allergic or afraid of it. It's just that I used to drink a lot — too much — and now I don't." Jeremy paused again, awkwardly holding a corkscrew in one hand and an unopened bottle of wine in the other. Davis, laughing that same soft chuckle again, got up and crossed the room. He sidled up next to Jeremy, smelling of leather and fresh earth, and gingerly plucked the bottle out of Jeremy's left hand. "May I?" he asked before taking the corkscrew. Jeremy focused on the way Davis's hand wrapped around the wine bottle, his fingers meeting around the width of the bottle. With an ease that told Jeremy this wasn't the first time, he wiggled the cork out with a satisfying pop. "Glass?" Davis asked casually. Jeremy, still unsure of what to say next — *don't break your sobriety for me*, though that seemed a tad bit dramatic, even for Jeremy — took a crystal glass from the bottom of his liquor cabinet (art deco, covered in bakelite decorations, purchased at a vintage market in Fort Collins) and set it on the top. Davis swiftly poured a glass of wine, popped the cork back in the bottle, and handed it to Jeremy.

"Thank you?"

"A lot of people don't believe me when I tell them that I can be around alcohol. I like having options to drink *something* when people are having booze, but there's always a glass of water." Davis said it like it was so simple, the way he navigated his life without this cornerstone of social culture. But to Jeremy, who couldn't handle more than one glass of wine without falling asleep or blurting out what he really thought, was stunned.

It was so impressive. The work, the confidence, the continual thought. It was something Jeremy had never encountered. It was even kind of sexy, the way Davis announced his sobriety and his adjustments to Jeremy without batting an eye.

But it would be inappropriate to say that to Davis. A client who had become a coworker who seemed like he was on the way to becoming a friend. And though Jeremy knew that the world wasn't about equality, he felt like the scale of their blossoming friendship had shifted. Davis had shared this kernel of his soul with Jeremy, so Jeremy needed to share something in return.

A truth for a truth.

He took a sip of wine and sat down in his Eames chair, nodding toward his couch for Davis to sit on, which he did. While the Eames chair was, admittedly, not the most comfortable chair, it was one of the first purchases he had made for *this* house with the windfall of money. It had made him feel like a real adult, something to hold on to when everything else he had taken for granted had crumbled.

"You asked how I ended up here," Jeremy said. Davis took a sip from a Nalgene water bottle covered in stickers and nodded. "I went to undergrad in New York City — art history and studio art — and then was doing graduate school in Philadelphia. A master of fine arts in exhibition design. I think — no, I know — I chose this path because of my parents." Another sip of wine. "My dad was an engineer and my mom illustrated children's books. You're right — I am a city boy. I was constantly at museums and art shows and the library, and when I went to NYU, I wanted to do something that would honor both of my parents." A slightly larger sip. "I'm their only child."

Davis, to his credit, remained quiet, only shifting to interlace his fingers and hook them over his knee.

"So I was in Philly for grad school and was deep into the preparation for my final thesis, which was an exhibition on the development of carbon-14 testing, and I got a phone call. I knew Mom was sick, but I didn't realize it was as bad as it was." Jeremy's nose stung. "She went quickly. I was able to get back for the funeral, then my dad was able to attend my graduation but, um." His eyes were leaking now. "But right after, the doctor said his heart just gave out."

Davis made an empathetic noise but didn't say *I'm sorry*, which Jeremy appreciated. He knew that people often didn't know how to react to this kind of news, but it was never their fault. Just random chance.

"Did you know that there's a medical diagnosis for a broken heart? *Takotsbuo cardiomyopathy*," Jeremy recited the syllables with care, something he had spent hours trying to learn after his boyfriend had left him, saying that he was "moping all the time."

"I can see that," Davis said quietly. "My Gram wasn't the same after Pap died."

"So yeah, I was kind of a mess then, going through their things. I ended up chasing anything that reminded me of them. Mom and Dad met attending Vanberg as undergrads. They lived on the same floor their freshman year, and my dad, as corny as it was, had packed a guitar and played her a song. They both said it was love at first sight."

"Wow."

"Yeah, so I moved here with no plan and a double inheritance and bought this house. I did a bit of consulting work — which I've recently restarted, as you may know — and then the university had an opening for an exhibit designer." He drained his glass. "I love what I do. I love my friends that I get to work with."

Davis sat for a moment, and Jeremy imagined, again, that words hung in the air between them. But instead of a heavy cloud of worry, it was something that seemed to sparkle above them. A truth for a truth, and mutual acceptance of two difficult stories.

"Thank you for sharing," Davis said simply.

"Well, you did it first," Jeremy replied, sounding annoyingly like the children he worked with at the museum from time to time.

"Nah, I just told you something about myself. You shared something deep." Davis let out a warm laugh. "I'd toast to you if I had something to drink."

"I have seltzers," Jeremy said, hoping that was okay.

"That's great. I tend to drink a lot of carbonated water or Diet Coke. Don't tell my dentist. I mean, not like I ever had one growing up anyway, but, you know." Davis chuckled, and Jeremy gave a sympathetic laugh, which was what he thought was the right move.

Davis

It usually took a lot longer for Davis to share these parts of his history. There had been coworkers that he had gone out on longer trail work trips with in West Virginia who didn't even know he was from the state. He had bitten his tongue while these foresters from New England and the Pacific Northwest talked about dumb hicks and the decimated forests, like it was the fault of the people who lived there. Not the government that had spent the better part of the twentieth century disconnecting people from the land and turning the forest into something to be used, rather than something to be cultivated in peace and sustainability for future generations.

When he first met Jeremy, all poised and perfect, Davis had thought about lying about where he was from. Most people in Colorado — shit, most people he'd ever met, even in Pittsburgh — couldn't tell a West Virginia holler accent from a southern accent. There were cities in the south, full of culture and history that wasn't just about finding various ways to evade the law and scrape out a living. But after Jeremy had taken his corrections in stride and listened to Davis, then had given his ideas the respect that Davis barely gave himself, he knew that he'd be honest. Honest about his upbringing, honest about his drinking.

Honest about his sexuality, if a lie of omission was considered honest.

"So a master of fine arts?" Davis asked, taking the can of seltzer from Jeremy, doing his best to ignore the way that Jeremy's fingers were able to wrap around the entire can.

"Yep." He shrugged, folding himself back into that uncomfortable-looking chair. "And yes, before you say anything, I've heard the *master of farts* joke about a million times."

Davis let out an unexpected laugh, hearing Jeremy, who should have been talking about art history or philosophy, say the word *fart*. "Well, I mean, it makes sense. Anytime I've been to an art museum, everyone walks around like there's a stick up their ass." Jeremy was quiet a moment, and Davis had a brief flash of panic, an *oh I fucked up and offended someone* panic, before Jeremy produced a noise that was indescribable. The closest thing Davis could think of was the one time he had done an internship at a wildlife rescue program and had watched an injured Canadian Goose be brought in, hissing and spitting and honking. That's what Jeremy's laugh was like — loud and unrestrained, but oddly full of joy. "I didn't think it was that funny," Davis said, laughing as he felt his ears heat.

"It's refreshing," Jeremy said. "Art museums *are* full of pretentious pricks, but people don't usually say that to me. Well, with the exception of my friend Emmy, who is convinced that fine art is just a tax shelter for the rich."

"Isn't it?" Davis said, raising an eyebrow.

"I mean, *yes*, but I've seen pieces of art that encapsulate entire moments in time. I mean, take, for example, the impressionists — Monet? The water lilies?" Davis nodded, even though he didn't know what Jeremy was referring to, thinking instead about the tea candles that floated on water, surrounded by potpourri, in his gram's bathroom. "The ability to capture *movement* and *air* and *light* in this painting was a rejection of the encroachment of industrialization and business into their lives."

"Like how Zahniser believed that Americans needed spaces without cars and trains," Davis said.

Jeremy cocked his head. "I'm not familiar. What do you mean?"

Davis took a deep breath, wondering if he would be able to communicate the modern idea of *wilderness* in a way that was as succinct as Jeremy had explained *expressionism*.

Davis stayed until he finished his seltzer, with Jeremy chatting about his plans for the weekend. He was going to go to an exercise class with a friend, then he was planning on checking out an exhibition in Denver with other friends, and then, he said he "would see where the night took him," which sounded more interesting than Davis's plans, which were video games and a marathon snuggle session with Mary Anne. Maybe a bike ride. He had been teaching the dog to run behind him as he pedaled, and he was thinking she might be ready to take it out to the trail. Mary Anne could try out her new backpack and see how she liked it. Which meant Davis would need to get her backpack. Probably more treats, too.

"I should head up," Davis said, slapping his hands on his thighs as he stood up. "I have a few things I need to pick up in town before it gets too dark."

"Thank you for coming down to the city," Jeremy said, standing up alongside him and taking his empty can. Davis wished that he could use that as a pretense to see what Jeremy's long fingers would feel like intertwined with his own or wrapped around his wrists.

"No worries," he said. "Like I said, I was going to be down here anyway." A lie, but one small enough to not be consequential.

"See you next week for another session?" Jeremy asked, his cheeks flushed a bit red from the glass of wine he had drunk.

"Of course," Davis replied. "My forest or your house?" Davis asked, cringing at the way it sounded like a date.

"Your forest," Jeremy confirmed. "I think we'll make some great progress." Davis waved at Jeremy as he headed out to his truck, tossing his backpack into the back seat before he realized he needed his phone to navigate this city. Swearing to himself as he grabbed it, he took a moment to google "water lilies painting" and saved it for later before punching in the address of the pet store.

Jeremy

Jeremy was blessed (if he believed in that kind of thing) with friends who would truly do anything for him. Phoebe had once driven down from skiing in the middle of a blizzard to help him move a particular couch he wanted from a vintage store in Denver. Foster had taken to keeping a tool bag in the back of his car, just in case Jeremy needed help with one little thing. That little sense of community was one of the many reasons that Jeremy couldn't imagine leaving Vanberg after all this time, little ways that this strange mountain town had started to feel more like home than bustling east coast cities ever did.

He had been chatting to Davis after their last collaborative session at the national forest, one in which they had decided on a main narrative for the visitor center, working to break down the binary of inside versus outside and create a space in which the two could flow back and forth in a spectrum. Jeremy had developed the idea when Davis sent him a YouTube video on the ways that people interacted with public land and how the boundaries were constantly shifting over what was protected versus what was used. The exhibit, as they had planned, involved a lot of natural light, sound baths, and stories of people who had used the forest for a variety of different uses, from sacred to commercial, throughout the known history. Jeremy had been giving Davis a list of contractors and production agencies who could print the various panels he needed, as well as a list of places where the Forest Service could buy new vitrines and display cases for some of the small exhibits they had planned.

"People pay *that much* for that cabinet?" Davis had said, a look of disgust taking residence on his face.

"Well, yeah. I know it seems absurd, but it's solid construction, and the back panel is removable." Jeremy had ordered these exact display cases for Emmy and Ryan's exhibit on science salons and had been especially happy with the way that they made changing out artifacts easier.

"I could build that for one eighth of that cost," Davis had scoffed. He had sounded so confident, so sure. Davis grabbed a scrap of paper from the side of his desk and began to scribble numbers and sketch a tiny diagram of how he could construct it. It was rudimentary, of course, but Jeremy was able to see that it would more than get the job done.

"Impressive," Jeremy had said. "I wish I had someone like you to help me out around my house, building things." It had been something that Jeremy mentioned without thinking about it, talking to Davis the way that he would have talked to any of his friends. He had meant it as a joke, as an aside, but Davis had fixed him with a *look* and a tiny grin and asked, "What do you need help with?" Like it was something so easy, so simple.

And so Jeremy had opened his big, stupid mouth and rattled off a list of the current projects that were on his mind. Fix his garbage disposal. Replace wiring in the hallway closet. Ideally, make the sink a bit higher so he didn't have to hunch over while he did dishes. One day, build a huge dining table that he could host dinners around. He left out the part where he imagined hosting dinner parties like his parents did, all of their New York friends and family squeezed around one table, talking and laughing so hard that you could probably hear them from the street.

"I can come down on Sunday, if you're free," Davis said. Which was why Jeremy was up earlier than he ever was on a Sunday, looking at his living room in a slight panic. Did the Eames chair need to be at *that* angle? Did he have a nice selection of magazines and design books on the coffee table? Was it a type of wood that Davis would respect? Jeremy was proud of the eclectic decoration he'd accumulated, everything designed or built before 1960, but now he was worried that it looked like a shitty design museum, rather than a cohesive home. He adjusted a poster from MoMA, pursing his lips and wondering if he should exchange it for a print he had of Mondrian's *Composition*. He looked at his throw pillows and was all of a sudden second-guessing the color palette he had chosen for the living room. Mauve pillows with a leather couch?

A knock at his door, and Jeremy tossed the pillow down, figuring that the best type of design was one that he didn't overthink (as if he hadn't overthought everything in his life since he had gotten the email from NDavis). And there was Davis, dressed in his usual uniform of sweatshirt and work-ready pants, holding a tool bag in his left hand and a coffee in his right.

"Good morning!" Davis said, waiting at the entrance to be invited in.

"Morning," Jeremy replied, awkwardly formal. He stepped to the side and nodded for Davis to come in, then asked another ridiculous question. "How was traffic?" Like Davis lived in Los Angeles and not in a cabin that was only accessed by one road.

Davis, as usual, took it in stride. "Surprisingly, there was no traffic jam. I think most people head out to the mountains on the weekend, rather than us weird mountain folk heading down to the city."

"Do you come down often?" Jeremy called over his shoulder, having crossed toward to the kitchen to make himself a cup of tea. Something with ginger that would settle his stomach. He wondered if he'd eaten something weird last night.

"Nah," Davis said, setting his tool bag on the ground. He took out a small towel and placed it on the coffee table before moving his bag on top of it. A thoughtful little gesture that made Jeremy's heart stutter. He should avoid any tea with caffeine in it this morning. "I tend to stay away from busy events and cities. I lived in one for a bit, when I finished my undergraduate degree, and it was fine, but I like the quiet more. When I do come down for, like, supplies and groceries, it tends to be on a Monday or a Tuesday. Less traffic, and everyone is at work, so there are fewer people at the store."

"Smart," Jeremy said, not knowing what more to add to the conversation. Luckily, Davis was a man on a mission.

"Okay, so what projects do you have in mind for the day?"

Davis

Davis knew he didn't have to drive down the mountain to help Jeremy. He could have easily sent him three YouTube videos that would have explained how to do everything and a list of basic tools he would need to have in his house. But, as he so rarely did these days, Davis indulged himself in being a bit selfish. He could go down the mountain, spend some time with his new friend, and swing by the bike shop afterward. Maybe even splurge on something new for the kitchen at the cabin. A new mug. Some artisan ginger beer. And, of course, Mary Anne needed treats. He should probably buy Alex a thank-you gift for all the times he ended up watching Mary Anne. But from the photographs and videos that Alex had sent in the past hour, it looked like Caveman and Mary Anne were best friends.

And if he thought a little about how his new friend was unfairly gorgeous, well, that just came with the territory. Lots of people were attractive.

Jeremy took a sip of his tea and looked around his living room. "This room is mostly done, but the kitchen has been giving me a bit of trouble. They're all little things, but other than the living room and the back porch, it's the room I'm in the most."

Davis didn't think about the fact that Jeremy's bedroom was not on the list of the most used places in his house.

"Do you like to cook?" Davis asked. It wasn't what he had *intended* to ask. He had meant to ask what projects, specifically, Jeremy needed done today, but he wanted to know why these rooms were the most used.

"I do," Jeremy said, smiling. "It's one of the ways I like to unwind after work. I occasionally still sketch and paint a bit, but I do a lot of design work at, well, work, so I like to turn that part of my brain off sometimes."

Davis chuckled. "I know what you mean. There's nothing better for me to clear my head than a hike, but when I've been hiking all day, I tend to just sit on my couch and play video games." Wow, could he sound more boring?

"Nice," Jeremy said. "I think the last video game I played was *Spyro the Dragon*." Because he probably read giant hardback books about smart, artsy things that would give Davis a headache. "Anyway, the kitchen is there." Davis followed him down the hallway and to the right, to a kitchen that was smaller than would be currently designed, but seemed, surprisingly, to fit Jeremy well. An expansive window above the sink overlooked a small backyard. Davis could see a table, chairs, a few plants in pots. Cozy. Not his style of nature, obviously, but enough soil and greenery to restore the soul. Plus, a view of the mountains. "That view is one of the reasons I chose this house," Jeremy said, interrupting Davis's perusal. "I have a dishwasher, of course, but I like to do dishes by hand and look at the mountains in the evening."

"That sounds lovely."

"It is. However, that sink is giving me trouble recently. I think I need to replace the garbage disposal. Every time I start to look up videos of replacements, they all recommend cleaning it first, and I can't get over the idea of sticking my hand into that." He shivered, and Davis suppressed a laugh.

"That's an easy fix," Davis said, grateful that he had lived in a house in Huntington with one of those *newfangled sinks that eat your scraps*, as his uncle had called it the one time he visited. "Can you show me where your electrical panel is first? We can turn off the power to the kitchen so no one's hand gets eaten."

Davis didn't know why he used the word *we*. Clearly, only one person was needed to flip a switch. Davis followed Jeremy to the back door, opened the panel, and saw that the switches weren't labeled. He made a mental note to label all the circuits after he fixed this.

"Hey, can you go in the kitchen and let me know when the lights there go off?" Davis asked. Jeremy complied. It was silly, but he missed his presence around him. A few flips, then Jeremy shouted, "That one!" Davis made his way back to the living room and grabbed the necessary tools and a flashlight.

He knelt down and opened the cabinet under the sink. It was tidy and organized underneath, all organic cleaning solutions and folded towels. New sponges, still wrapped in plastic. While Davis was looking, Jeremy was explaining the issue, that the garbage disposal sometimes backed up and sometimes didn't work. Davis thought it could be a motor issue, perhaps a full replacement if it had finally crapped out. If it wasn't that, it could be a seal or a pipe fitting issue, and he would have to run to the store and —

"Jeremy?" Davis asked, pulling his lips between his teeth to stop from laughing.

"Yeah? Need a tool? I used to help my mom with the plumbing sometimes in our apartment so she didn't have to call the super." A laugh. "What I mean is that I'm really good at holding a flashlight."

"No, just a quick question." Davis didn't know how to ask this without sounding like an ass, so he just barged ahead and did it. "Did you press the reset button?"

"There's a reset button?"

Well. That answered that question. Davis pressed the small button that had popped out on the bottom of the disposal, then stood up. "Be right back," he said to Jeremy. He flipped the circuit on, then hustled back to the kitchen. "Okay, try it now," he instructed Jeremy, who looked a bit bashful. It was adorable.

"This is why the IT staff at the university hate me," Jeremy said after he turned on the faucet and flipped the switch for the disposal, which roared to life, chomping at the water and the imaginary food waste.

"It's something that anyone could overlook," Davis said, overcome with a desire to make Jeremy feel better.

"I mostly feel bad that you drove all this way to press a button."

"Well, I'm here. Do you have any other projects that you need help with?" Once again, Davis's words were tumbling out faster than his brain could catch up with. His brain would have come up with a sentence like *oh, that's fine, I have other things to do in town*. "I can help label your circuit breakers for you. It's easier with two people."

That took less time than expected, becoming almost a game as Jeremy sprinted from room to room, trying to figure out which circuit connected to which set of lights and sockets. Davis cringed at his labels, at his messy handwriting that had gotten him last place in the third-grade handwriting competition back in Anthracite Springs.

They met in the kitchen, and again, Davis was planning on saying something like *well, that was something easy, and now*

I will be on my way to the store when, instead, he said, "You do know that your cabinet doors are all a bit...off, right?"

Jeremy blushed. "I do know that. Is it something else that's easier to fix with two people?" Davis must have been imagining things at this point, because Jeremy's face looked almost hopeful.

The cabinets took longer, which led to Jeremy putting on music to accompany their work, and Davis was surprised to find that it was a playlist of 1950s and 1960s pop hits, things that his mother and her sisters would have sung along to on the oldies station they could pick up at the big farmhouse, laughing about stories from their childhood and singing along to the Beach Boys or the Supremes. When Davis asked why Jeremy had chosen the music, he had simply replied that he preferred the simplicity of the pop music of that era, the way the songs followed a nice pattern and were easy to sing along to. Davis couldn't argue with him there.

It was dusk by the time Jeremy hung the final cabinet door, having progressed from simply holding them in place to leading the alignment of the last few doors. There were two above the refrigerator that Davis couldn't reach if he tried, anyway, and Jeremy had lifted up on his tiptoes with the grace of a ballet dancer, his limbs stretching and reaching to screw the last hinge into place.

"*Voila*," Jeremy said with a flourish. "Though I really should be saying thank you."

"It wasn't a bad way to spend a day," Davis said. "I like feeling helpful."

"You should meet my friend Phoebe," Jeremy laughed. And just when Davis was about to take his leave — for *real* this time, packing up his tools and everything else — his stomach growled. Not in a way that he could pass off as a groan when he stretched or maybe a ghost in the house. It was hunger.

He'd grab a sandwich on the way back home. It was getting late anyway. The bike store would be closed, and he really didn't need anything special from the store for the next week, but Mary Anne did need a raincoat for the rain that was forecasted, and —

"I can order something for us for dinner?" Jeremy said, a question hidden in a statement. "I owe you *something* for all the help you've given me today."

That was logical. It made sense. "Okay," Davis replied, setting down his tools. Food was always good. Food was something you did with friends.

Jeremy

"Any dietary restrictions?" Jeremy asked, pulling up a food delivery app on his phone.

"I try to not eat a lot of red meat, but I'm not picky," Davis responded, putting his hands in his pockets.

Jeremy pushed down the impulse to offer to cook for him, to pull out what was left in his pantry and fridge and impress Davis with what he could pull together. He knew that he had gotten at least a few blowjobs after making carbonara.

"Breakfast?" Jeremy asked.

"It's seven p.m."

"Time is a social construct," Jeremy replied, inadvertently quoting a rambling that Phoebe had gone on recently when she was extra high at the bar next to the museum.

"I'll take your word for it." Davis chuckled. "Yeah, sure. Why not? Breakfast sounds excellent."

"Have you ever had breakfast at the Fox?" Jeremy asked, assuming an answer, but swiping on his phone. He pulled up a delivery app and showed Davis the menu on his phone. Davis looked briefly and nodded.

"No, I mean. I don't spend much time down here, and I don't have that much in common with the college kids that live here." A wry laugh. "I barely had things in common with kids in college when I was in college."

"We'll go next time. I really love their Belgian waffles," Jeremy said before realizing what he'd implied. A moment of panic, then trying to rationalize it to himself. Friends hung out. He got coffee with Foster once a week. More than that, usually. He grabbed dinner with Emmy all the time, cooked for Phoebe, and at one time even agreed to watch a sports game with Ryan. Friends hung out.

"Do they have biscuits and gravy?" Davis asked, apparently unaware of Jeremy's inner turmoil.

"I don't know. Uh, here," he said, passing the phone to Davis awkwardly. Food was ordered, and the two men made small talk while waiting for it. Finally, Jeremy realized he was being the worst host of all time and offered Davis a drink.

"Not a *drink* drink, but, like, like a liquid to consume." Had he been replaced by a robot? Who the fuck talked like this? "I got some beverages without alcohol." Overwhelmed by his inability to form a normal sentence, Jeremy got up and crossed to the kitchen. He had picked up some seltzers and other drinks at the store last weekend, a tiny voice in his head saying *just in case*. That tiny voice's entire goal had been to make Davis feel more comfortable, and here Jeremy was, being the most uncomfortable he had ever been in his tenuous friendship with Davis, so he couldn't imagine how Davis felt.

Davis, to his credit, gave a light laugh. "What do you have?"

"Uh, a lot." He felt Davis's presence behind him as he opened up the refrigerator, surrounded by the cabinets that Davis had helped to realign.

"Oh, I love this one." He reached around Jeremy, their arms brushing, and picked up a light green bottle. A type of ginger beer that Jeremy had only picked up because the design on the bottle was especially eye-catching. He had to support businesses that employed good designers.

Jeremy grabbed a seltzer, and the two men settled around the dining room table, Davis leaning back in his chair and kicking one leg across the other. One of the knees in his work pants had ripped, exposing a small patch of skin, and Jeremy was overcome by an odd desire to mend the knee of those pants.

"What's that from?" Jeremy said to distract himself, pointing to a spiderweb of scar tissue that spread across Davis's left knee.

"Mountain biking," Davis said, taking a deep pull of the ginger beer. Jeremy made a mental note to keep more of those in the house, along with the flavors of seltzer that Davis liked. Huckleberry. Peach. Flavors that were fresh and earthy, like him.

"That seems intense," Jeremy said stupidly. He made another mental note to ask Phoebe and Emmy to look up the history of mountain biking so he could sound intelligent the next time he saw Davis.

"It's not that bad," Davis said, stretching. Jeremy tried very hard not to look at the slice of stomach and flash of hair that was revealed. He failed. "Have you ever been mountain biking before?"

"Huh?" Jeremy asked, again stupidly. He always felt stupid around Davis. He could hold his own with PhDs and professional scientists, but there was something about this sincere, open, genuine man that unraveled him. Davis was unlike anyone Jeremy had met before, and it still had him off-kilter. He was beginning to think that he liked it.

Because he wasn't allowed to like *him*.

"Mountain biking. You could come out with me, if you'd like. We've got some good trails in the national forest. Plus, it would be a good way for you to see some different ecosystems." Davis finished his ginger beer, asked where the recycling was.

Jeremy thought for a second. He could hold his own in a spin class, had been going with Foster three to four times a week since everything had reopened. He had been complimented on his legs before by men during the summer. Those skills could transfer, right?

"Yeah, it's been a while, but it'd be nice to go out again." A white lie. Which was fine. He told those all the time, about deadlines for deliverables and when he would show up to meetings on time.

"Great. Do you have a bike?" Davis looked so excited, so *pure*, that Jeremy told another white lie.

"It's in the shop."

"You can borrow my friend Alex's. He's about your height." Davis's eyes flicked up and down Jeremy's body, and he had to try not to preen. Because you didn't preen in front of men who were just being friendly.

"Great, what day?"

And so, Jeremy Rinci ended his weekend eating breakfast at seven thirty p.m. and making plans to go mountain biking — a sport he had never tried — with Davis, a man he could never have. At least the pancakes were excellent.

Davis

A good way to see some ecosystems. God damn, Davis had said a lot of dumb shit in his life, whether it was to hide his drinking, his crushes, or the way he struggled to read, but this had to take the cake.

"Do you want to try out the disc golf course next weekend?" Alex asked, interrupting Davis's mental spiral. "We can take the dogs. Caveman couldn't catch a disc if his life depended on it, so he won't mess up your score."

"I've never been frisbee golfing," Davis admitted, watching the dogs wrestle in the soft patch of grass outside.

"It's *disc golf,*" Alex emphasized. "You can borrow a few of my old discs."

"Mary Anne might eat it." Davis grimaced. He had already lost his extra game controller to Mary Anne's tendency to chew when she was bored.

"Eh, it's worth it. Sharing is caring, right?" Alex whistled, and Caveman galloped over to him. Mary Anne, having lost her play partner, looked at Davis as if it was his fault.

"Hush, girl," he said to the dog, laughing. "You're going on a playdate with Caveman, anyway." He turned back to Alex, who was engaged in a deep conversation of his own with Caveman, the subject apparently how stupid and cute the dog was. "Thank you for taking her today. This is a new friend, and I don't know whether he likes dogs."

"No sweat," Alex said, because for him, it was easy. No worries about if a male friend would get the wrong idea or misinterpret a friendly hug. No worries about if he had pressed his luck by acting on his crush — a totally unattainable, pie-in-the-sky, *ridiculous* idea of a crush. But he liked Jeremy. As a friend. Because he had to.

He liked sharing things that he loved with his friends, and he guessed that Jeremy had decidedly moved from the "coworker" category to "friend" category.

As he reminded himself, he did things with friends all the time.

Well, at least he had back in West Virginia.

So it wasn't weird to invite Jeremy out to go mountain biking, he rationalized. It wasn't weird to make sure that Davis had a few different types of teas on hand because he had suggested that they start in the morning, right as the dew was burning off. Davis told himself it was because he knew that traffic was bad coming from the foothill cities, but deep in his heart, he knew it was because early morning was his favorite time to go mountain biking. The way the mist hovered right about the floor, the way the rising sun from the east caught the tips of the mountains and made the aspens shine in a manner that took his breath away. It was unlike anything he had ever seen in West Virginia, which was gorgeous in its own way. He wasn't cut from the same type of cloth as Muir or Carson or Kimmerer. Words weren't the way he was able to communicate nature. He could only show someone the beauty in person, not write about it.

And he wanted to show Jeremy.

Jeremy knew about words and colors and theories of design. Jeremy's brain was fascinating to Davis, and he relished the times he got to pick it.

His ass wasn't terrible, either.

After Alex, Mary Anne, and Caveman headed to Alex's cabin, Davis put a kettle of water on in his kitchen and turned on the electric burner that reminded him of home. It'd take a few minutes to warm up, even more for the water to heat. Which gave him time to brew coffee because, even though he liked the sassafras tea, every other flavor he had tried at Jeremy's house was *disgusting*. With the beverages prepped, Davis went outside to check on their bikes and was happy — and, frankly, shocked — to see that Jeremy had shown up early.

"Hi," Davis said, trying not to stare. Jeremy had swapped his typical dress clothes for athletic gear — compression leggings under shorts that had to be at least two inches above his knee. A technical T-shirt that had a pattern laser cut along the shoulders. For ventilation, Davis assumed, though it let just enough skin show through. He was reminded how the girls at his high school used to wear shirts that showed just hints of skin, how he had always liked those hints of skin more than the full reveal.

"Traffic was great," Jeremy said, answering a question that Davis hadn't even asked.

"Awesome," Davis responded. "I, uh, started coffee inside." Davis nodded his head toward his cabin. As Jeremy opened his mouth to reply, probably something like *I don't drink coffee because it's how I keep my skin glowing*, Davis quickly added, "I boiled water for tea, too."

The side of Jeremy's mouth quirked up. "Do you mean microwave?"

Davis rolled his eyes. "I may be a hick from West Virginnie, but I had a roommate in college who studied abroad in London and came back telling us that microwaving water was a sin."

Jeremy's face split into a full grin. "Well, I guess I could go for a cuppa," he said, adopting an over-the-top cockney accent.

"If you keep talking like that, I'm sending you the wrong GPS coordinates," Davis replied, opening the screen door. He felt Jeremy follow him into the cabin and then realized it was the first time that Jeremy had been in his personal space. Davis had been in Jeremy's house, had drunk his ginger beer and used his bathroom and gotten frustrated with the way he had decided to organize his kitchen as he fixed the doors. But now Jeremy was in Davis's house, and it felt so much more precious. Fragile.

Fucking terrifying.

The man had fancy chairs that looked amazing but were wildly uncomfortable to sit on and a leather couch (he couldn't imagine how terrible it would feel in the summer). Davis had a quilt from his aunt tossed over the back of his couch. The couch that Davis now realized had just *been here* when he moved in. He wished he had listened when his gram had taught him how to clean a couch, probably at some point in high school after he was learning to do laundry on his own.

"So, this is my mansion," Davis said, the screen door slamming shut loudly behind him. It was a small place, but something about moving out of his home state and moving up in his career made this his tiny little kingdom. He had begun to personalize it more, with vintage national park posters, in addition to a concert flier from his friends' band from back in West Virginia, made before they had gotten that small fifteen minutes of fame, and a few photos of Mary Anne. A portrait of Gram and all her grandchildren that had been taken at Sears in 1994. His slippers were by the door, his favorite seltzers in the fridge. His favorite video games that he could replay as many times as he wanted without roommates judging him. He liked that it was a place that he had to himself, a place where he didn't have to worry about anyone looking over his shoulder.

Until now.

"It's gorgeous," Jeremy breathed out. "I mean, I know it's just a little rustic cabin —"

"*Hey*," Davis said, half-jokingly, half-defensively.

"No, no, shit — ah. That wasn't the right phrase. It's perfect because it's a rustic cabin, but you can tell that whoever built it, care was taken in the construction." Jeremy pointed to a small detail on the window frame, something that Davis had never noticed. A tiny little lip in the frame, between the top and bottom pane. "That's called a lamb's tongue, and it means that these are original windows. I'd guess they keep the heat in nicely?"

"Yeah, they do." So well that on this crisp spring morning, Davis felt like the room was on fire.

"Amazing the way craftsmanship used to be," Jeremy said, reaching one delicate finger out and running it along the windowsill. Davis had an absurd desire to pull that finger away from the window and pull it into his mouth, to suck and allow his cheeks to hollow out, to hint at other things he could do with his mouth.

Instead, he said *yeah* like a fucking idiot.

Jeremy blushed a bit. "Sorry, I loved the one architectural history class I took in undergrad, but I was dead set on my majors. Plus, well, architecture had too much math for me." He flashed a dazzling smile at Davis and pointed to his own chest. "Art kid."

"I'm happy with the place," Davis said, moving away to look anywhere but at Jeremy. "I've lived in some odd places in my day."

"My friend's brother runs a summer camp not too far away from here, and he has some stories." A shiver ran down Jeremy's spine, and Davis remembered his house, everything so ornate and perfectly arranged. Of course Jeremy could never be comfortable in a cabin like Davis loved.

Of course.

"Before we head out, you should see the back porch," Davis said. He nodded away from where Jeremy was looking at his couch before he could ask questions about the quilt. He opened the back door, the squeak of the hinge a small thing that reminded him of the quiet nights in the summer back home, when the lightning bugs would dance just above the grass. He felt Jeremy come out onto the porch behind him and heard the door close, but Jeremy remained silent. Davis filled that space. "I know it's silly, but I remember how you talked about the view from your kitchen, and I thought you would like this view. You can see that peak over there. It's one of the first ones to get snow in the winter, and there's a fire watch tower up on top of it that's now owned by the Forest Service, and the view from it is really cool and — sorry, that's silly, you don't care."

He was nervous, and his accent got worse when he was nervous, his stupid twangy accent that made people think he was dumber than he already was —

"Not silly," Jeremy said, his voice catching slightly. "Incredibly thoughtful." He made a pleasant little noise, the type of sound that Davis would make when he found an especially rare wildflower. "Like you."

Davis could have floated into the air with how he felt.

And instead of spilling out what he wanted to say, which was *hey I'm queer, and I like you more than as a friend*, he resorted back to his old habit of distracting himself with physical activity.

"Ready to ride?"

Jeremy

There weren't many places to ride a bike in New York City. Not for little Jeremy Rinci, the son of a children's book illustrator and a mechanical engineer, who was, for lack of a better phrase, not given any genetic inclination toward sports. He had learned how to ride a bike in college while dating a Bed-Stuy hipster who rode a fixed gear and played bicycle polo, but he never really did anything with it until the stress of his MFA caused him to find some type of physical outlet. A few people in his cohort had decided to try a spin class, and Jeremy had fallen in love. The lights, the sounds, the way he could feel as though he was a part of something else, to push himself but still embrace that individualized self-confidence that came with dancing alone in his apartment. The best spin classes reminded him of the best nights out at clubs, that fiery mix of dopamine and sweat and a good beat that was worth any headache you would wake up with.

However, Jeremy was quickly finding that his previous history of Ladies of the '80s spin classes and hipster bikes was essentially useless when it came to mountain biking.

Oh, he could pedal fine, all right. The first few minutes, just down a gravel service road, were easy and gave Jeremy a false sense of confidence. *Look at me, being outdoorsy and shit.* He couldn't wait to rub it in Emmy's face.

And then, following Davis, who made this seem like it was second nature, he went around a curve and began to pedal *up*. He was even doing that thing where he could stand up and pedal, which, to Jeremy, seemed like it was in defiance of gravity.

"You good back there?" Davis called from what seemed like four miles up the trail.

"Yeah, I'm great," Jeremy lied, tipping to the side again. How did you manage to get momentum to move the bike at all? He was a designer and art historian, he was *not* the type of man who could comprehend basic physics on a *mountain*.

"This hill can be a bit tough, especially with the altitude," Davis was saying. "Feel free to hop off and push your bike."

Thank fuck, Jeremy thought to himself as he sprung off the bike. He had at least hiked before. It wasn't something he necessarily sought out, but you couldn't live in Colorado for longer than three months without accidentally being roped into climbing a 14'er. He spent at least a few days each summer hiking in the mountains with Emmy and Foster, and he liked to go for long, rambling walks with Phoebe and Declan through the city as they chatted about art. He was almost entirely sure that he would not make a total ass out of himself if he could get away with hiking up this hill. As if realizing what he had suggested, Davis hopped off and began to push his own bike up the hill. It gave Jeremy a distracting view of how the thick muscles in Davis's back rippled as he held on to the handlebars.

Unfortunately for Jeremy — and even more unfortunately for his Achilles tendon — none of the myriad hikes he had gone on in Colorado involved a bicycle. He held it out from himself to the left, mimicking what he saw Davis do, grateful for his long arms and the way he ensured he wasn't impaled by the handles, but he kept forgetting about the pedals. Every four steps, it seemed, the back of his left leg would be smacked with the pedal, which somehow felt like he was taking a dagger to his calf. He would bet that there was either a bruise or a trail of blood that would stain his socks.

And these were his nice sweat-wicking socks.

"Almost there!" Jeremy called to Davis. Or maybe it was more of a bit of motivation for himself, because it finally looked like there was a bit of light at the top of the trail that meant the trail would flatten out. He could handle that. It'd be a bit rocky, but it was something he could control. Jeremy pushed his bike up and over, pulling in deep breaths of air in a way he hoped told Davis that he was invigorated, not on the edge of dying.

"Uh, we'll head over that way." Davis pointed his arm over to the left, and Jeremy caught a whiff of pine and earth and a bit of something sharp and spicy. He almost forgot the pain in his lungs and the throbbing in the back of his heel with that breath, with the way that Davis, when he was surrounded by trees with a light breeze rustling a wayward piece of hair that had escaped from his helmet, smiled a bit broader. His eyes shone out here. Davis in the trees is how Jeremy felt when he was in a figure drawing class, completely in his element.

"Great," Jeremy said, not investigating if his breathlessness was from the elevation, pushing a bike up a mountain, or the way Davis looked right now. He hopped on his bike and tentatively followed Davis, enjoying the fact that he was going slowly (Jeremy hoped it wasn't for his own benefit. He did have a little bit of pride, after all). He was finally getting the hang of the fact that he had to let the terrain move the handlebars for him — less trying to control the bike and more that he was along for the ride, though pedaling forward.

He could do this. Maybe he could impress Davis after all.

"Okay, here we go!" Davis called, and Jeremy looked up just to see him disappear over the edge of the trail.

Oh, so now they were going *down*.

You can do this, you can do this. Jeremy repeated the phrase on a loop. He'd learned that it was about letting the bike lead. Vaguely, somewhere in the back of his brain, he remembered advice from the first time his father had taken him out to Long Island to learn how to drive a car.

The minute you try to control everything, you stiffen up, and you'll overcorrect everywhere.

The thing about Jeremy Rinci was, however, that the more he told himself *not* to do something, the more his body instinctively *did* the thing. And while he had learned to manage it in certain situations (sex, looking at Davis during their work sessions, looking unfazed when he showed up late to a meeting), it turned out that he was not able to manage it now.

The front wheel of his bike went over the edge, and Jeremy, smartly, didn't look at the trail in front of him. He figured he would just go and see how it went.

And that did not go well, because he forgot that gravity would be on the side of his bike.

Art kid.

His breath was forced out of his lungs multiple times as he careened down the trail, miraculously able to keep his bike up because the trail was straight. *Shit, shit, shit, shit.* He could get to the bottom of the hill, and then he would be able to just tell Davis that he would hike the bike back, tail between his legs. He'd probably have to cancel his contract with the national forest, because this was embarrassing and — oh *fuck*, there was a turn in the trail.

"Way to go!" Davis, who had apparently pulled to the side of the trail on the curve, called.

Jeremy let out a screech that reminded him of what he thought a pterodactyl would probably have made in response. Then his front tire caught a rock that was in the middle of the trail, and he was falling, tumbling, crashing.

He wished that something more eloquent had gone through his head in what he thought would be his final moment of consciousness, but *fucking shit* was what repeated.

"Fucking shit," he said out loud when his body came to a stop. He had done his best to tuck into a tiny ball and roll down the hill, tiny branches and little rocks flying in every direction. Once he established that he still had all his limbs attached, he made to get up, assuming that he had probably ruined Davis's friend's bike.

"Stay there!" Davis yelled, scrambling down the hill toward him, and Jeremy agreed this was the right thing to do. Mercifully, he sat down and noticed the blood dripping from his knee, the way his shoulder burned.

Fucking shit indeed.

Davis

Fuck.

Davis had been trained in first aid since a high school class, had maintained his CPR and first aid certs every year since he had started interning with state parks in college. Hell, just a few years ago, when the world was waking back up, Davis had spent a week struggling through a wilderness first responder course, learning how to set broken bones and to properly carry someone who had had their pelvis crushed by a falling tree. He had assisted on a lot of injuries and rescues, had found people who followed their GPS down an abandoned access road to a mine back in West Virginia.

But his stomach had never dropped like this. He had never felt an entire chill course through his body and render him motionless like he did when Jeremy hit a rock and flew over his handlebars.

A credit to Jeremy, though, to the way that he was able to tuck his body and roll so his shoulder and side took the brunt of the fall. Davis ditched his bike to the side and scrambled down the mountain, pulling at the pack he had grabbed at the last minute.

"Ow, dammit," Jeremy was saying, taking a few seconds to stand up. He was moving, he was talking, which meant he was breathing and hadn't hit his head in any significant way.

"Don't move," Davis said, his voice coming out sharper than he intended. Jeremy, to his credit, sat back down, legs out in front of him. He had torn the knee of his leggings, bright red blood showing through, and the shoulder of his shirt was torn and his wrists were muddy. But Davis wasn't thinking of any of that as he tossed his bag over to the side and pulled up Jeremy's shirt, exposing a pale, toned abdomen.

"What are you —" But Davis wasn't listening to any protests. He remembered a scenario in his wilderness first responder class. He had been playing the victim of a mountain biking accident for the other members of the class, and the instructor had pulled his shirt up and used stage makeup to paint a tiny bruise on the right side of his stomach. When none of the "rescuers" had managed to look for that type of injury, the instructor had grimly informed the class that, in this scenario, Davis would have died.

Handlebars on mountain bikes are incredibly dangerous. They often press into the stomach and cause the appendix to rupture.

And while Davis couldn't remember shit from most text-books, he could remember things from hands-on practical experience, even though he had never anticipated that he would have to use these skills on someone he cared about in this way.

Pulling Jeremy's shirt up toward his chest, Davis looked over his stomach for any immediate bruising that would indicate internal bleeding of any kind. "Let me know if you feel anything painful," he said sternly to Jeremy, gently pressing his fingers into the soft skin of his stomach in various places.

"Other than my fucking hands and knee," Jeremy grumbled.

"Those aren't important," Davis said, continuing his investigation of his organs. His fingers moved up, pressing against his ribs, until Jeremy let out a painful *hiss*.

"God damn, they're important," Jeremy replied. "I'm a fucking *artist*, and my hands — ow!"

"No internal bleeding. Organs seem good. Now I need to check bones —" Davis spoke more to himself than to Jeremy, trying to keep his mind on the task in front of him instead of the image of Jeremy's lean body flying through the air. "Jeremy!"

"Yes?"

"Can you breathe?"

"Well, obviously. I'm talking to you." Jeremy took a breath, as if to prove a point. "Ow, fuck."

"Don't do that."

"Breathe? Davis, you can say my hands aren't important, but I do need to breathe —"

"No, just not deeply. You've probably bruised a rib."

"But how are my hands?"

"You won't care about your hands if you've broken a rib and punctured a lung," Davis responded, definitely harsher than he intended. He finished his assessment of Jeremy's torso with a sweep of his collarbone, then finally felt like he could breathe again. He sat back on his heels and swiped a palm over his face. "Sorry, I just—" He took a deep breath in and out. "I wanted to see if I needed to radio SAR or anything."

"SAR?"

"Search and Rescue."

Jeremy scoffed. "I don't need to be rescued."

Davis couldn't help the skeptical look on his face and the way his eyes darted to Jeremy's shoulder and knee. "Do I need to recount what just happened?"

"Well, you know, this was a bit more, uh, intense of a trail than I anticipated," he said, looking away.

"It's not your fault you caught a rock," Davis said, making sure his voice was more gentle. He had a tendency to turn gruff and almost mean when he was worried about someone.

"It's more the fact that I wasn't entirely honest with you," Jeremy said, looking back at Davis. He was surprised to see Jeremy's cheeks turning bright red.

"How?" Davis reached for his bag and unzipped it, looking for his first aid kit.

"Well, I might have not had the same type of experience with mountain biking," Jeremy began.

"I mean, biking around the city is fine—"

"I tend to bike more stationary," Jeremy admitted. "Like in a room with thirty other people and loud music. Or on my Peloton at home."

"What good is a bike that doesn't go anywhere?" Davis said without thinking.

"Uh, it's great cardiovascular fitness," Jeremy sniffed.

"I didn't mean that," Davis said apologetically. "You could have just told me that you didn't want to go mountain biking."

"Yeah, but..." Jeremy looked away again. "You seemed so excited about it. I didn't want to disappoint you."

Davis didn't know *what* to say to that, so he said the first thing that came to his mind. "Let me fix up your knee so we can hike back."

Jeremy

Not that Jeremy had ever anticipated injuring himself mountain biking, but common sense told him that he should be focusing on the injuries and the fact that the initial adrenaline was wearing off, causing a stinging pain to radiate from his knee and wrists. Not a good sign, and having an MFA was nothing close to being an MD. However, all he could focus on was the fact that this was the first time he and Davis had touched skin-to-skin.

Davis, who had apparently assuaged his fear that Jeremy was critically injured and was digging through a small blue zipped bag that he had retrieved from a larger backpack. Jeremy hoped that Davis had more in that bag than the first aid kit Foster had made him invest in during COVID, which seemed to just hold a variety of different sizes of bandages and some small packets of triple antibiotic ointment.

Trying to make light of the fact that he had not been prepared to see genuine fear on Davis's face, not to mention the fact that his knee and wrist really did burn something fierce, Jeremy tried to make a joke about it. "I bet you do this to all the exhibit contractors. Just bring us out here to the forest to injure us."

Davis's eyes shot up, looking almost pained, and Jeremy regretted the joke immediately. "I would never do anything that would cause anyone pain, least of all you."

"I —" Jeremy began, then added, more softly, "I'm sorry. I was just making a joke. I *am* glad that you're prepared with that kit. I would bet a million dollars you were a top-notch boy scout."

Davis's eyes relaxed, and he smiled. "Yeah, well, there wasn't much else to do in my hometown besides play baseball and become an eagle scout."

"I bet it's how you got all the girls," Jeremy said, wondering if the slight ache when he said that phrase was related to his injuries.

Davis looked away for a moment, then laughed. "I'll have you know I was not very cool in high school and didn't date at all."

"Well, I mean, you should just show off this first aid kit in town, and the women will come flocking," Jeremy said, waving a hand at the contents of the bag, which seemed to include everything from a flare to a heat blanket. He wouldn't have been surprised to find a kit for Davis to stitch him up out here in the wilderness.

"Sure," Davis replied, pulling out a bottle of hand sanitizer. "Okay, so I'm gonna wash my hands and put on gloves, but you should probably get to a doctor at some point, just to make sure nothing gets infected." Jeremy knew that Davis was thorough and prepared from their work together. Usually, in Jeremy's experience, the designer was the one who would bring ideas, and the client would shoot them down or agree. Davis always brought ideas to the meetings, from color schemes to label text, often with evidence of multiple drafts. But it was different to see Davis in action, the way he methodically took out all the supplies that he would need and placed them on a plastic cloth he had unfolded. Jeremy saw antiseptic, gauze, bandages, and a wrap of some kind. "Let's start with your hands," he said after putting gloves on. Jeremy held out his palms, feeling equal parts like he was a little kid who skinned his knee and a damsel in distress.

He felt safe in Davis's hands, he realized.

"This will sting," Davis whispered, taking Jeremy's right hand in his because *of course* he knew that it was Jeremy's dominant hand and he wanted to work on it first. Davis dabbed a wipe on Jeremy's palm and, *oh fuck*, he was right; it did hurt. *Fuck.* "There we go," Davis whispered as he pulled away, more to Jeremy's hand than to his face, but Jeremy felt his face heat any way. "Just a few more steps. This should feel better." A cooling gel was smeared on Jeremy's skin, then a gauze pressed over. "I'll just wrap it up," Davis said, and began to unwind a small roll of what, to Jeremy, felt like a lighter ACE bandage around his palm and wrist, tucking the end in neatly. He then repeated the same process with Jeremy's left hand, just as careful and just as cautious.

"Do you want me to work on your knee?" Davis asked, holding his hands about a half foot above Jeremy's knee. And while Jeremy was pretty sure that he would be fine to walk on it, that he was more worried about his hands, he felt like being just a tiny bit indulgent.

He had done *mountain biking*. Surely that meant he deserved a bit of special treatment. "Yeah, that might be great. Just so it doesn't get infected. And you can make sure there are no rocks or dirt in the scrape." Davis gave him an odd look, and Jeremy was worried he had said a little too much.

Davis

Davis was grateful that he had asked Jeremy out to go mountain biking on a weekend, as the hike back to Davis's cabin took longer than he would have anticipated. Having a bruised knee would do that to you, but Davis was impressed with the way that Jeremy kept a good face on while they walked.

Davis spent most of the hike talking about the various species of trees around him, partially because he thought it would get Jeremy's mind off the fact that he was injured and mostly because Davis needed to keep himself distracted because Jeremy's injury was *his fault*.

Jeremy, bless his sweet heart, listened to Davis detail the difference between ponderosa and lodgepole pines and even tried to point out aspens on the walk back, because they were, according to him, "the only tree I learned about in Colorado." Blessedly, finally, they made it back to Davis's cabin. They had decided to leave the bike Jeremy was riding on the trail, Davis having marked the GPS coordinates on his phone so he could hike out and get it tomorrow. He figured it would be a little like penance for injuring Jeremy. Plus he would have to fix it before he gave it back to Alex. Davis leaned his own bike against the front of his cabin, then turned to Jeremy. "I'm sorry," he said for what had to have been the thousandth time. "Can I offer you some food or a seltzer? A tea?"

"It's not your fault," Jeremy replied, also for the thousandth time. "But I almost never say no to tea." Davis nearly sprinted to the kitchen to heat up water, though he heard Jeremy's pained groan as he sat down on this couch. A few minutes later, Davis came out with a cup of chamomile tea in a mug. He had only second-guessed the choice of mug three times, settling on one with Smokey Bear reminding the user that only they could prevent forest fires.

"Here," Davis said.

Jeremy took the cup and smiled, then took a sip. His injured knee was stretched out on Davis's couch, so long it seemed to take up the entire length. Davis perched on a nearby foot cushion so Jeremy didn't have to move.

There was an awkward silence, the only noise Jeremy sipping his tea and Davis cracking a can of seltzer. "I'm sorry," Davis said again.

"You should be," Jeremy said. Davis's heart dropped somewhere into the inner core of the earth, but only for a moment, because Jeremy smirked, a sly smile that Davis had only received from men at very specific bars, and never on his couch in the national forest. "You should be sorry that you didn't tell me how much more comfortable this couch is over my own."

Davis let out a relieved laugh that bordered on frantic. "I mean, really? A leather couch? You should know better." Davis waggled his fingers. "Design and all."

"I've never subscribed to form always following function," Jeremy said.

"I mean, it *looks* nice," Davis said, laughing.

"Fine, fine," Jeremy said. "I'll just live here on this couch forever, then. You can take my leather couch." Davis would probably agree to that, suffer through a loud and uncomfortable piece of furniture for the chance to keep Jeremy here, laughing and smiling, drinking tea in his cabin.

"I'm going to have to charge you rent," Davis joked back. "I mean, the federal government shuts down at least once a year at this point, so I do need a steady source of income."

"Oh?" Jeremy said, shifting up and setting his teacup down. "Not a second career as a paramedic?"

Davis rolled his eyes. "Too much math. Forest kid," he said, pointing to himself in an imitation of Jeremy earlier. "Speaking of, how is your knee?"

"It doesn't hurt as bad," Jeremy said, gingerly bending the knee. "I think I'll live."

"And your wrists?" Davis, without thinking, held out his hands. Jeremy placed his wrists in Davis's open palms. Davis studied the bandages, which looked good, and delicately pressed the skin just above the wrap. "Does that hurt?"

"No," Jeremy said, his voice getting a bit softer.

"Good," Davis whispered back. He leaned a bit closer, his hands still holding Jeremy's wrists the same way he would hold a rare wildflower. Cautious. Protective.

"Hey, I saw that your bike was back and thought I could drop off Mary Anne." Davis heard Alex's voice a millisecond before he would have crossed the point of no return and closed the gap between Jeremy's lips and his own. He pulled back quickly and, Davis was grateful to realize, Jeremy had also reclined back on the couch. His brain was lagging like the dial-up at his parents' house, because before Davis could open his mouth to ask Alex to keep Mary Anne outside, there came the noise of his front door opening, followed by the unmistakable sound of eighty pounds of a loving pit mix barreling through the house.

"Mary Anne!" Davis said, leaping up and just barely getting a hand on her harness. Mary Anne, excited by a new person to meet, whined and pulled, wanting to get to Jeremy. Davis couldn't blame him. Like dog dad, like dog daughter, apparently.

"Who is this?" Jeremy said, releasing that same goose honk of a laugh Davis had begun to crave.

"This is Mary Anne," Davis said, pulling back on the dog's harness. "Sorry, I didn't get a chance to see if you liked dogs. Alex, my coworker, was watching her today and apparently, just dropped her off."

"Is she friendly?" Jeremy asked.

"She wouldn't hurt a fly," Davis responded. Jeremy shifted, only wincing slightly as he bent his legs and placed both his feet on the floor.

"Hey, girl," he said softly, placing his bandaged wrist out in front of him. Davis, still keeping a light grip on her harness, led Mary Anne over to Jeremy. "I promise I usually don't smell like this much dirt," he joked to the dog, then added, "You probably like that, though." Mary Anne, to her credit, sniffed Jeremy's palm and, after a moment, pressed her head into Jeremy's hand.

"She likes it when you scratch behind her ear," Davis said, suddenly feeling like his heart was growing too big for his chest.

"She likes me!" Jeremy exclaimed, almost in awe, as he followed Davis's guidance. Mary Anne looked at Davis just once, as if to check, then turned back to Jeremy. "She really likes me," Jeremy repeated.

Who wouldn't? Davis thought. "She's a good dog" is what he said instead.

"I always wanted a dog," Jeremy said, shifting to scratch Mary Anne's other ear. "It's kind of hard in a fourth-floor walkup in Greenwich Village, or when you're in art school." Davis wouldn't know what it was like to be an art student or what it would be like to live in New York City. But he did know dogs.

"I always had 'em growing up," Davis explained. "Always some kind of mutt running around our house. I, uh, didn't get Mary Anne until recently." Davis focused on scratching the dog's back rather than watching Jeremy gently stroke the dog's ears.

"Why?"

"I wanted to make sure I was staying. It wouldn't have been fair to get a dog and then move somewhere else." Mary Anne, to underscore the gravity of what Davis said, rolled over on her back, demanding belly rubs.

"You were thinking about leaving?" Jeremy asked, rubbing the dog's belly.

"When I first moved, I wasn't sure. But now, Colorado, for some reason, feels right." He chanced it then, and looked up at Jeremy, who was looking back at him, smiling.

"I know the feeling" is all he said.

Jeremy

Jeremy felt like he could have sat on that couch and talked to Davis for hours, a snoring dog somehow the white noise machine Jeremy didn't know he needed. He did need to get back to the city, back to his life, back to where people were neatly slotted into their roles in his life. Friends, coworkers, et cetera. Davis, in the past two weeks, had apparently defied any categorization of friendship in Jeremy's taxonomy.

The moment Jeremy closed his car door after he gingerly sat down in the driver's seat and waved to Davis, who was standing on his porch, Mary Anne seated next to him, looking like something out of a Norman Rockwell painting, he began to panic a bit. Because *something* had happened between the men, somewhere between Jeremy's injury and their conversation on the couch. A rumble that foretold of something, like the moment when you knew a subway train was arriving, the way that the entire station would shake and heads would snap up.

Damn the lack of cell phone reception. He needed to run this past Foster. Which was annoying in its own way, because nothing fluffed Foster's feathers and caused him to preen like being needed for advice. Jeremy pushed his hybrid car as fast as it could go up the last hill before he got to coast down seven miles of warning signs about the steep grade.

"Come on, come on, come on." Jeremy had been out to the national forest enough times now that he knew the exact moment that cell phone reception would come back, the moment the screen on his car would begin to light up with text messages that his friends had sent and work emails he could probably get away with ignoring. It was right as he began to see the growing urban sprawl of Denver and the constant construction on the highways, the reminder that over the past few years, the beauty and quiet of the Front Range had become less and less of a secret to his fellow millennials who had left the coasts in search of houses and places to raise families. As he crested the top, he punched the screen that connected his phone to his car, searching for Foster's number.

"Yellooo," Foster drawled.

"Help!" Jeremy whined.

He could almost imagine the way that Foster's face would twist into a sly grin. There was nothing that Foster loved more than giving advice to his friends, even if he was pretty garbage at it most of the time. "Did you call for your friend or Uncle Foster?"

"I'm not calling you that —" Jeremy replied through gritted teeth but was cut off by Foster.

"Listen, I've known you for the better part of four years, and it counts double because you let me crash on your couch for the first three months of lockdown. We work out together three to four times a week. We're basically a platonic married couple at this point. I know your whine." He heard Foster take a sip of something, probably a mai tai or a daiquiri. Though he worked at a brewery, he tended to not drink beer unless he was drinking his sister's recipes.

"Fine, I need advice."

"Comic sans or papyrus. The only fonts you should use."

"Not design advice," Jeremy said, his finger hovering over the *end call* button. He should call Phoebe instead. She'd know what to do, having finally acted on her long-time crush. But, Jeremy reminded himself, he didn't have a crush. Because you didn't get crushes on straight men you worked with who were just being nice to you. Even if that niceness came with surprisingly tender hands and a gentle touch on a scraped knee. And an expertly wrapped bandage around both his wrists. As if to remind him, Jeremy's wrist gave an uncomfortable twinge as he switched lanes.

"*Oh*," Foster said, playing along. "Is it boy advice?"

"You're still straight, right?"

"Last time I checked, which was about thirty minutes ago, yep."

"Ew." Jeremy pulled a face in his car. "And single, right?"

A short pause. "Er...yeah. Single."

"You've never thought about, like, making a pass at me, right?" Jeremy rolled his eyes, feeling stupid for even asking the question.

"Nah, man. Like, you're objectively attractive, but ladies are where it's at for me."

"And, like, we're friendly and give hugs, but you've never, like, caressed another man's hand?"

"Not even when Dec got those sexy-ass hand tattoos." Foster laughed. "I think there's an unspoken rule of places on the body that you don't touch or *caress*, in your words, unless you're sending out signals."

"What about, like, in an emergency? Like, say, your hand is bruised and someone has to wrap it? And then you have to check the bandage?" Jeremy could feel himself scraping at the bottom of the barrel of excuses.

"Nope. I think then you're even more clinical. Oh, but, in Hallmark movies, there's always the moment when one character gets sick and then the other has to take care of them." Foster paused, and Jeremy knew that a lightbulb had gone off in his head. "Who is this about?"

"No one. It's hypothetical."

"Hush. I know everyone you know down in the city, and Dec is seeing Phoebe now — finally — and Ryan is very straight and very taken. You haven't hired anyone new at the museum, and there hasn't been a new spin instructor in the past four months, and you swore off apps for a while and haven't been on any dates, because you would have told me." Foster, when he got his mind on something, was like a squirrel who was convinced he could find the nut he buried. And, occasionally, and unfortunately for Jeremy, sometimes squirrel-Foster found that nut. "It's that forest guy."

"His name is Davis," Jeremy said, worried his voice would give him away.

It did. "You like him?"

"That's not a question. I can't like him. I don't mix business and pleasure. Plus, he's not my type."

"What, is he unintelligent?" Foster had shifted to being a cat now, playing with its prey.

"No, he's incredibly knowledgeable about the national forest's ecology and its history..."

"Is he mean?"

"No, he's absurdly nice and welcoming. He made me leave with leftovers today..." Jeremy eyed the stack of plastic containers that Davis had loaded into his car, saying that he had made too much lasagne anyway and that Jeremy should rest his wrist and not do too much chopping. It was a flimsy excuse, but Jeremy, who had apparently become a pushover, took all the food with a grateful smile.

"Is he unattractive?"

Jeremy turned up his AC. "No, he's not. Objectively speaking."

"Bring him to my birthday party next week. I want to meet this mystery man."

"I'm not bringing him around everyone. Between you and Emmy, it'll be like hyenas around a baby gazelle."

"I'm taking that as a compliment. Wait. Isn't it a Saturday?" Foster wondered. "It is, because tomorrow is Sunday, and that's the day that the direct flight to Iceland leaves..." his voice trailed off. "Why are you working on the weekend?"

"He invited me to go mountain biking," Jeremy groaned. "And I thought that my spin class experience would translate over."

"You fucking idiot," Foster cackled. "You fell, didn't you?"

"Hard."

"And not just off the bike, huh?"

"I'm hanging up now."

"Don't keep Uncle Foster waiting. I want details!" Jeremy hung up and knocked his head against the steering wheel.

Fuck.

He did have a crush on Davis.

And what was worse? He was not sure anymore that it was unrequited.

Davis

Davis had spent Monday morning alternating between tuning up Alex's bike (Jeremy had really fucked it up, though he would never tell him that), taking Mary Anne through miles and miles of the forest, and doing anything he could imagine to get his mind off how fucking awkward that had been. Even the baseball game in the background and replaying of his favorite level in *Halo* hadn't provided a distraction. He had shown his hand, and god knew he was a horrible poker player at the end of the day.

They had struck up a friendship. Davis wouldn't have thought twice about inviting any other guy to go mountain biking with him. But he had to admit to himself that there was something different about inviting Jeremy. Maybe it was that selfish part of him that craved some hit of dopamine, but he wanted to show Jeremy something he liked. And something he was good at.

Which had backfired in his face.

He had gotten Jeremy injured, something he would never get over and. If he was fifteen again, he would go to church with his gram and complete upward of twenty-five Hail Marys to try to make it right, even though he always lost count and felt bad because he couldn't even get through confession and penance right.

As if on command, Mary Anne released a giant snore from the couch next to him, and Davis smiled. He was reminded of the awed smile on Jeremy's face when Mary Anne had sniffed his hand, the way he had sounded wistful at his want for a dog. How Mary Anne had stayed by Jeremy's side, leaning her brick of a head on his legs as the two men talked about nothing and certainly didn't address the elephant in the room, how Davis's thumbs had swiped over Jeremy's wrists as a definite prelude to something more.

Dogs had always been constants in his childhood. Davis didn't know one family back home that didn't have some type of mutt roaming around their property or trotting out in the woods throughout the summer. Jeremy spoke fondly of his parents, in the distant, detached way that Davis knew meant he still grieved their loss in his life, so he knew Jeremy had had an amazing childhood, one that was full of subways, museums, and probably eating sushi or whatever kids who grew up in a city ate. The things that would have terrified Davis had brought joy to Jeremy, and Davis suppressed a laugh as he imagined how a younger Jeremy would have looked on his pap's farm, or his long legs dangling off a bar seat. He wondered if he would have tried to sneak sips of the beer foam like Davis did as a kid. He wondered if a young Jeremy would have loved the dog that Davis had adored as a child — a horrible-smelling, stubborn hound mix named Boomer that followed Davis as he tramped around the woods, a version of Shiloh without the backstory that made Davis cry in fourth grade.

"I should call him, right, Mary Anne?" Davis asked the dog, setting down his controller and looking at her. She had previously been curled up in a donut, apparently trying to make her sausage-like body as small as possible, and lifted her head when she heard Davis's voice.

"Or maybe a call is too intimate. A text?" Mary Anne cocked her head. "You're right, texting is too intimate. An email?" Davis took the fact that Mary Anne laid her head back down as encouragement that he was on the right path.

Davis crossed over to his desk and opened up his personal computer and typed an email from his personal account to Jeremy's email. Tapping the tiny microphone, he spoke to his computer, never quite comfortable with the way he had to slow down his speech for the machine to understand it.

"Dear Jeremy *comma* I want to apologize for how you got hurt yesterday *period* I feel very horrible and will understand if you do not want to work with me and the forest again *period* Also *comma* how are your wrists and you knee *question mark* Make sure that you are changing out the bandages and let the wound breathe but wash it after any exercise and keep it clean because you do not want an infection *period* Someone told me that they are an artist and need their hands *period* Enter Mary Anne says hello *period* Let me know if you would like to refer the forest to another designer *period* We will still pay your contract *period Enter* Have a good week *comma Enter* Davis"

He clicked the microphone and scanned the email, making small corrections to words that had been misunderstood and turning the *do not*s into *don't*s" to make it sound more natural. With one more look back at Mary Anne, he clicked send, and Davis imagined that the *whoosh* that emanated from his computer was the physical manifestation of the email zooming across cyberspace or the information superhighway or the cloud. Whatever the young kids were calling it these days.

Nearly five minutes later, as Davis was trying to rapidly click through a cutscene between Master Chief and Cortana, a soft *ding* from Davis's computer drew his attention to a new email.

D —

You have nothing to apologize for. If anyone understands that accidents happen and life is random chance, it's me. If you hire another exhibit designer, there will be hell to pay (not from me, but I have friends who are much stronger than me).

My wrists are healing nicely, thanks to you. My knee was a bit bruised, but I think it's okay. Will I still see you next week for our meeting?

J.

Pulling his computer onto his lap, Davis tapped out a quick response.

Good! I am glad to know that your friends have your back. That is important.

Ice your knee today and then use a heat pad to help it move better.

The meeting time is still good.

D.

He had just picked up his controller again when his computer *ding*ed.

I think my friends would like you. I don't think any of them know as much about trees as you do, and it's always good to put them in their place when someone is smarter than them.

Davis read the email about seven times. *Smarter than them.* Davis had looked at the people that Jeremy worked with at the museum, read their bios on the website. There were PhDs and other degrees that Davis had never heard of, a list of alphabet soup titles after their names.

Before Davis had a chance to respond, another email appeared, nested under the previous from Jeremy.

My friend Foster has a birthday party next weekend. It's a costume party, which is absolutely ridiculous, but it makes him happy. You should come down and meet everyone.

Davis looked at his seltzer. Took a sip. Swished it around in his mouth like he used to do with whiskey. The one downside to sobriety was that all stupid decisions were his and his alone. He wouldn't be able to blame what he sent back on alcohol or the social pressure of a group of people at the bar egging each other on in the way that felt like the only socially acceptable way for Davis to find community with other men back in Morgantown. Mary Anne, who really should take up a second career as a therapist, uncurled herself from her tiny dog ball and delicately stepped on Davis's lap (as delicate as a dog who weighed as much as a wheelbarrow of bricks could, that is). She gave a tender lick to Davis's chin, then sprawled across his lap, looking pointedly at Davis as if saying *you know you want to go.*

"You're too smart for a dog," Davis said, reaching over her to get his laptop. "Imma send you back and get some dumb hound instead." Davis swore she rolled her eyes, and he chuckled, setting the computer on her back and typed:

Sounds fun. Send me the address. I'll get a hotel room for the evening. I'll even dress up.

Davis's phone lit up just then, Jeremy having texted an address in Vanberg along with a message.

Jeremy: You don't have to dress up if you don't want to. Or you can, like, be a lumberjack. Or a forest ranger.

Davis: Are you saying that I dress like a lumberjack every day?

Jeremy: Am I wrong?

Davis: I'm dressing up.

Jeremy: As what?

And Davis, who felt a tingle in his spine that reminded him of when he took his at-bat to hit a homer during the WVSSAC Regional Championship, the closest he ever got to winning a big game in his not-so-illustrious career as a backup varsity catcher, typed *it's a surprise.*

Davis

"This is fucking stupid," Davis said out loud to his reflection in the half-rusted mirror in the bathroom of his cabin. Which, somehow, made him feel even stupider. He was thirty-eight years old, had been living independently since he was eighteen years old, had moved across the country and established a career in a notoriously difficult federal agency, and here he was, unable to decide how he was going to slick back his hair to impress a boy.

Good god, if his friends from back home could see him now.

"Knock, knock," came a voice. He had always been frustrated by the way seasonal work functioned as a kind of extended college dorm experience, which meant a lot of loud parties and people barging into your room at all hours of the day. Not that he had a college dorm experience, but he knew what it was like from movies. It had gotten a bit easier when he'd finally gotten full-time jobs, which meant that he didn't share an entire home with other people. But it still meant that he shared a campus of tiny cabins with other rangers. Most of them were weird loners who liked trees more than people, but people would still randomly walk into his house.

Thank god he never brought anyone home here. His few attempts in Denver left him feeling like he didn't belong in the bars that showed up on particular Yelp lists. Not like Davis had been on any dates since he moved to Colorado, but he had opened a few apps during his first week and realized that there was no one he wanted to fuck within a thirty-mile radius of his tiny mountain town.

And, if he was being honest, that was even a lie. There was no one he could trust within a thirty-mile radius of Klarluft. But that had changed. He trusted Jeremy, had plans to see how far that trust would extend this evening.

"I know you're in there!" Alex yelled from somewhere near the front door. Then he heard Alex talk to Mary Anne, who had left Davis's side to investigate and was, apparently, the world's worst guard dog.

Davis also, surprisingly, trusted Alex, who had started to show up when Davis felt bored and demonstrated decent skills during co-op play on the Xbox. And Yesenia, too, who had shared a hilarious story about her two grandmothers that had gotten Davis confused until she clarified that her Abuela Olivia and her Grandma Doris were married.

"Hello?" Davis asked, hastily tucking his shirt into his dress pants and walking out into the living room. Alex stood there, Caveman at his side, with two sets of baseball mitts. He let out a low whistle, and Davis wished he didn't blush so easily.

"Damn, you're looking fancy tonight. I guess you're not down for a game of catch, huh?" He tossed the gloves onto the coffee table and flopped down into the recliner. Davis had finally agreed to play disc golf with Alex and had hated every second of it, but during their chatter on the course, Davis had mentioned that he played baseball in high school and could go for a game of catch. Alex, it seemed, had come to take him up on that.

"I'd rather toss a ball around, I think," Davis said, trying not to cringe at the phrase *tossing a ball*, which, at previous jobs, would have resulted in a cascade of homophobic jokes that

Davis would have had to endure until he decided to fake a stomachache or just secretly leave the group.

Alex, to his credit, just shrugged. "Next time, then. Date tonight?"

Davis hesitated. "Something like that." It was a bit closer to the truth than he was usually willing to admit, even to himself.

"How'd you meet them?" Alex's use of a non-gendered pronoun wasn't lost on Davis. Was this an opening?

"Uh, well, the exhibit designer that I've been working with around here invited me down to a party in Vanberg tonight," Davis began, and a grin split Alex's face.

"That tall guy? With the hair?" Alex asked, and mimed Jeremy's curls.

"Yeah. Um. Him. Jeremy. Jeremy Rinci is his name." An admission, even if he didn't say the details in the words that clattered around his brain almost constantly.

"Nice," Alex said in the same tone that Davis imagined he would compliment a man on a girlfriend.

Davis fiddled with his tie. "You're...you're okay with that?"

"I mean, he's hot, and if he's into tree nerd shit, then that works for you." He made it sound so simple. Alex was a hydrologist by training. He spent his time wondering about acre-feet of water, as if an acre-foot was a measurement that made any kind of logical sense. He let out another laugh. "Plus, Yesenia owes me twenty bucks now. I bet her that you had a crush on him."

"So." He swallowed again. "You're fine working with a—" Another pause. *Fuck*, this was harder than telling people he was sober. "A queer ranger?"

"Does it affect your ability to do a job any differently than if you were getting railed by a woman?" Alex asked bluntly.

"Well, no." Davis swallowed. "And, just for the record, I, uh, like women, too. I'm bisexual." This was only the third or fourth time Davis had said the words out loud to someone, and it still felt new, a bit clunky on his tongue, like he was trying to sound out a new word he had never seen before.

"Then who cares? I mean, statistically, you're not the only one." Alex gave a sly smile. "Plus, like, I've kissed men before. Probably dated one, if you want to consider what my college roommate and I did 'dating.'"

"Oh," Davis said, allowing himself to smile. "That's cool. Was he a good a kisser?"

"The beard took a bit to get used to, but yeah. He was good. It was different, but good." Alex smiled. A faraway glance told Davis that maybe he wasn't quite done thinking about his college roommate. "I've mostly dated women, but I don't know if anything is truly ever off the table." Mary Anne, who had finished her standard sniff of Caveman, looked at Alex as if begging for a walk. "So what kind of party is it?"

"It's a costume party." Davis groaned, wishing that there was something he could do to take the edge off his nerves that wasn't exercise or masturbation, which were both out of the question now that he had put on his costume.

"Oh, fun!" Alex looked him over. "Who are you?"

"It's fucking stupid, but I'm this old actor. Rock Hudson. He was queer, and everyone knew it but didn't say it." Davis rubbed two palms over his face, probably fucking up the hair that he had actually done for the first time in years.

"Wait," Alex said, getting up and walking over to Davis. He put his hands on his shoulders and looked him straight in the eye. It was ridiculous, but Davis was always worried that when one of his male coworkers would find out about his sexuality, they would be afraid of him. Wouldn't use the same bathroom or give him bro hugs, not to mention the fears that had taken root in Davis's mind when he had attended a performance of *The Laramie Project.*

Alex's grip on his shoulders was the same as it was yesterday when he had asked a question about the predicted output of the Colorado River. "Wait. You're telling me that Jeremy doesn't know that you're queer? So he doesn't even know it's a possibility that you could be into him?" A stern look. "You're into him, right?"

At this point, Davis was too far gone in this conversation with Alex to think about the words that came out of his mouth next. "Fuck yes, I'm into him. Have you *seen* him?" Davis could have waxed poetic about the one curl in the center of Jeremy's forehead or the way that there was this one specific vein that crossed the top of his hand. He figured that might have been a bit too much for Alex at this particular moment.

"Okay, good. So he doesn't know you're queer. And this costume" — Alex pointedly looked up and down — "is how you're going to tell him?"

"Yeah." So dumb.

"Stealthy," Alex said, slapping his thighs and standing up. "Welp, best of luck. You're staying down in the city? Want me to watch Mary Anne?"

"Yesenia is going to come over and check on her." Actually, Yesenia had confronted Davis as to why Alex got to be the favorite dog uncle. "I'm staying the night — I have a hotel room," Davis replied, though what he wanted to add was *I would love it if I didn't need it.*

"Good. Don't drink and drive." Alex, he remembered, was from some state where there was a lot of corn. Iowa or Nebraska. Seemed like a good guy who would always take care of his friends. Shit, Davis had already told him one of his secrets. Why not dump everything on him at once?

"I'll be fine. I, er, actually don't drink. Like at all. I'm sober." He needed to practice how he would tell people here, but for a first attempt, Davis figured it wasn't bad.

"Oh. Cool. Good to know." Alex shrugged again. Davis was beginning to think that he could tell Alex that he was actually a lizard person sent to control the Forest Service and he would just go *a'ight* and ask Davis his opinion on what team would probably be joining the SEC next season. "Anyway, good luck. Let me know how things go."

"I will," Davis said, and he believed it. He wanted to tell Alex how much it meant that he could be honest with him, that he could let him know a version of his true self, but, well, he had already revealed so much. "Thanks, dude." The same way he would have always covered as a man pretending to be straight.

"I got you," Alex replied, picking up the baseball mitts. "And if your man has a friend, well. I wouldn't say no to some fun down in the city."

"I have to make sure that I'm welcome," Davis said. "Uh, Alex? Do I look okay?" An awkward question, one that admitted too much again.

"You're great. Knock 'em dead." And with that, Alex and Caveman headed out of the cabin, probably to meander and find another to play catch with or to go back to his own space, Davis didn't know. And, frankly, Davis didn't care. Because letting one person out here, in the forest, know details about his true self was giving him the confidence to head down to the city and let Jeremy know.

Jeremy, I'm bi.

Or maybe he would say —

Jeremy, I'm queer.

Or just lead with something direct like —

Jeremy, I like you.

Or —

Jeremy, I want to kiss you.

Davis shoved his duffel bag into the back of his truck cab, then slid into the driver's seat. He put on a playlist of bluegrass music, one that featured the band he had gone to school with, of Tiff on banjo and Caleb on guitar, with a new vocalist. He maneuvered through the mountain passes, sure that he could show up and wow Jeremy with his costume and maybe, if he was brave, get a kiss out of it.

Jeremy

Adjusting his wig one last time, Jeremy looked in the mirror in Foster's guest bathroom. "This is stupid," he said to himself. He wiped a smudge of eyeliner — Dec's suggestion, when he had admitted his costume at a post-work happy hour last week — and tried to imagine what Andy Warhol would say to him. Probably something like *stop being so stupid and just go fuck someone random at the party*, which was advice that would have worked before lockdown. Maybe he had changed even before then, though he wouldn't lie and say that having another body close to his was something that was a struggle to deal with.

Walking out of the bathroom, he saw Emmy, dressed as her research subject, emerging from a closet, adjusting her hair, and slipping one of her shoes back on, followed closely by Ryan, who was tucking his shirt into his pants and, quite obviously, wiping his mouth. *Straights*, Jeremy thought, laughing at the way they thought they were being inconspicuous. While he loved them, those two wouldn't have known discretion if it hit them in the face. Looking around the room, he saw Dec enter with Phoebe. He knew they were both queer, and they were much better at letting people know only what *they* wanted them to know. Dec had tingled Jeremy's gaydar the first time he was dragged to Next Door by Emmy and Phoebe, but Phoebe'd had to spell it out for Jeremy for him to realize, and Jeremy had realized that his assumptions about being able to suss out someone's sexuality had been developed in a very specific east coast urban setting. Not for the first time this evening, Jeremy thought about Davis in the way that he had suspicions he knew it was uncouth to voice.

The words had tumbled out of his fingers, and he had clicked *send* before he could even process what he had been doing when he invited Davis to this party. A moment of panic, then a wish that he had installed the program that allows him to unsend emails. Then a resolution. They were friends. It had been established when Davis came to help him out at the house (god knew Foster couldn't use a drill to save his life), and when Jeremy had gone on that ill-fated bike ride. His wrists and knee were healing nicely. He never would have thought to use a gentle heating pad, borrowed from Emmy, to help his knee move smoother, if Davis hadn't suggested it, which had allowed him to return to his very stationary bike. There was only a small hint of pain in his ribs when he breathed during that class, and he felt physically almost back to normal.

Emotionally? Well, did anyone over the age of thirty feel emotionally normal ever?

Following the class, Foster had fixed Jeremy with a pointed expression and said, "Coffee shop. Now." Which meant Jeremy was going to be interrogated about that phone call he had made coming down the mountain. He should have called Emmy. Her advice would have been blunter, but at least she knew how to keep her mouth shut. Over Jeremy's blend of too sweet chai and Foster's caramel something-or-other, Jeremy had cleared his throat. "So, your birthday party..."

"Yes, the event of the season. I'm aware." Foster licked a bit of whipped cream off his finger but didn't toss his typical coy glance at whatever poor barista he decided to flirt with. Interesting.

"Yes, the party to end all parties. I made sure to tell the Met to cancel their gala this year," Jeremy replied, unable to keep from rolling his eyes. "Were you serious when you told me I could invite people?"

"I mean, if they're cool and they show up in costume." He grunted. "I think that's what should have really been the first red flag about Flo's ex-husband. He would never dress up for our parties. Couldn't even put in the smallest bit of effort. Fucker." Foster took a moment to breathe in deep through his nose, a technique that Jeremy noticed he had been using more in the past two years. He never pried much into Foster's sister's life, only knew that she had forgone college to open the brewery and had gotten divorced in the past two years.

"Well, I did communicate to him that it's a costume party, so I'm sure he'll dress up."

That small hint of gossip caused Foster's eyes to snap open. "*Him?* You asked about *people*, but it's seeming like you wanted to ask about one very specific *person*."

"You're the worst."

"Love you, too, Jer Bear." Another obnoxious sip of his coffee drink. "Yes, please invite your forest crush. I'm dying to see what fair young gentleman has caught your eye."

Jeremy snorted. "Well, since the cat's out of the bag. He's not young — I'm pretty sure he's older than me — and he's, well," Jeremy scrambled for words, "burly."

"Burly." Foster deadpanned.

"Stout?"

"That's a beer."

"Robust."

"How you would describe coffee."

"He's, I dunno, rugged. Sexy. Not the type of man I'm usually attracted to, and I don't even know if he is interested in me or if he's even queer, which could make me a real fucking asshole." Once he started, it seemed like he couldn't stop. "He's thoughtful and kind and quiet. Unassuming. He thinks differently from anyone I've ever met, like someone who was born two hundred years ago. He's got strong convictions, brilliant ideas. He *cares*." *I want to be something he cares about* was the unspoken half of that sentence that Jeremy needed much more courage to ever voice.

"You're down bad, Jer Bear." Foster smirked.

"Don't make me start asking questions," Jeremy replied. "Don't think I haven't noticed that you've been quite silent about any new bedroom adventures recently." Foster's face blanched. "I'll be nice to you now, but only if you're nice to Davis at your party."

"Ugh, fine."

So there Jeremy was, recycling his standard Halloween costume of Andy Warhol — white wig and all — and hoping that Davis would come down the mountain. He had agreed to attend, had even hinted at dressing up, but then had gone radio silent about the party, their conversations returning to progress on the cabinets Davis was making and feedback on narrative text Jeremy wrote. After sending him the elaborate digital invitation that Foster had created on Thursday, he hadn't heard anything else and didn't want to push.

Push further, that was.

But there had been moments over the past two weeks when images had flashed into his head. The way his rough hands had searched over his torso and chest, checking for injuries. The tenderness with which he had wrapped bandages around his wrist. *Will you be able to draw if I wrap it like this?*

"New person!" Flo, dressed as Stevie Nicks, called from the front door, holding a glass bottle of light beer that reminded Jeremy of cash only bars in Bed-Stuy, a contrast to the flavorful craft IPAs and stouts she was known for. "New person who looks fancy who I don't know!"

"Jeremy!" Foster's voice joined his sister. "I think this guy's for you!"

Christ, Foster. Make it more obvious, why don't you.

He crossed the room, noticed Ryan arguing about a ruling in beer pong, confirming to Jeremy that Ryan was still the straightest man he had ever met, and laughed to himself again. Davis would probably fit in well here. Emmy and Phoebe were chatting by the door, Emmy showing Phoebe a photo on her phone.

"Hey," came Davis's voice. And there he was, standing in the doorway, broad shoulders taking up most of the space of the opening. Davis, who Jeremy had never seen out of flannels and sweatshirts, was in a short-sleeved button up, his hair slicked in a way that reminded Jeremy of *West Side Story*. He had shiny patent-leather shoes and khaki pants that hugged his thighs in an obscene manner, even if they had a pleated front.

"Davis! You came!"

"I did," he replied, blushing a little. "This is quite an elaborate setup."

"Hello, I'm Foster Sterling, Jeremy's best friend, birthday boy, and general all-around amazing human." Foster, who had rented a full Shakespeare costume from the University's theater department, including neck ruff, brocade vest, and knee-length boots, was gesturing dramatically. Emmy and Phoebe looked up simultaneously and made their way over to join Foster. *Now he had a fucking audience.*

"Uh, hi. I'm Davis."

"Just Davis? Like Cher?"

"No, Davis, as in *no one has called me by my actual first name in three decades*," he responded quickly.

Foster grinned. "Oh, I like you." He turned to Jeremy and gave what could only be described as a shit-eating grin. "I'm really glad Emmy and Phoebe sent me that special list. I have suggestions for you later." Jeremy felt his face flush as Emmy and Phoebe shared a knowing giggle. Foster was opening his mouth to say something to Davis, but by some miracle of technology, Foster was distracted by his phone buzzing in his pocket.

"Well, welcome to the chaos," Jeremy said, moving closer to Davis so he could be heard better. In addition to beer pong, which Ryan hadn't left all evening and Foster was being called to in order to rule on a dispute, there was a karaoke machine in the corner, a photo booth, a spread of catered food, and a trough for drinks. "These are my friends. They're kind of idiots."

"I'll fit in just fine." Davis laughed. They had found themselves near the drinks, and Davis was frowning.

"What's going on?" Jeremy wanted to fix it, whatever it was.

"I don't see any drinks that are non-alcoholic here." Jeremy was going to find Foster and wring his neck. He needed to fix this.

Now.

"I'll find something," he said quickly, turning on his heel and heading toward the kitchen.

Davis

Davis, a bit stunned by Jeremy's abrupt departure, had sat down in the closest unoccupied space, a couch tucked near a coffee table that contained a chess set and a stack of books on Shakespeare and self-empowerment. Davis wished he could pick up the chess pieces and make sense of it, but he only knew that the horse moved in an L shape. Checkers was more his speed, but this clearly was a crowd who understood chess. He was here to meet people, to meet Jeremy's friends, but this was an entirely different environment from what he was used to. Everyone here was so, well, *cool* and urban, and Davis felt like an ogre who needed to go back to his swamp. He would *not* take his phone out and distract himself by scrolling.

"Do you know how to play chess?" A small woman wearing a finely tailored suit and a top hat had sat down next to him and begun talking.

"Not at all," Davis replied.

"Me neither. It's way too confusing. I prefer checkers, though there was a moment when I watched that show about, like, a chess prodigy and considered learning chess if it meant I could meet gorgeous women like that." She set her glass of wine down and looked at Davis. "You're new here."

"I guess?"

"I saw you come in. Who do you know?" She took a sip of her wine, her cheeks a bit red.

"Uh, do you know Jeremy? Jeremy Rinci?"

Her eyes widened in understanding. "I know Jeremy, of course! We work together. He's one of my best friends." She was bubbly and energetic, like a sprite from a fairy tale.

The pieces began to slot together in Davis's brain. "You work at the museum? Then you're either Emmy or Phoebe, and considering the fact that you're talking to me with a smile on your face, I'm assuming that you're Phoebe."

The smile on the woman's face grew wider, and she nodded. "Jeremy notices everything. He's talked about us?"

"He mentions his friends a lot. Foster certainly lives up to his reputation. Which one is Emmy?" Phoebe pointed to a woman in an elaborate turn-of-the-century gown who was laughing with a woman dressed as Lucille Ball.

"I'm Davis. I work out at the national forest, and Jeremy —"

"Is working on an exhibit out there. I know! It sounds amazing. My brother lives out in Klarluft." Davis's shoulders relaxed a few inches as he chatted to Phoebe about a summer camp that her brother ran. "He's over there" — she pointed to someone wearing an extra-long beard — "and Lucille Ball is his fiancée, and the man who is some sort of old-timey paleontologist is an actual paleontologist."

"Ryan?" Another name from all the times that Jeremy had talked about his friends. The way Jeremy talked about Ryan reminded Davis of the way his uncle talked about the dog that he swore he was never going to get but bought a matching recliner for. Phoebe chattered away, filling in Davis's silences with stories about her friends and family.

"And he's married to Emmy?"

Phoebe laughed. "Not married. Never married. But together."

"And you're dating someone too?"

"Declan," she said, and Davis could practically see her eyes turning into cartoon hearts. "He's the sweetest. You'll recognize him. He's dressed up as a historic animator named Ub Iwerks, and he's got these sexy tattoos, and he can draw." She sighed. "He sometimes seems grumpy, but I promise he's nice!"

I sometimes seem straight, but I promise, I'm queer! Davis thought.

"Do you want me to get you a drink?"

"No thanks, I —" Davis prepared himself to say something *again*, when Jeremy appeared, holding two cans, accompanied by the aforementioned Declan. And while Davis knew he had *a type*, he wasn't expecting for Jeremy's friend to be nearly as gorgeous as Davis found Jeremy. Phoebe had really won the hot boyfriend lottery, it seemed.

"Davis," Jeremy said, looking a tad bit uncomfortable, like he was wearing shoes that were too small. "This is Declan. Declan, this is Davis."

He wanted to make Jeremy comfortable, to show him that he liked his friends and, even though he wasn't completely comfortable, he was having a good time. So Davis stood up, brushing an imaginary crumb off his shirt, and presented his hand. "Ah, the famous Declan. Phoebe — I mean Ms. Dietrich — saw me sitting alone and started chatting. She's been raving about her phenomenal partner, and here you are."

"Uh, here," Jeremy said, holding two cans out toward Davis with stiff arms. "Dec said this is a beer without booze, and this is seltzer." Something warm and delightful bubbled in Davis's chest at the fact that he had *remembered*, not as an afterthought when everyone else was ordering. It explained Jeremy's quick departure and the length of time he was gone. He was looking for something for Davis to drink.

"You sober too?" Davis asked Declan as he took the cans from Jeremy. He set the beer down and opened the seltzer. Something about the taste of beer didn't work for him anymore.

"Ironically, I'm a bartender."

"And bar owner," Phoebe added, grinning with pride.

"I make a mean mocktail if you're ever near campus," Declan said. He addressed Davis, but watched for Phoebe's reaction. Davis scanned the gathered group, and that warm feeling returned when he saw Jeremy watching him.

"I'd like that. I tend not to venture down from the mountains, but —"

And at that moment, Davis had the type of energy surging through his veins that made him think that he should buy a lottery ticket, knowing that the numbers he chose would be said on television before the evening news. That these people, in this hot, loud apartment that smelled like bodies, beer, and a hint of weed, were somehow *his* people. An unmistakable undercurrent that there could be someone in this room that could be *his* person.

How funny.

"— there might be a reason to soon."

Jeremy opened his mouth to say something, but was cut off by Phoebe, who barreled her way into the conversation like a delightful little freight train. "Who are you, anyway? I've been trying to guess your costume all night. I know it's an actor —" She prattled on, and Davis vaguely caught that she was talking about how her partner liked old films. But Davis was looking at Jeremy, wondering if he should push his luck and go all in. Declan cleared his throat and met Davis's eye, and at that moment, Davis knew that, somehow, Dec *knew*. Knew who he was dressed as and knew what he *was*.

"Rock Hudson," Davis said, taking the words from Dec's mouth.

"Who's that?" Jeremy asked, his sky-blue eyes seeking out Davis's own.

Davis took a moment and glanced over at Declan, who almost imperceptibly raised an eyebrow to ask a question. Davis nodded once, not sure if his voice could be trusted to explain it and say everything that needed to be said.

"A very famous actor who," Dec cleared his throat, "was definitely not straight."

Jeremy, who had apparently decided to sip on the NA beer Davis didn't want, choked.

"Emmy!" Phoebe was calling across the room, cutting through the silence. The tall woman with severe bangs who had shoulders that could fill up a doorway came over to the group. "Tell us what you know about Rock Hudson!"

"Did someone ask about rocks?" Ryan had joined the group, and all of a sudden, Davis was swept up into a whirlwind conversation that somehow jumped from film history to paleontology history and ended up with Declan, the quiet, tattooed one, grinning as he talked about how one of the first animated films was about a cute dinosaur.

"Foster!" Ryan called. "Get off your fucking phone and join us in the present."

"I'm about to throw this phone into a volcano in Iceland," Foster grumbled, coming to join the group.

"You know my sister has been working in Rejavik," Ryan said to Emmy.

Jeremy

The moment that Ryan had called over Foster and pulled him into a headlock, giving Foster a noogie and asking him who he was texting all night, Jeremy felt that the room had gotten too crowded. For one of the first times in his entire life, Jeremy wanted to be outside, wanted to be out in the mountains, where everyone wasn't so damn loud and he could just sit on Davis's back porch and figure this all out.

So he did, turning abruptly on his heel and heading out to Foster's back patio, and he put the pieces together from the last few minutes. One moment, he had been watching Davis tentatively slot in with his friends, and the next, Dec had blown Jeremy's mind wide open.

Davis was dressed as an actor who was "definitely not straight."

Which meant...

Davis wasn't *straight*.

That explained the *looking*.

Davis wasn't *straight*.

That explained the tension that had pulled between them recently.

Davis wasn't straight.

Which meant he wasn't imagining things and he could potentially —

"Hey, you good?" And there Davis was, sliding the door open and poking his handsome head out.

"I'm fine, just —" Jeremy took a breath in and let it out, a small cloud of cool air emerging from his lips. "Actually. We should talk."

"Your friends are nice," Davis answered.

"They're a goddamned nuisance."

He smiled. "Yeah, that, too."

"We should talk."

"I can drive back up to the mountains, if you'd like." Davis looked at the ground. "Sorry if I made things weird."

"No, please don't drive back up. It's dark, and that road is very dangerous." That felt overprotective, not caring. Not sexy. Jeremy sighed.

"I have headlights, Jeremy." Davis laughed.

"Maybe I want you to stay." And Jeremy just opened his fucking mouth and said that.

"Okay," Davis responded. "I have a hotel room, so do you want to meet for tea tomorrow morning? Give you some space?"

"I don't think space is what I want right now," Jeremy breathed.

"Oh."

"I can drive you to my place," Jeremy said, more to the creek below than to Davis.

"Okay, but, um." Davis took a deep breath, swallowed, then continued. "Should I grab my bag from my truck?"

Jeremy felt a flame of hope burn bright in his chest, like the first catch of a match before it settled. "I mean, that's up to you. I can always drive you back to your truck. After we talk."

"I'll get it, just in case," Davis said, leaving the doorway. *Makes sense*, Jeremy thought to himself, the fact that Davis was always prepared. Remembered that he had been an eagle scout, which Jeremy had then learned took more commitment than he would have had at seventeen. His brain immediately went to wondering if he had gotten a merit badge in knot tying.

There was a commotion inside, and Jeremy heard Foster cry out "*You just got here!*" Jeremy went back inside to where Davis and Foster were talking by the door, Davis with his keys in his hand.

"Jeremy," Foster whined, drawing out the last syllable. "He's *leaving.*" *Shit, Foster was a bit drunk.* Which, in Jeremy's experience, meant that he usually was the one encouraging everyone to stay out for "just one more drink" or, more recently, he had tended to get oddly morose and prone to talking about desires and goals and a lot of other maudlin topics that Jeremy didn't want Davis to experience. "You finally brought him *here*, and now you're *leaving?* You should *stay*, and you should want *him* to stay, because everything is so fucking *transitory* now, and no one *stays.*"

"Easy, Foster," Flo said, pulling his arm away. She made eye contact with Jeremy and gave him a nod that said *I got it from here.* "Plus, it does seem that he's not leaving alone." Her eyes knowingly flicked to Davis, who had attempted to sneak out the front door behind Jeremy.

"He's new in town," Jeremy stumbled to explain. "I'm gonna just, uh, make sure he gets somewhere safe."

"Good," Foster said. "At least someone will get some tonight." Jeremy felt his face heat while Flo guided Foster back to the beer pong table. If Jeremy knew anything about Foster, it was that his mood wouldn't last, and he'd be back to the life of the party in a few minutes.

"My team!" Ryan was yelling, corralling Foster to be his teammate in a game of beer pong. He'd be fine.

"Are you ready?" Davis said, bringing Jeremy back to the present moment.

"Yeah, just —" Jeremy dug his keys out and made an awkward gesture toward where his car was parked, a functional, perfectly fine sedan that Jeremy now was concerned was too small for Davis's broad body to fit into.

Which was stupid, he reflected as he folded himself into the driver's seat, because Jeremy had always been the tallest person in a room, and he fit into this car, occasionally, in his younger days, into the back seat with men who were shorter than him.

Davis sat in the passenger seat with his bag on his lap, looking a little like he was a kid whom someone's mom was driving to school.

"You can toss that in the back," Jeremy suggested. Davis turned and set it, gently, in the back seat. Because, of course, Davis was a large man who could move with the grace of a small kitten when he wanted to. Jeremy started the engine, an uncomfortable silence blossoming between the men.

"So," Jeremy said, awkwardly drumming his fingers on the steering wheel as he eased onto Broadway. "Your costume."

"What about it?" He could feel Davis getting defensive.

"I, uh, well. Um." God, where had his suave nature gone? Where had the guy gone who could dance up to anyone and find a good time? "I didn't, uh, well, realize—"

"You didn't realize I was queer?" Davis said, a dry laugh in his voice.

"Well, no," Jeremy said, feeling stupid.

"Good," Davis replied smugly.

"Why good?"

"Because I didn't want — don't want — anyone at work to know."

"But I'm gay! And we work together!" Jeremy flapped a hand between them as he pulled up to a red light.

"Jeremy, have you seen yourself? Your friends? Vanberg? You walk through and work in a world that is very different from mine," Davis said simply.

"But, well," Jeremy sputtered again, "I just feel like you could have told me. Like, I'm *gay*. I'm not going to be upset that I get to work with another queer man. I would think you would want the community." Jeremy parked in front of his house, unsure of where the evening was going. There was something bubbling deep in his stomach, and he wasn't sure if, when it rose to a boil, it would turn into anger or excitement or an emotion wholly unfamiliar to him.

"Are you mad at me?" Davis asked, turning toward him, a tinge of red high on his cheeks.

"No!" Jeremy almost shouted.

"Then why are you yelling?"

"Because I *like* you, you pain in the ass. I like you and didn't think I could like you, so I tried not to. But you're so damn endearing talking about trees and the elk rut that I couldn't help it!"

"Well, try being me!" Davis spat back. "You show up with your pretty hair and your design ideas and your long fingers, and then you listen to me? Shit, a guy gets ideas."

"Wait," Jeremy said, Davis's comment slotting together with his thoughts in his mind like Tetris pieces. "You like me?"

"Yes!"

"Like, well, *like* like?" Jeremy felt like this was high school again.

Davis let out a frustrated noise and turned toward Jeremy, grabbed his face between his rough palms, and kissed him.

Jeremy would be lying if he said he hadn't imagined what it would be like to kiss Davis, but there was nothing like the reality of a situation, the heat and desperation. It wasn't a gentle kiss, nothing like the way that Jeremy sketched or Davis pointed out a specific type of fern. It was bruising and needy, progressing from closed lips to panting mouths in the space of a second. Davis's tongue was hot as it slid against Jeremy's own, and Jeremy was delighted to find that Davis moaned when Jeremy wrapped his hands around Davis's wrists. He captured Davis's lower lip between his teeth and was rewarded with a *goddammit* that was breathed into his own mouth.

"Wait," Jeremy said, pulling back, pleased to find both men were winded. "This costume. Rock Hudson. This was your way of coming out to me?"

Davis's lips were kiss bitten and red and delicious, peeking out from his scruff, as he smiled at Jeremy. "After mountain biking, I was sure you *knew*, but you didn't, so I decided to be a little more, well, obvious."

"You know what's obvious?" Jeremy said, moving closer. "Telling me."

"Jeremy," Davis whispered against his lips, his breath hot and warm, hinting at what could come. "I'm bi. I like you. Now kiss me."

And Jeremy did. The car grew steamy, and Jeremy felt, foolishly, for the first time in his life, like he was in a teen movie, being able to neck with a boy outside in a car. Two men making out in a subway car was something that most New Yorkers didn't bat an eye at, and Philadelphia was too damn cold in the winter to do anything that wasn't inside with the heat turned on, and it was too damn hot in the summer.

Jeremy licked up his neck, cursing the fact that Davis's stupid, brilliant costume had buttons and that Jeremy's fingers were too long and too awkward right now to even think about undoing them in this car. This car, which was getting too hot and humid and was not large enough for all the things that

Jeremy wanted to do to Davis tonight. All the things that he had not allowed himself to even think were possible spun through his mind, but one thought had bubbled to the surface.

He needed to get Davis in a bed.

Now.

Pulling Davis's earlobe between his teeth, Jeremy was rewarded with a pleased groan from Davis. "Cancel your hotel room," Jeremy whispered. "Come to my place."

"We're at your place," Davis smiled back. "Well, outside it."

"Stay here."

It had been a while, Jeremy realized, and he had forgotten how this other side of him came out during sex. A bit more demanding, more dominant than he was in his daily life. He hoped it wouldn't scare Davis off. "Please," Jeremy added, hoping it would take the edge off his request.

Davis, who was bulky and thick and delicious underneath his fingers.

Davis, who was nodding his agreement and fumbling for his cell phone.

Davis, who whispered "fuck it" and kissed Jeremy again, telling him, against his lips, that he'd just eat the cancelation fee if it would get him to Jeremy's bed faster.

Davis

Davis was pushed into the door that he had walked through a few times before, the sturdy wood pressing against his back. There was something that Davis always enjoyed about the pressure of someone on him, no matter the gender, but Jeremy's height was really working for him right now. The way that Jeremy's knee was tracing up the inside of Davis's thigh and how Davis's mouth was being simply ravaged, and Jeremy's hands? well...

Jeremy's hands were in Davis's hair, tugging, pulling it out of the slicked back style for the costume and sending it into disarray. Davis, as soon as he regained the use of his mouth and his wits, was going to beg Jeremy to wrap those delicate fingers around his throat. Lovingly, of course. But Jeremy was mumbling against his lips, something that sounded close to *fucking hell*, and found his keys and opened the door, moving near Davis's right hip.

As Davis tried to regain his balance, grateful for his low center of gravity, he took a giant step backward. He took a moment to look at Jeremy, really look at him, his curls tumbling a thousand different directions and his already lush lips even more full and kiss bitten. He was already hard, but seeing Jeremy, who was always so put together and effortless, look so casually debauched, made Davis a thousand times harder.

What was worse, though, was the ache in Davis's chest when he looked at Jeremy and saw him looking back. He had noticed, of course, the way that Jeremy sometimes looked, his long eyelashes fluttering a bit as his eyes danced over the breadth of Davis's chest. But those were always stealthy glances. This was the full force of Jeremy Rinci's gaze, and it made Davis feel a buzz in his bloodstream he hadn't felt in years.

"I've imagined you here," Jeremy said, eyes bouncing from Davis's arms to his crotch.

"I've been here before," Davis replied, slipping off his shoes. The dress shoes that he had to dig out of a closet, laughing to himself about the deep metaphor there.

"You've not been here like this," Jeremy said, unbuttoning his own shirt, revealing a pale chest, a thin gold chain. He crossed the room and took Davis's chin in one hand, while the other slipped below his waist.

"That's true," Davis laughed against his lips. "I like being here like this."

"You're good with...more?" Jeremy asked.

"God yes," Davis panted.

"How do you like it?" Jeremy said, gritting his teeth. Davis licked his lips, watched Jeremy's blue eyes trace every movement. He had anticipated soft from Jeremy, when he had allowed his mind to wander in the cramped shower of his mountain cabin. Soft, delicate kisses, with Davis assuming the role that so many people expected of someone who was built like he was. But Jeremy was gripping his side under his shirt just this side of gentle, each fingertip a brand against Davis's skin, and Davis got the sense that, though nothing about them would suggest it, the dynamic between the two men would fit into place, the way that trees made space for each other to reach the sunlight. Davis could be tossed around, and Jeremy could toss.

"I like it rough. Uh, you can, like, manhandle me," Davis said, a rasp in his voice that might have been a plea or might have been a challenge.

"Thank fuck," Jeremy replied, slotting his mouth against Davis's. Then he was pulling him backward, back to the far hallway toward Jeremy's bedroom, the mysterious hallway that Davis had imagined more than he wanted to admit.

Davis lay on the bed, pausing for a moment, resting back on his palms. Jeremy was studying him, the way he imagined that he had done in art school, studying life models. *Draw me like one of your French girls.*

Jeremy's white button-down shirt was now completely undone, and Davis could just see the light sheen of sweat that put his lean muscles into relief. Davis's own shirt, one of only a few dress shirts he owned, had been tossed somewhere in the hallway. And even though he was so fucking overjoyed to be here, so proud of himself for making an initial move on a man for the first time in his life, he couldn't help but compare himself to Jeremy. Jeremy, who was tall and lithe and nearly hairless, some type of ethereal elven creature that would have been better suited within a scene from the *Lord of the Rings* films. And if Jeremy was an elf, then Davis was a dwarf. Shorter, with a slight belly and hair that drifted from his chest down below his boxers.

His pants had gone missing in the hallway, too, it seemed.

"Look at you," Jeremy was saying, snapping him back to the present. "You know, I wondered," he continued.

"Wondered what?" Davis asked, desperate for him to keep talking.

"Wondered what you'd look like under the flannels and the sweatshirts. But only in moments." He swallowed, and

Davis tracked the movement of his Adam's apple, the way his nipples had hardened in the cool evening. Jeremy kept a window open in his bedroom, and a soft breeze drifted across Davis's stomach, causing him to shiver as Jeremy continued talking. "But I was good. I didn't let myself think about you like that."

"I'm not as good as you," Davis admitted, though he figured the bulge in his boxers could have spoken for him.

Jeremy prowled closer, feline in the way he came onto the bed and kneeled, continuing to *look* at Davis in a way that made Davis's blood hot. "Are you saying that you've been bad?"

"Yes," Davis hissed.

"You've had bad thoughts about me?" Jeremy knee-walked forward on the bed, and Davis glanced at his waist and took in the fact that he had unzipped his fly and the ruddy tip of his dick was peeking out. Davis wanted it in his hands, his mouth, his soul.

"Terrible thoughts," Davis admitted, loving the way Jeremy was approaching him, as if he had nefarious plans for Davis's body.

"Good." Jeremy smiled. Davis braced himself for the weight of the other man on top of him, but Jeremy sat back on his heels, one hand grazing over his own chest, catching on a nipple. "Show me."

"Huh?"

"Come on, baby," Jeremy purred. "Show me what you did when you thought about me." Davis had never been called *baby* before, had tried to say it to girls in high school, but it never felt right. But something about the way Jeremy said it to him slipped from his ears, down his spine, and sizzled through his nerves.

"Okay," Davis breathed, and hooked his thumbs in the waistband of his boxers. "Can I?" He wanted to double check, to make sure that he had correctly understood what Jeremy wanted him to do.

"Fuck, please," Jeremy replied.

Davis lifted his hips and shimmied his boxers down his legs, trying his damndest to avoid getting them caught on his toe, and flicking them off the bed. He spread his legs farther, as if to say *here I am, flaws and all* and, mimicking Jeremy, ran his hand over his chest and down his stomach.

"Yeah, baby," Jeremy continued. Davis wrapped his hand around the base of his cock, already hard and throbbing. He had to be careful not to stroke too hard, not to tug too much, unless he wanted this to be over in thirty seconds. "You need lube?"

"Yeah," Davis responded, and Jeremy reached next to Davis, close but not touching, and pulled out a slim bottle. "Optimistic?" Davis quipped.

"I wasn't a boy scout, but I like to be prepared," Jeremy quipped right back. Again, when Davis expected Jeremy to just hand him the bottle, he watched as those long, elegant fingers flicked open the cap and tilted it over Davis's hand and cock. "Open your hand," he commanded, and Davis watched, almost out of body, as his hand followed the command. A spurt of cool liquid splashed onto his hand, and he returned it to his dick, hissing a bit until the temperature adjusted.

"What do you like, baby?" Jeremy asked, leaning closer as Davis picked up the movement with his hand, an obscene noise echoing through the bedroom. "You want me to blow you?"

"No," Davis ground out.

"No?" Jeremy repeated, pulling back up, but leaving a hand on Davis's thigh.

"No, I want that, *god, fuck I do*, but I'm so close already." Davis's hand was speeding up, out of his control, his body chasing the orgasm that his mind was trying to stave off.

"That's sexy," Jeremy said, planting a kiss on his chest.

"Touch me," Davis was able to say.

"Where?"

"Anywhere, Jeremy, you're —" and whatever Davis was about to say or admit was cut off by Jeremy's mouth crashing down on top of his own, his tongue thrusting into Davis's mouth. Those hands he had watched for what felt like years now roamed up and down his chest, fingers bumping over a nipple while Jeremy's other hand joined Davis's. Their fingers tangled over Davis's leaking dick, his hips moving in an erratic rhythm. Jeremy pulled their joined hands tighter, the kind of pressure that Davis loved — just *this side* of too much — and he came.

"Fuck," he breathed into Jeremy's mouth, cum slipping between their hands. A moan may have escaped somewhere in there as well. Jeremy, still proving that he was truly always prepared, reached his clean hand off the bed and grabbed for a pack of wipes.

"Are you some kind of sexual Mary Poppins?" Davis asked, then immediately wanted to kick himself for saying the least sexy phrase in the world.

"You know I'd look phenomenal in that jaunty little cap that she wore," Jeremy said. "I live alone, and I don't trust men to bring anything they need because, well, *men*." Davis watched Jeremy hastily wipe his hand, fantasized about having the courage one day to ask him to lick his fingers.

"You've never, uh, with a woman...?" Davis let the end of the question hang in the air as he was passed the wipes. He had forgotten this part of sex with men, how it could be messy, which was sometimes the best, but was, most of the time, an inconvenience.

"Nope," Jeremy said, popping the *p* at the end. "I knew early on. Pretty sure I came out of the birth canal fashionably late, listening to Cher, and having strong opinions on esoteric design choices." Jeremy chuckled but fell silent when Davis didn't join him, the fear of not being *enough* hammering through his body.

Jeremy

There was a moment, just a flash, when Jeremy was worried that Davis would achieve that fabled post-orgasm clarity and remember that he was actually straight, whatever experimentation he wanted with Jeremy cleaned up with the same wipes that Jeremy had used to wipe away the evidence of his orgasm.

Jeremy was sure that fear had come to fruition when Davis had asked him about his sexual history. There was nothing about women that had ever interested him sexually. It was just a fact about him, like the fact that he was six-five and his favorite color was a light teal. Jeremy Rinci was gay.

But as he watched Davis, his cock softening against the gorgeous hair on his thighs, Jeremy pieced things together. How Davis would catch himself watching Jeremy and look away, a light blush on his cheeks. How he used his costume to come out to Jeremy instead of putting it in words.

"Davis?" Jeremy asked softly.

"Sorry," he said, taking a deep breath.

"Am I the first man you've slept with?" Jeremy figured he should prepare himself to be disappointed sooner rather than later.

"No," Davis said. "You're not an experiment to me." A wave of calm settled over Jeremy. "It's just, well, I've never hooked up with someone I work with." He coughed a bit and looked away. "I kind of keep this part of myself, uh, well, hidden at work. It's not their business."

Jeremy felt a slight burning in his chest that accompanied a feeling of sadness. "Baby," he whispered. "You never have to hide who you are with me." *I want it to be my business*. Too much, too open for a first hookup, Jeremy knew that. But they hadn't met on an app or on a dance floor. They'd known each other for months at this point.

The apprehension returned, and Jeremy was sure that Davis would pull on his clothes and leave right now. That fear, however, was replaced with something very close to joy when Davis kissed him after cleaning his hand. Well, doing a decent enough job of cleaning his hand, because his right hand on Jeremy's neck was still a bit sticky.

"Thank you," Davis was whispering against his lips, sucking his lower lip into his mouth. "Thank you." And then Davis was kissing down his chest, licking over a nipple, and continuing his path downward. Before Davis made his way entirely south, Jeremy tapped him on the shoulder.

"I'm on PReP," Jeremy said. "And I haven't been with any-one since I was last tested." He nodded to his phone, which had been tossed onto the floor next to the bed. "I can pull them up if you want."

Davis blushed. "I trust you. I have to get a full physical every year, and my results are negative. My right hand is also regularly cleaned." Davis smiled up at him. "Jeremy, can I?"

Whereas Jeremy loved using names in bed, he very rarely heard his own name said to him. And he found that he *liked* it a lot. "Can you do what, baby?"

"Can I suck you?" Davis growled, seeming a little desperate. And while the conversation had taken the edge off his erec-tion, the need in Davis's rasp had him hardening again.

"Yeah, baby. Use that pretty mouth." And Jeremy idly wondered if anyone had ever called Davis *pretty* before, because his cheeks flushed bright pink right before he took the head into his mouth.

If there had been any part of Jeremy that still wondered if he was an experiment, the way Davis was able to take him to the back of his throat would have been an indication that either the man had practice or had been blessed with an absent gag reflex. Jeremy held his hips still, running his fingers along the stubble of Davis's beard, feeling the way his cheeks hollowed as he pulled back to breathe. Jeremy was close already, but the way Davis let a small stream of saliva slip out of his mouth and onto Jeremy's cock had him near the edge. He worked him with both hands, the calluses from whatever lumberjack shit he did in the forest providing a fantastic level of friction.

"You like that?" Davis asked, and the way he said it wasn't the way Jeremy was used to hearing. Not a self-assured manner that confirmed it, not *Yeah, you like that, huh, you slut*, but a genuine question.

"Yeah, baby," Jeremy hissed. "I like it."

"I'm doing well?" A bit coy, his ranger was, asking such a pertinent question before pressing his tongue into the slit at the head of his dick.

"You like praise, baby?" Jeremy was rewarded with another blush on Davis's cheeks. "What else do you like?"

"You can, uh." Davis's hands stopped for a second. "I'm not used to talking this much. Do guys say *fuck my face* in bed?"

"Guys say whatever turns them on," Jeremy replied, taking a deep breath to hold off his impending orgasm.

"Well, then." Davis took him down again, then popped off to say, "Can you fuck my face?"

"You sure?" Jeremy must have hit the lottery, because here was this fucking perfect man asking Jeremy to own his throat, just for a little bit this evening.

"*Yes*." And then Jeremy was thrusting, and Davis was making the best kind of noises, breathing through his nose as Jeremy's hips worked. As he kept working himself in and out of that pretty mouth, Jeremy pulled back for just a second.

"I'm close —"

"Down my throat, please," Davis begged. And who was Jeremy to deny someone who asked so nicely?

Davis

Davis hadn't used an alarm in years. He had gotten up early in high school, the result of attending a school that started at seven a.m. and was a thirty-minute drive from his house. That had continued through his time working and attending community college, trying to fit in shifts at various jobs around the classes and the hours of studying he had to do to make sense of all the textbooks, and well into his time in Morgantown, then back to the New River. There was a tiny part of him that, he admitted, felt a little better than everyone else when he was able to complete tasks before the rest of the world had risen. Early coffees, early bike rides, early hikes — excellent ways to experience the world. So when the first hint of sunlight slid between the blinds in Jeremy's bedroom, Davis was already awake and only panicking slightly.

He had awoken with their legs tangled together, Jeremy's limbs that seemingly went on forever twisted and braided around his own. Jeremy, it seemed, was not the type of person that believed in personal space in bed. If Davis was estimating correctly, he had roughly three centimeters before he would tumble off the side, while Jeremy's left arm was tossed out with what seemed like miles of mattress to spare.

Davis gingerly lifted an arm and a leg from his body and ignored how those places went cold the minute Jeremy's limbs were gone. Quietly — well, as quietly as a man of his bulk could — Davis crept into the bathroom to relieve himself.

Taking a glance in the mirror as he was washing his hands, Davis was surprised to find that he had scratch marks down his stomach, little whispers of pink and red that flashed between the hair on his torso. He shouldn't have been surprised, based on the way he had begged to feel more.

Jeremy, he was learning, was full of surprises. The wry, witty man became dominant and all-encompassing in bed. He had *wanted* Davis, had shown him that by pressing him against the door and the bed and had opened his perfect mouth and called him *baby*. So Davis was learning not to assume anything about Jeremy Rinci. But he did assume that he would have woken up before nine a.m.

Davis assumed wrong.

He needed something to do, and he couldn't just slip out Jeremy's front door and spin away in his truck because *they worked together*. And, also, Jeremy had driven him to his place, and Davis, lust drunk in a way that sent him for a loop more than whiskey had ever done, had no idea where Foster lived. More than that, Davis *liked* Jeremy. Liked him as something more than just a hookup, and that meant that Jeremy deserved to have a morning conversation. Which, based on the way that his eyelids were fluttering when Davis peeked back into the bedroom, was looking like it would be more like an early afternoon conversation.

So Davis did what he always did in the morning and made himself useful. He emptied Jeremy's dishwasher, grinning as he found a light yellow Fiesta Ware mug that he hadn't seen in his previous visits to *Casa di Rinci*. He snooped a bit. It was something that his Pap would have called him a nebnoser for, but he found a load of towels in the dryer that he could fold. He perused Jeremy's bookshelf, flipped through a heavy text filled with high-quality photographs of art by names Davis didn't recognize — Clyfford Still, Mark Rothko — and one he did — Jackson Pollock. Davis didn't know the first thing about art, but when he looked at one page, at a print that was blazes of sharp colors dripping into one another, he felt something in his chest that reminded him of the first time he had seen Yosemite Valley.

This matters, that feeling said to him.

"Which book did you choose?" Jeremy's voice came, and Davis was so startled that he closed the book with a slam, then worried he had ruined the page with that one painting.

"Uh, I dunno," Davis said, embarrassed. "I just grabbed this one."

Jeremy walked over, his hair a mess and his eyes only half awake. He had not put on a shirt, but he had slipped on pants that looked so soft that Davis wanted to touch them. He curled his hand into a fist. Then he remembered that he *had* touched, *could* touch, and he did, rubbing the material between his thumb and forefinger. It was as soft as it looked.

"Abstract Modernism," Jeremy said as Davis opened up to the page he had been looking at. Davis was sitting on a stool, and Jeremy was over him, leaning into him slightly, the way Mary Anne did when she liked a new person.

"I have no idea what that means."

Jeremy opened his mouth to respond, then closed it. "It's hard to explain. It's better to experience?" He leaned down, reached over Davis's shoulder, and tapped one long finger on *that* painting, the one with the colors that looked like they had been torn away. "This was done by Clyfford Still. There's an entire museum dedicated to his work in Denver." A pause. "We should go."

Davis gently set the book down and rotated on the plush stool toward Jeremy, who was still standing above him. "You'd want to go with me to an art museum?"

"I want to go a lot of places with you, Nathaniel Davis," he responded, and Davis almost fell out of the chair. He had been sure that at some point this morning, Jeremy would have given him a very honorable and deep sigh and said something like *we are better as colleagues*.

"Oh," Davis replied eloquently.

Jeremy scratched the side of his head, a nervous gesture, and Davis's heart smiled. "Would you like that? Doing things together?"

"Yeah, Jeremy," Davis said, standing up and pressing a kiss to his shoulder. "I would."

"Good, because we got an invite to a brunch with everyone."

"We?"

"Well, Dec texted me that he's organizing a brunch, but I doubt he'll care if you show up."

Davis did a quick scan of the litany of faces he had met last night and remembered Dec. Tall, tattooed, dating Phoebe, the small, chatty woman. Dec had known his costume. "Oh, that'd be great. I have a change of clothes in my bag, so I don't have to wear that stupid costume." He cringed, thinking that he had brought a forest service hoodie and a standard pair of jeans. Nothing sexy or interesting to meet Jeremy's friends in the light of day.

"That stupid costume made for a very enjoyable evening." Jeremy shifted and paused again. "Uh, the brunch is at the bar Dec owns. Is that okay? With, well, you know."

"With my sobriety?" Davis asked, maybe a bit more forcefully than he intended. He ran a hand down Jeremy's arm and was rewarded with a little shiver from the taller man. "Yeah,

Jeremy. I'm good. Thank you for checking." A little spark of hope flared in Davis's chest that there would be a day that Jeremy wouldn't have to ask because he would just *know*.

"Perfect," Jeremy said, smiling. "I'm going to grab a shower."

"Okay, I'll grab my stuff while you're in there."

"I think you misunderstood me," Jeremy said again, his voice dropping and his fingers curling into the T-shirt Davis had tossed on. "*I'm* going to shower. *You're* going to join me."

"Oh. *Yes.*"

Jeremy

Jeremy and Davis were a bit late to Dec's impromptu brunch, first because of the way they had taken turns on their knees in the shower, Jeremy finally getting the chance to show off his own admirable deep throat skills, and then they were made later as Jeremy struggled to decide what type of tea he wanted for the morning. He could have picked his standard morning blend, but he purposefully waffled, knowing that each moment was another second he got to keep Davis to himself. At some point, even Jeremy had to admit he was stalling, and Davis followed him out to his car, hands tucked in his hoodie pocket.

Dec's bar was hard to find, the entrance an unassuming door that you would have to know led to a bar to open it, but Jeremy had been there enough times he could probably find it with his eyes closed. Jeremy opened the door, and Davis followed him, a comfortable presence behind Jeremy's back.

Dec was at the door, looking like he could barely tolerate the group of hungover thirtysomethings surrounding him, but Jeremy knew better. Still, Jeremy wanted to make sure it was okay to bring a new person.

"Uh, you remember Davis," Jeremy said, nodding back to Dec. "He's still in town."

"More the merrier," Dec said, only a tiny glint in his eye giving Jeremy a clue that he knew exactly why Davis was still in town. While there was a part of Jeremy that wanted to climb onto Davis's back and yell to his friends, "I fucked this super-hot, rugged man," a bigger part of him wanted to let Davis take the lead with how to progress. Plus, Jeremy didn't want to get ahead of himself.

Ahead of himself further, he thought, kicking himself as Dec headed back to the bar. The words about inviting Davis to a museum had tumbled out of his mouth this morning before he was even fully awake, but seeing that gorgeous man looking at his art books had unlocked something inside him. He wanted to take Davis everywhere and show him all his favorite pieces of art. Show him the dorm he had lived in during his time at NYU and kiss him, then take him to the Stonewall Inn and talk about how important it was that queer history was being recognized at the federal level.

But he had no clue if Davis wanted the same.

"Here," Dec said, shaking Jeremy out of his thoughts, the two men still lingering by the door. He pulled out two flavored seltzers from his hoodie pocket and passed them to Davis. "I've got lime and cranberry. Choose what you like. I can also make you something if you want. Like a fancy drink without booze."

Davis looked stunned, like a fish taken out of water for a moment too long. "I, uh, these are great. Fine. Perfect. Thank you."

Dec gave him a quick nod and then turned back, being drawn to Phoebe like a moth to a flame. Phoebe, who was looking at a glass of water as if it had wronged her, was seated next to Ryan and Emmy, who were doing a terrible job of attempting to prop each other up in the bar. Joe, the older, original owner of the bar, bustled about, setting out an array of food that had been ordered.

"Breakfast food," Davis said quietly. He looked up at Jeremy, and their eyes met, a moment of quiet heat passing between the two men. "Remember when you ordered me breakfast food at your house?"

"I do," Jeremy said, keeping his voice low.

"I thought about you touching my knee for the entire week following," Davis said, pitching his voice low. It was a confession of sorts, it seemed, a way for Davis to admit that his attraction to Jeremy had been lingering in the air for a long time.

"I wanted to touch more than just your knee, Nathaniel Davis," Jeremy replied, feeling raw and exposed.

Davis began to speak but was interrupted by Foster and Flo bursting through the door.

"I am *starving*!" Foster proclaimed, dramatically collapsing into a booth. "Who let me drink alcohol last night?"

Flo rolled her eyes. "At least your friends got to see you in your happy drunk phase." She rolled her eyes at Jeremy, who knew that Foster's happy-go-lucky attitude could turn into a moody pout as fast as the snow could come down from Greeley when the winds changed.

"I have feelings, Florence," Foster said.

"Well, at least someone in this family does," she replied, setting a cooler of beer down, then turning to the rest of the bar. "The rest of you degenerates, who needs some Henrik Hund?" She picked up an unlabeled can of beer and offered it to Emmy, who turned a pale shade of green.

"I'll take it," Ryan said, reaching past her and opening the can. "What's got you down, Foster?"

"Nothing," Foster said, sliding farther into the booth.

Flo pursed her lips and looked between Ryan and Foster, as if to say something, but settled for helping Dec behind the bar.

"Uh," Davis said a bit awkwardly. "I'm gonna go get a coffee from Dec." And he walked away, leaving Jeremy to take in the room. Dec and Phoebe flirted as they set up the buffet further, Ryan turned his attention back to Emmy, and Foster, sensing that others' attention had turned away from him, slid his eyes to Jeremy.

Shit.

"So," Foster said, sitting up and leaning over the back of the booth. "You left my party last night."

"That's correct," Jeremy said, sipping his tea.

"You left my party with Davis last night."

Damn his friends. "That is...also correct."

"You showed up this morning with Davis."

"Your powers of perception astound me, Foster," Jeremy deadpanned.

"You got laid, didn't you?" A feline smile spread across Foster's face. "Yes! At least one of us is getting some from our crush."

"Shut up," Jeremy hissed. "Don't say it too loud. Emmy and Phoebe will never let him leave until they interrogate him." Jeremy looked up to where Davis was chatting with Joe. Davis mimed swinging a baseball bat, and Joe laughed.

Jeremy had never *not* been proud of his sexuality. He'd never questioned it or felt the terror at coming out that he read about in the news. He had grown up in the center of east coast queer culture and had been lucky to have elder gay mentors from a generation that had lost so many. Jeremy loved being gay, loved gay culture and bars and Pride and everything that came with it. He never felt like he was missing out on the parts of the world that were meant for straight men, whether they were advertisements featuring women eating cheeseburgers or fantasy football.

But Davis wasn't like Jeremy. And Jeremy suddenly became nervous that the parts of his culture he loved and the parts of the world that Davis felt comfortable existing within were somehow fundamentally incompatible.

He wished he could call his dad and ask him about baseball.

He wished he could tell his mom about Davis.

"Jer?" Foster said, a bit softer.

"Yeah?"

"I didn't mean to push," Foster said, picking at a seam on the booth. "I'll be good."

Jeremy shook his head as Davis approached. "It's fine." Jeremy caught an unusual timbre in his friend's voice. "Are you okay?"

Foster waved it away and pushed up from the seat. "I'm fine. I'll be better when I get a mimosa."

Davis sidled up to Jeremy, a cup of black coffee in his hand, while Foster had moved on to bothering Dec for a mimosa.

"Hey," Davis said.

"Hey, yourself."

"Your friend suspects something, yeah?" Davis said, more to his coffee than to Jeremy.

With anyone else, Jeremy would have told a white lie, but he felt the need to be honest with Davis, since they had been deeply honest with each other last night. "Yeah, he does."

Davis smiled a bit. "That's cool. I mean, not exactly subtle, right?"

Jeremy smiled down at Davis, feeling like his heart would burst with how happy he was in this moment. "I mean, I have some ideas about how to be a bit more obvious..."

Davis rolled his eyes. "Later. I need sustenance."

Jeremy followed him to the buffet and began to feel like he might want to follow him anywhere.

Jeremy

He had driven out last night after hanging with Emmy, Phoebe, and Ryan at Next Door after the workday, sipping a ginger beer with bitters that Dec had prepared for him. He had been pointedly vague about where he was going for the long weekend, though Emmy's and Phoebe's shared glances told him that the two women knew exactly what he was up to. Ryan, bless his heart, told Jeremy that he hoped he had a nice time.

Part of Jeremy's mind still believed that he would show up, and Davis would see him and act as if nothing happened. He had selected a chamomile and lavender blend for his tea today to soothe his nerves. Chamomile was what his dad had always prepared for Jeremy before he had tests at school, and Jeremy had continued the habit when he began college, sipping a cup before exhibition openings or studio critique sessions. And now, apparently, before he went to the national forest to see a man that he may or may not be starting a relationship with.

He shouldn't have worried, though, with Davis greeting him with a knowing smile and, once he was inside Davis's cabin, pulling him into a hungry kiss, whispering *I missed you* against his jaw.

They worked better now, after acknowledging (and repeatedly acting on) their mutual attraction, an elephant in the room that had shrunk to something smaller than Mary Anne.

Ideas flowed smoother, the division between their work relationship and personal relationship becoming translucent. An idea shared in the dark, faces turned toward each other on pillows or a tangent about a childhood memory that derailed a work session. No worries, because, though there was a deadline connected to the grant funding, Jeremy felt like there was no possible end in sight, a trail that would continue for miles, like the Appalachian Trail that Davis had a map of in his bedroom, the sections he had completed highlighted in bright yellow.

"So I'll be sending this out to the regional office for a final approval, though it might take a while with the holiday," Davis said, clicking send on an email in his office in the admin building. "And then once we get the okay from them, we can put the signage into production and begin the install." Davis looked over at the paper calendar taped to his wall, a Pittsburgh Pirates giveaway that his cousin had sent in a care package along with a photocopied recipe for pepperoni rolls and a handful of morel mushrooms. "Is it too ambitious to hope for an installation in the summer?"

"I don't think so," Jeremy said, doing a series of mental calculations in his head.

"Oh, I wasn't worried about *us*," Davis said, and Jeremy tried — and failed — not to read a double meaning in that sentence. "It's just that summer is our busiest season."

"Why?"

"The highest number of visitors — lots of people camping because we're cheaper and less busy than Rocky Mountain National Park, and it's also fire season, so there's a chance the forest would deal with closures or we'd get called out to help with the fire management," Davis explained.

"What can't you do?" Jeremy asked, smiling at him. His gaze flicked down to his lips, skimmed over the stubble of his beard. wanted to kiss him, but he knew he had to be respectful of Davis's boundaries on the forest property — no PDA in his office, and only in Davis's cabin when the blinds were down.

"I was thinking that we'd send out most of the signage to a fabricator that my friend has used down in Denver. They can do a quick turnaround, so that's one less thing that you have to worry about," Jeremy said, turning back to business.

"That makes sense," Davis said. "Somewhere on my computer, I have the national forest design guidelines for signage. I skimmed through it, and it seems like we have free rein of font and panel design." Davis' face turned an adorable shade of pink. "I, uh, mean you have free rein of design." He gave a nervous cough "There's a list of approved paint colors, too, for most of the major paint brands." Davis quickly attempted to change the subject and began to tell Jeremy how he worked at the hardware store in his hometown in high school when Jeremy laid a gentle hand on his arm. A gentle redirection, Davis' hazel eyes snapping to his own.

"Davis," Jeremy said. "I was thinking that you could help with the signs."

"How?"

"I'd like you to make them," Jeremy continued, his long fingers tapping a delicate rhythm on Davis's forearm. "Like the one you made for the trail. The one you took me on the day we met."

"You remember that?" Davis whispered.

Jeremy smiled, soft and satisfied. "I was impressed. Here was this rugged beast of a man who was able to craft an exquisite design with his hands." Jeremy slipped his palm down Davis's forearm, leaving warm sparks in the wake, until he was able to interlace their fingers under Davis's desk, hidden away from any eyes that could peek into his office. "And I like your hands."

"You trust me?" Davis said. "With the sign?"

Jeremy shrugged casually. "It's your forest."

"Technically, they're owned collectively by all United States citizens," Davis replied, being intentionally difficult. Jeremy huffed an affectionate laugh. "So it's your forest, too."

"Our forest," Jeremy said, pressing a kiss to his knuckles. "Do you have your wood burning stuff here? In *our* forest?"

Davis

Davis kept all his wood burning equipment in a dusty workshop. It wasn't much, just some nicer pencils, a printer, the solid-point burner that he had brought from West Virginia, and a wire-nib burner that he had splurged on the first time he'd gone into Vanberg and found a store that sold the equipment. He was still processing Jeremy's request about the signage; Davis still didn't feel like he was contributing a lot to the exhibit, mostly vague ideas and the occasional tangent about a keystone species and the importance of old-growth forests.

"So how did you get into this?" Jeremy asked, leaning against the table.

"Community college," Davis replied, plugging in the solid-point burner. "I entered with no major and no idea of what I wanted to do, just the vague sense that I should probably do something with my life after high school that wasn't just working." He pulled out a piece of scrap wood, a nice piece of poplar that would be easy to burn. Davis preferred a harder wood when he worked on signs, but this would be perfect to teach Jeremy. "I lucked out with an adviser who had me try a lot of things, including a bunch of one-credit classes that met for, like, forty-five minutes once a week. I was trash at the child development class, but woodburning was fun. It's just tracing, so you don't really need many art skills."

Jeremy rolled his eyes. "That's hogwash."

Davis laughed and mouthed *hogwash?* back at Jeremy.

"I dunno, I was trying to be folksy, out here in the mountains," he laughed. "But, like, we started my art classes by doing our own replications of artistic styles. Tracing to understand how a figure was put together. That takes skill, too. Plus, it's something you do with your hands, so there's technique there."

"Okay, Picasso, I trust you," Davis laughed back. "Anyway, I will sketch out what I want to burn in the wood, and then you trace it. There are different pieces for shading and different textures and thicknesses, but it's very simple at its core."

Jeremy picked up a pencil and twirled it in his hand, then drew a simple heart on the piece of wood. "So I can just burn this?" he asked.

"Basically," Davis said, then proceeded to let Jeremy know where he should and shouldn't touch on the burner, showed him a scar on the inside of his right ring finger that came from gripping the burner too close to the tip. Davis enjoyed the way Jeremy focused as he put the burner to the wood, then bit down on his tongue as he immediately applied too much pressure, then pulled back to apply too little, creating an inconsistent line. "Lines are tricky," Davis said by way of encouragement.

"I'll stick to charcoals and leave the wood to you," Jeremy said, cocking his head and taking in the uneven heart.

"It's beautiful, but it needs one more thing," Davis said, picking up the burner from its rest. Jeremy made a steady stream of comments — all positive, all full of praise that went straight to Davis's heart — about Davis's grip and the steadiness of his technique. "There," Davis announced, setting down the burner again.

He stood up and showed Jeremy the $D + J$ he had drawn in the heart.

"A true work of art," Jeremy said, pressing a kiss to the back of Davis's neck, and Davis felt his smile against his skin.

Jeremy

Following a dinner of mushroom carbonara, after Davis had shared stories about hunting for morels and sheepshead mushrooms, the two men walked out to the back porch of Davis's small cabin to a pair of rocking chairs. Davis held a can of seltzer with a peach shrub added to it, Jeremy cradling a steaming cup of tea. He had started bringing up small stashes of his favorite seasonal flavors with each work visit, just to make sure they were always around if the work session was extended late into the evening or even into the next morning.

Jeremy and Davis were quite committed to the success of this visitor center redesign as of late, the nights where spring was burning off into summer.

"You know how old couples love a set of rocking chairs on a porch?" Davis asked. Jeremy did not. He knew that old people in certain neighborhoods in the cities loved stoops and public parks, diners and chess tables, but he assumed the concept was the same.

"A place to gossip and learn everyone's business?" Jeremy joked.

"Somethin' like that." Jeremy loved the way that the longer Davis talked and the more he got away from work, the looser his speech got. When he dropped letters off words and let his vowels elongate, Jeremy knew he was relaxed. Davis, in those moments, was more introspective, unraveling his thoughts through speech. Jeremy, a child who'd spent most of his evenings watching documentaries or sketching, liked that Davis was happy to take the burden of the conversation.

"Are you imagining being an old man, baby? In your rocking chair?"

Jeremy had meant it as a joke, poking Davis for being a couple of years older than him, but instead of the quiet chuckle he expected, Davis let out a sigh.

"Jeremy, I don't think you know a lot about where I'm from, and that's on purpose. Anthracite Springs is, well, it's a place you move from. It's a place that ages you. *Everyone* was either in high school or old. You take a job at the mill or the mine or Walmart if you stay, and all of a sudden you're twenty-four with a child and you look *old*." Davis took a sip of his seltzer. "And so when I imagined being old, it was with a wife and children, and I was probably the age I am now." He looked over at Jeremy. "I never allowed myself to think about sitting on a porch with another man, or even someplace that wasn't West Virginia." A smile. "I like it."

"Oh," Jeremy said, because what exactly did you say to something that vulnerable?

Another sip of seltzer while Jeremy blew a cool stream of air over the top of his tea. He was reminded, as he often was in quieter moments, of his parents. The Rinci family had been three only children who often existed in individual spheres in a shared space. Jeremy was often sprawled across the floor in his parents' apartment sketching while his mother painted on the easel that was in the sunroom. It was an open floor plan, so they could always see each other, and occasionally, she would look over her shoulder and give him a soft smile while he got a peek at what imaginative landscape she was creating. And, usually, at the dining room table, was his father, who was working on his ham radio or reading an article, humming softly to the faint strains of the public radio station that was a constant presence in the kitchen. As an adult, he liked working on his own thing, but alongside other people. Different from Emmy, also an only child, who preferred solitude. Different from Phoebe, who needed constant noise and energy. Different from Foster, who was constantly juggling seven things and doing none of them well.

But Davis seemed to operate at a similar pace. In the mornings, he would make coffee for himself and tea for Jeremy, and they would each scroll on their phones, sipping their individual drinks, quietly together.

"Do you have siblings?" Jeremy asked, breaking the silence.

"Two, but we're not close," he responded. "But three if you count my cousin who came to live with us when my uncle died."

"Sorry," Jeremy said automatically.

"Don't be. He was a piece of shit," Davis said tersely. "But my cousin is amazing. He was the first person I told. About me." Davis waved a hand between them.

Jeremy knew that he needed to tread lightly with the next question, knew that there was some sort of hurt that Davis was nursing behind the wall he had built up around himself about his family. Jeremy knew, because he recognized it. The way that, for years, he had quickly pivoted a conversation away from the topic of parents, because there were days where even thinking about the change in verb — his parents *were* alive and now they weren't — felt like pouring salt into the wound.

"How did that go?" Jeremy asked gingerly.

"He was fine with it," Davis replied, beginning to gently jiggle his left leg. Something he did, Jeremy knew, when he was nervous. It was miraculous how many little things he had picked up about Davis, how many bits of minutiae he'd discovered about a man that he had firmly filed under the category of *friend*. "He laughed and punched me in the arm when I told him, actually." Davis chuckled slightly. Jeremy didn't know if he should laugh. "I had to be like, *no dude, I actually like guys* and then, like, back it up with the name and a photo of the first guy I had hooked up with."

"Why wouldn't he just believe you?" Jeremy asked.

Davis shot him a look. "Anthracite Springs isn't San Fran, Jeremy. I was home from living in Morgantown, and I had only gotten the courage to go to a bar in Pittsburgh because someone had told me that's where *Queer as Folk* was set. I didn't — I don't — exactly look like what people in my hometown thought queer men look like."

"What are they supposed to look like?" Jeremy asked again, a bit absentmindedly.

"Have you looked at yourself in a mirror recently?" Davis resounded wryly. "You're all thin and *pretty*, and I'm what people back home refer to as a *brick shit house*."

"I think you're pretty," Jeremy said defensively.

"I know, baby," Davis said, and Jeremy's insides turned upside down at the use of the pet name he loved to use on him. "But yeah, I ended up spilling all my secrets to Bruce over half a bottle of Seagram's Seven, and at the end, he just shrugged and said *hope that Henry guy is cool and isn't a Pitt fan*. Which, for where I'm from? That's as good as it's gonna get."

"What was Henry like? Did you date?"

Davis gave another snort that previously, Jeremy would have read as dismissive, but he knew now was a unique brand of self-deprecation only Davis embodied. "Date, heh. I barely dated girls in high school and during community college, trying to not fail out of school and pay my rent. No, Henry was, well —" A soft, wistful smile grew on Davis's face, and Jeremy immediately regretted ever asking about stupid Henry from stupid Pittsburgh. "Henry was a friend who taught me a lot over a few years." Davis's smile turned into a slight frown when he added, "We stopped hanging out a lot when I stopped drinking. Some people can't handle a mirror to their own behavior, you know?"

Jeremy remained silent.

"Anyway, Bruce kept my secret and didn't even tell Gram or Pap, and he tells them everything. When I told my dad, though — *shit*." The last word was extended, drawn out, and Jeremy was reminded of an iconic scene from *The Wire*. "That didn't go well. Ended up crashing with Barry for the rest of the time I was home." He swallowed, his eyes a bit misty. "After that, when I went home, I stayed with Bruce or Tiff, but Tiff had her kid to worry about. So, yeah. I ended up not going home much after undergrad. I worked for a few state parks and only went home for Pap's funeral. And then the world shut down, and then I moved to Colorado." He made pointed eye contact with Jeremy. "And then I met you. And you feel safe." Jeremy would not cry. "What was it like when you came out?"

"I mean, my parents *knew*," he said, laughing.

"How so?"

"Straight little boys tend not to beg their parents to go to school as Delta Burke from *Designing Women* in first grade. Here, I have a photo saved on my phone somewhere." He dug around in his pocket and, with a few swipes, had a photo of himself, a gangly little boy with hair so light it was nearly white, dressed in a sequined muumuu with bright eyeshadow.

"My aunt and her best friend loved that show," Davis said. "They've been roommates for years..." And just like that, Jeremy saw the lightbulb go on behind Davis's eyes. "Holy fuck, do you think Aunt Susan is gay?"

"That's for Aunt Susan to decide." Jeremy gave a bit of a chuckle. "I'm lucky. And it's hard to say, because, you know, it's not safe to be openly queer everywhere, but...well...I've never experienced that. My high school was super accepting, and then I studied art history at NYU, then earned a master of fine arts." Jeremy gave a laugh and an exaggerated limp wrist. "Vanberg isn't exactly Castro Street, but no one looks at me differently."

"What's Castro Street?" Davis asked, and Jeremy felt stupid. Stupid to assume that every queer man knew the same references or cared about the same shit that he did.

"It's the center of the gayborhood in San Fran," Jeremy explained.

"Have you been?" Jeremy nodded. Davis smiled. "Tell me about it."

"Why?"

Davis gave a faux-exasperated sigh. "Because I've never been further west than Yosemite, so I don't know what San Francisco is like."

Davis

Davis liked to listen to Jeremy speak, the way he added details to his speech with elegant gesticulations of his hands and pointed grimaces and smiles to emphasize his jokes. He wasn't loud funny, like Alex or Barry back home, but he had a quiet humor. More Moe than Larry or Curly. A straight man who brought the house down.

And wasn't that an ironic role for him to play.

Jeremy started talking about his trips to San Francisco, about an art museum that had a hideous new building but an amazing collection. Jeremy's stories expanded like fractals, like how tree branches grew and meandered, yet retained the same trunk and roots.

The museum in San Francisco led to Jeremy talking about a visit to a train station that became a museum in France. That deviated to how Jeremy had been following the reconstruction of Notre Dame and then casually moved to how there was a church that he wanted to see be completed in Spain.

"Have you been to Europe?" Jeremy asked, licking his lips and looking at Davis.

Davis snorted. "Jeremy Rinci, the first time I was on a plane was when I flew out here to interview." He swallowed a laugh as Jeremy tried — and failed — to hide his surprise at that fact. Davis imagined that Jeremy had grown up attending art openings and, well, whatever fancy people did, whereas Davis was lucky if they could drive to the New River for a few days on summer vacation.

"Wow," Jeremy said.

"I know, I know, dumb hillbilly," Davis said, more to defuse any potential fight than anything else.

"No, amazing. You're still experiencing new things as an adult. That's brave." Jeremy looked at him as if he could peer into his soul, sort through his memories. Previously, that type of closeness, especially with a man, had made Davis want to run to the trees and never return. Now, however, he still craved the forest surrounding him, but he also wanted to bring Jeremy around him.

The sun had mostly set, just a faint glow behind the mountains, and Davis could just make out the outline of a bird. A dark-eyed junco, he thought.

It felt like a protective bubble had settled around Jeremy and Davis, the two men held in the protective bosom of some beautiful earth mother, allowing them to exist in a world that was just the two of them.

And Mary Anne, who was snoring, her chin on Jeremy's left shoe.

"I want to take you to Europe," Jeremy said a bit dreamily.

Davis allowed himself to live in this dream world, just for a moment. They were safe here.

"I want to take you to Yellowstone, show you Old Faithful," Davis replied. Eyes met and a smile was shared. Jeremy reached out and picked up Davis's forefinger between his fingers, pinched it just enough to say *I'm here.* Davis interlaced his fingers with Jeremy's, squeezed back.

"I want to take you to the top of the Eiffel Tower."

"I want to climb Half Dome with you."

"I want to take you to the Parthenon."

"I want to show you my hometown."

"I want to go back in time so you can meet my parents."

Davis didn't know what he could say after that, so he said the first thing on his mind. "I want to kiss you."

And he did.

Davis

Davis had never been on a surprise date, something that one of Jeremy's friends would probably say was an issue of the patriarchy. When he had *dated* before, it was within the "confines of the expectations of the gendered binary," as Emmy had said one night after too many gin and tonics when Ryan tried to pay for her dinner. But he liked this, the idea that someone was taking care of him. He had never imagined it could be like this.

Davis had received a mysterious text from Jeremy during the week, which just said *Are you free Saturday?* Davis had responded with a thumbs-up, and Jeremy then texted that he would drive out to the mountains and pick Davis up for a date.

As long as Davis didn't mind spending the night at Jeremy's house.

And while Davis still liked his cabin better than Jeremy's house, he had gotten used to spending evenings there. And, usually once a week, Davis returned the favor as host, enjoying evenings in the rocking chairs on the back porch, looking at the mountains.

A part of Davis — the part that still wondered if he could stop with just one drink, the part that wondered if he had done the wrong thing by moving out to Colorado instead of taking up space in his hometown, his parents be damned —

wondered how long he could continue to exist in these two separate worlds.

Jeremy had picked Davis up with a bouquet of wildflowers ("I made sure the florist only used local Colorado wildflowers," he had said) and a treat for Mary Anne. Alex agreed to watch the dog for the day, and Davis left a set of probably too-detailed instructions for his friend, along with Davis's number, the number for the local vet, and three emergency vets if something went wrong.

"Baby, it's just one night," Jeremy said, scratching behind the dog's ear. "She's stayed with Alex before." Jeremy nodded to the other man.

"I know, Jeremy, but I worry about her," he said, handing the leash over to Alex. He turned and looked at the other ranger. "Will she sleep in your bed?"

"No," Alex replied. "Just I sleep in my bed."

Davis rolled his eyes and watched Mary Anne trot past Alex, give Caveman a loving sniff and begin to explore the house. "I will bet you five bucks that she's on your bed right now."

Alex leaned back, far enough to see down the hallway and into his bedroom, if his cabin had the same layout as Davis's. A small sigh, a laugh, and a tiny shake of the head told Davis that Mary Anne had commandeered Alex's bed.

"You gonna go show her whose house this is?" Davis asked.

"She looks so happy there," Alex said, defeated.

"Pushover," Davis replied, while Jeremy giggled in the corner.

Davis sat in Jeremy's car, still a bit concerned that even his nice boots were too dirty for the car. It was immaculate, not a speck of dirt anywhere. "Your car looks like you just drove it off the lot."

"Thanks," Jeremy said. "I didn't own a car until I moved out to Colorado —"

"What? How?"

"I grew up in a city that actually believes in public transportation," Jeremy replied. "Like, I knew the fundamentals of driving — my dad made me learn on Long Island — but I never had to use it. I went to college in Philadelphia and could either walk or take the train anywhere."

"Whew," Davis said, blowing out air through his teeth in a whistle that reminded him a bit too much of his Pap. "I've been driving since I was ten? I dunno, probably sometime around then."

"Isn't that illegal?"

"Oh, you sweet summer child." Davis laughed. "Of course it's illegal, but who is gonna tell anyone? Plus, every one of my friends had a story about having to go drag some aunt or uncle or parent out of a dive bar before they had their learner's permit. It came with the territory. Plus, you could always make a few extra bucks each summer if you knew how to drive a tractor or a riding mower to cut grass or pick up a farm shift, so it came in handy."

"You had a difficult life, huh?" Jeremy said. And when Davis had heard those words before, from a counselor or people in undergrad or at conferences he had been to, it had usually been accompanied by his least favorite emotion — pity. But Jeremy never made Davis feel like a charity project, never made it seem like Jeremy felt sorry for him. It was just a fact.

"Yeah, it was a bit rough, but..." Davis raised one shoulder a bit uncomfortably in Jeremy's thin car. "There's a lot of good there, too. A lot of good people, even if they're a bit rough around the edges. Like me."

"You're not rough around the edges," Jeremy said. "You're...weathered. Like a beautiful piece of driftwood or something."

"That's almost sweet," Davis said, deflecting the compliment.

"Plus, you have a gooey center. I've seen you with Mary Anne." Jeremy reached across the center console and placed his hand on Davis's thigh, his palm a comforting warmth. "I've seen you with me."

Davis's heart flopped around and probably did a few somersaults, and it was at that moment that Davis realized that he had never felt about anyone the way that he felt about Jeremy.

Jeremy

This was unlike Jeremy. He was not the one in the group who made plans ahead of time (that was Emmy), or could plan elaborate surprises (that was Foster), or could rally a group of people to try something new (that was Phoebe). Jeremy went along for the ride, preferring his own company if no one suggested anything. Something about Davis made him want to go above and beyond, to plan dates and show up at his house with wildflowers.

You love him, a voice in the back of his mind whispered, sounding annoyingly like a combination of all of his friends' voices at once.

"Where are we headed?" Davis asked as Jeremy took the exit ramp off I-70 and merged onto 6th Avenue.

"Remember that morning that you were looking through the art book in my house?" Jeremy said softly.

"You mean the first morning, we, uh —" Davis blushed, and Jeremy wanted to pull to the side of the road and kiss him senseless.

"Yeah, that morning, baby," Jeremy muttered. "This museum is full of his art. And there's a special exhibition on art restoration and," his voice trailed off, "I just really think you'll like it."

"Oh," Davis said.

"Oh, in that you're excited, or oh, in that you're not excited?" Jeremy asked, willing to throw out all the plans and do literally anything Davis wanted to make him happy today.

Maybe not skydiving, but most things.

"Oh meaning I'm excited, but I don't know how to go to an art museum," Davis said, looking out the window, a sure tell that he was embarrassed. Jeremy knew that he had a lucky upbringing just by virtue of living in New York City. Most museums were free and strangely accepting of letting pre-teens wander through them, as long as they didn't cause much trouble. He vaguely remembered a meeting, not long after the history museum and the science museum had merged, where Emmy and Phoebe had taken umbrage with a science outreach coordinator's suggestion that part of their curriculum should be to teach kids how to act in a museum.

Jeremy parked, having scored a parking pass from an old coworker from Vanberg University who now worked in donor relations at the museum, and they exited the car. Davis studied the museum building, a boxy building of patterned concrete that was more complex than it looked on an initial viewing.

"This doesn't look like the museums I saw growing up," Davis said as they walked toward the building. "I mean, it was mostly small, old buildings and covered bridges, but in sixth grade, we took a bus to DC, and once, in high school, we all went to Pittsburgh on a big trip." Davis grinned. "I liked the dinosaurs. Thought it would be cool to play in the dirt all the time."

Jeremy laughed. "Don't tell Ryan that. He'll never let it go."

"I didn't really go on the big field trips in high school, like how the French club went to Montreal or the Spanish club went to Mexico City," Davis explained as they waited in line to purchase their tickets. "I was bad at languages, and I never had the energy to sell enough chocolate bars to go on some of them, so I just didn't go. Plus, the trips were all far, and I preferred to save that money for new baseball gear."

"What was your hometown like?" Jeremy asked, sensing that Davis was in a good state to answer more questions.

"Small. But friendly. But alienating," Davis laughed. "Probably just imagine the exact opposite of anything you experienced growing up, and that's accurate. Like, what was your first job?"

They settled into the queue for tickets. Jeremy had considered purchasing them ahead of time but didn't want to add on the special exhibition if Davis wasn't interested. "I worked at an after-school art program that my mom ran," Jeremy answered. "And then, in college, I worked as a figure model. Then I was a waiter for three minutes before I realized that I didn't like having people boss me around. Mostly, I've been an exhibit designer or an artist."

"My first job was cleaning out the chicken fryer at the gas station," Davis said. "I did shifts at my friend's dad's farm, and for a while, I was a janitor, because it was easy to do hours for that around community college classes." He smiled. "Look at you, slumming it with me. I'm surprised they even let me in the museum."

Jeremy never wanted Davis to feel like that, never wanted Davis to feel like he didn't deserve to take up space anywhere he wanted to be. "Baby," he said, turning Davis by the shoulders so he faced him. Davis's eyes instinctively left Jeremy's face and scanned over his shoulder, a quick look around him before looking pointedly at Jeremy's hands on his shoulders. Jeremy quickly removed his hands and let them hang by his side.

"Yeah?" Davis said after a moment.

"You good?" Jeremy asked, dropping his voice to a whisper.

It took Davis another moment, another scan of the room, then Jeremy saw his shoulders relax, just a millimeter. A flash of something over his face, something Jeremy might call *determination*, then Davis reached out and took Jeremy's hands in his own. "Sorry I'm like this. I don't know how to, well..." He let the sentence linger.

"Baby, I'm lucky as hell to be with you." Jeremy leaned down and placed a light kiss across Davis's lips to remind him that he was valued and desired, but also so Jeremy could see the little blush that bloomed on his cheeks. It was similar to the way he blushed during sex, and Jeremy loved that little reminder of what they shared. "And if anyone tries to prevent you from getting into this museum, I will fight them off with my bare hands."

"Jeremy, you're a doll, but those hands are soft as hell. Unless you're talking about the callus where you hold your pencil," Davis laughed. "I appreciate it. Now, show me some art."

Davis

Davis had liked the art in those books at Jeremy's house and imagined that it would be neat to see them in person, but it wasn't something that he craved doing. He didn't have the heart to tell Jeremy, because he had looked so proud when they pulled into the parking lot and Davis took in the odd building. Davis was brainstorming the ways in which he could pretend to love what he saw when they approached the first gallery, after he had told Jeremy that, of course, he wanted to go to the special exhibition, which was on art conservation science. At least he would like the science.

It was nothing that Davis could ever have expected.

Davis had been speechless before, but that was when he saw astounding locations in nature. The first and only time Davis had seen a sequoia, he had looked up and up and up until his neck hurt, thinking about the amount of time the tree had existed for. He had stayed there, at the base of the tree, for nearly forty-five minutes, thinking about the ways sequoias could only drop their seeds when there was a forest fire. About the ways that enormous tree represented the cycles of life and death. Davis wasn't religious in any formal way, but he was spiritual, and when he saw a sequoia, it connected him to something larger than himself.

The first time he had stood on top of a fourteen-thousand-foot peak, having crossed the tree line where it was just a collection of sparse flora and the occasional marmot skittering by. There, Davis was reminded that even in the harshest environments, there were creatures that seemed imbued with the tenacity to survive and thrive.

When he had driven through Yellowstone and seen Old Faithful and had been guided on a hike through the bubbling mud pots by a married set of rangers who tossed jokes back and forth. Not only was Davis reminded of the power of the earth beneath his feet, but of the way that love and connection could exist between two people and be shared with others.

Davis had assumed that these moments of spiritual revelation were reserved for the natural world.

Until he stood in front of the painting he had first seen in a book and took it all in.

This was the type of painting that his dad would have seen on the news and said was some big city bullshit. "A toddler could do that. It ain't special."

It was *just* color, a logical part of Davis's brain said. In the way a sequoia was *just* a tree. But the color seemed to consume him, flow between his organs and into the spaces between his cells. He felt an ache in his chest, one that alternatively could mean he was tragically sad or ecstatically happy. Either way, it was a *big* emotion, something that couldn't be contained in his physical body. Davis touched his cheek and found that it was wet, soft tears leaking from his eyes.

Moving a bit closer, Davis could see the individual brushstrokes, and he had the subsequent realization that a *man* made this. A real human, with thoughts and feelings like Davis had, stood in front of this giant canvas and made a series of thoughtful, intentional brushstrokes that were able to pull this emotion out of Davis.

This is what people must feel like when they read books and cry, Davis realized. Words had never evoked this emotion in him, but this painting had. In the same way nature did.

Davis worked to have a moment where he wasn't analyzing his thoughts but just experiencing them, remembering the way his counselor told him that he should think of thoughts floating past him like leaves in a river. And then he remembered that he wasn't here alone and turned around to see Jeremy watching him. In a way, Davis and Jeremy found the same things stunning, found the same things reminded them of the beauty of this precious, fragile life.

"Sorry," Davis said, wiping at his eyes.

"Thank you," Jeremy said.

"For what?"

"For allowing me to experience *you* having that experience." He pulled his lips between his teeth to suppress a smile, but his clear blue eyes shone with all the emotion that he wasn't saying. "I got to see something that no one else has ever seen."

"Shut up," Davis said bashfully.

"You know there are, like, hundreds of other paintings in this museum," Jeremy joked.

"I'm leaving," Davis said, walking to the next painting, preparing himself to understand what this field of red would evoke in him. They meandered through the first exhibition, slower than Davis ever would have guessed he would be in a museum. The space seemed endless, with a new gallery appearing every time Davis thought he had seen it all. He didn't grow bored until the end, when the exhibit on conservation was filled with signs with too much writing and big words that stopped making sense in Davis's brain.

He shook his head and turned to Jeremy. "I think I'm museumed out," he said honestly.

"Even I have to take breaks sometime," he joked back, slipping his hand into Davis's and leading him out of the museum, somehow able to remember what seemed to Davis to have been a maze.

"If I would have known it was this easy to woo you, I would have brought you here weeks ago," Jeremy said when Davis insisted on going to the gift shop to purchase a sticker.

"Thank you," Davis said, turning around and lifting up to kiss Jeremy deeply after he paid for the sticker, an outline of the strange building that now meant something to him. "I never would have done this without you."

"Well, you took me mountain biking."

"Am I going to be injured here?"

"Only if you trip, baby."

Jeremy

Jeremy drove them to his house while Davis FaceTimed Alex to check on Mary Anne. Jeremy tried not to laugh as Davis insisted that Alex "put Mary Anne on the phone," and his heart felt like it might burst out of his chest when Davis told Mary Anne about his day at the museum.

"You know," Jeremy said, once Davis had hung up, telling Mary Anne that he would see her tomorrow. "You can bring Mary Anne down to Vanberg if you want."

Davis looked over at him, his face full of surprise. "You sure?"

"Why would I not be sure?" Jeremy said, slightly offended. "I just offered it."

"Well, you know," Davis said, smirking, "your place is…tidy. Mary Anne is a dog."

"I like dogs."

"Yes, but —"

"I like Mary Anne."

"I know, and —"

"Does Mary Anne not like me?" Jeremy suddenly decided that one dog's approval meant the world to him.

"No." Davis chuckled. "She does. Well, she likes everyone —" Jeremy scoffed "— But she especially likes you. It's just, I don't want to ruin your space. I know how important your house is to you, and I would feel terrible if Mary Anne ruined your uncomfortable couch or that weird chair you never sit on."

"I doubt many dogs are drawn to Eames chairs." Jeremy laughed as he parked the car in front of his house.

"Did you name your chair?"

"It's after the designers."

"Sound like a bunch of weirdos," Davis said, hopping out of the car.

"Most artists are," Jeremy replied.

Davis shot him a grin that was pure joy, with an undercurrent of lust. "I like weirdos." He stayed close to Jeremy as he unlocked the door, his rough hands already sliding around his hips. Shoes were kicked off, bags tossed on the floor, and Jeremy turned to Davis, one last futile attempt to be a host before he dragged Davis into his bedroom.

"Do you want a seltzer?" Jeremy asked.

"I think there are other things that I'd like to have," Davis said, unbuttoning his jeans.

"Oh, well, in that case," Jeremy said, smiling like a fool as he took Davis's hand and headed back to his bedroom. They tumbled onto the bed, laughing in a way that felt euphoric, the way he felt the one time he had gone to Vail and gotten altitude sickness. He'd purchased a small canister of pure oxygen, and on one quick inhale, his mind had cleared, and everything had immediately felt better.

With Davis underneath him, his strong thighs pressing out against Jeremy's own legs, loose and supple, Jeremy felt the same way.

"What did you have in mind tonight?" Jeremy asked, slipping his fingers underneath the hem of Davis's shirt, enjoying the sensation of the hair that led both up and down.

"Um," Davis hedged. "I'm good with anything."

Jeremy gave him *a look*. "Baby, anything is a broad concept."

Davis laughed in agreement. "Okay, fine. I was more concerned with getting our clothes off, and then my brain kind of went hazy afterward." He blushed. "I mean, maybe we stick to hands and mouths tonight?"

Jeremy could work with that. He preferred to be fucked anyway, didn't want to be the one to do the fucking, but as long as Davis was involved, Jeremy was sure that it would end in a good time, and they would both be boneless.

Before Jeremy could communicate the rest of that to Davis, he kept talking. "I mean, definitely, yeah, *everything* eventually, but it's been a while since I've fucked anyone, and I want to make sure I don't shoot off in three seconds."

Jeremy pressed a kiss to Davis's belly. "I'm on your schedule. For what it's worth, I'm not into topping, if that's okay. Hands and mouths anywhere, though."

"Hands and mouths," Davis repeated. "So that means shirt off, yeah?"

"That means everything off, baby," Jeremy said, helping Davis with his shirt, and then his pants. Keeping his own clothes on, a bit more of that control seeping into his blood, Jeremy made his way toward Davis's cock, hard and thick, his hands gripping Davis's hips, the fingertips digging in. Jeremy loved the way Davis was softer, muscle underneath, but flesh that gave and curved.

"Jeremy," Davis said, his voice straining. Which made sense, as Jeremy had just placed a tentative, teasing lick to the ridge of his cock.

"Yeah, baby?" Jeremy teased, letting the tip of Davis's cock rest against his lower lip.

"Can you put" — he took a breath — "can you put your hands on me?"

"Where?"

"Can you reach my mouth?"

Jeremy maneuvered himself to the side, hiding his grin in Davis's hip, using it as an excuse to scrape his teeth at the dip where his thigh met his hip, which earned him a pleased moan from Davis. Keeping his right hand cupping Davis's balls, fingers toying with the space just behind, Jeremy slid his left hand up the contours of Davis's chest, through the hair, over the bump of his collarbone, and pressed two fingers against his lips. Davis opened for him eagerly, pulling his fingers into his mouth in a way that had Jeremy grinding his hips against the bed. Davis continued to suck, and Jeremy went back to his previous task, the sideways angle creating a new sensation in his own mouth. Grazing his teeth along the shaft, Jeremy smiled, then took him deeper, humming and willing his throat to open just a bit more.

"Dear god, babe, *fuck*," Davis hissed against Jeremy's fingers. "I'm gonna —"

"In my mouth," Jeremy said, pulling off long enough to get the words out before returning. He was glad he was quick, because it took two more deep sucks, two more jerks of Davis's hips, before he spilled down the back of Jeremy's throat, a salty wave that reminded Jeremy of how much he enjoyed sex, especially when it got a little messy. Testing the limits, he sat up, made eye contact with Davis, his lips open slightly so he could see, then swallowed.

"*Fuck*," Davis said, his head falling back on the pillows. "All right, my turn," he continued, but made no movement. "Okay, just kidding. You may have killed me."

Jeremy laughed, kissing that spot on his thigh one more time, then sat up and quickly took his own clothes off. He pulled off his briefs, found himself leaking already. Running his thumb over the head, Jeremy collected the bit of precum there, then tapped Davis's lip. "Baby, you don't need to do anything," he said, pressing down, feeling a jump in his cock when Davis's tongue swiped at the pad of his thumb. "Can I just look at you? And —" Jeremy looked down at himself and gave a stroke that he hoped emphasized what he was hoping for.

"On me?" Davis asked sweetly, and Jeremy thought he might come right then and there. It wasn't much longer, though, with Davis's lower lip pulled between his teeth and his gold-green eyes bouncing between Jeremy's face, Jeremy's hand on his cock, and Jeremy's left hand, which he used to brace himself over Davis's torso.

"Close," Jeremy warned, and Davis made eye contact, sending him over the edge, painting Davis's chest and stomach. He groaned through the last vestiges of his orgasm, gaze glued to the way Davis looked down at his body, a bit in awe, like he couldn't believe this was happening. Jeremy slipped his pointer finger through his release, smearing it around a patch of chest hair. "That was fucking sexy," he said.

"Yeah," Davis agreed. Jeremy took one more moment to look, to capture this mental image, then turned and found the pack of wipes in his drawer. He pulled one out and used it to clean the majority of the cum. "I can get it," Davis said, his hand wrapping over Jeremy's own.

"You let me get you messy. Let me clean you up." He gave one more wipe, then chucked the wipe into the trash. "Be back. I'm getting a washcloth. Want a seltzer?"

Davis laughed and got up himself. "I can get it. I know where the kitchen is." He aimed himself toward the hallway before Jeremy reached out and grabbed his arm, pulling him back.

"Baby, I have neighbors, and my blinds are open," he said. "Mrs. Anderson might keel over dead if she sees you walking through my kitchen *au natural.*"

"Good point." Davis laughed, sitting back down. "Cities are a bit different." He looked a bit embarrassed when he added, "You know that."

"Yeah, but different is good," Jeremy added, kissing Davis's knuckles once before he headed to the bathroom.

Jeremy

"You know, I've never *dated* anyone like you," Davis muttered.

"Wildly good looking and phenomenal in bed?" Jeremy loved seeing the way Davis's cheeks got pink.

"I sleep with myself every night," he replied, and Jeremy gave him a playful shove. "No, you know what I mean. A man."

"Yeah, baby. I am a man," Jeremy said, pressing a kiss to his cheek as they walked up to the brewery. "You sure you're fine with this? We don't have to go."

"Jer, I promised Foster I would check out his brewery. Plus, they're showing one of my favorite movies of all time." Earlier in the week, Jeremy had called Foster and asked if the brewery was dog friendly, to which Foster had replied, "Duh, it's Colorado." So Davis had driven down with the dog, and Jeremy had greeted Davis with a kiss and Mary Anne with a Mountain Friend dog T-shirt, which Davis had put on her before showing the dog to the guest bedroom, telling Jeremy that he wanted to focus more on his friends than his dog. Jeremy was slightly disappointed. He had wanted to show off Mary Anne, who he had been increasingly thinking of as *their* dog.

"Foster is always showing movies here. He does a Hallmark marathon throughout December," Jeremy explained, walking toward the entrance. "What is it tonight?"

"*The Sandlot.*"

"Huh, never heard of it." Jeremy shrugged, thinking it wouldn't be a big deal, but Davis had stopped in his tracks.

"That is the most offensive thing you've ever said to me, Jeremy Rinci," he said. "This movie is a *classic*."

"Hmm, well, we'll see," Jeremy joked, reaching for Davis's hand. Davis took it, then quickly dropped it as they headed inside. "It's okay, baby. It's just my friends tonight. Soft launch, as the kids say," Jeremy said, lowering his voice to a quiet whisper. Jeremy watched Davis's shoulders straighten, and then he took Jeremy's hand definitively. Something deep in Jeremy's chest purred, and he felt like a cat in a sunbeam with the way Davis was claiming him. As if he was something that Davis — strong, beautiful Nathaniel Davis — could be proud of.

Jeremy led Davis into the brewery and reflected on the space. It was an industrial space that he had walked into a few years ago on a horrible date, one where the other man spent too much time talking about his new climbing gear and his plans to head to Burning Man. Jeremy got up to get a second round of drinks and had met Foster, who was bartending, and struck up a conversation with him and hadn't even noticed his date leave.

"Do you want this beer?" Jeremy said, sipping his pinot and indicating the glass of lager on the bar. "The guy I was with apparently left, and I hate beer."

"I don't like beer either," Foster had said.

"But you work here?" Jeremy asked, feeling a sense of kinship with this man that had heralded friendship without one iota of sexual attraction. Foster gave off straight man pheromones or something, because Jeremy just *knew*.

"My sister is the brewer," he said, nodding toward Flo, who had been wrestling with a complicated series of pipes and hoses, her hair tied up in a colorful scarf. "I manage the business side of things. I'm Foster," he had said, holding out his hand.

Jeremy and Foster had become unlikely friends, the male equivalent of a house cat and a Clydesdale that had become barnyard pals. Jeremy was excited for all of his friends to meet Davis, to meet Davis as his boyfriend, but he was especially excited for Foster to meet Davis as his boyfriend. It mattered what Davis thought of Foster and what Foster thought of Davis. Since his dad had passed, these were the two most important men in his life.

Which was a shocking development, Jeremy reflected, seeing Ryan and Emmy together in a corner, drinking beers with their hands interlaced. How quickly this former stranger turned colleague turned lover had turned into someone who mattered.

"Do they have something for me here?" Davis asked, breaking Jeremy out of his thought cycle.

"Yes," Jeremy said, turning around and pulling his knuckles to his lips. "I asked Foster to make sure there was Diet Coke, seltzer, and NA beer." He pronounced it "en ay," the way he had heard it said in the YouTube videos he had watched about the brewing process to make sure that there actually wasn't alcohol.

"Thanks, Jeremy," Davis said quietly. "People usually don't check."

"People should," he replied simply. "Anyway, you met a lot of these folks at Foster's party, but, uh." He swallowed, wishing he had a glass of wine to help assuage his nerves and lubricate his voice. "If it's okay, I'd like to introduce you as my boyfriend?"

Davis

Boyfriend.
  Boyfriend.
  Boyfriend.
  The word rang through Davis's skull like a dining bell at a camp cookout. It wasn't that he was scared of the word or didn't think that it was the appropriate word for how he felt about Jeremy. It was a word that he knew, in theory, could apply to him with another man, but here it was. He'd had a few girlfriends, and he imagined that what he had with Henry could have been called dating, even if they never used the word. But Davis's life had been centered around working toward his career and taking steps to fashion himself into a man he was proud of. He had never had time for a boyfriend, it seemed.

  And it wasn't just the fact that Davis still couldn't believe that he had pulled a guy like Jeremy who, daily, stunned him with his beauty and grace. It was the fact that he was thoughtful, too. Previous dates or even friends had learned to *tolerate* or *deal* with his sobriety, but it always felt like something that was a burden or an afterthought. Jeremy, however, factored it in and ensured that it was smooth and natural. And what was even more surprising was that Jeremy didn't even think twice about it and seemed to not believe the fact that no one else had done this for Davis.

Jeremy led him into the brewery, which was a comfortable space, less like a bar and more like a coffee shop or a social club. It was smaller than he had anticipated, and it still smelled like a brewery, but it also had a comfortable-looking couch. There was a stack of games and puzzles that looked well played, not like they had been picked up from the Goodwill. The DVD menu of *The Sandlot* showed on the wall of a small side room, with well-designed posters with the names of the beers hung throughout. Davis tried to remember the names of Jeremy's friends, out of costumes and less hungover than they were the morning he had spent the night with Jeremy. He recognized Emmy and Ryan immediately, not only by the way they seemed to be bickering as foreplay, but by the way they were both tall and took up space. Another couple — Phoebe, laughing, and Dec, tattooed — joined the two. Phoebe's laugh echoed through the entire brewery, while Declan's blackwork tattoos on pale skin made a statement of their own. Davis had spent a lot of his life trying to disappear, and here were these people, and Jeremy wanted them to see Davis. See them together.

Davis was beginning to think he wanted that, too.

"Hey!" Jeremy said, dragging Davis along.

"Hello," Ryan said, pulling his hand away from Emmy's neck and waving. "We have spots over here." His eyes flicked down to where Davis held Jeremy's hand like it was a life ring tossed into the ocean. "Jeremy, do you have news?"

"Shut up, Andersson," Jeremy said, rolling his eyes. Davis suppressed a smile. "You all remember Davis?" Nods all around. "Well, this is Davis. Again. This is Davis as my boyfriend."

"Hi." Davis gave a weird wave. "I'm Davis. The boyfriend."

"Cute," Phoebe said as Davis slid into a chair next to her. She was nice. She had been welcoming.

"Baby, what do you want to drink?" Jeremy asked, placing a hand on Davis's shoulder.

"Diet Coke?" Davis said, his cheeks warming.

"Oh!" Phoebe said, looking toward Dec with a smile. "A Diet Coke sounds great for me, too. Can you get me one?"

"On it, Feathers," Dec replied, walking away with Jeremy. Walking away with his lifeline and stable force here in this tiny corner of a brewery.

"You should go, too," Emmy said to Ryan.

"Huh? Why?"

"Because, Doc, you love me and want to get me a beer," she replied. Ryan scoffed jokingly but leaned down and placed a light kiss on Emmy's forehead before joining the other two men.

"So, Davis," Emmy said, turning back to Davis and interlacing her fingers under her chin. "How's it going?"

"Good?" Davis got the impression that every question with Emmy was a challenge, a chance to say the right or the wrong thing. "Fuck, I dunno. I'm nervous. I like Jeremy, so I want his friends to like me." Always a bit *too* honest, the minute that he decided to open up.

Emmy quirked her lips up, but her face didn't soften with the smile. "We like Jeremy, too."

"She can be a lot," Phoebe said, pressing a kiss to her friend's shoulder. "But she means well. Jeremy has been happy recently. I've noticed a change in him. He's calmer?"

"He's super efficient at work, too. Are you the reason he shows up on time now?" Emmy laughed.

"I wish," Davis said. "He's horrible in the mornings." Was he allowed to admit that they slept together? That he knew exactly how Jeremy was in the morning, all rumpled hair and sleepy eyes? At least he didn't tell the women what he usually did to Jeremy after he saw him wake up. "Jeremy could sleep through a foghorn or a tornado siren, I'm sure of it." That was better.

"Phoebe's a disaster in the morning, too," Dec said, coming back with a beer for himself and a Diet Coke placed in front of his partner, pressing a kiss to her temple. "I think the last time I checked her phone, she was setting, on average, five alarms each morning."

"Excuse me," Phoebe said, crossing her arms. "I enjoy my sleep."

"You enjoy high-powered edibles after you stay up too late reading," Dec replied. "But I enjoy you when you're in my blankets." He leaned down and pressed a kiss to her shoulder, mumbling something in her ear that resulted in a squeaked laugh.

"He's an early riser, too," Emmy said, pointing her beer at Ryan.

"My college coach insisted on morning swim practices, even in the depth of winter in Minnesota," he whined. "It's been beaten into me." Ryan faked a swoon, knocking his glasses off in the process. "Take pity on me, Davis."

"You're on your own," Davis replied, pointedly not picking up Ryan's glasses. He peeked at Emmy and was rewarded with a small, feline smile from the taller woman, a hearty laugh from Dec. *They might like me.* "I had to get up early all the time for work growing up, and even now, so I don't even need an alarm."

"Were you like that in college?" Emmy asked, picking up Ryan's glasses and turning toward Davis.

Davis's mind scrambled for an easy answer, even as he opened his mouth, hoping that the words would miraculously appear. In the Forest Service, in state parks, it was a motley crew of rangers. Some had served in the military and had then chosen to serve their country in the silence of nature, in a way that was kinder to their mind. Some had gone to vocational school and found their way to parks and forests because of their ability to tinker, to fix whatever was broken away from the hustle of civilization. Some were scientists who hated being in a lab or at a university. And some, like Davis, took a bit longer to figure things out, did school on their own schedule.

Not like Jeremy, who had jumped into the conversation, telling a story about a time he slept through a poli sci final, whatever that meant. Emmy was talking about her time in undergraduate and how she had to wake up early to open a coffee shop. Phoebe joined in, adding a story about how, during her freshman year, there was a lemon poppyseed muffin that was the only thing that got her out of bed for her chemistry lab.

And Davis, having taken a tiny step toward making himself visible, felt himself slipping back into the sides of the room, like a wallflower in those old romance novels his aunt used to read. Back to the safety of not being noticed.

"Hey," came a softer voice at his elbow. Declan was standing there, holding a pint of beer. He nodded toward the bar. Davis, still having nothing to contribute to the conversation, followed him to where a woman was standing behind the bar, a riot of tight curls spilling out from a scarf wrapped around her head.

"Flo, this is Davis. Davis, this is Flo. She brews the beer here."

"Nice to meet you. I'd ask for one but, uh, I don't drink," Davis said quietly. He felt like the wind had gone out of his sails.

"No sweat," she said. "Seltzer or Diet Coke?"

"I have a drink back —" he began, but Dec cut in, telling her *Diet Coke*. "Thanks," he said, reeling from the roller coaster of emotions, of new faces.

"Sorry. We had to escape. All the academics were chatting again," Dec said, pulling a face.

"College talk?" she asked, clinking a beer against Dec's glass.

"Always," Dec said. "I love Phoebe so much it's stupid, but I can't sit there and listen to all that *school* nonsense when I have nothing to add." Dec could have stolen the words right out of Davis's mouth. "Sorry if I dragged you away. It's just, as a bartender, you get a sense of when people are uncomfortable."

"No, I uh — thank you. I mean, I went to school, like, I have a degree in forestry. But, you know, I went to community college first and worked. It took me years to get my degree." Davis looked over at Jeremy, his honking laugh joining in with his coworkers and friends. *They belong together, and I don't fit there.*

"Hey, better than me," Dec snorted. "I'm a dropout. Flo didn't even start."

"Excuse me," she said, drawing out the syllables. "I participated in an apprenticeship, like an old-timey blacksmith."

"You know," Davis said, getting a tiny bit of courage back. "I have some great stories from community college. Like, back in West Virginia, my study group consisted of a retired coal miner, a former football star, and a bar back. We took turns making dinner for our study sessions until we got to Sam, the coal miner, and found out that he could make the best pierogies. He worked it out so that for every question we got right, we got an extra pierogi." Davis laughed, then added, "We destroyed that biology final, along with our digestive systems."

"I just hated school," Dec said. "It seemed like a waste of time and money."

"Community college was all I could afford," Davis said. "And, well, my grades weren't good enough to get into a four-year school." Something he wouldn't have admitted to Jeremy or the people laughing across the bar. He flicked the tab of the pop can with his thumb. "Sometimes I think I'm too dumb to be around Jeremy, not to mention his friends."

Dec raised his eyebrows. "I know the feeling. I've known that group for what, six years now?" Flo nodded in confirmation, and Dec continued. "They're all brilliant, but sometimes they forget that there are other ways of being smart."

"What do you mean?" Davis, oddly, wanted to defend Jeremy, to tell Dec and Flo that he had never felt that from Jeremy. But it was close to a feeling that he had felt before, the way Jeremy referred to design and art history like he had an encyclopedia in his brain. Davis knew a lot about forestry, loved what he did, but he also spent a lot of time *confirming* that he was right before he spoke. Quiet searches spoken into his phone or googled facts as he was in meetings on his computer.

"I mean, I know more about beer from *making* beer than anyone who has never set foot in a brewery," Flo said. "You can study it all you want in these new college programs, but nothing replicates *doing it*."

"I don't have a business degree," Dec added. "But I've been managing a bar for almost a decade now, and I've owned it for five. What can school tell me that experience hasn't?" He took a sip of his beer and looked back, and Davis knew that he was looking at Phoebe from the way his smile grew fond. "The best combination is when you *understand* each other and know that you've got different paths, but somehow those paths work together."

"Bringing out the ole Irish blessings, Dec?" Flo joked.

"I want that," Davis said. "But how much difference is too far to bridge?"

"I think anything can be bridged with enough work and communication," Dec said. "I mean, it might take time, but it will." Davis thought of the New River Bridge, the steel arch that spanned the gorge, how it made the valley even more beautiful and accessible to people.

Flo gave a sarcastic smile. "It took you six years to stop being an idiot." Dec picked up the beer she had been drinking and pointedly moved it down the bar.

"I know we just met, and excuse me if I'm speaking out of turn," Flo said, turning to Davis. She cleared her throat, and Davis felt an immediate kinship, as if she was someone else who was beginning to stand on her own and be confident. "But I've never known Jeremy to be judgmental, and that's saying something, because his best friend is my idiot brother." She reached for her beer and took a hearty sip and a deep breath. "There are people who accept you for who you are, warts and wrinkles and all, and there are people who will constantly try to make you get plastic surgery." She sighed. "Choose the ones who love your wrinkles."

"Phoebe loves my wrinkles," Dec said, preening. Flo threw a bar rag at him.

"Jeremy has no wrinkles," Davis said, too honest again.

"Everyone has wrinkles, honey," Flo said. "It shows we've lived."

Jeremy

"So then, I'm standing there, realizing that agreeing to swim in a lake in Minnesota in the middle of winter is not the best way to, uh, show off my assets," Ryan was saying, earning a laugh from the entire group.

"Were your toes cold?" Emmy asked slyly, and Jeremy turned to explain the inside joke to Davis, to find that he wasn't there.

He left. An immediate thought, a fear that shot straight through Jeremy's bloodstream. He shouldn't have brought him to a *bar*, he should have told his stupid friends to *shut up*, he —

He was walking back, chuckling softly with Dec while Flo rolled her eyes behind the bar. A flash of jealousy replaced the fear in Jeremy's stomach.

It was stupid, Jeremy knew. Even though Dec was open about his sexuality, he was happily partnered with Phoebe. And even if they played around outside their committed relationship, Jeremy knew that it was all consensual, and he wouldn't just *hit on Davis* right in front of him.

But there was still some odd, untouched, feral part of Jeremy that made him want to run over and suck on Davis's tongue to make a claim.

"Hey, you," Davis said in a quiet voice, coming up next to Jeremy. *Sotto vocce*, his mom would have said, reading the music to Jeremy as a little boy, her hands so large over his little boy palms on the keys.

"Hey, baby," Jeremy replied just as quietly. "You good? We can leave if you want."

"No, no, no," Davis said, smiling. "Dec and Flo want me to stay."

I want you to stay. "Cool" is what Jeremy said instead.

"Jeremy said you have a dog?" Ryan asked Davis. Oddly, Jeremy was relieved that Ryan remembered this detail. Ryan, who had just finished a story that involved more detail about his testicles than Jeremy ever wanted to know.

"Yeah." Davis grinned. "She's the best girl."

"Do you have a picture?" Phoebe asked.

"Only a thousand," Davis replied, and Jeremy loved the way that he was bashful. A safe kind of embarrassment.

"Emmy had to buy extra storage on her phone when we got Mary Anning," Ryan said, poking Emmy in the side.

"She's a very photogenic dog," Emmy replied.

"Davis, show her the one where Mary Anne was in the field with all the flowers." Jeremy had saved that photograph as the background on his computer. He didn't realize that dogs could *smile* like Mary Anne did, her mouth as wide as a whale's, her tan fur a beautiful contrast against the green meadow, dotted with small purple wildflowers.

"Here," Davis said, swiping and showing the picture to the group.

"She's perfect," Phoebe said, reaching across the table and grabbing Davis's forearm. "What's her name?" Davis was pulled to the other side of the table by Phoebe, who demanded more photographs and videos.

"Mary Anne," Jeremy said. "Like *Gilligan's Island*."

"Name twins!" Ryan said. "Mary Anning —" He took Emmy's phone and held it up, showing a photograph of a black and white border collie perched on Emmy's lap. "Mary Anning is named after a paleontologist."

"She's also better behaved than Ryan," Emmy added wryly.

"Is that so much to brag about?" Dec said, grinning.

Foster drifted around the table, tossing out comments about how his leopard gecko was also very cute, and was suddenly next to Jeremy.

"How's dog dad life?" Foster asked.

"She's Davis's dog," Jeremy replied.

Foster huffed out a skeptical laugh. "Sure, sure. You've never bought Ryan and Emmy a shirt for their dog." He leaned closer to Jeremy and dropped his voice. "You like him, don't you?"

Jeremy nodded.

"You more than like him, huh?"

Jeremy nodded again.

"He's good for you," Foster said. "You kind of, I dunno, light up around him."

"I hope I'm good for him," Jeremy whispered back, taking a sip of seltzer and meeting Davis's eyes across the table. "I hope I'm enough."

Davis

Davis was listening to an audiobook and perusing Jeremy's spice cabinet when he felt the footsteps behind him. He turned around, and his jaw nearly fell to the floor. "Jeremy, I know you've made jokes about baseball pants, but did you have to order them in that size?"

"Do you not like them?" Jeremy preened, shifting his weight from one hip to the other. The pants were so tight that Davis could almost see the definition of all four muscles of his quadriceps. He had spent time studying prefixes and whatever the other one was called — the ending of words — in high school, hoping that it would give him an advantage on the SAT. It had not worked, but the word came back to him, unbidden, as he studied the curve of Jeremy's thigh.

Damn, he was a lucky man.

"No, I like them," Davis said, groping around on the counter to find the seltzer he had forgotten about. Jeremy's eyelashes fluttered. As rough as he could be, the man was always desperate for praise. "You're relieving a lot of fantasies I had in high school when I watched my best friend on the baseball team."

"You were into your best friend?"

"No!" Davis felt his cheeks flush. "He was in love with one of our other friends, but those boys from visiting schools? Well..." Davis finished his seltzer and crushed the can, some remnant of his closeted high school self. "I could pretend that there was a guy on the other school's team that was like me." He looked away. "That's stupid."

Jeremy crossed the room and slipped his palm to Davis's cheek. "It's not stupid, baby." A light kiss. "We all dreamed. You just had different ones."

Davis drove them down to Denver, only stopping to pick up Foster and Flo. Foster spent most of the time in the back seat texting someone while Flo maintained a one-woman monologue about the market pressures of the craft beer industry. Jeremy, as was usual, made sarcastic jabs at Foster and empathetic comments to Flo. Davis, also as usual, stayed quiet, focused on adjusting the music so everyone would be able to have a conversation. Parking was easy, courtesy of Emmy, who had pre-purchased parking for everyone, which Jeremy had explained was the way she covered for her own anxiety. The whole group gathered at the gate, and Davis took a moment to take it all in. He had a group of friends. He was queer. He had a group of friends who knew he was queer and didn't care. A flash, just the briefest instant of that old, terrifying thought — *I want a drink* — then it was gone.

Because Jeremy was poking him in the thigh and asking him where the tickets were, and Davis found himself embraced in the hug of a large, blond man.

"Ryan is still learning how to behave in public," Jeremy said, rolling his eyes as Davis extricated himself. "Maybe one day he'll be housebroken." Jeremy shot Ryan a look, like this was a conversation that he had with him a dozen times. "Down, boy."

Ryan rolled his eyes behind thick glasses. "Only she can tell me that." Emmy grinned and pulled a baseball cap down on her head, looking tentatively excited, just as Davis did the first time he had gone to a gay bar, not sure if he would belong or be accepted.

Now that they had admitted that they were something to each other and Jeremy's friends knew him as Jeremy's *boyfriend*, there was a new, unfamiliar need for Davis to show Jeremy things he liked. What was terrifying, though, was Davis's constant worry that what he liked sucked.

His gram had always turned on the radio to listen to Pittsburgh sports teams, and something about the way that Greg Brown called the games was comforting, a family member whose voice was always in the kitchen. Baseball made sense to Davis in the same way that nature did. It was in his bones. Hockey moved too fast, football a touch too violent, but baseball was perfect for a quiet kid who struggled with reading and was prone to spending long periods of time by himself. It helped, too, that Davis was decent at the sport, giving him a way to make friends in a community he was comfortable in. Davis spent most of his time in classes, with his head down, hoping a teacher didn't call on him or counting paragraphs until the one he would be reading aloud, practicing to himself so he didn't mispronounce a word.

So when Dec and Flo had asked about a baseball game, brought the idea up to the entire group, Davis felt a familiar sense of belonging, a chance to show this group of Jeremy's friends that he wasn't stupid, that he was competent. The group found their seats without much struggle, with Jeremy telling Foster that *no, he didn't want ice cream in a tiny helmet at eleven a.m.* and Foster getting the ice cream anyway. Davis settled in and took in the familiar sensation of a baseball game. Nothing would beat the first time he and Gram went to Three Rivers, a trip for just the two of them, the Pirates so bad that they could afford decent tickets, popcorn, and an IC Lite for Gram.

Davis looked up at the wispy clouds drifting over the Colorado sky and hoped that Gram could see him now. Surrounded by friends with a soda, a hot dog, and a platter of nachos with extra jalapenos. He smiled and took a bite of his hot dog, being careful not to splatter ketchup on his Clemente jersey, one of the reminders of home he had packed up in a truck for his cross-country move.

"What are you thinkin' about?" Jeremy asked, curls being ruffled in the slight breeze.

"My gram." Davis smiled. "She loved baseball. She died when I was sixteen, and every time I turn on a game, I think about her."

"I think about my mom every time I'm in an art museum," Jeremy said, his voice dropping to a softer register. "We carry their memories on, eh?" He reached over and slid his palm onto Davis's thigh. Instinctively, and with immediate regret, Davis pulled his leg away and looked behind him.

"Baby," Jeremy whispered, casually moving his left hand to the soda between them. "It's okay here."

"Are you sure?" Davis felt a rush of sweat, like the first time he knew he was going to kiss a man, a classmate in evolutionary biology who had asked Davis to study at his apartment. The blinds were down, their textbooks open, and Davis had looked up from highlighting Thomas Hunt Morgan's name and seen Tim looking back at him and *knew*. Emotions had warred in his body, excitement and fear, and Tim had smiled and leaned over and taken the highlighter from Davis's hand. Similar battles were occurring in his stomach now. His trust in Jeremy wrangled with the familiarity of keeping that space between him and Jeremy in the forest.

"Nathaniel," Jeremy said in a low voice, causing goose bumps to spring up along Davis's neck, bringing him back to the present moment. "I was dragged to the Pride game last year with Dec. Denver is an accepting place."

"Dec is...?" Davis let the question hang in the air as he watched Dec's tattooed fingers brush along the back of Phoebe's neck.

"Yeah. So is Phoebe. So is Lina." Jeremy nodded at the woman with an undercut who was trying to wave down the cotton candy seller.

"Oh," Davis said. He felt stupid, to not realize this about Jeremy's friends. He looked down the row at Lina, who noticed him looking and smiled, her eyebrow piercing winking in the sun of the midday game. Yeah, he probably could have guessed that Lina was queer, even though Davis's gaydar (queerdar?) probably wasn't calculated correctly, having been developed in Anthracite Springs and Morgantown, West Virginia, instead of New York or San Fran. He looked at Dec and Phoebe, the way their bodies were drawn together like a pair of magnets, and felt some type of connection. Phoebe whispered something to Declan, popping a small gummy candy into her mouth, and Dec rolled his eyes but smiled, wrapping his hand around her forearm and squeezing. Dec looked up and made eye contact, and Davis felt embarrassed, felt like he was caught looking at a private moment. But Dec simply smiled and gave him a small head nod, the same one that he had given Davis the night of Foster's party. Retroactively, Davis realized what that head nod had meant.

Davis had thought it was a standard head nod, the kind that straight men gave each other instead of communicating with words. But now Davis realized that Dec's head nod was a form of solidarity, a way of saying *I see you* and *We're part of the same team*. And while Davis would never wear colors that weren't black and gold, he did feel like he was on the same team as Dec, wearing a black shirt with a purple logo — and

Phoebe, in a plain white T-shirt, and Lina, in a tank top that showed off an impressive shoulder tattoo and a silver sports bra. A reminder that he wasn't ever alone.

"But it's up to you, babe." Jeremy crossed his legs, his feet pointing away from Davis.

"No." Davis swallowed, then took Jeremy's hand. "I can try new things." Jeremy shot him a hot smile. "After all, you're at a sports event."

"Watch yourself," Jeremy replied, squeezing his hand.

"Counting on it."

Jeremy

When Dec and Joe, the original owner of the bar near campus, took out notebooks and began to keep score, Jeremy did the next best thing. He stared at butts in baseball pants and wondered how that one extremely tall player got his curls to look so damn good during the game.

It wasn't that Jeremy didn't like athletics. He loved spinning and had even attempted cross country in high school. He had admired athletic forms of all genders in his figure drawing courses. But something about professional sports seemed off-limits for him. His parents were more likely to take him to a talk at the New York Public Library than take him to a Yankees game, and he had never had much interest, other than to hate the Mets like his dad had taught him. He knew, logically, that there was no reason that gay men couldn't like sports, but there was something inside him, some internalized message that said *not for Jeremy Rinci*.

"How'd you get into baseball?" Jeremy asked Davis.

"It was cheap to play," Davis replied. "Football cost too much for equipment, but every tiny town in West Virginia has a T-ball team sponsored by the local Dairy Queen or Tractor Supply."

"What was your team?" Jeremy asked.

Davis chuckled. "I began my hall of fame career as a member of the Junior Mountaineers T-ball team, then I played for

Whiting Savings and Loan before Little League, then I was catcher for my high school team."

"How come I never get to see you in baseball pants and a mask?" Jeremy asked, nodding at the catcher who was heading to the pitcher with the same energy that Emmy had when Ryan was being purposefully difficult.

"Because you've never asked," Davis said. "I do have this fantasy —"

Jeremy didn't get to hear the rest of it, because Emmy, speak of the devil, appeared at the end of the row and sat down.

"Did you know the inventor of the high five was the first openly gay baseball player?" Emmy said by way of greeting, sipping from a canned cocktail and holding a beer for Ryan. "I was in line and bored, so I was reading the Wikipedia entry about baseball traditions." She reached around the men and passed the beer to Ryan, who was asking Dec to explain why K meant a strikeout, much to the tattooed man's chagrin. "History's fucked, though, because I did read that he ended up unhoused. Of course he did, because why would anyone good ever get a happy ending?"

"You've really got a knack for bringing the mood down," Jeremy said, wondering if it was acceptable to strangle one of his closest friends.

"Well, you're partially right," Davis interrupted, surprising Jeremy. "His name was Glenn Burke. He was out to his teammates, though. Not the media." Jeremy looked, a bit wide eyed, at Davis. It wasn't like him to correct people, and it wasn't like most people to correct Emmy when she began to chat about history.

"Really?" she asked, looking at Davis.

"Yeah, I mean, the media outed him after he retired and he struggled with addiction and was diagnosed with AIDS, but he still played baseball as *himself*. I don't like to think of him as an entirely sad story." Davis, seeming to realize that he had begun to raise his voice, took a sip of his soda. "I listened to a podcast on it."

"Can you send me the episode?" Emmy asked.

"Sure."

"Have there been other queer baseball players? I mean, like, if there were, you'd know, right?" Emmy's words, as they usually did, tumbled out of her mouth faster than her good sense. Jeremy thought back to his plan to find a way to cover her mouth with a baseball glove.

"Why are you asking me? Because I date men?" Davis said, his voice a bit tough.

"I mean, yeah, but also because you love baseball."

"Would you ask Ryan about the queer history of...whatever his sport of choice is?"

"He's a swimmer. We share a love of Ian Thorpe, thank you very much," Emmy said primly.

"Do you know the history of every woman who does your sport?" Davis asked. Jeremy, for a moment, felt like he was at a tennis match with Davis and Emmy volleying responses back and forth. "I mean, I figure that there have been gay baseball players as long as there has been baseball," Davis continued, using a nacho to push a jalapeño around in the cheese. Jeremy wanted to jump in front of Davis and tell Emmy that no one owed anyone an explanation of their sexuality, but if there was one thing Emmy hated, it was hypocrisy.

And Jeremy had told Emmy and Phoebe that Davis wasn't out at work.

And Jeremy had let them know that he didn't understand it.

And Emmy had a memory like an elephant.

"I guess that's a good point," Emmy said, her head moving from side to side as she thought over it. "I just feel like by *now*, we would have someone who is out."

"Billy Beane came out after he retired, and there's an out player in the league right now," Dec called, not looking away from the field. "And can we not argue about this? What I care about right now is the fact that this damned player on deck hits a home run every time something bad happens, so stop arguing so we can get him out."

"He's superstitious," Phoebe stage whispered, then stole a bite of Dec's hotdog.

"Maybe that's it," Jeremy said, looking for an opening. "Maybe the baseball players are too superstitious to come out." And even Jeremy knew that it was a sad excuse to end this...not quite an argument, but *tension* between his boyfriend and one of his best friends.

"Nah," Davis said. "I think it's more an issue of people thinking they're owed every bit of a person all the time."

"What do you mean?" Emmy said, and Jeremy couldn't tell if she was genuinely curious or setting Davis up for failure. He hoped it was the former but worried it was the latter.

"Like, why does a baseball player need to come out? Baseball is a job about focus, about milliseconds, and the last thing anyone wants is a distraction." Davis took a frustrated bite of his nacho. "If a player can field his position and maintain a decent batting average, and he's fine keeping himself focused that way, why is it any of our business what he does off the field? He's a baseball player. He gets paid to play baseball."

"But what about little kids?" Emmy asked. "What about other people who need that encouragement?"

"I played baseball just fine for fourteen years with no queer men as role models," Davis said, his face hardening. "I'm a damn good forester, too." And Jeremy got the feeling that Davis wasn't talking about baseball at all.

"What do you think, Phoebes?" Emmy said, calling down the seats.

"I think that baseball is like white noise," she replied, focused more on the snacks in front of her than the men on the field.

"Ryan?"

"Nope," he replied. "I'm learning how to score, not talking about the sociopolitical implications of baseball." He looked at Jeremy, making very pointed eye contact and raised his eyebrows as if to say *get your man in line*.

But Jeremy, out of loyalty to Emmy's friendship, but also maybe made a bit silly by love, wanted to hear more of Davis's perspective. Because Jeremy had never questioned that coming out was a good thing. He'd never thought anything but the more queer people the world knew about, the better it would be for everyone.

Davis was still talking to Emmy, though his voice strained a bit. "I just think, and, like, I don't know, 'cause I'm just me, but I think that people need to worry about themselves first. Like take care of your own backyard before you go tellin' the neighbors what to do."

Emmy opened her mouth to say something, but Davis set his soda down. "Gotta piss," he said abruptly.

Emmy turned to Jeremy with a questioning look on her face.

"What the fuck?" is what Jeremy said.

"What?" She looked genuinely surprised.

"Why were you like that?"

"It's just talking," Emmy replied. "I wanted to figure out what he thought."

"Emmy, I *really like* him, and I would *really appreciate* it if you didn't, like, question his sexuality," Jeremy said through gritted teeth.

"Where did I do that?" she asked, digging in. "We're talking about baseball."

"No you weren't," Ryan called, then leaned around Dec to continue talking.

"Andersson," Dec whispered, wrapping tattooed fingers around Ryan's forearm. "I swear to god, if you block this at-bat, I'm calling in favors with everyone I know in this state and making your life hell."

"Fine, fine," Ryan said, climbing over the back of his seat and making his way toward an empty seat behind Jeremy and Emmy.

"Yes, Doc?" Emmy asked.

"Look, I love you, but you're being weird." Ryan said it simply.

"I'm just being me," Emmy defended.

"And you're weird. I like your weird, but it takes getting used to. Especially to new people." Jeremy suppressed a laugh, remembering the months Emmy had fervently declared that she hated her co-curator before a snowy evening, where Jeremy looked at the two of them and knew it was endgame.

He looked down at Dec and Phoebe, whose edible had clearly kicked in. She was now focused on the plate of nachos she had ordered instead of the way Dec was explaining scoring to her.

Davis came back and next on the other side of Phoebe, a pointed choice to avoid the conversation that had been occurring before. Jeremy got up and headed to the bathroom, hoping that a few moments away from that tension would help it all dissipate from the group the way that he sometimes took a midday spin class when he missed his parents something fierce. Something to distract him, to assuage the ache that threatened to split his chest open with the beat of the music and surroundings. Other times, he would call Yuna, or she would call him, and they would meet at her studio, a sunlit room at the back of a tattoo shop, and the two of them would play loud music and sketch, and they never asked each other questions about why they needed distractions. Since he was at a professional baseball stadium, he settled for the next best thing — heading to the men's bathroom, which had a *trough* instead of urinals. He followed it with an aggressive hand washing and then waited in line for a soda, even though Jeremy really wanted a glass of the red wine that came in a small plastic cup. Taking his slightly flat, overpriced artisan soda back to his seat, Jeremy sat down next to Davis, who looked back over his shoulder and gave Jeremy a small smile. Jeremy watched the way he asked a question about Dec's scorecard, then noticed — oh, Jeremy gripped his soda with all of his fingers as his heart clenched — Davis tentatively correcting something on Dec's scorecard.

He looked down the line, to where Emmy was asking Ryan about college football coach salaries while he tried to listen to Dec explain scoring. To where Joe was asking Lina about her arm sleeve, pulling up his T-shirt sleeve to show a faded, vaguely military-looking tattoo.

The baseball game proceeded as baseball games were wont to do, in Jeremy's limited experience — lots of talking between his friends in the seats, with the occasional interruption of the game on the field, a diving catch made by a player with a feral-looking beard or the crack of a home run, followed by the crowd cheering when a little girl held up the ball in the stands. The game ended with a home team loss, but a win for Jeremy, because as they left their seats and threw away their trash, Davis was smiling, talking to Joe and Dec about why someone named Rose should be in the Hall of Fame.

As they were walking out toward the cars, Jeremy saw Emmy tap on Davis's shoulder and pull him aside. The two of them had a quick conversation and seemed to swap phone numbers, then rejoined the group. Jeremy breathed a small sigh of relief. Maybe things would be okay. Maybe Jeremy could have everything he wanted and more. Foster and Flo piled into the car, grumbling about how Mountain Friend still didn't have the capital to get a satellite tap room at Coors Field, which expanded to a larger conversation about the present decline of craft beer after the boom of the 2000s.

"Did you notice they had Red Herring on tap?" Foster asked his sister.

"That damn beer has been a monkey on my back since Craig got hired by ABInBev," Flo said, blowing a curl out of her face. "I'll get a better red ale back, though."

Jeremy, driving, looked over at Davis, who was doing a poor job at trying not to listen. "Craig was Flo's ex-husband. Opened the brewery with her," he explained, quietly. "They divorced during the pandemic lockdown, and he took one of her best-selling beers and sold the recipe to a big brewery."

"Shit," Davis breathed, then smiled at Jeremy. "Good thing you won't be able to steal my dendrology knowledge."

"Even if I could," Jeremy smiled back, "I wouldn't want to."

Davis

By the time Foster and Flo were dropped off — Foster to his apartment, Flo to the brewery to check on the canning line — it was too late for Davis to drive back to the mountains. Not that he wanted to, enjoying his weekends spent down in the city with Jeremy. In return, Jeremy spent an evening or two up in the mountains, joking that he was taking advantage of the University's new flexible remote work policy.

"Hey, girl," Davis said to Mary Anne, who lifted her head up from her crate as the men entered Jeremy's house. Her crate that Jeremy had purchased and kept in his house, saying it was silly for Davis to drive a crate back and forth all the time. Let out, Mary Anne gave a kiss to Davis's hand and then pawed at Jeremy's thigh until he scratched behind her ears, smiling. Jeremy went to the door and let Mary Anne out in the backyard. Davis joined him and wrapped his arms around Jeremy's slim waist.

"I had fun today," Davis said against Jeremy's back.

"You honestly like my friends?" Jeremy asked, sliding his hands over Davis's own resting on his hips.

"Yes," Davis replied honestly. "I do. They're...unique. But they love you." *Who wouldn't love you?* The word had been banging around in Davis's head, louder and more distracting than the time a red-tailed hawk had flown through a window in his childhood home.

"They like you, too," Jeremy said, turning around.

"Well, good," Davis mumbled against Jeremy's lips. "Because I like you, too."

"Mm-hmm," Jeremy mumbled back, reaching his long arms around and sliding the tips of his fingers into the waistband of Davis's jeans. Davis felt his cock twitch and knew that it was the night that he needed to ask for what he wanted. Plus, he'd had to suffer the entire day watching Jeremy in those baseball pants, so he deserved something for how he was able to control himself.

"Can we have fun tonight?" Davis said, and Jeremy's fingers inched lower.

"Fun like this?" The tip of Jeremy's finger dipped into Davis's ass crack.

"Fun like we fuck," Davis said and, like he had hoped, Jeremy's fingers dug into his ass, and he pressed a hard kiss to Davis's mouth, forced his mouth open and plunged his tongue inside. "Jer, please. Tonight, can I fuck you?"

"God yes," Jeremy replied. He pulled back for a second, and Davis watched his clear blue eyes, knew that he was running through logistics. Jeremy may joke that he had never been a boy scout, but he planned like the best of them. "Showers," Jeremy said definitively.

"Together?" Davis asked hopefully.

"No," Jeremy said, and Davis was sad for a moment before Jeremy added, "You know that we can't shower together without one of us ending up on our knees." Davis huffed out a laugh at the fact. Jeremy continued. "I'm going first, then I'll start to get myself ready." He turned around and gave his own ass a suggestive grab, and Davis groaned, his cock already uncomfortably hard in his pants.

Davis fed Mary Anne to distract himself from the sound of Jeremy showering. The water turned off, and he called *your turn*, and Davis put Mary Anne in her crate. She turned around twice, then dropped into a small ball on the dog bed that Jeremy had purchased last week, telling Davis that he was excited to find one in a color scheme that matched his living room.

"I'll be back in a bit, girl," he said to the dog, feeling a bit stupid and a lot excited. "I promise you'll get to sleep in the bed after we're done." Mary Anne, to her credit, gave a canine sigh that Davis took to mean *go get some*.

Davis showered as quickly as humanly possible, doing everything in his mind not to think of how Jeremy was preparing himself. He used to think about baseball statistics when he needed a distraction from his own libido. RBIs, batting averages, and OBP. But now even baseball reminded him of Jeremy. At this point, what wouldn't?

Turning off the water, he dried off in milliseconds, thought about wrapping the towel around his waist until he realized that the light friction would be too much. He wanted to last, wanted to let Jeremy use him in the best way, to fill him up until he was begging.

Davis rounded the corner into the bedroom, and Jeremy was on the bed, a large towel laid out on the sheets while he toyed with a teal plug in his ass. Suddenly, teal was one of Davis's favorite colors.

"Fuck," Jeremy hissed. "Been waiting for you. I'm starting to open."

As if Davis hadn't been hard already, the remaining drops of blood in his body all ran straight to his cock, leaving him incapable of speech. Thank god for Jeremy, the way he liked to run his mouth during sex and tell Davis what to do, and thank god that Davis had experience with this before. Davis walked over and knelt next to the bed, pressing a gentle kiss on the inside of Jeremy's thigh before reaching to Jeremy's Mary

Poppins box of sexual treasures and grabbing for the bottle of lube and tossing a strip of condoms on the bed. Jeremy looked at the condoms and then back at Davis, a subtle question.

"Can we?" Davis asked. "I've —" his voice disappeared, and he summoned his strength to bring it back. "I've only done this when using condoms." He circled his fingers around Jeremy's ankle, his eyes focusing on the place where silicone met skin, reminding himself he'd replace that toy soon enough.

"Of course, baby," Jeremy said. "But I'm gonna need you to do a little bit more than watch right now."

"I want to touch you," Davis said, growing braver by the second.

"Then touch me," Jeremy said. Davis crept his fingers up the inside of Jeremy's thigh, watching the way tiny shivers ran through his body in response. He placed his fingers over the flared base of the toy, and Jeremy removed his hand, placing it on his chest. Davis gave the toy a gentle push, watching Jeremy's face, rotating it slightly, which rewarded him with a moan. Davis felt his arousal down to his toes as he remembered how this worked, the action at once familiar and new. Jeremy's hand danced across the slight muscle of his chest, idly playing with a nipple as Davis found a comfortable rhythm with the toy, occasionally mouthing at his balls and sliding his lips up and down Jeremy's shaft, avoiding the sensitive head. He pulled the toy out and slid up Jeremy's body, kissing him softly.

"Baby, I'm empty," Jeremy whined. There was no heat in his complaint as he watched Davis give himself a stroke. He reached for the condom, ready to slide it on and slick himself up and slide into Jeremy, but, suddenly brave, he asked for something else. Something that appeared in his mind as he saw Jeremy there, squirming with want, his hole pink and waiting, and the want and desire to prolong this experience for eternity washed over Davis.

Something had shifted between the men, and Davis couldn't pinpoint the moment, art museum or brewery or baseball, but he trusted. He wanted.

"Can I use my tongue?" Davis asked in a hushed tone.

Jeremy

"Only if you want," Jeremy responded, and prayed that Davis wanted.

"I mean..." Davis gave a nervous laugh, and Jeremy watched a blush spread under his chest hair. "I like it done to me, and girls I've been with said I was good with my tongue. It can't be that much different, can it?"

"As I have never had a vulva, I wouldn't know," Jeremy replied without thinking, and then he let out his loud laugh. That damn laugh, the same as his father's, and now Jeremy was worried that he had ruined the mood. But he felt a brush of air on his ass in the staccato rhythm of Davis's chuckle. Davis was laughing, too.

The minute that Davis's tongue made contact with Jeremy's opening, though, Jeremy's laugh was replaced by a moan. Tentative at first, more of a tickle than a touch, and Jeremy could feel Davis lose his hesitation, much to Jeremy's benefit.

"Tell me what to do," Davis said, coming up for air. "I love it when you tell me what to do."

"Make it sloppy," Jeremy said, stepping into his more dominant role, and Davis complied, slicking up his hole with his saliva, the sounds vulgar and wonderful in the small bedroom. "Fuck, that's good. Grab the lube, baby. I need a finger." Davis complied again, circling Jeremy's hole with one finger. Jeremy had done a fair job of getting himself open with the toy and his own hand, but the press of Davis's blunt fingers inside him was better than the slide of silicone.

"More," Jeremy commanded, sweat beading across his forehead. Another finger, and maybe Jeremy was imaging it, but he swore he could feel the calluses of Davis's hand, the reminder of how different they were. When Davis pressed in farther, tucking a third finger inside Jeremy, he leaned down and kissed him, panting in a way that made it seem like Davis was as full as Jeremy was.

"Jeremy," Davis breathed into his mouth. "Jeremy, please, soon."

"Please," Jeremy hissed, somewhere between demanding and begging. He kept a hand on his cock, stroking it to stay in the moment, and watched as Davis slid the condom on and added lube, maybe more than was necessary, but Jeremy didn't care.

Because it was Davis.

And he was *there*, pressing Jeremy's knees up toward his ribs to keep him open, then he was positioning the blunt head of his cock against Jeremy and then —

"Come on, baby," Jeremy said, bearing down and helping to ease Davis's entry, being rewarded with the nearly indescribable sensation of being *full*. Davis looked at Jeremy in amazement, a reverence that reminded Jeremy of when he looked at an old-growth forest or when he had seen the Still paintings in person. Like Jeremy was something to be stunned by in this universe.

Jeremy was sure that his face looked the same, his lips pulled between his teeth as Davis worked himself deeper.

"Fuck me," Jeremy babbled, not sure if he was asking or just in awe. But Davis complied, beginning to pump his hips.

Jeremy had once attended a lecture by a physicist, something that a new coworker from the science center thought would have made a good exhibit. Jeremy didn't understand one third of the words that were said, but he remembered something about how time went strange around a black hole. Davis and Jeremy must have been on the edge of a black hole. It was the only way to explain the way that Jeremy's sense of time slipped away from him as his body grew soft and warm. The way Davis grunted every time he got close to coming and their eyes would meet for quick moments, just before Davis's eyes would roll back in his head as he slid into Jeremy again.

Davis gripped Jeremy's hip with his left and used his right to stroke Jeremy. "I need to see you come," he said.

"Make me, baby," Jeremy said, pressing his hands into the headboard above him and pushing back against Davis. It took a well-timed thrust from Davis that hit Jeremy's prostate at the same time that his hand skimmed over the head of his cock, and Jeremy was coming over his stomach and Davis's hand. He released one hand from the headboard, Davis still thrusting, his rhythm faltering and swiped his fingers through the cum on his stomach.

"My mouth," Davis pleaded, and the minute that his tongue touched Jeremy's messy fingers, he was coming, too. Davis rode out his orgasm, a full-body experience for Jeremy as well, feeling Davis suck around his fingers and pulse within him.

And then it was silent, Davis collapsing on Jeremy's chest, a moment where they were smeared and stuck together, just the noise of their frantic breathing and the pounding of Davis's heartbeat against Jeremy's own.

Jeremy

Installation of the exhibit had been progressing, and Davis had sent him various photos of the new taxidermy display cases, complete with their new signage. Davis had been insistent that they hire someone to narrate the labels for accessibility, a series of audio clips that could be accessed by QR codes on each label. When there was no budget to be found for a professional narrator, Yesenia, a fellow Ranger, had mentioned that she had done theater productions in undergrad and had offered to narrate and refused compensation. "You're doing something special here," she had told Davis, and Jeremy had to clench his fists under the table to stop from leaping across the room and hugging Davis.

Jeremy listened to the label narration as he drove up, surprised at the warm timbre of Davis's coworker's voice, then switched to the audiobook of *Braiding Sweetgrass* that Davis had recommended. Davis was waiting on the front porch with Mary Anne when Jeremy pulled into the gravel parking lot. The dog had bolted off the front porch when his engine quieted, her cold nose immediately bumping against Jeremy's hand when he opened his car door.

"Well, at least someone is happy to see me," Jeremy said, to which Davis rolled his eyes. Jeremy pulled his small leather duffel out of the back seat, to which Mary Anne had given her standard sniff test, then sauntered over to the porch. "Hey, baby," he said to Davis, who was sitting on the three steps that led to his porch. He wanted to wrap his arms around Davis, kiss him on that stoop, but he waited until they were inside, the door locked, the blinds drawn.

Jeremy found out that the more time he spent in the mountains, in the national forest, the more at ease he was. He wouldn't call himself "comfortable" while out here, and he certainly wasn't going to attempt mountain biking in the next decade or so, but he found that he could find small bits of beauty in the lack of urbanization, the quiet moments when it was just a low hum of insects buzzing while Davis and Jeremy watched Mary Anne sprint down the trail while they walked (he refused to admit he was hiking) or when they shared a cup of tea in the rocking chairs on Davis's back porch. He had even, last week, purchased a new pair of hiking shoes which were a beautiful dusty violet color. Jeremy left them at Davis's house, along with a few shirts, boxers, and a pair of joggers that had found their way into a drawer in the top left of Davis's dresser. In return, Davis had left a pair of shorts, three pairs of socks, and a sweatshirt that Jeremy absolutely, definitely did not wear to sleep.

He absolutely was not borrowing another sweatshirt right now, walking (*not* hiking) to an unknown destination on a Saturday morning. Davis had woken Jeremy up when he got up, which was unusual, and then said he was going to leave Mary Anne at home, saying that Mary Anne wouldn't enjoy where they were headed, which was even more unusual. Jeremy slid his feet into his hiking boots, already a bit dirty from their walk with Mary Anne the night before, and hopped into Davis's truck. Davis pulled up a playlist of Motown that accompanied the men as they bounced down a forest service road. Davis shared stories of his aunt and gram singing Motown, and Jeremy talked about the public radio station that had been a constant presence in his home growing up. Sharing memories with Davis didn't bring up the constant pain in his chest that often accompanied talking about his parents. In fact, it sometimes felt like they were still around, two people who were unalike and in love watching over Davis and Jeremy, an odd match themselves.

Davis navigated the truck onto a road that was less clear, and they began to climb up.

"I'm glad we're not biking this," Jeremy quipped.

"It's not even that bad of an incline," Davis quipped back, shaking his head. "I'll get you back on a bike someday."

"Doubtful. I'm very happy to have you just drive me around. Where are we headed, anyway?"

Davis swerved to avoid a large boulder in the middle of the road, then grinned. "I wanted to show you something." Reaching the top of the road, Davis pulled into a turnoff and cut the engine, then hopped out of the truck. He quickly maneuvered around to the passenger side, opening the door for Jeremy.

"Is it a long hike?" Jeremy said, looking at the new metallic water bottle he had purchased last week. "Should I bring water?"

"Nah," Davis said. "It's a five-minute walk at best." Jeremy followed Davis up a small path, which revealed a small structure on the rocky top of the mountain. A study base, constructed of what, to Jeremy, looked like an older way to form concrete, topped by a small wood building with windows. A simple staircase led to a single door, painted a forest green with the USFS logo on the outside, locked with a padlock and heavy metal chain.

"What is this?" Jeremy asked, searching his brain for an architectural style that seemed right.

"It's a fire watchtower, built around 1908. People used to staff these all the time. They'd live here to try and spot fires so rangers knew where to go." Davis climbed the staircase, then fished in his pocket, pulled out a key, and unlocked the padlock. "Come on in and look." Jeremy took the stairs two at a time and followed Davis into a single room. It was crowded with an older metal desk on one side and a few cabinets, all in a mint green color that told Jeremy they had been installed during the 1940s. The windows allowed in the light, tiny specks of dust dancing in the sunbeams. Davis stood by a large circular table, smiling. "The national forest owns the tower, but this one isn't staffed right now. I made sure that I took the only key, told my boss that I wanted to do a survey of the towers now that fire season is starting. To see if we want to use them." He looked out the window, then back at Jeremy. "But really, I just wanted to make sure that no one would interrupt us."

And Jeremy knew what this meant to Davis, realized that he had taken a number of precautions to create this space for the two of them in the forest. Jeremy looked at the windows, not a blind in sight, and appreciated the view that much more.

"This was updated by the CCC during the Depression and doubled as an air raid lookout during World War II," he explained. "It's like the mountain version of a lighthouse," Davis explained. "We still rely on people in some of these towers during fire season to spot the first signs of a fire. Even in this day and age of drones and satellites, putting a real person here is the most effective way." Davis ran his fingertip over the map on the table next to him, complete with complicated-looking equipment on it. "I thought that, you know, after the art museum, you would appreciate this. Because of the human element."

Jeremy opened his mouth to answer, but no words came out. He loved it when Davis talked about his expertise, impressed with the way he could connect science and history in a simple message. But it was the fact that he'd thought about *Jeremy* and how he would understand all of this that left him almost speechless. Honored. *Loved.*

"How does it work?" Jeremy asked, taking in the collection of old photographs, metal equipment, and topographic maps that looked like nothing more than squiggles to Jeremy. Davis had tried to explain what the distances between the lines meant last week, but Jeremy's brain had focused on the way that Davis's fingers had tapped over the map rather than the cartography lesson.

"It works like this," Davis said, turning him around and pressing him against the counter that projected from the windows. "You look out at the trees and make sure we're safe. Let me know if you see smoke, because that means a fire."

Jeremy scoffed. "I know what smoke means," he protested, but he did scan the horizon, imagining how daunting it would be to survey this entire landscape. "And what will you do while I watch?"

Davis answered by dropping to his knees.

Davis

It was a bit of an awkward angle to be sure, but there was something about the risk here that was playing to a fantasy that he didn't even know he had. Usually, Jeremy took the lead during sex, but something about being out here, away from everyone, in a place where Davis felt confident and in control with someone he deeply cared about — well, it made him bold. And it made him creative. Thank god for the years he spent crouching as a catcher.

Davis caressed Jeremy's ass through his shorts, gently nuzzling one ass cheek through the thin fabric. He shifted both hands to the front of Jeremy's waist and palmed him, feeling the initial stirs of an erection. Running his hands up to the waistband, Davis slipped his fingertips inside and pulled them down.

"This okay?" Davis asked.

"Fuck yes," Jeremy hissed.

Still kneeling, Davis took Jeremy's cock in his hand, stroking it lightly. He quickly licked his palm and then replaced his hand, the combination of saliva and precum easing the way. Davis, realizing he was in a fantastic position for one of his new favorite activities, reached his left hand up and pressed down on Jeremy's lower back. The taller man acquiesced with a contented groan, spreading his legs wider, as if he knew what he was doing. Davis spread him wide and pressed his face in, tongue flicking over the puckered entrance.

"What are you—" Jeremy began, but Davis quieted him with a gentle kiss at the base of his spine.

"Shh, baby," Davis said. "You have to keep watch."

"Are you gonna stay back there all day?" Jeremy moaned. "Or are you going to help me keep watch?"

"What do you want?"

"I don't have —" Davis began, but Jeremy cut him off with directions to check the back left pocket of his daypack.

"I told you that you would have made a great scout," Davis said upon finding lube. He left the condoms in the bag, knowing he didn't have enough time to prep Jeremy. Davis stood up and shoved his own shorts down, pressing his own erection to the cleft of Jeremy's ass.

"Mmm, I'm learning from the best," Jeremy replied, looking over his shoulder. Davis lifted up onto his toes and kissed him, feeling brave and bold and powerful. Because he was here, in a building that was central to his job as a Ranger, and he was with Jeremy, and just for this moment, these two parts of his brain — two parts of his heart — were able to be fused into one.

Davis kicked a small stool over and stepped on it, grateful for the way it lifted his hips to a perfect height. He tapped Jeremy's thighs open just a bit, then slid his cock between them, the tight friction causing him to press his teeth into Jeremy's shoulder.

"Watch for fires, baby," Davis said, picking up the pace of his hips. He reached around and wrapped a slick hand around Jeremy. Davis wasn't the most coordinated, had faked sick in school the week they learned square dancing, so it took a bit to properly time the rhythm of his thrusts with the movements of his hands. Jeremy looked down, watching the movement, and Davis removed his hand, scraped his teeth against the side of his neck. "You have to watch."

"I'm watching," Jeremy said, the muscles in his neck straining.

"Attaboy," Davis said, feeling Jeremy's release cascade over his hand. "Now you can watch me." He pulled back, out of the grip of Jeremy's thighs, took a sticky hand to himself, and used Jeremy's cum to help him finish, just avoiding his shorts.

"Davis —" Jeremy began, still breathing heavily.

"Wait a second," Davis said. "I want to remember this." A few seconds, just the space of a breath or two, and Davis grabbed for Jeremy's bag, pulling out the travel package. He grinned at Jeremy, who grinned back. "See? I told you. Boy scout."

Jeremy

"No one is going to come to this," Davis muttered, awkwardly adjusting his tie. Jeremy thought that he would be more comfortable wearing literally anything, including a shirt made of cactus needles.

Scratch that. He'd probably like that. Would say something about how it's a smart way of honoring the local flora and fauna.

And just like how, once, Jeremy googled "Colorado Rockies" in order to learn a bit about Davis's favorite sport, he found himself opening up an app he had downloaded that was supposed to be a guide to local plants in the state.

"Why are you looking up native cacti in southeastern Colorado?" Davis asked, peeking over to look at Jeremy's phone.

"No reason," he replied, embarrassed. Jeremy had dressed a bit more conservatively than he was used to, out here. He knew Davis still wasn't ready to let his coworkers know about their relationship. He didn't anticipate any outward, active homophobia from people who would come to a visitor center opening on a Tuesday evening in the middle of nowhere. But he didn't want to make Davis uncomfortable. So Jeremy had forgone one of his standard exhibit-opening suits — a gorgeous, dark green velvet with a stunning paisley shirt — and settled for the straightest outfit he owned, a black suit paired with a white shirt. He did wear a violet pocket square because, well, he needed to make sure that *someone* knew he was queer at some point. Even if it was just himself.

Davis had asked Jeremy if he would be interested in attending the exhibit opening, and while, of course, Jeremy said yes, he had suppressed the desire to ask if he was attending the opening as the exhibit designer, Davis's boyfriend, or both. Those worries had taken more of a back seat, however, when Jeremy showed up to the visitor center and saw how nervous Davis was.

Davis, who had so much to be proud of in this exhibition. This should be an entire night to celebrate his brilliance.

"Um, hi," Davis said, clearing his throat and stepping up to the small podium. "My name is Davis and, uh, this is the exhibit that we're opening." He winced, and Jeremy had this mad desire to leap up on stage and wrestle the mic away. But he also knew from conversations with his friends that a partner wasn't supposed to fix something for the other one. They were supposed to work on it together and find a mutually agreed upon solution. Or something like that. Jeremy had only been half listening when Emmy and Phoebe had been discussing their approach to conflict and consent in their relationships. He made a mental note to participate in the *relationship* chat next time, even if Davis was only his boyfriend in Vanberg and in his cabin.

Davis's eyes scanned the crowd and found his own. Jeremy gave a slow blink, like a cat, and a small, secret smile that was just for the two of them. He wished he had the ability to telecommunicate and send Davis a tiny whisper in his ear. *I love you. You're amazing. I'm proud of you.*

Davis smiled back and took a deep breath and seemed to regain his confidence from somewhere. "My apologies. I spend more time chatting with the trees and elk than I do with humans some weeks." A polite wave of laughter rolled through the crowd. "Anyway, I'm here to say a few words of thanks before I pass it over to the tribal reps who have generously offered to provide a blessing over the exhibit. First, I'd like to send our appreciation to the National Science Foundation and National Endowment for the Arts..." Jeremy zoned out as Davis worked his way through the list of government offices that had provided funding, but he paid attention enough to realize that Davis had maneuvered a variety of interdepartmental funding at the federal and state level to make this exhibit a possibility. "And I'd like to finally thank Jeremy Rinci, of Rinci Consulting, for the design and interpretation of the exhibit. If we would have stuck with my sketches, well, let's just say no one would want to be at this exhibition except my coworkers, and only if they were getting paid." Another round of polite laughter. "Okay, well, I'm sweating, so I'm done talking, and I'm passing it off to my supervisor and an enrolled member of the ancestral stewards of this land we are on."

Davis practically ran off stage, and Jeremy had to clench his fists to keep himself from wrapping his arms around him. Maybe it wasn't the type of homophobia that he had been warned about by elder gay men, but this was a special type of torture. He was standing next to the man he loved, in front of a project that was the culmination of both of their professional expertise, a series of panels and artifacts and specimens that had brought them together, and he couldn't even reach out to congratulate him. Couldn't kiss him in front of *their* exhibit and claim him as *his*.

Was this how Davis felt daily? How was he able to manage it?

A terrifying thought as Davis gulped from a can of seltzer next to him — what if he didn't love Jeremy the way that Jeremy loved him? Was that why he didn't talk about him?

Jeremy felt like he had to actively work not to bring up Davis in every conversation, even ones that had nothing to do with him.

"Congratulations, gentleman," Eric said after his speech and the blessing were finished, walking over to Jeremy and Davis, shaking Jeremy out of his thoughts. "When Davis first proposed this opening, I couldn't believe that anyone would actually come to it."

"I keep telling you, people want to connect with nature," Davis said quietly, but Jeremy knew that he was proud, saw the smile that spread across his face that was usually only reserved for the way Jeremy was able to tease him in bed. It was that smile that said *I told you so*, and he loved it.

Loved him. Eric and Davis chatted for a bit, mostly about the exhibition, before Eric excused himself to go connect with some visitors. Davis went to follow, to answer a question one had about lichen or moss or something, but Jeremy reached out and grabbed him by the sleeve.

"Wait, Davis," he said, pulling the shorter man into a corner and whispering. "*Nathaniel.*" He may have added his full first name just to watch the way he shivered with delight. "You've been nervous about this entire opening. And you're telling me that you are the one who planned it all?"

Davis blushed a brilliant crimson that would put even Phoebe's redheaded sister-in-law to shame. "I've been trying this thing where I take chances on things that scare me." He gave Jeremy another secret, private smile, and Jeremy swore he could feel that smile pressed against his own lips.

He hoped to god that he was something Davis felt comfortable taking a chance on, and he hoped even more that it didn't scare him.

Davis crossed the room to where Eric was standing with Alex and Yesenia. Alex leaned down, and Jeremy saw his lips form the phrase *so you're dating now?* Davis gave another short nod. A blink-and-you'd-miss-it nod.

Jeremy, overcome and needing a distraction, meandered over to the appetizers and picked at a piece of cheese, then picked up a small plastic glass of seltzer, recalling a similar museum party where he had teased Emmy about developing feelings for her coworker. How the shoe was on the other foot now, because here he was, staring like a lovesick idiot while Davis talked with a visitor, pointed out the different leaf shapes that made up the border to one of the panels.

Taking a sip of the seltzer and enjoying the way the bubbles tickled his nose, Jeremy thought back on his previous relationships. He supposed that he had thought he had been in love before, maybe with his first boyfriend in high school — a foolish, silly, superficial love that felt like it was more important than oxygen — and perhaps with his partner in grad school. He had told both of them that he loved them, and he was sure that he did, in a way.

But no one had warned him that love like the love he felt for Davis could be painful. He imagined that it was something he would have been able to fly back to New York to figure out with his parents over a bottle of red wine at their favorite restaurant in the Village.

If only.

He guessed he was being a bit morose and existential, but what good was it being in love if you couldn't be a little dramatic about it?

Perhaps it was a small miracle his parents had passed so quickly in succession. Because when Jeremy imagined losing Davis, his heart seized up and his limbs went a tiny bit numb. It felt unnatural. Davis, in some strange way, had woven himself into the fibers of his heart. Davis would probably have some beautiful metaphor about nature and co-evolution to share, but Jeremy just thought of a classics professor who had taught about Achilles and Patroclus, and how Patroclus had wished his ashes to be mixed with Achilles' upon his death. Or how Emily Dickinson had written that she "tore open the letter and licked the envelope to get a taste of you."

Even historically, he had always felt a connection to the most dramatic of queers, had dressed up as Oscar Wilde for Halloween for years until he replaced the costume with his now-standard Andy Warhol costume.

Was it also telling, Jeremy wondered, tossing his seltzer in the recycling, that he was most drawn to the stories of queer love that ended in tragedy or was kept a secret?

Achilles was killed in battle.

Emily Dickinson died alone and unknown, with the identity of the love letters' recipient a mystery.

Oscar Wilde was imprisoned for sodomy, betrayed by a lover.

Andy Warhol was shot.

Jeremy sighed, feeling more morose than he should be at an exhibition opening he designed, until he heard a chorus of familiar voices.

Davis

Davis was in the corner, explaining plans for trail expansions to the regional director, who had come down for this exhibit, when he heard the voices.

"Please. He's *with* Jeremy. You know he has to expect lateness at this point."

"We would have been here on time if Foster hadn't made us wait until his phone was fully charged."

"Please, you and Ryan still found time for a quickie make-out in Phoebe's bathroom while you were waiting."

"God *dammit*, Andersson, is there any time you can keep your hands to yourself?"

"Why would I when I have such great hands and Emmy has such a great — hi, Jeremy!"

Davis, who was doing his best to pretend that the emotional equivalent of a herd of hippos hadn't arrived in his forest, snuck a look out of the corner of his eye. Jeremy was surrounded and entirely engulfed by his friends, who were dressed in various overly nice outfits. Jeremy, though, being the tallest, was able to see over the heads of all his friends to make eye contact with Davis. There was a part of Davis that wanted to hide, because all of these people *knew*. They had seen him hold hands with Jeremy, had watched them kiss at dinner in those small moments where Davis felt like he was *just like everyone else*. But that group was now here, in the world that he carefully planned and protected, and Davis was scared.

But another part of Davis, a part that seemed to be growing by each second, was happy. Because *these people knew*. These people saw him. These people knew and had somehow driven out to the mountains to see Davis's exhibit.

"Where's Davis?" Emmy was saying. "I'm so curious to hear his approach to the narrative in the design." Quickly extricating herself from the rest of the group, she spotted him quickly and headed over. "Congrats!" she said to him, then added, "I'd give you a hug, but I'm really not a hugger." She rolled her eyes. "I put up with it for everyone else."

"I'm not a huge hugger either," Davis admitted, feeling like he had found an opening in the fortress that was the tall woman.

"Good, and, um." She chewed her left thumbnail and shifted her weight from one foot to the other. "Sorry."

"For what? You said sorry at the game?" Davis wasn't used to people apologizing, let alone twice. It wasn't done where he was from. You just grunted and moved on with what you were doing in life, preferably minding your own damn business.

"Yeah, but Ryan and Phoebe both laid into me about being an asshole to you the other week, brought up that I needed to explain myself better," she said, walking farther away from the group, as if afraid that the rest of her friends would hear her being emotional. "I mean, they're right. They always are. But I..." She scrunched her face and then let out a deep breath. "I'm protective of my friends. I worked really hard to build a life here, and there has been a lot of change in the past year and, well, I don't want things to just crumble."

"Oh. Thank you."

"Yeah, so, but Jeremy loves you and, as my therapist is constantly reminding me, I have to trust people and let life be something I experience and not control." She picked idly at a bracelet on her right wrist, a thin silver chain which had a series of waves as charms. "I grew up in a house and city that wasn't big on talking about feelings."

"Fuck," Davis laughed. "Did you grow up in West Virginia, too?"

Emmy laughed. "Youngstown, Ohio. So replace your coal mines with steel mills," she said it like his uncle did, *still mills*, "and you've got my neck of the woods."

Davis felt a flicker of a connection with her, suspected that she was someone who also hid her vulnerable, soft belly. "Do you feel like this is enough feelings talk?"

"Fuck, thank you," she said. She looked at him out of the corner of her eyes and gave a soft smile. Davis had to give it to Ryan. She was terrifying, but she was also beautiful. "Could you give me a tour through the exhibit?"

"Can we all come?" Phoebe asked, heading over with Dec in tow. Davis looked to Jeremy, who was smiling at him while Ryan chattered away at him.

"Okay, I get why I'd be out here a lot, because this forest is amazing and there are a million trails to hike, but you're not really a nature person, right?" Ryan asked, peeking out the window of the visitor center.

"It's beautiful. Peaceful." Jeremy looked right at Davis. "I love being here."

It was only as Davis was showing Emmy the way he had made sure to highlight the efforts of early White settlers to preserve some of the forest as a wildlife preserve that Davis remembered something Emmy had mentioned, almost in an off-hand manner.

But Jeremy loves you.

Davis

"Where are you taking me?"

"Hush," Davis said, swerving to avoid a tiny bird that was perched on the side of the road. He laughed, thinking about how, when he was learning how to drive, his older brother would screech every time there was a squirrel or bird near the highway. "It's a surprise." The word *baby* died on his tongue. Jeremy called Davis that all the time, and Davis relished it, like a cat that had found the perfect sunbeam, but it didn't feel right for Davis to use. He wanted a name for Jeremy, wanted something that would communicate that Davis was Jeremy's and Jeremy was his to the entire world.

"I'm not into ropes like Dec or feet like Ryan," Jeremy said, chuckling.

"Your friends overshare," Davis replied.

"Like yours don't?" Jeremy tossed back.

No. Only Alex knew that Davis was queer, and only Alex knew that Jeremy was the person that Davis was partnered with, though he was pretty sure Yesenia suspected something. He hadn't even called his friends and cousins back home, the ones he still talked to, to let him know that he was dating anyone. It wasn't that Davis didn't want to, because there was a part of him that wanted to climb up to the tallest point in Colorado (Mount Elbert) and scream that he was in love with Jeremy Rinci and all of his persnickety quirks. But there was a bigger part of him — most of him, if he was being honest — that didn't even trust himself to admit that to Jeremy.

Because what if he didn't feel the same?

As Davis maneuvered his truck into the parking lot, he considered Jeremy. Considered the fact that one day, this tall, elegant man was going to look at Davis, all dumpy and scraggled, and realize that he was just a whim. A chance to play in the dirt before going back to his ivory tower. But he'd take Jeremy for as long as he could get him.

"Ta-da!" Davis said, turning the truck off.

"What is this?" Jeremy asked, raising one eyebrow in a way that still made Davis jealous. "This looks like it would be a brewery or" — Davis watched him try to get his emotions in check — "is it a climbing gym?"

"Honey," Davis said, the nickname surprising even him. "It's something I know you'll like. Even with your legs, I know you would hate climbing."

Jeremy sniffed. "I like climbing some things." His eyes scanned Davis's legs and crotch.

"Just trust me." He hopped out of the truck, and Jeremy did the same. "Follow me." Davis pulled out his phone to check the instructions that had been emailed to him last week when he had set everything up.

"I trust you, baby," Jeremy said, pulling his knuckles to his mouth. "More than you know." There was something there that Davis should poke at, should pull to expose what was underneath, but not now, now today. Not when Davis had been racking his brain to think of something that he could do to show Jeremy how much he cared for him.

How much he loved him.

Davis pressed a doorbell near a pedestrian entrance next to a garage door and spoke his full name into the speaker.

"Why don't you use your full name?" Jeremy asked.

"Because it was my pap's name," Davis said, turning around. "I didn't feel like I could ever live up to the man he was, so I didn't feel like I could ever use his name." He swallowed, then told him something he had never told anyone else in Colorado. "I went by Nate as a little kid."

"Nate," Jeremy said, seeming to test out the way the name rolled off his tongue.

"Don't you start," Davis warned.

Then Jeremy's breath was hot against his ear. "I prefer you as my Nathaniel anyway, baby." The door opened before Davis could do something foolish, like wrap his entire body around Jeremy's or confess his undying love to his man.

"Welcome to Clever Fox," the woman who opened the door said, two long braids hanging out of a beanie with the distinctive logo on the front.

"Wait," Jeremy said, turning around. "Clever Fox, as in my favorite tea?"

Davis grinned wide in a way he hadn't for the longest time. "Clever Fox, as in a place I had to scour the internet for so I could find out how to tour the factory." He smiled at the woman. "Luckily, a friend from forestry school works in their sourcing department and was able to connect me with Dani here." She winked.

"Jeremy, I'm told that your favorite tea is the chamomile or the mint blend. Is that correct?" she asked, her voice deep and scratchy but full of warmth.

"I drink it every day," he responded, smiling.

"How do you feel about seeing the entire process from leaf to cup?" she asked.

Jeremy nearly bounced on his toes. Davis's heart fluttered, seeing the man he loved so happy about something as small as tea. "I've been curious about the way you blend spearmint and catnip in the proprietary..." Davis couldn't pay attention to what he was saying, only took in the way his curls bounced as he chatted, as Dani welcomed them inside.

"Do you want a photo with the mascot?" she asked, pointing to a large stuffed fox nearly the size of a human, which was curled up on a recliner with a sign above it that said *Even the cleverest need to rest*.

Jeremy let out his signature loud, honking laugh. "Of course!" He sprinted over and curled himself around the fox. "Davis, give her your phone." Davis chuckled as he passed over his phone to her, clad in its shatterproof case that was standard for all forest rangers. She snapped a few pictures of Jeremy lounging, looking more like a dandy than anyone in the twenty-first century had a right to.

"Are you ready for a tour?" Dani asked, passing the phone back to Davis.

"No!" Jeremy said, surpassing them both. Then, he added, "Can you take a few photos of me and my boyfriend?"

There was something about the way that Jeremy said *boyfriend* that made Davis feel like he could fly. Something about that phrase, which to some may seem so juvenile, made Davis feel like he was living a life he hadn't expected. Like he had truly come into his own and was living as authentically as he knew how.

But who are you authentic with? Came the voice from the back of his head, the same voice that sometimes asked him if he was sure he couldn't just have *one* drink with friends.

Davis told that voice to shut up as he went over to the fox, and Jeremy wrapped his arms around him for the photo.

Jeremy

They had walked along the main strip downtown following the tour of the tea factory. Jeremy could have stayed for three more hours asking about tea, but even he could see that Davis's attention was fading, so he suggested heading downtown. It wasn't anything close to a true gayborhood, nothing that Jeremy had remembered from his days in Philadelphia or when he would go out in New York visiting his parents...before. Denver had a few gay bars, but it was nowhere close to the same.

It was nice, though, Jeremy thought, that he could walk down the street in front of all the hipster couples and older wealthy people drinking and hold his boyfriend's hand. He could pull Davis close and press a kiss to his messy hair and enjoy the way he would blush and become a bit shy. But he would never press Davis to do more, would always check in before he pulled him into an alleyway and sucked his tongue and ran his hands up the stocky column of his neck and squeezed until Davis would whimper and beg *Jeremy, please*.

"Oh," Davis said, pulling up in front of an Italian restaurant. "It's been so long since I've had homemade Italian food."

"Davis doesn't exactly strike me as an Italian name."

Davis rolled his eyes. "I'm some kind of mountain mongrel, and you know that." He gave Jeremy that type of look that said he would be a bit of a brat when he got home, which was Jeremy's favorite type of evening. Because they had been together enough to know that there was a *dynamic*, a way that one or the other could push and pull to get the other to capitulate in a really sexy way.

It was inexplicable, but they worked. The exhibit designer and the forest ranger.

Jeremy and Davis.

"My best friend growing up was only second-generation Italian," he said, his eyes growing as big as saucers. "I would head over to his house when I needed something to distract me, and his mother would cook and cook and tell me I was too skinny, which," he laughed, "was clearly never a problem for me, but I still took extra gnocchi."

"I love Italian food, too," Jeremy said, which was a better thing to say instead of *I love you, Davis*, which was a thought that had taken to banging around in Jeremy's head a lot, even more than his thoughts about the utility of midcentury design. Which was saying something. "Do you want to get dinner?"

"Can we?"

When Davis turned his eyes on Jeremy, he felt as if he couldn't say no to a puppy. He would give Davis everything in the world, if only he would ask. They were seated quickly at a table in the corner, one candlestick lit between them, and Jeremy had a flash of a similar dinner in the future. A dinner where he would ask Davis a question that would have a much more serious answer than if they wanted to split an appetizer.

"Drinks for you gentlemen?" the waitress asked, her hair sparkling silver and pink in the candles of the restaurant.

"Just a sparkling water for me," Davis said.

Jeremy wanted a glass of wine, not for any reason to get drunk, but because he missed the taste of a Willamette Valley pinot with a marinara. His eyes bounced around the menu, from the wine portion to the food. He opened his mouth but hesitated.

Davis, who had such attention to detail he could see what looked like a speck moving against a cloud and be able to talk about specific bird migration patterns, caught his hesitation. "Babe," he said, softly. "Jeremy, if you want a glass of wine, get a glass of wine." A squeeze of his hand from Davis's rough palm.

"Uh, yeah," Jeremy said, clearing his throat. "A glass of the pinot noir, please." He knew his cheeks were flushed before he even took a sip of the wine that hadn't even been delivered to the table.

"Jeremy," Davis said, still not having let go of his hand. "You've watched me be around people who were drinking for, well, weeks now." Not that Jeremy knew exactly how many weeks and days they had been together. That would have been silly.

"Yeah, but..." Jeremy swallowed, now almost as red as the wine he had ordered. "Did you notice that I haven't had a drink since we've been dating?"

"I guess I didn't."

Jeremy covered his face, which was liable to cause a forest fire at this point because it was so hot, said through his hands, "I was worried you wouldn't kiss me if I tasted like alcohol."

"I, uh..."

"And I won't get drunk or anything, I just really love the taste of a good glass of pinot and they have my favorite here and —"

"I appreciate what you've been doing," Davis said, seeming to pick his words carefully. "But I want you to enjoy what you like." Jeremy checked one more time, just a nod, and smiled into his menu.

Davis

Another step in their relationship, Davis imagined as he un-locked the door to Jeremy's house. A date that involved time between them and a glass of wine in Jeremy's hand and noth-ing was odd about it. Sitting down at a table in an Italian restaurant that reminded him of the ones in his hometown, with the red and white checkered tablecloths and someone's nonna's recipe used for the sauce with a healthy pinch of sugar.

Davis had kissed people who had been drinking since he'd become sober, but he hadn't given it the time of day. But Jeremy, sweet, wonderful Jeremy, had been giving up a small, simple pleasure of his to make sure that he could kiss Davis.

He had driven them back after Jeremy had thrust the key into his hand.

"My tolerance was always shit," Jeremy said, walking un-steadily into the house and plopping onto his couch. He kicked at his shoes before Davis came over and helped him out of his designer boots that wouldn't actually last as much as a mile on the trail that was meant for elderly guests.

I should buy him a better pair of hiking boots.

"But it's even worse now, which is fine," he giggled, that loud honk of a laugh that warmed Davis's heart.

"Let me get you a water, babe," Davis said, pushing off the couch and heading to the kitchen. He loved Jeremy's kitchen, with its shelves meant for small, prewar humans who were Davis's height, but he still missed his kitchen. Jeremy had, in Davis's opinion, an absolutely nonsensical way of organizing his dishes (bowls on *top* of plates?) and he put the wrong size of fork up front in the silverware drawer. He poured Jeremy a glass of water from the purifier in the fridge, then grabbed a sparkling water for himself. His heart thudded an extra beat when he realized that all the flavors that Jeremy kept were Davis's favorites.

They were making space for each other in these small ways that led up to something huge.

"Here, take this and drink it," Davis said, and Jeremy did. Davis sipped a seltzer and drew idle lines up and down Jeremy's arm, enjoying the way tiny goose bumps sprouted in the wake of his fingertip.

"Can we watch a movie or something?" Jeremy asked, his clear blue eyes turning into pleading circles.

Davis scoffed, as if it was the most difficult task in the world. "What are you in the mood for?"

"The one with the rat that cooks," Jeremy said, sliding himself sideways.

"Nope, uh-uh," Davis said, getting up.

"Do you hate the French?" Jeremy asked.

"No, I have no thoughts on the Fr — no, it's the fact that rats shouldn't be in a kitchen. I saw too many things when I cleaned the chicken fryer and when I worked at a diner in Morgantown. I don't want to entertain the idea that rats are anything but nuisances and carriers of the plague," Davis explained.

Jeremy, to his credit, burst out laughing, that goose-like honk echoing throughout the living room.

"I love your laugh," Davis said when Jeremy had settled down and caught his breath.

"It's my dad's laugh," Jeremy said. "I hated it all the time growing up, tried to hide it, but when he was gone, I missed hearing it. So I laugh like that." He smiled. "My dad would have liked you, I think. He was good with his hands, liked to tinker with things."

"I bet my gram would have liked you. She didn't finish high school, but she read all the time. Probably knew about all those artists on your bookshelf. May have been the smartest person I ever met, even though she had an accent thicker than my own."

"I like your accent," Jeremy replied. "It's like a little history book of where Nathaniel Davis is from."

"You're gonna make a man full of himself," Davis said as Jeremy nestled his head against Davis's neck. Three deep breaths, and Jeremy was almost falling asleep.

"Ah-ah. No, no, no," Davis said, poking Jeremy in the side to wake him up. "You're not going to make me fall asleep on this couch."

"You've grown to appreciate my couch," Jeremy mumbled.

"I tolerate it. But I'm not sleeping here." With that, he poked Jeremy again, to get him to move, but also so he could hear that laugh again.

"I love you," Jeremy said, seeming like the words tumbled out of his mouth as his laughter subsided.
Davis froze.

Jeremy loved him.

You should say something, you fucking idiot.

Jeremy tucked his face into Davis's shoulder, his lanky body wrapping around Davis's own. "You don't have to say it back. I know it's soon. I just...I just had to say it to you."

"I'm sorry" is how Davis responded, which was the worst fucking way that he could imagine responding to his dream man confessing his love to him. "I'm not sorry for, uh, what you said. But, well, I'm sorry that I can't — *fuck* — words are so hard for me, Jeremy, but —"

And Davis decided that he could use his mouth in a different way to show Jeremy all the mixed-up and confused feelings that were swirling around in his chest. So he dropped his mouth to Jeremy's temple and whispered, "I'm glad you're in my life."

Davis

When Davis had been drinking, there was a time, usually around two a.m., where Davis would wake up and have an uncomfortable reckoning. What had he said? Who had he fought? Had he kissed anyone he shouldn't have?

Now that he wasn't drinking, he still woke up occasionally, and he still used that time to think over his day, even more so now that he was with Jeremy. A bit of clarity in the witching hour, when Davis could spend a moment with his own thoughts, think about his life in a clearer way. As he wiped the sleep out of his eyes and looked over at Jeremy, curls tossed elegantly over his forehead and snoring softly, *he knew*. He knew that he loved Jeremy, too, and he wished like hell that he had the ability to tell him.

How did you tell someone that not only did you love them, but that they had become more than your wildest dreams?

How did you tell someone that the thought of them leaving you made your chest feel like it was splitting open?

How did you tell someone that you didn't deserve them but that you were grateful for their presence in your life, even if you knew they should move on?

Davis didn't have those words. So he pressed a kiss to Jeremy's shoulder and slipped out of bed to fold his towels. That, he could do, even at two a.m. Before he could make his way to the dryer, a vibration distracted him.

"Your phone is ringing," Davis said, pushing on Jeremy's arm.

"S'on silent," Jeremy grumbled into the pillow.

As Davis listened again, he was aware that it wasn't the typical vibration pattern for Jeremy's phone. Which meant that it was Davis's phone that was vibrating. Which was odd. No one ever *called* Davis. His friends from back home communicated through various group threads on social media, while his coworkers at the national forest were as averse to phone calls as Davis was, so it was a text-only coordination for mountain biking or dog watching.

The only person who had called Davis in the past year was Jeremy, and he had already fallen back asleep, if the soft snores were any indication.

Davis pressed another kiss to Jeremy's shoulder and made his way over to the dresser, which he had been surprised to learn was all a wireless charging stand, and picked up his phone.

"Hello?"

"Davis? It's Eric. There's a fire out by Pine Valley that's started spreading tonight with the winds."

"Shit," Davis said, snapping into wakefulness.

"Haines index kicked up to six last night," Eric explained, referring to the system that forest agencies used to quantify the dryness of the air. "We think it was a backcountry fire that got out of control and joined the smaller one in progress." Eric sighed, and Davis could hear the stress in his voice. Like all rangers, Davis had training in fire management, and even though he was primarily an interpretive ranger, he had a second job for when it was an all-hands-on-deck moment. And as Eric continued to describe the conditions and which fire divisions had been activated, Davis realized that this was an all-hands-on-deck moment. Davis scrambled for a scrap of paper and began to write down the basic information Eric was telling him — when he needed to report, the equipment he needed, the forms that needed to be filed for the emergency response database.

"Got it, got it," Davis said. "I, er, I'm down in Vanberg for the night, but I'll head out soon."

Eric grunted his acknowledgment, then hung up, saying that he needed to call Yesenia, too. Alex would stay in Klarluft, holding down the fort. He needed to check and see if Alex could watch Mary Anne, didn't think it would be safe to take her out to where the command center would be.

As he found his pants and shoved his legs into them, Davis mentally scanned his cabin back in the forest. He had a go-bag packed and knew that he'd be part of the incident control team, not actually fighting the fire. He hoped to god they wouldn't put him in front of a camera to update the new stations. He was better, he assumed, at the logistic aspects. Which crews would go where, what equipment needed to be deployed, all the ways he could —

"Where are you going?" Jeremy said.

So much for being a logistic expert, if Davis had forgotten that his boyfriend was asleep in the same room with him.

"There's a fire," Davis said, buckling his belt.

"Where?" Jeremy sat up, and Davis surpassed the need to run over and smooth his curls back into place.

"Out past Klarluft. Pine Valley area." Davis peeked at his phone and tried to scan the email that had been sent out. "They're evacuating the closest town now, and the support trailers are setting up at the fairgrounds."

"Wait," Jeremy said, his feet hitting the floor. "People are evacuating, but you're going there. Isn't that dangerous?"

Davis resisted the urge to roll his eyes. "Jeremy, that's what we do as rangers. We keep people safe. It's part of the job."

"Who keeps you safe?" Jeremy asked quietly.

Davis shrugged. "You don't have to worry. I'm not one of the hotshots or on the wildfire team. I'll be helping to coordinate the response. I'll be fine."

"I won't be," Jeremy said. Davis didn't know what to say to that, so he walked out into Jeremy's living room and began to boot up his computer.

"Jeremy, this is routine for us," he said, even though this was Davis's first wildfire in the Mountain West and, from the looks of it, the fire was shaping up to be a significant one. And a dangerous one, if the wind projections were accurate.

"What are you doing now?" Jeremy said, having tossed on a T-shirt, watching Davis struggle to enter his password. He was flustered, partially from being up at two a.m., but also because Jeremy didn't seem to understand that Davis had no choice.

"I'm looking at where I need to go," Davis said, his eyes bouncing over the map Eric had sent over. The assembly point was clearly marked, and they had gotten reservations at the motel in the nearest city. Dogs weren't allowed, and Davis didn't have time to drive Mary Anne down to the city. Grabbing his phone, he sent off a quick text to Alex.

"You have to leave now?" Jeremy asked, beginning to pace.

"I need to upload these forms, then I'll be out," Davis said. "I'm only usually out there for two weeks, max." Couldn't Jeremy see that this was part of his job?

Clicking into the emergency response portal, Davis double-checked his contact information, which hadn't changed since he moved to Colorado.

Under emergency contact, Davis had written 911, followed by a number of a friend who still lived in West Virginia. It was easier that way, he had figured. He'd get help immediately, then Tiff would eventually be notified, and she could disseminate the information to anyone who cared.

His mouse hovered over the box, and he felt Jeremy come up behind him.

"Who's Tiff?" Jeremy asked.

"A friend from high school."

"Why is she your emergency contact?"

"She's always got her phone on her. She's got a kid, so I figured it would be easier."

"What about me?"

Davis didn't turn around, just clicked *accept* and closed his computer.

"Davis, why am I not your emergency contact?" Jeremy asked again.

"I didn't get a chance to update it," Davis lied.

"I just watched you. Why didn't you put me?"

"I can text you when I'm out in the forest —"

"Davis." Jeremy's voice had gone cold. "Why won't you put me?"

"It's not the Forest Service's business to know about us," Davis muttered, sliding away from the table and beginning to put his computer into his backpack.

"It's very much *my* business to know if you're in danger or hurt."

"I'm not going to —"

"You don't know!" Jeremy ran a frustrated hand over his face. "You know you're my contact, right? It used to be Foster, but I changed it to you. Because you're the most important person in my life, Davis."

Jeremy

Jeremy was reminded of the time he had fallen while mountain biking, that sense that gravity had taken over and he was unable to stop it, just prepare for the fact that he would be injured and hope it wouldn't be fatal.

"Jeremy, I can't have this conversation right now," Davis said, gritting his teeth and grabbing his bag, shoving a sweatshirt into the zippered opening. "I need to focus."

"Am I just a distraction to you?" Out of control. That's how he felt. The same sensation that had taken over when he had heard his dad had passed, the knowledge that something had slipped through his fingers before he had a chance to appreciate it.

"No, I'm tired and I need to get back to the mountains." He continued packing.

"You don't even have your family down as an emergency contact." Jeremy kept at it. Something had to make sense. He could find an explanation for this.

"What can they do? They're in West Virginia. Gram is dead, and my aunt is in an old folk's home." Davis seemed frustrated, getting angry with Jeremy when it was Jeremy who was getting his heart ripped out.

"Have you told your parents about me?" Jeremy asked, his nose dripping as his eyes watered.

"No, Jeremy. I don't tell them shit about my life because they've made it very clear that it doesn't *matter* to them. So fuck 'em. They don't get to know what makes me happy."

"If I make you happy, why won't you tell them?"

"Because they're dead to me!"

And that, of all things in this conversation, struck a nerve. Jeremy took Davis's duffel from his hands and began to pack his things, even opening the drawer reserved from him and shoving boxers and T-shirts in. "My parents *are* dead, Davis. And almost every day, I think about what it would be like to tell them that I love you. And I can't, and you won't even tell a fucking piece of paper what I mean to you." He was shaking now, his fingers trembling as he packed up more of Davis's things. "I hope to god that you're safe out there, but I can't sit at home like a wife waiting for a sailor. I deserve *more*."

"Jeremy, can we please just have this conversation later?" Davis begged, and for the first time, Jeremy looked at Davis. Through his own tears, he saw that Davis's eyes were red and watery. Torn between wanting to hold Davis and push him out the front door, Jeremy settled for neither.

"Davis, I don't think you want to have this conversation ever," Jeremy said, dropping his bag at his feet. "And I can't wait forever."

"Jeremy —"

"*Nathaniel Davis*," Jeremy said, his voice cracking as tears flowed. "Please be safe."

"I'm sorry. I can't do this right now." He picked up his duffel, slung his backpack over a shoulder, and headed to the front door. "You deserve someone better," Davis whispered, opening the door.

You deserve someone who can fit around your life.
I want to be that someone, but I don't know how.
Help me, Davis.

"Be safe, baby," Jeremy whispered through his tears.

He stood there, in a T-shirt and shorts, for just a moment, hoping that Davis would burst back through the door.

It was just silence.

Jeremy crumpled onto the couch and cried until he fell asleep again.

Jeremy

"You need to get moving," Foster said later that evening, when Jeremy asked him to come over and told him that he had broken up with Davis. He was beginning to regret it. "It's how I get my mind off breakups. Get your blood pumping and your mind on something that isn't how much it sucks to be single." Foster's history of two- or three-week relationships didn't seem to have any comparison to watching the man Jeremy thought he would grow old with walk out his front door.

"Is that why you set the record for classes attended last year?" Jeremy shot back, testy. "Because you've been bouncing between women like they're a new fashion to try on?"

Foster's eyebrows shot up, and he huffed a dry laugh. "I'm going to allow that one because it used to be kind of true and I know you're hurting right now." He looked at his phone and then flipped it over, screen down. "I'll also excuse you for not having our normal Sunday morning catch-ups over the past few weeks."

"Sorry, I've been a shitty friend," Jeremy said.

"No you haven't," Foster said, smiling. "You just fell in love, and it sucks."

"You would know."

"You know, Jer Bear, I thought I did know. But it turns out, when you're actually in love, it blows all that other shit out of the water."

This was surprisingly insightful for Foster, and Jeremy began to slot a few puzzle pieces of what he'd seen of his friend's life together. "Foster, are you in love right now?"

Foster took a deep breath and let it out slowly. "I think I might be. And that's why I know how shitty you feel."

"Are you also broken up with?" Jeremy's mind was spinning. He felt like he had skipped three seasons of a television show and was trying to figure out what characters were doing when he had only seen the premier episode. Talking about his friend's problems would help get his mind off his own. This was a needed distraction. A lifeline.

"No," Foster said delicately. "Technically, I was never dating her, so it can't be considered a breakup. But I'm pretty sure that she doesn't feel like I do."

"Want to talk about it?" Jeremy asked.

"Do you mind?" Foster asked, uncommonly serious.

"Never, my darling. Never."

The next morning, Jeremy was dismayed to find that Foster, doing what Foster did, had rallied Declan and Ryan to join them for spin class.

"I've been there," Ryan said, clapping a hand on Jeremy's shoulder. Jeremy was reminded of how he and Foster had found Ryan halfway through a bottle of bourbon, moping on his couch, after he had pissed Emmy off enough for them to break up.

"He doesn't want advice," Dec said. "Dammit, Andersson. Just let him process."

"What's got your goat?" Ryan said, moving his attention to Foster, who was playing with a gym towel. Jeremy, now privy to an absolutely stunning revelation from Foster, watched their interactions closely.

"I slept like shit," Foster said, deflecting. Ryan shrugged, and the four men went inside the studio.

Foster was right, Jeremy figured. He needed to get back to his usual routine. No more trips to the mountains. More trips to Denver. Spin class four days a week, and maybe he would actually flirt with one of the new instructors —

Who was he kidding? Jeremy was nowhere near ready to get back "out there." He wasn't even sure if he ever wanted to get back out there again. But he could get back on his usual spin bike.

It was a standard class, with a decent playlist and an instructor who didn't try to make the spin class about their life coaching business. But something felt *off* the entire time for Jeremy. He figured he would need a nap later (he'd slept like shit), and he was probably dehydrated from crying. But all of a sudden, the room became too loud, and his heart — his heart wouldn't stop racing.

Shit.

It was just like what happened to his dad after his mom had died, and now Jeremy was going to — well, he didn't know, but he knew he needed to leave the studio. Unclipping from the pedals, trying to catch his breath, Jeremy headed out of the studio, growing dizzier with every second.

If he could just get to the locker room, he'd be fine, but the reception area was too bright, and he was just so *damn* dizzy, and his chest hurt. His heart wouldn't slow down. His sight tunneled, black spots at the edges of his vision growing larger and blending together. Leaning against the wall, he slid down to a seat, head between his legs, hoping that this would eventually be over. Either he would die or he would pass out, but something would end the way he felt.

"Jeremy?" Ryan's big body was silhouetted in the door to the studio. "Jeremy," Ryan said, kneeling down next to him and speaking in a soft yet firm voice. "You're okay."

"I'm not okay," Jeremy whispered, shaking. "I'm dying?"

"You're having a panic attack," Ryan said slowly.

Is that what this was? How could his brain make it feel like he was having a heart attack? It couldn't be a panic attack. It was the fact that he had lost the man he was in love with. He was dying from a broken heart, the same way his father had. This is why he knew that love wasn't for him. It would be the thing that killed him —

"Jeremy." Ryan's voice again, followed by a solid palm between his shoulder blades. "Take a deep breath in." Jeremy could do that. "Now let it out slowly. Imagine that you're blowing out a thousand birthday candles." He could follow that instruction, too. "Good, great. Now do it again." Jeremy breathed, felt his pulse drop a tiny bit. "Okay, now I'm going to count inhales and exhales to make sure that they stay nice and long, is that okay?" Jeremy nodded, and his vision began to get a bit clearer, enough that he could see Dec and Foster had joined them, forming a wall to shield Jeremy from anyone who would see. Ryan counted in that same soft and firm voice, only stopping to see if Dec could get a water bottle. "All right, there. Take a sip of water when you're ready. Hey, Foster?"

"Yeah?"

"Can you grab Jeremy's stuff so he doesn't have to worry about it?"

Foster held up the bag Jeremy had brought. "Already got it all."

Ryan smiled at Foster. "Look at you. I guess you're responsible." And it was a testament to the fact that Jeremy must have been feeling better, because he was able to notice the way that Foster breathed out a tiny sigh of relief at Ryan's approval.

"I can get up now," Jeremy said.

"You sure? Sometimes during panic attacks, Emmy's hands and feet go numb, so just be careful," Ryan said, and Jeremy found that he was seeing this man in another light. He had always written Ryan off as being a bit of a goof, but he tolerated him for their working relationship and the fact that Emmy loved him. But it was clear that he had done his homework when it came to living with someone with anxiety, and Jeremy was able to get the firsthand benefit from that.

"Thanks," Jeremy said. "I'm kind of embarrassed." He was incredibly embarrassed, actually.

"Dude, fuck that," Ryan said. "It happens to a lot of people."

"Was that your first one?" Dec asked, handing over a cold bottle of water.

"I think so? Fuck, man. I really thought I was dying there for a bit," Jeremy said.

"Emmy says she feels hungover afterward," Ryan said.

"They fucking suck," Foster said. "I had one in high school, right after my parents got divorced." He shivered. "No thank you."

Later, Jeremy, who had been chauffeured home by Foster, with Dec and Ryan in tow and had to promise that he was fine and would call if he needed anything, turned to his phone. Opening to his favorite contacts, he hovered a thumb over Davis's name for just a second before he clicked on Emmy's name. He wasn't quite ready to have this conversation with her over the phone so, in a classic millennial move, he sent a text.

Jeremy: Hey, are you busy?

Emmy: No

It took him a few minutes to get the courage to put the words on paper, because if he put it in writing, sent it across the airwaves or however texting worked to Emmy, she would never forget, and it would mean it was real. That Jeremy was hurting in a way he had tried to prevent for years, and it was affecting him more than he cared to admit. Finally, he typed.

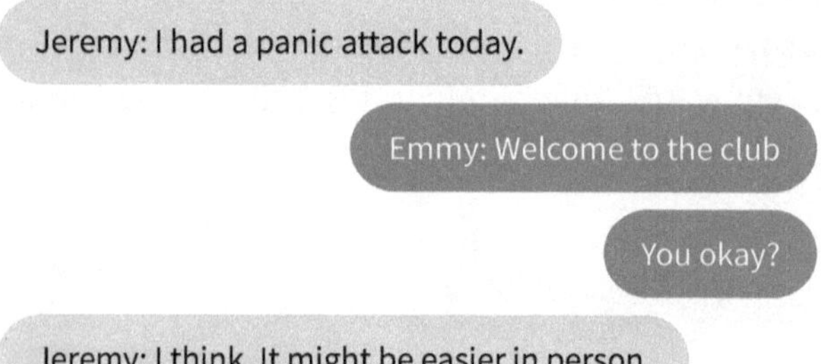

Emmy: Tea?

Jeremy: Wine

And that's how Jeremy found himself heading to Next Door. Emmy was already there, and Jeremy joined her at the bar. He waved to Lina, Dec's bartender, who had recently taken over more management responsibilities, and ordered a glass of pinot noir, knowing that Dec tended to stock his favorite varietal.

"I thought you weren't drinking," Emmy said by way of greeting, taking a sip of her own clear drink, which Jeremy knew to be a gin and tonic.

"Well, until yesterday, I was also dating someone, so things can change at the drop of a hat." He sniffed the wine. "Sorry, that was unnecessarily harsh."

"Hello?" Emmy waved a hand in front of Jeremy's face. "You're talking to me. Emmeline Bonaire, Ice Queen of Unnecessarily Harsh? Do you not remember my initial few months with Ryan?" Jeremy laughed and took a sip of wine. "The way I was a complete dick to Davis?"

"About that — Davis wouldn't commit. We broke up."

"You proposed?" Emmy asked, her eyebrows disappearing into her bangs with surprise.

"No. God, no. That's — no. It's stupid, but he's headed out to do work with that fire and, shit, I got *scared*, Emmy. I mean, you know about my parents. You know why I never wanted the entire drama of falling in love. I just wanted to know that he was safe." He rubbed his eyes to try to stave off the sting that heralded tears. "He wouldn't even put me as an emergency contact. He's out in a *forest fire*, and he could *die*, and I wouldn't know."

"Jer," Emmy said, placing a hand on his arm. "That fucking sucks."

Jeremy rolled his eyes. "I'm calling Phoebe. She's more comforting."

"No, but that's life. And I know it's rich, coming from me, because I literally check Colorado Fire's website four times a day during the summer if I haven't taken my meds and gone to therapy, but Davis is smart."

"He's so smart," Jeremy agreed, unable to keep the admiration out of his voice.

"That man is the most competent person I know." Emmy took a pointed drink. "And I know myself." There was a moment of silence as Emmy rattled the ice in her glass and Jeremy traced a finger around the rim of a glass. Emmy, as she usually did, broke the silence.

"Did you ask him why he didn't put you down as an emergency contact?"

"He said it's none of the Forest Service's business. But there has to be more to it than that," Jeremy said. "It's pretty clear he doesn't want to be associated with me, doesn't want to be out at work."

"Have you asked why?"

Jeremy responded with silence.

"Jer, when you introduced us to Davis, I did some digging." Jeremy fixed her with a pointed stare, and she rolled her eyes. "Okay. Well, yes, first it started with wanting to know the history of where he worked, but then I stumbled upon stories. Short documentaries. The Forest Service was — and is — in a lot of places, a good ole boys club."

"I mean, what isn't?" Jeremy said. "I'm in academia and openly queer. I have been my entire career."

"No, Jeremy." Emmy's voice took on a harder tone. "Not in a *these men promote their friends who go golfing with them* type of way, but in a way that normalizes sexual assault, racism, and homophobia. Davis being out could —"

"Be riskier than the fires," Jeremy finished, feeling foolish.

"Yeah, and like, small towns are still sometimes *small towns*," Emmy said. "I'm not saying that everyone in a mountain town is carrying pitchforks or tiki torches, but, well, is it self-preservation? Phoebe didn't tell me she was bi until, like, three years after I knew her. She didn't want our friendship to change."

Jeremy felt oddly guilty, a strange sensation where he knew he was right to be upset with Davis and trusted his emotions but also knew that what Emmy was saying made perfect sense. That disconnect made him feel like a petulant teenager, confused about new emotions and the reality of being able to understand the wider world.

"But *he knows* about my parents, and he knows how afraid I am of losing him."

"Did you tell him that?"

"Of course! And then, when he wouldn't respond right then, I realized that it meant he didn't love me like I loved him. So I pushed him out, made him leave." He shrugged. "And here I am. Oh, and every single man I'm friends with saw me have a panic attack this morning, so that was great for my reputation."

"You can't do that, Jer," Emmy said, rolling the glass between her hands. "It's not fair."

"What do you mean?" Jeremy asked, setting his wineglass to the side.

"You and I, well, we're only children. We don't like to rely on people, especially because we've been hurt in different ways by our parents."

"How have my parents hurt me?" Jeremy asked, feeling a rage beginning to grow in his gut. "They did *everything* for me. They were the best."

"But they died," she said in the blunt-but-kind way that only Emmy could pull off. "And that hurts."

"Yeah, well, it's not *their fault*."

"Never said it was," Emmy said simply, giving a sad smile. "Did you go to therapy afterward?"

He had meant to. It's what people *did*. It wasn't like he grew up in a family that avoided therapy. His mom taught art therapy for a bit and his father had often spoken about sessions with his therapist. It was normalized. Therapists came to holiday parties and summer cookouts. He had talked to a therapist during college when he was figuring out what to do with his career. But after his parents died, he moved to Colorado and never contacted them again.

He thought that throwing himself into his career and into the house would fix it. If he could make a home that was something like his parents had, wouldn't a partner slip right into that world? But Davis had taught Jeremy that you could make a habitat physically perfect for an animal, but they had to feel comfortable there. Somewhere, in his rambles about reintroducing endangered species, bred in captivity, to the wild, Jeremy had picked up on that. Jeremy had made a nest for someone, but Davis didn't fit that nest. And Jeremy didn't fit in Davis's nest in the mountains. But somehow, they worked together.

They *had* worked together.

"Fuck," Jeremy said to his glass of wine.

"Yes?" Emmy said, raising her eyebrows into her bangs.

"You're right."

"I know."

"I hate it when you're right."

"You and Ryan can form a club." She smirked.

"How did you manage it?" Jeremy asked, draining his glass of wine.

"Being right? It's innate, darling," she said, affecting a dramatic accent.

Jeremy rolled his eyes. "No, um, well. I never asked. How did you manage being with Ryan? With, well, everything?"

"With my asshole brain and mouth that works faster than my good sense?" she asked, wincing. "Listen, I'm my own worst enemy. I know." She sighed and took a sip of her drink. "I want to say that it's the work I did in therapy and my ability to communicate, but the honest truth is, I got lucky."

"By living here?"

"By meeting Ryan. By meeting someone who would be patient with me. Who'd wait while I figured things out. Who wouldn't run at the first sign of trouble. Ugh, I hate to sound like your wise old aunt —"

"You're my age," Jeremy interjected.

"Hush. But relationships take *work*. You have to fight for love." Emmy gagged and made a face. "Can you believe I'm sitting here waxing poetic about love?"

"What about marriage?" Jeremy asked.

"I'm happy for Phoebe and Dec. The photos looked perfect, and she's been waggling that ring in my face all week. I'm happy for Colin and June, whenever they decide to ever go through with it." Emmy sighed. "I think that the best part about our shit show of a generation is that we've realized that we're only doing things that feel right to us."

Jeremy felt a flicker of hope. "Can you say more?"

"Yes, but I'm going to need another drink." Jeremy hadn't had two glasses of wine in the same night since he'd started dating Davis. Having ended it, it felt pertinent to drown his sorrows in his favorite pinot. Emmy waved at Dec, and he quickly brought over a gin and tonic for her and a second glass of wine for Jeremy. Jeremy's eyes shot to the silver band on his left fourth finger, an Irish ring that he and Phoebe had returned from Ireland wearing together, along with a hyphenated last name. Phoebe and Declan Whitford-McFadden, like a couple that transported from the Gilded Era, sparkling and joyous, like the best kind of champagne.

He wanted that, but on his own terms.

"What were you saying?" Jeremy said, swirling his wine.

Emmy thought for a moment and took a sip. "So, like, I don't want kids. Ryan doesn't want kids. I think a generation ago, we would have had them because it's what you were supposed to do. Dec and Phoebe wanted to get married, which works for them. Ryan asked why I didn't want to."

If Jeremy wasn't mistaken, Emmy — the ice queen with a sharp tongue and an even sharper wit — was tearing up.

"And he understands. And we're committed, in our own way." She coughed and brushed her cheek, surreptitiously removing the one tear that dared to fall.

A few days later, Jeremy clicked on a link that had been emailed to him.

A new website opened on his computer. He confirmed that his connection was strong and connected to the video portal. Looking at his own face, Jeremy took stock of the man staring back at him. For a long time, his mental image of himself was lodged somewhere in his midtwenties. But he was older now. Late thirties. An age that he had known his parents at. He looked a bit closer, at the lines that spiderwebbed out from the corners of his eyes, the way that the skin below his eyes had gotten just a bit thinner. Maybe his lips had gotten thinner and there were frown lines around them.

Smile lines, he remembered his mom saying. *I want my face to show that I have lived.* She had said that to a friend once, with Jeremy overhearing it from the other room while his mom gossiped with a group of friends that she had known in art school.

Jeremy smiled at the camera. He liked himself. This was the face of someone who had been in love. Who loved.

The video blinked to life.

"Jeremy Rinci?" a soft-spoken gray-haired Black man asked.

"Uh, hi." It seemed his headphones were working.

"Nervous about therapy?"

Jeremy smiled. "Who isn't?"

Davis

It was easy to lose himself in the controlled chaos of the fire. The vast majority of people in this part of the mountains knew that fire was a true part of their life, had prepared and followed the evacuation orders without much difficulty.

At night, the sky glowed a hazy red, making it difficult to fall asleep. During the day, smoke clogged the sky, shifting it to a dirty orange. Davis didn't see the sun for the entire week he was out on fire duty.

He had sent a message to Foster, Ryan, and Dec on day four. A simple message: *If he asks, I'm doing okay*. His phone stayed in his pocket, and he didn't open his messages, with the exception of the photographs that Alex sent of Mary Anne and Caveman.

Alex: I think they're in love!

Davis hadn't had the energy to respond back with anything other than a heart emoji. At least his dog was faring better in love than he was.

Jeremy hadn't said the words *I'm breaking up with you*, but even Davis could read between the lines there. He turned back to the computer and looked at the current updates for the fire, which was currently sitting at 25 percent containment. Not even good enough for a minor league batting average. A new team of firefighters was coming in from Fort Collins, and Davis confirmed that they would be working on a firebreak on the northwest edge. Logistics helped keep his mind at ease. Davis had been placed in charge of ensuring that crews heading out to dig firebreaks had the appropriate equipment. Managing dozers, excavators, backhoes, shovels, and hydration powders was easier than thinking about how Davis had blown up his relationship.

A reminder popped up on his screen. *Coordination Update Meeting – 5 min!* It was one of three in-person meetings at the command site, a chance to get updates and ask questions in person instead of over IM and email. Davis was grateful for it. He liked having the information shown and spoken to him, rather than having to read the text-heavy forecasts and updates that flooded his inbox. Leaving his makeshift desk in one of the trailers, Davis crossed to the main area, an outdoor stage where they probably held sheep-shearing contests, which had been covered by a temporary tent. Davis headed down the side, sitting near the front but not close enough that anyone would call on him, a strategy adopted in high school classes that he continued here.

A man sat down next to him, and they each grunted their hellos. The other man stretched, and Davis caught a glimpse of a tattoo — *my unconquerable soul.* And Davis was struck, because he remembered the stanza, the poem he recited to himself each morning.

I thank whatever gods may be / For my unconquerable soul

Davis, at that moment, listening to an update on evacuation orders, thanked whatever gods may be. For everyone helping and working on the fire. For the resources he'd been using.

He looked out at the distant glow that reminded him that the fire was an ever-present threat.

So he kept thanking *whatever gods may be.*

For Gram and her love of baseball.

For his counselor and her advice.

For his friends in West Virginia who had been patient with him.

For Henry, who'd taught him about his body and love.

For his cousin Bruce.

The list grew all-encompassing to include more abstract ideas, less tangible things.

For creating a path that Davis could walk all the way to Colorado.

For allowing Davis to get to know himself here.

For bringing Jeremy into his life.

And, he hoped, for Jeremy's ability to forgive.

Later than night, Davis took a deep breath and picked up his cell phone, double-checking that it was connected to Wi-Fi to make the call clearer.

"Hello?" a man's voice answered the phone.

"Is Tiff there?" Davis asked. He was a bad friend. Tiff was apparently dating someone new, and he didn't even know.

"Whose calling?"

"Davis."

"Uncle Davis!" It wasn't Tiff's new boyfriend, but her son, Corey. Corey, who had been starting middle school the last time Davis saw him, was apparently a grown man now.

"Corey! How old are you these days? I didn't even recognize your voice."

"I turn eighteen next month. I'm headed to WVU in the fall. Like you did." There was awe in Corey's voice that Davis didn't deserve.

"Proud of you, little guy," Davis said, wiping his eye. In the background, he heard Tiff ask who Corey was talking to. Then, suddenly, she was on the phone.

"Nathaniel Davis, you goddamn pain in the ass. Move out to Colorado and forget all of us back home like your shit don't stink."

"Hi, Tiff." Davis smiled. People back in West Virginia loved in a different way than in Colorado. "Sorry I didn't call."

"Yeah, well, you're not the only one who didn't." She coughed. "Phone works both ways, y'know?" He could tell she pulled her face away from the phone as she told Corey to *leave her alone so she could catch up with Uncle Davis.* "Sorry 'bout that. Almost eighteen, and he thinks he's grown."

Davis laughed. "I can't believe he's that old already!" It seemed like just yesterday that Tiff had told their lunch table that she was pregnant and had to keep the baby.

"He's growing like a weed. He's been taller than me since he was ten." The conversation, much to Davis's surprise, flowed easily, and there were moments that he felt transported back to a bonfire in Anthracite Springs. Tiff had been promoted at work, and Corey had gotten a scholarship.

"So why'd you call?" Tiff asked finally.

"What do you mean?"

"Nathaniel Davis, I've known you since we were playing in a sandbox together. I *know* you."

"I was seeing someone, and I think I ruined it," Davis replied.

"What did you do?"

"I don't know how to tell him I love him. I think I waited too long." Tiff was silent for a moment, and Davis had a moment of panic that she had hung up when she registered the pronoun. Then she laughed.

"What's funny?"

"You know that Corey still thinks you're the coolest guy ever?"

"I didn't, but that's an honor." Davis braced himself for the inevitable realization that his queerness would mean Corey wouldn't think he was cool.

"He's gonna think you're even cooler now," Tiff said, and Davis knew she was rolling her eyes and shaking her head. "He told me a few years ago he knew he was not straight when he started looking differently at his Sidney Crosby poster."

"Oh! That's...that's great," Davis said.

"Things have changed round here," Tiff said. "Not the whole way, but there's a GSA club at the high school, and two of the girls on the basketball team took each other to prom last year." Tiff asked gentle questions about Davis, reminded him that she had coached Corey through first crushes and first loves and first breakups and was convinced it never got easier. As they spoke, the knot in Davis's chest unraveled and was replaced by a soft, warm feeling. The kind he got when he drove through the part of the national forest that had been decimated by Pine Bark beetles and saw dozens of saplings had been planted by the Youth Conservation Corps.

Hope for the future.

And then, suddenly, on a Wednesday a few weeks later, the wind changed, followed by enough rain for the crews to get the fire contained, a reminder of how so much in life was up to random chance. A few days to finish the containment and take stock of the effects of the fire, then Davis would be back to his regular responsibilities.

And maybe back to Jeremy.

Davis

Davis got home late on Friday evening. He could have stayed the night at the hotel, but after checking his paystub and ensuring the overtime was correct, he drove back to his cabin, calling Alex on the way and waking him up so he could get Mary Anne.

"Happy to be home, Mary Anne?" he asked as the dog leapt out of the truck cab and sprinted toward the front door. The dog pawed at the door and whined as Davis unloaded the bag with what he would need for the evening. The rest of his gear could wait. Davis wanted a shower and to fall asleep for seven to ten business days.

He opened the door, and Mary Anne ran to her bed, spun around three times, and flopped onto the pillowed circle.

"Well, didn't take you long to ease back into things," he said wryly. His voice echoed through the cabin, which felt emptier than it should. Which was stupid, of course, because Davis had lived alone for the vast majority of his adult life, which, he considered, was over half of his life. He liked being by himself.

Three months with Jeremy Rinci had changed that.

But as he toweled off and slid into a pair of soft pajama pants, Davis reflected that the change had started even before the tall man had sauntered into his life. He had moved to Colorado. He had gotten the dog. He had taken tentative steps to living more authentically, like a toddler learning to walk, until Jeremy had held his hand as he gained confidence.

Slipping under a blanket in his bed that felt much too big and much too cold, Davis was sure that right now, the only thing he was confident of was that he was lonely. He knew that progress wasn't linear, but he wished he could have channeled some of that hope he felt back at the fire.

The next morning, Davis brewed a cup of coffee and walked to his back porch as Mary Anne made her standard perusal of the meadow. He had been looking forward to seeing this view again, had realized how much it grounded him every morning, and whispered *this is your home*.

"Cooper's hawk," Davis whispered, wishing that he could tell Jeremy about the striking blond bird that floated on a thermal.

It would get better. He'd get used to the silence again.

It didn't get much better. Davis had spent enough time moping around his cabin that Alex had come over, barging in with all the subtlety of an avalanche, and told Davis that he needed to go outside and remind himself that humanity existed.

"You haven't even gone on a ride with Yesenia and me," Alex said. Which was only half-true. He had planned on joining both of them for a ride yesterday but had gotten distracted by a half-finished idea that had taken root in his brain.

"I mean, it's just..." Davis began.

"I'm taking your daughter" — Alex scratched behind the dog's ear — "For a playdate with Caveman. Go somewhere. Go to the city. Go to a sporting goods store. I don't know, go anywhere."

"I don't want to head down the mountain."

"Shit, just get out of this cabin. It smells like sadness."

So that is how Davis, who'd spent the vast majority of his non-traditional college experience processing his feelings at the bottom of pints of beer at bars, found himself processing his feelings at the bottom of a Diet Coke at a bar in a mountain town in Colorado.

He had driven past the bar dozens of times, laughed at cheesy sayings on the sign outside, but had never gone in. He opened the door to find a fire blazing and soft folk music playing off a speaker. He didn't know what he had been expecting — something more harsh, something more like the bars he and his father knew in Anthracite Springs — but this place seemed more like a coffee shop that happened to serve alcohol.

Davis walked up to the bar and slid onto a stool, repeating a mantra to himself as he tapped his fingers on the bar.

"You're new here," the bartender, a tall White man with a pale gray ponytail, said with a smile.

"Simon, be nice," came a familiar voice. Davis turned to the side to see a face he knew he had seen before. The man wearing a flannel was tallish, with brown hair pulled into a small bun. He turned his body toward Davis to show long legs clad in jeans with a pair of wool socks and, oddly, sandals. "I know him."

"Last time you brought someone new in the bar, you fell in love with her," Simon said, laughing. "Go easy on this one."

"You're Phoebe's brother, right?" Davis was hit with a bit of recognition from the night he met Jeremy's friends and the brunch after. Another time, too, at Phoebe's surprise birthday party.

"The one and only Colin Whitford," the man said, tipping his pint of beer toward Davis. "Phoebes told me that you live out here. I was surprised I hadn't seen you before." He laughed. "It's not like we get a lot of new blood out here. Can I buy you a beer?"

"I, uh, don't drink, so bars really aren't my scene," Davis replied.

"All good. Mind if I do?" Colin asked simply.

"Of course not." He looked to the bartender and asked for a Diet Coke, Colin insisting he would pay. It had been shocking to Davis, the way this group of friends had not only never questioned his sobriety, but accommodated him in the most subtle, soft, and caring ways.

"What brings you here tonight?"

"I needed to get out of my house and clear my head," Davis muttered.

"I get that. June — that's my fiancée, I think you met her. Curly red hair, bump on her nose, hips for days?" Davis swore he saw Colin's eyes turn into hearts. "Even more hips now that she's pregnant." Colin's voice caught.

"Congrats?" Davis asked, still in that in-between phase of life where he wasn't sure whether people wanted children. He couldn't keep a boyfriend. He shouldn't think about a tiny life.

"It was planned." Colin grinned.

"Do you know what you're having?" Davis asked, thinking about Tiff, who had her son in eleventh grade.

"A daughter," Colin said, and Davis was sure he saw tears in the other man's eyes. "There are days that I wake up and still can't believe it." He took a sip of his beer. "June lovingly told me to leave the house tonight because I was making her nervous." He fiddled with a napkin, tearing off a corner. "I just wanted to check the bag one more time. I know she's not due for another two months, but things could happen any time." He chuckled. "Anyway, I came here because it's where we met. Even if I can't be with her right now, I'm still thinking about her. Hell, I'm always thinking about her." Davis gave a small smile, even though his heart ached. This was how he had felt about Jeremy while he was working on the forest fire. Every single time he touched a McLeod, he wanted to turn and tell Jeremy that they should do an exhibit on Malcom McLeod, who had fought the largest wildfire in US history and was an icon to forest rangers everywhere. He wanted to ask Jeremy exactly how he would have described the ridiculous art in the Best Western they were staying at. He wanted to turn on another movie from the '90s that Jeremy had never seen and watch him find a queer subtext.

He took a pause, hesitant to continue further. He'd only met this man once before and, Christ, he had a daughter on the way. Something beautiful and new and full of hope.

"So you need to clear your head?" Colin asked again, continuing the conversation. And as much as Davis wanted to sit here and sulk and watch the baseball game (and sulk that it would never be *his team* making it far in the playoffs), something about Colin made Davis open up. He searched his mind to remember what he did and came up with *something to do with children*, which made sense.

"I'm here because I can't drink away my problems anymore, but this is the only place where it's socially acceptable to sit by myself and mope," Davis said honestly.

"What kind of problems?" Colin asked.

"Guy problems," Davis replied.

"Right," Colin said. "You and Jeremy are together, right?"

"Was. Were. I dunno. Words have always been hard for me," Davis said. "Which is probably what got me into this situation in the first place." Colin waited patiently, leaving space for Davis to talk. "I, uh, I had to leave for the fire, and, well. I didn't handle it well. Wasn't able to say what he meant to me. He deserves someone who would fight for him, who would think about him in those kinds of ways."

"So he wanted you to stay, but he didn't ask."

"I couldn't stay," Davis explained. "I wasn't at the place where I could have that kind of big conversation. So I didn't. I just left for the fire." Davis looked at his glass. "I assume that he's already moved on, because he lives a more interesting life than the one I do."

Colin made a thoughtful noise, then asked. "Did you ask him to wait for you?"

Colin let out a wry chuckle. "No, personal experience. June and I met and fell...quickly. She left, and I didn't ask her to stay. Even though all I wanted to do was ask her to stay. It's terrifying. What if she said no? I thought that I wanted the universe to decide for me, that if it was meant to be, it would fall into place." Colin laughed dryly. "The universe doesn't know shit."

"You went to her?" Davis started formulating a plan.

"No, I got lucky." Colin's eyes were misty again. "She came back to me."

The door opened, the pounding of rain giving Colin a chance to dry his eyes and Davis a chance to think. He was surprised to see Yesenia at the door. She looked around the bar until her eyes settled on him. She gave him a small head nod, and Davis responded in kind, indicating that she should join them.

"This seat taken?" she asked, touching the stool next to Davis.

"All yours. Colin, this is Yesenia. Yesenia, this is Colin. His sister works with, uh, Jeremy."

"You mean your ex-boyfriend?" Yesenia said.

Davis whipped his head around. "How did you know?"

"Dude, you're not subtle. Also, there are three people I see almost every single day. You've been off since you got back from the fire." She flagged down the bartender and ordered a

Diet Coke to replace Davis's own and a lager for herself. "Alex told me that you went out, and I wanted to be here if," she shrugged uncomfortably, "well, if you felt like you were going to drink tonight."

"Thank you," Davis said, touched by her thoughtfulness. "I just needed to get out of my house, and I ran into Colin, and he's been helping." Colin gave a salute.

"Did the fire fuck you guys up?" Yesenia asked.

"No, my camp is fine," Colin responded.

"I'm fine, no issues with the logistics," Davis added. Yesenia had been at an outpost on the other side of the burn. She should have known that.

Yesenia rolled her eyes and muttered *men* to her beer. "Not, like, structurally. And while I'm glad you're fine, with your camp or whatever." She looked to Colin, then back to Davis. "I meant you and Jeremy."

"How did you know?" Davis asked for a second time.

"The same thing happened to my husband."

"You're married?" Davis asked.

"Congrats," Colin said, looking at his phone.

Yesenia gave an affectionate chuckle. "Davis, you spent the first year keeping everyone at arm's length. Of course you didn't know. I don't wear a ring at work most days, anyway."

"Where's he living?" Davis knew he missed a lot, but he didn't realize he had missed an entire other person living on their site.

"He's in the Pacific Northwest, on the Olympic Peninsula. He's a biologist, too, and they had an opening for his specialty. We had a discussion one night and figured that if he didn't take it, he'd regret that chance, right?" She smiled to herself. "I still choose him every day, and he chooses me. And, like, well, if it works for us and we're happy, why does it bother anyone else?"

A vibration on the table, and Colin's phone lit up. "Hey, darling," he said, answering it. "Yeah, I'll pick up some ice cream on the way back." He laughed. "And yes, hot dogs for dinner are fine. All right, love you." Hanging up, he looked at Yesenia and Davis. "Don't ever tell her, but I am so sick of eating hot dogs for dinner during her cravings," Colin laughed. After paying for his drink, he turned to Davis. "Do you want my number? June and I are always looking for more friends who actually live out here so we don't always have to head down to the city."

"Yeah, actually, that would be lovely." Davis awkwardly maneuvered his phone out of his pocket and passed it over for Colin to type his number into it. "I'm available for babysitting when your daughter arrives, too."

Colin smiled. "You think I'm gonna leave that girl's side? Please." With Colin gone, Davis turned back to Yesenia.

"I should tell you thank you. I didn't feel like I wanted to drink, but it's good to know you're around if I need someone."

"My stepmom was sober. People are weird about it, but I dunno, they don't need to be." She sipped her beer. "Want to talk about your boy problems?"

"No," Davis said honestly. "I'm kind of talked out."

Yesenia nodded. "Want to sit here in silence and pretend we give a shit about this baseball game?"

"That sounds perfect."

She bumped her shoulder into his, and Davis was reminded that not everything had gone to shit. He still had his job. He still had friends here. Davis felt a tiny flicker of that hope.

Jeremy

"You owe me," Yuna said by way of greeting, showing up in sunglasses at Jeremy's doorstep.

"You're my only friend that doesn't work with me or know people I work with," Jeremy explained as he let her in and led her to the backyard. "If this goes wrong, they'll never let me live it down, and I'll have to move to a different state." He paused, then added, "Probably a different country."

"Okay, so what's the plan?" she asked, putting her hands on her hips and surveying the two large boxes in front of them.

It had been a middle-of-the night idea, something that Jeremy hadn't had since undergrad, back when his sleep schedule was less regular. Foster had come over before and insisted on watching a series of increasingly corny romance movies, telling Jeremy that *it helps him deal with shit*. Jeremy wasn't sure why he needed to watch another straight couple figure out how to make their bookshop-slash-cheese shop work, but he was humoring Foster. And maybe it was because he thought constantly about Davis and wanted to know how to reach out to him, or maybe it was because he saw that the Pine Valley fire had been 100 percent contained, but when he'd woken up at midnight, Jeremy wanted to make a grand gesture. Something that would make even the most hard-hearted of big city businesswoman realize that her dream was to own a specialty cupcake store.

Or something that would make a Country Forest Ranger give a Big City Exhibit Designer another chance.

Which is how Jeremy — and now Yuna — ended up with two boxes to build one large rocking chair that could fit two people.

"Did you do any big sculptural projects during your MFA?" Yuna asked, cutting open one of the boxes.

"Unless you count the furniture I assembled with an Allen wrench? No," Jeremy replied, taking out a booklet of instructions that seemed to be roughly the size of a Cheesecake Factory menu.

"We're smart, though," Yuna said. "Two artists, understanding of spatial relationships and scale? We'll be done in no time."

An hour later, Jeremy and Yuna had managed to do...nothing significant.

"Call someone," Yuna said, throwing a piece of wood across the lawn. "These instructions are too difficult to follow."

"The website said that *even a child could put it together*," Jeremy said, setting down two pieces of wood that he couldn't figure out how to assemble correctly.

"Well, maybe you need to call your friend who's most child-like," Yuna suggested.

Within fifteen minutes, Foster was knocking on Jeremy's door, holding a drill. But he wasn't alone.

"What part of *don't tell anyone* did you not understand?" Jeremy asked, looking past him to see seven people that he knew and loved and did not want to see.

"Well, I figured I'd ask Dec a question about some tool-related things, and then he offered to help because he fixes things at the bar all the time. And then he told Phoebe, who told Emmy, so she and Ryan joined, too. And Dec asked to borrow a tool from Joe, and Lina said she had some in her car, but Joe said that Cynthia was curious about it when Dec explained it, so..." He gave the drill trigger a squeeze for emphasis.

"Y'all need more lesbians in your life," Lina said, rolling her eyes. "Foster, give me that drill before you hurt yourself."

"Yuna hasn't been helping," Jeremy muttered, standing to the side to allow everyone to parade into his house.

The assembled group was, in Jeremy's estimation, one of the smartest groups of people in Colorado at any given moment, and it still took them the better part of a day to finish the rocking chair. June and Colin had even come down. In the end, Jeremy's biggest contribution was ordering food and drinks for the group and making sure Dec didn't accidentally take a hammer to Ryan's head for being a "back seat carpenter." Davis would have loved it here, and, honestly, probably would have assembled the chair faster than the entire group combined.

Next time, Jeremy told himself.

Some force inside Jeremy told him that this entire plan would work. It was the same sense of calm, some silly breeze of assurance, that Jeremy felt when he had first looked at his house.

The same scratch at the back of his brain that Jeremy had felt when he looked at Davis the first time.

He knew.

This matters.

Later, as six large pizzas were consumed in record time, Jeremy took a moment to look around at his friends. Phoebe and Dec sat on the floor. Emmy and Ryan each had brought a chair in from the dining room. Flo had taken a pillow from the couch and was using it as a chair. Joe leaned against the wall while his new wife, Cynthia, leaned against his legs. June, eight months pregnant, sat in the Eames chair while Colin took the footstool. He turned to Foster, who had joined him on the couch.

"I need a big dining room table, huh?" Jeremy asked him.

"Yeah," Foster said around a piece of crust. "I don't know why you don't have more people over. You have the best space of all of us that isn't the bar or the brewery."

"I want to have people over," Jeremy said, then, louder, to the rest of the group, he asked, "Would y'all like to do a weekly dinner here?"

"Potluck?" Phoebe suggested.

"Are dogs welcome?" Emmy asked.

"Can we bring kids?" Dec and Colin asked in unison.

"Yes, yes, and yes," Jeremy said. "I'll bring Davis."

Davis

"Jeremy, from the bottom of my heart, I am *so* sorry, and I want to prove to you that you're the best thing that ever happened to me." A pause, a moment to see the reception.

Mary Anne sneezed.

"That bad, huh? Too corny, right?" Davis asked her. She cocked her head and lay her head on the arm of the couch. "You're right, you're right. I know." Davis tried to remember what he had learned from the podcast episode on *how to apologize*. It had, essentially, boiled down to "be authentic and be yourself," which was the thing that Davis had a lifetime of experience avoiding doing. Davis could do authentic.

"Jeremy, I fucked up, and it made me feel like shit." Davis looked at Mary Anne again and found out that dogs could roll their eyes. He flopped down on the couch on his stomach and looked Mary Anne in the eyes. "I don't know how to do this."

He knew that you couldn't apologize with just things, even though that hadn't stopped Davis from purchasing two ridiculous items to be shipped to Jeremy's house. He had started mountain biking again with Alex and Yesenia and had asked them what he should do. Their advice had been to call Jeremy like a civilized person, but Davis knew that wasn't right. Calling people on the phone was what you did for average people. Jeremy was amazing and special and deserved to have something to remind him of that, to let him know.

But Jeremy also needed *words*, and words were the hardest thing for Davis to do.

"We can do this, right, Mary Anne?" She didn't respond, but Davis knew she would agree. "We're gonna learn how to do the best damn apology in the entire world and tell Jeremy we love him. I love him," he corrected. "God willin' and the creek don't rise, right, girl?" he added as an afterthought.

Mary Anne let out a tiny bark in her dreams.

Davis took that as a yes.

Davis

"Atta girl, Mary Anne!" Davis said to the dog as she bounded down the trail after his bike. "You're the best mountain dog of all time." She cut to the side, and all of a sudden, he was chasing her, an elated giggle escaping his mouth as he watched her completely in her element. She waited at the bottom of the trail, just like she had been trained to do, and Davis dismounted his bike when he got to her. He rubbed behind her ears and continued to babble his affection to her until she rolled over, exposing her belly.

And it struck Davis, again, that *this* was his home. He had a dog and access to an untold number of trails and mountains. He had the belief of his coworkers and boss and a job he felt passionate about.

He'd *had* Jeremy, and he guessed that he considered himself lucky to have experienced that kind of love. The next time someone took a chance on him, was able to see inside his soul the way Jeremy did, Davis would make sure to grab on with both hands and never let go.

He still hadn't gotten the courage to reach out to Jeremy. His gifts had been delayed by supply chain issues, so he had decided that he would head down to Vanberg and apologize in person after they arrived.

Having a plan felt good, he reflected, getting back on his bike and slowly pedaling to his cabin, Mary Anne contently trotting next to him. "Go on, girl. You can head to the cabin," Davis commanded, and Mary Anne took off. The dog was smarter than most humans he had ever encountered. He would put money on it. Mary Anne let out a pleased bark, which meant that she had seen one of her favorite people. Alex or Yesenia, Davis guessed.

But then Mary Anne appeared back on the trail, and Davis felt like he was in one of the old black-and-white *Lassie* reruns. Like Mary Anne was here to tell him that Timmy had fallen into a well.

"What is it, girl?" he asked the dog, playing into the part. She gave another pleased bark, and Davis pedaled a bit faster, and then —

For a moment, Davis thought that he must have been dehydrated and hallucinating. Because there weren't a lot of hybrid cars that went through the national forest, and there weren't many that pulled up in front of Davis's house. And Davis had only encountered one light blue Prius that had both NYU and Vanberg stickers on the rear window. And that specific car was parked in front of his cabin at the moment.

And if to confirm it, there he was. Jeremy Rinci, in all of his lanky, gorgeous beauty, leaning against the car, wearing those same damn suede boots he had worn the first time he had ever set foot in Davis's life.

Mary Anne, the traitor she was, ran over to him and slobbered all over his hand. "Hey, girl," he said, scratching the dog behind her ears.

"She'll slobber all over those fancy shoes of yours," Davis called, taking off his helmet and realizing that he was still damp with sweat.

"Eh, shoes can be replaced," Jeremy replied. "Hi, Davis."

"Jeremy," Davis said, and his brain, which had momentarily blanked, was all of a sudden full of too many thoughts. Jeremy was *here*, which meant that he didn't completely hate him. Davis had practiced for this, made sure that he had the words ready in his mind, right there on the surface, easy to grab. Like those ducks he used to pull at the county fair, the ones that meant he went home with three sandwich bags of goldfish.

"Jeremy!" he said, louder this time. "Sorry! I love you!"

"What?" Jeremy asked, looking stunned.

"I, uh, *shit*. I'm sorry. And I love you. I love you and I'm sorry." He wasn't making things any clearer.

"Thank you," Jeremy said, laughing slightly.

"Why are you laughing?"

"Because I wanted to apologize, too," Jeremy said, kicking at a rock in a gesture that was familiar to Davis. It was what he did when he was being stubborn about things.

"Why do you need to apologize?"

"I pushed you away," he said.

"I sprinted away," Davis admitted.

"I made you something," Jeremy said, sticking his hands in his pockets. "I had some help installing it, so, uh." He kicked another rock. "Can we go to your backyard?" Davis was, for a second, worried that it was going to be a surprise party, which would have been Davis's nightmare. But no one else was there, just a double wide rocking chair with lush cushions, different from the cheap ones that had been there before.

"What, what are these?" Davis said, looking them over. They looked solid, sturdy, with a hint of craftsmanship that even Davis's uncles would have been proud of.

"Rocking chairs," Jeremy replied, using his forefinger to nudge one into movement.

"Why?"

Jeremy looked up at him, his eyes a bit shiny. "Because you deserve to dream about being on a porch with a partner, no matter who it is."

Davis laughed, wet and messy, like the tears he was told boys shouldn't cry as a child. "This is ironic. Like that story with the comb and the watch we read in school."

"Huh?"

Davis pulled up his phone, swiped to his email, and pulled up an order confirmation, then a shipping notification, and showed Jeremy.

"You bought me two Eames rockers?"

"They're not originals," Davis said quickly. "Even with the overtime pay from the fire, there's no way I could ever justify paying eight hundred dollars for a chair, let alone two of them." Jeremy wrapped his arms around Davis, and Davis pressed his face into Jeremy's chest, then added, "I also bought you a tool set. If I wasn't going to be around to fix your shitty door hangings and hang your shelves, you needed good tools to do it."

"I started therapy," Jeremy said.

"I told Tiff about you. She said she's proud of me. That she wouldn't tell anyone back home."

"You didn't have to do that."

"I know," Davis whispered. "I wanted to."

"My therapist says that, well, he talks a lot about how I was lucky. Growing up where I did, working how I have. That the idea of coming out once and being done is bullshit." Davis smiled as Jeremy sniffled, then continued. "I trust you to do what feels right for you."

"I trust you to trust me," Davis said. "But I need a push from time to time. My counselor told me that. I started seeing her again."

"Therapy twins," Jeremy said, letting out a small, uncomfortable laugh.

"Are we okay?" Davis asked.

"I think we're going to be," Jeremy replied. He reached for him, and Davis had the impulse to run back inside, tuck himself away with Jeremy. But he didn't. He just let Jeremy kiss him, here in the parking lot, next to the sign that had previously read *Visitor Cunter*. Davis had kept that sign, tucked into a corner of his office. He'd give it to Jeremy on the one-year anniversary of the day they met.

A truck pulled up, and Jeremy pulled away, giving Davis space. Eric, Yesenia, and Alex piled out of the truck.

"Welcome back, Davis," Eric said, nodding.

"Uh, hi, everyone. Eric, Alex, Yesenia." Davis took a deep breath and felt just the whisper of Jeremy's pinky against his own. He could do this. He would do this. He took Jeremy's hand and gripped it tightly, the way he would grip an axe that he would use to fell a tree. He'd fell the tree of homophobia, if necessary.

There was a reason Davis had been in that remedial English class. "You remember Jeremy, right?"

"We've had loads of compliments on the visitor center, Jeremy," Eric said. "Are you here for work on the exhibit?"

"No," Davis said, speaking up, his voice cracking slightly, like he was in high school all over again. "No, he's here because he's my boyfriend."

"Congrats," Eric said. Davis had been ready, he supposed, to argue. To cite all the anti-discrimination laws that he had listened to podcasts about, learning about workers' rights and how at-will employment didn't apply to federal employees. Shit, he had been ready to teach these men a lesson about the Lavender Scare, the lesser-known Cold War moral panic that Emmy had sent him a podcast on.

"Thank you," Jeremy said, giving Davis's hand a squeeze.

"Okay," Eric said. "Does your boyfriend want to come out to the bar with the rest of us?"

Later, at the bar, Eric came up next to Davis and offered to buy him a beer to congratulate him on his new relationship.

"It's not *that* new," Davis said, feeling his cheeks heat.

"Let me do something nice for you, because I doubt we're getting a bigger budget from the White House this year," Eric laughed. Another moment of truth, because Davis could get the beer and let it sit, warming up, or pass it to Jeremy, who would drink it for him and not say a second word. But he was being open and honest. He had called his old counselor last week and admitted that he was still nervous about telling people. He had also come out to her, explained what had happened with Jeremy and how they were healing.

"Good for you," she had joked. "Twice the number of hot people to look at."

She had talked him through his fears, using her way of posing questions and having Davis share answers he already knew deep within his soul. That he would be seen as weak or somehow broken. How the idea of alcoholism as an illness worked for some people but let others think it was contagious or incurable. How Davis didn't want to care about what other people thought, but he did.

"Sweetie, we're never done learning about ourselves," she had said. "It ain't a bad thing to update people on what you've learned about yourself."

"I actually don't drink," Davis said confidently. Or as confidently as he could, talking to the toughest person he had ever met.

"Okay. My wife doesn't either. Diet Coke?" Said like it was nothing at all. Davis supposed it wasn't to people who could see the nuance of shades of gray in the world. He liked being around people who could understand the spectrum of experience, whether that be people's paths to careers, sexuality, or life choices.

"Diet Coke is great," Davis smiled back.

Epilogue

Davis made a cup of tea, something he had taken to sipping on in the evenings as it got colder, not only because it heated his core and made the evening feel a bit more cozy, but because the warm beverage always reminded him of Jeremy. It turned out that he loved mint and herbal teas, just not black tea. Another thing he learned about himself.

He flicked the back porch light on and headed outside, pulling a beanie onto his head. Settling into his rocking chair, he pulled the crocheted afghan over his lap — something his grandmother had won at the church festival back when they still allowed you to gamble at church — and pulled out his e-reader. It had been a gift from Phoebe, mailed to Davis's cabin after he had spent the weekend down in Vanberg. While at a bookstore, Davis had unintentionally shared about how reading was a struggle for him, how the letters sometimes danced around on the page and didn't form into sounds in his brain. The message that accompanied the thin device from Phoebe told him that there was a setting on this e-reader for a font that was supposed to help people with dyslexia.

On second thought, it probably hadn't been unintentional that Davis shared something he was self-conscious about with Jeremy's friends. Because they were his friends, too. Just like how Yesenia and Alex were Jeremy's friends, along with Alex's new partner, a younger ranger who was hired to assist on the outreach program. On day one, they had introduced themselves as "Sam, she/they," and Yesenia and Davis had shared a knowing look as Alex's eyes had turned into cartoon hearts instantly. Sam had encouraged Davis to attend the national forest's LGBTQ+ employee resource group. And even if Davis still left his camera off and didn't say much in meetings, it was nice to know that he had other rangers like him in a digital connection.

At seven fifteen, Davis's phone lit up with a FaceTime call. He swiped to answer it, and his heart was full. He'd never get tired of seeing Jeremy's face on the other end of the phone.

"Let me see my girl" was how he greeted Davis.

"What am I, chopped liver?"

"Show me Mary Anne," Jeremy demanded. Laughing, Davis turned the phone to face the dog, rolling his eyes at the way Jeremy cooed and praised Mary Anne.

"You know, you could get a dog of your own."

Jeremy scoffed. "It wouldn't be the same. It's not *Mary Anne*."

"How was your day?"

Jeremy filled Davis in on the minute details of the day, which centered around an exhibition opening. He had dropped down to part time at the University, working there Monday, Wednesday, and half days on Friday. Rinci Consulting was taking off, enough that Jeremy was able to bring on a paid intern. Which was good, because Rocky Mountain National Park had contacted Davis, asking for the contact information of the new visitor center's exhibit designer.

Davis wanted to share that news in person, though.

"And yours, baby?" Jeremy asked. Then it was Davis's turn to share, about the youth group he had led on a hike today, the way the kids had introduced themselves with pronouns without a second thought. How Sam was applying for a grant with

OUTdoors, an organization that helped queer youth explore nature.

"Can I join their programs?" Jeremy asked jokingly.

"Nope, it's only mountain biking." Jeremy pulled a face, having still refused to get on a bike that moved out in the mountains. For his part, Davis refused to spend money on a bike that went nowhere.

"Talk tomorrow?"

"Can we do six?" Davis asked. "There's a band playing at the bar that Yesenia wants to go see." Because every day, some-how, they saw each other's face, whether it was a FaceTime call or a selfie taken in the evening. Keeping their respective homes, their separate paths for careers, was what worked for Jeremy and Davis. Jeremy was searching for an electric car to make the drive cheaper, and Davis had traded in his truck for a hybrid for the same reason. Perhaps not the most efficient or economical, but at this point, Davis was happy. Jeremy was happy. They were happy together.

"Of course, baby," Jeremy said. "I love you."

"I love you."

"I was talking to Mary Anne."

"Sure you were."

Four Years Later

Jeremy looked at the table and hoped it would be big enough. When he had bought it two years ago, it seemed enormous, big enough to seat everyone Jeremy had ever known. But over the past two years, it had become crowded, which, he supposed, was a good thing.

"It's big enough, baby," Davis said, reading Jeremy's mind.

"You flatter me," Jeremy replied.

"It's gonna be fine. The entrees are resting, and people are bringing sides and desserts." Davis held a stack of plates in his arms, setting them down one by one as he rounded the table. The doorbell rang earlier than Jeremy expected, but most of his friends were always earlier than he expected. "Go answer your door, Jeremy. I'll set the table." Jeremy blew him a kiss, then headed to the other room to answer the door.

"I know we're early, but we just dropped River off with Kevin and are trying to enjoy every single moment of child-free time we can get tonight," June said once the door was opened, pressing a kiss to Jeremy's cheek.

"We can leave if you want," Colin added, setting down a package of cookies.

"It's fine. No worries," Jeremy said, waving away their concern. "Grab a glass of wine if you want. There's seltzer in the fridge, too."

"Darling, am I driving or you?" Colin asked.

"I carried a baby for nine months. You're driving," she said.

"June, our daughter is four now. How long are you going to say that?"

"Probably a solid fourteen more years," June replied. Colin let out a half-hearted *boo* as he left, and there was a knock at the door. "Oh, I bet that's Dec and Phoebes."

"Freedom!" Phoebe cried as she opened the door. "Adults! If I have to hear Raffi one more time today, I'm moving to the forest with Davis."

"I swear we love our daughter," Dec said wryly. "Also, we brought potatoes."

Colin returned with a seltzer for himself and a glass of rosé for June. He gave the glass of wine to his wife, then headed to his sister and gave her a huge hug.

"I get it," she said to him. "I get why you're one and done with children." Behind them, Dec rolled his eyes. "Declan Sean Whitford-McFadden, I can *hear* you rolling your eyes. I know that it's in your Irish blood to have, like, seven children, but let me be dramatic."

"I don't want seven kids," he said to Jeremy.

"Last I heard, you wanted ten," Davis said, joining the group with a glass of wine for Jeremy and a seltzer for himself.

"Still none for you all?" Dec asked Davis.

"Nah, dogs are enough," Davis replied, smiling at Jeremy. Being uncles to this group's overly precocious children was more than enough for the two men, not to mention the costs associated with surrogacy.

"Hi, hello, hi!" Ryan and Emmy were next, arriving at the same time as Lina and Yuna.

"I made cheesy potatoes!"

"Dammit, Andersson. We were making potatoes," Dec growled.

"Oh no, more cheese and potatoes." Emmy grinned.

Ryan turned to her. "Were we supposed to bring vegetables?"

"Potatoes are a vegetable, right?"

"We brought broccoli," Yuna said, rolling her eyes.

"And cauliflower. And green beans." Lina looked between the other couples. "What? I didn't trust anyone to bring what they said. I know how this group gets about potatoes."

"Fair point." Davis laughed, leading Yuna and Dec to the kitchen to drop off their dishes as the door opened again.

"We brought beer," Flo said, dressed in a vintage dress and holding a six-pack in each of her hands.

"She brought beer," Reggie said. "I brought gin."

"Thank god," Emmy said, crossing the room and taking the bottle out of Flo's partner's hand.

"Where's Foster? I haven't seen him in *months*," Flo asked, looking around.

"Amanda said their flight was delayed," Ryan said.

"You don't track your sister's flights?" Emmy asked Ryan. "I don't know how I've been with you this long." She swiped at her phone, then announced that their flight had landed and they should be here shortly. Amanda, her hair now a bright purple, and Foster arrived shortly after everyone sat down to eat. Jeremy waited impatiently, letting his best friend hug his sister before Jeremy tackled him in a bear hug.

"Wedding planning looks good on you," he said to Foster after their hug.

"I mean, what else do you expect from me? I do own and operate Seattle's best event space." Foster had sent him the article last week, and Jeremy had printed it out and put it on his fridge, feeling a bit like an old man.

"The sooner this event happens, the better," Amanda added. She looked at her brother. "You did it right. No wedding."

"You could elope?" Phoebe suggested.

"I guess I should be happy it's not a destination wedding," Amanda said, taking a sip of her brother's wine.

"Oh, but what if we —" Foster began before Jeremy clapped a hand over his mouth.

"Foster, why don't you go get yourself a plate before Amanda decides to take the next plane back to Seattle without you?" Jeremy suggested, laughing.

"Get me one, too," Amanda called, draining Ryan's wine. "And Ryan needs more wine."

Dinner went long, and drinks went on even longer. Commandeering the TV, Yuna showed photographs of her latest tattoos, Dec and Phoebe followed, showing a video of their daughter's first steps.

"Jo is much more graceful than her mother," Colin said, earning him a sisterly shove from Phoebe.

"More graceful than her uncle, too," June added, then showed a photograph of her brother and his fiancée in front of a tornado. "I'm just hoping River is slightly less brave and a tad smarter than her Uncle Julian and Auntie Violet."

Ryan jostled for control of the screen to show photographs of their latest trip to Vietnam and deftly steered Emmy away from talking about the museums they went to in excruciating detail. A toast was made to Davis, who had been promoted, and Jeremy smiled so wide his face hurt.

When Reggie fell asleep on Flo's shoulder, she announced that it was time for them to head home. "Don't believe everything they tell you about younger men," she said to Davis as they left. "He can barely stay up past nine most nights." The Whitfords and Whitford-McFaddens headed out afterward to pick up their children, followed by Emmy and Ryan, who called a rideshare and headed outside to wait for it. Yuna and Lina offered to help clean, but Davis shooed them out. Jeremy spent a few minutes with just Foster, as Amanda went to the backyard to say hello to the dogs with Davis.

"I miss you," Jeremy said.

"I miss you, too."

"You like Seattle?"

"I think I'd like anywhere," his best friend replied. "But yes, I like Seattle. Amanda's company is expanding again, so who knows where we might end up."

"I'm proud of you," Jeremy said.

"I'm here for two weeks," Foster said, rolling his eyes. "Don't act like I'm leaving right now and you have to be all sentimental."

"Fine, fuck you. Spin tomorrow?"

"You know it."

"Where are you staying?"

"Down in Boulder, but I'll be up here most days, working with Flo and Reggie." Amanda came back to the room, and Jeremy watched his friend's face glow. When Davis came into the room, accompanied by their two dogs, Jeremy was sure his face looked similar. Final goodbyes were said, and then it was just Jeremy and Davis.

"Clean now?" Jeremy asked, looking at the mountain of dishes that was stacked near the sink.

"Leave the dishes until morning, baby," Davis answered as he came up behind him, wrapping his arms around Jeremy's waist. "I'll do them. I'm always up before you anyway."

"This is why I leave my dishes to pile up until you visit," Jeremy replied, pressing his body back into Davis's solid form.

"You ever think about moving up to the mountains?" Davis asked him later in bed, after Jeremy had taken them both in hand for their releases.

"No, baby," Jeremy laughed. "You ever think of moving down to the city?"

"Hell no," Davis said.

"Maybe when we retire," Jeremy said, twisting their hands together, matching silver-and-wood bands winking in the low light. "We'll buy a house somewhere between."

"Maybe," Davis replied, pressing a kiss to Jeremy's knuckles. "I'm happy now, though."

"Same, baby." Jeremy kissed him then, soft and gentle.

"We've got what we need." Mary Anne, who still slept at their feet, gave a snore in agreement. Ginger, a smaller beagle that Jeremy had fallen in love with at an event at the museum, crawled up between the two men. "Well, everything except personal space," Davis added.

"Who needs that?"

Acknowledgements

In August of 2021, I bought a brand new notebook for the upcoming school year (I was a teacher). The first thing I wrote in that notebook were ideas for three book titles, along with the couples: Curated (Emmy & Ryan), Educated (Phoebe & Bartender), Exhibited (Jeremiah & Forest Ranger). The bartender became Declan, Jeremiah turned into Jeremy, and the Forest Ranger, of course, is Davis.

Publishing Exhibited is an unexpectedly emotional moment. I've always been an ambitious person and I've begun a million huge projects but very rarely see them through. Getting my ADHD diagnosis during the drafting of Exhibited helped me to understand why that was, which makes finishing the trilogy something I'm even prouder of. It wasn't the easiest road, as I switched DayJob careers throughout this series and published three other titles along the way. I couldn't have published any of these books, let alone six, without a whole host of people who I am grateful for every single day. These acknowledgements are just the smallest way I can repay my community.

Sam – for making the hottest faceless men of all time and somehow still understanding my sketches and voice memos for cover development and for being my friend from the first time we met during the development of S'mores cover. Look at us now!

Beth – I'm constantly impressed with the way you are able to smooth the bumps in my writing but still retain my narrative voice. I am so happy that you're my editor and so proud of the success you've found.

To the authors that so graciously provided blurbs and early feedback (Anita, Jen, Livy, Tarah, Ari, KT, Aimee) — this is the hardest job and I am so grateful that you took time out of your bananas busy schedules to spend some time with Jeremy and Davis.

To the folks in San Diego who make me laugh and smile regularly so I can exist as a person that isn't just Nellie Wilson, romance author (Jordan, Jess, Anna, Angela, Nick, Marlie). Thanks for being my friend even though you know that I'm constantly mining your stories for weird details to include in my writing.

Kelsey – for being someone who always helped me process my struggles with being "A Creative" in the age of social media, for your love of Eames chairs, for our shared love of hockey and baseball now, and for the myriad conversations about queerness that influenced so many of the discussions Jeremy and Davis have on page.

Megan – for helping me to get REALLY into baseball and for improving my craft in our discussions, and for being someone who *deeply* understood Davis from the first moment he ever appeared on page. The way you encouraged me to trust the process and lean into the uncomfortable moments in the manuscript and see what those revealed about my characters has made this book infinitely better. The reference to Pete Rose's Hall of Fame snub is for you.

Eliza – I think i have a collection of twenty voice memos from you that are just positive affirmations about my writing and validation that this is all so hard and we wouldn't do anything else. The grind is cumulative and there are days that I think I would have chucked my computer in the Pacific ocean if not for you.

Tori and Ellen – our group chat has brought me so much incredible joy throughout the drafting of Exhibited (not to mention all the best pet photographs). I love talking about the landscape of Romancelandia with both of you and am so grateful for the way you provide your perspectives as readers and defenders of the genre.

Brady – You're the Carl Thomas Dean to my Dolly Parton.

Also By Nellie Wilson

<u>Museology Trilogy</u>
Curated – Emmy & Ryan
A cynical historian and a sunshine paleontologist are thrown together professionally and romantically when their museums merge.
Educated – Phoebe & Declan
Casual friends strike up a mutually beneficial relationship that helps them both understand boundaries and what it means to do life with a partner by your side.
Exhibited – Jeremy & Davis
Opposites attract when an exhibit designer and a forest ranger fall for each other while redesigning a visitor center, but how can their different lives work together?
<u>Standalones</u>
Need S'more Time – June & Colin
A burned out teacher meets a camp director on a school trip. Can she evaluate her life in this new normal and make room for love?
Storm Warning: A Novella – Violet & Julian
Two meteorologists who have a heated history with each other spend a summer chasing tornadoes.
Corporate Mandated Holiday Romance – Brooklyn & Max

Fake dating a journalist at Christmastime to take down a billionaire? Easier said than done.

Future Books
Mountain Friend Series
Figure It Stout (late 2024) – Foster & Amanda
Ale's Well that Ends Well (2025) – Flo & Reggie
Bold Will Hold (2025) – Yuna & Lina

About Nellie

Nellie Wilson is the pen name of a historian in her mid-30s who has an impossible-to-spell real name. Originally from western Pennsylvania, Nellie spent time in Ohio and Colorado before settling in San Diego with her partner and snaggletoothed dog (and a recent feline addition). She enjoys drinking beer, talking about medical history and city planning, listening to emo music from the 2000s, and taking up hobbies for six months. When not writing books, she works as an architectural historian and reads Wikipedia entries for fun. You can find her on Instagram under @woahnelliewrites and occasionally struggling on TikTok under the same username.

9 798869 374561